"LIFE HASN'T TREATED Darcy Lemarsh well and he considers himself a loser who paints houses for a living. Darcy is accepting of the life he has and drifts along, taking each day as it comes. That is, until he meets Angie.

Angie brings change to his life and it isn't necessarily good. They move in together and a bumpy relationship ensues with few smooth spots. Angie introduces Darcy to her grandfather and Darcy's life spins out of control from that point, slowly at first, but with gathering speed when he takes on a task for the old man that he isn't equipped to handle.

Talented author C. M. Albrecht opens a door for the reader to step into a world that exists on the fringes of our everyday society.

— Anne K. Edwards, www.mysteryfiction.net

Deadly Reception

"CHEF MERLE BLANC, he has the nose. And when millionaire Bernard Goldberg dies during his wedding luncheon in the chef's restaurant, Chef Blanc's nose, he smells the murder! What greater insult for Chef Blanc than that someone would be so callous as to commit a murder in his restaurant during a wedding reception he has so painstakingly prepared. But the doctors and police believe Goldberg's death was natural. Can Chef Blanc keep some forty guests and employees in his restaurant long enough for him to don his apron and cook a killer's goose before closing time? "A fun read with lots of red herrings and false trails. I'm pleased to recommend Deadly Reception as a well told tale worth the time. Surprises in store for you. You'll want to read other tales by this very able storyteller. Enjoy. I sure did."

— Anne K. Edwards, www.mysteryfiction.net

The Albrmarle Affair

"SOMETHING DIFFERENT in private detectives. Fun characters who pull the reader into the story and their lives. Any reader will enjoy this tale by C. M. Albrecht.

"Two young people, Keely Foster and Parker Hall, trying to make their way as private detectives, are open for business. They are in luck. They shortly have not one, but two clients. One is an investment firm wanting to know why it's losing money in a restaurant and the other is a girl who thinks some strange woman may be watching her and she wants to know why.

"I'm pleased to recommend *The Albemarle Affair* to any mystery fan. Talented amateurs Keely and Parker will make you want to read their other stories."

— Anne K. Edwards, author of *Shadows over Paradise*

Music

"A FAST-PACED THRILLER that you'll read with a sense of wonder, whether you are an opera fan or not. Steve Music does indeed march to a different drummer and his finale is both triumphant and sweet."

— Arline Chase, author of *Killraven*, *Ghost Dancer*, and the Spirit series

Evidence

"WITH *EVIDENCE*, book two in the Steve Music Mystery Series, C.M. Albrecht has penned a snappy crime novel reminiscent of the time_honored genre of Robert H. Parker's Spenser series. A tantalizing plot enhanced by tumbled characters brings to the forefront descriptive storytelling in short to_the_point narrative and hard_driving dialogue. Albrecht's series is a welcome addition to the bookshelf of classic crime fiction novels.

—Elizabeth Eagan-Cox, author of the Shannon Delaney paranormal mystery series, *A Ghost of a Chance*, *A Ghost in the Shadows*...

THE LITTLE MORNINGS

by C.M. Albrecht

Cambridge Books
an imprint of
WriteWords, Inc.
CAMBRIDGE, MD 21613

© 2011 C. M. Albrecht. All Rights Reserved
First Print Edition, August 2025

Publisher's Note: This is a work of fiction. All characters and events portrayed in this book are fictional, and any resemblance to real people or incidents is purely coincidental.

All rights reserved. No part of the book may be reproduced in any form or by any means without the prior written consent of the Author or Publisher, excepting brief quotes to be used in reviews.

𝕮𝖆𝖒𝖇𝖗𝖎𝖉𝖌𝖊 𝕭𝖔𝖔𝖐𝖘 is a subsidiary of:

Write Words, Inc.
2934 Old Route 50
Cambridge, MD 21613

ISBN 978-1-61386-205-6

Fax: 410-221-7510

Bowker Standard Address Number: 254-0304

Dedication

*For my loving wife, Irma.
She always sees through me.
She always sees me through...*

The characters in this book are:
Mad, bad, and dangerous to know.
—Lady Caroline Lamb

Also by C.M. Albrecht

Music
Evidence
Still Life with Music
River Road
Tape
Marta's Place
The Albemarle Affair
Deadly Reception
The Sand Bluff Murders
The Morgenstern Murders

Part One

**Awake, my darling, look!
Day is already breaking...**

Life's all about choices. Every time we turn around we have to make a choice. It's always choices. And most of the time we make bad ones. At least I do. I don't know why, but someway, somehow, I always make the wrong choice. It isn't because I don't know any better or lack sound advice. Time after time people—people who know—point out the error of my thinking and still by God, knowing that, and taking everything into account and admitting they're undoubtedly right, I still have to go and do it anyway. I sure made a bad choice when I started after Angie. Then again, it's almost like, maybe I didn't have a choice at all.

"So you knew that was a bad choice, Mr. Lemarsh? Or can I just call you Darcy?" Kirk's voice was low and confidential. A little bit hoarse. He wanted to be my friend. He wanted to help me. He was a big beefy guy with a paunch. His jowls were heavy and red as if he shaved too close, and he had kind of iron gray hair in a brush cut. His eyes were red and he looked tired—tired and discouraged. He wore a cheap short-sleeve shirt and a striped tie. Dark wet spots stained the armpits of the shirt. A year ago I wouldn't have noticed it was a cheap shirt, so I guess my short brush with fame and fortune taught me a couple of things. I just wish life could ever teach me something useful.

I rubbed my wrists where I'd been handcuffed. They were still tender. I took my writer's glasses out of my jacket pocket and held them in front of me. I guess I was figuring how to start. I looked at them. Big dark brown plastic frames with lightly tinted glass. I tapped them on the table a couple of times. I looked at them some more and laid them down.

The little room was painted thick cream enamel with a dark green trim around the window and the door. There was only the table and three metal chairs with green plastic seats. The big window faced me like a wide-screen television along the wall behind Kirk. I saw my dark reflection, a sad and lonely loser with unkempt hair. I could barely see my beautiful jacket reflected in the window; it was too dark. And I was back to needing a shave. I knew people could stand on the other side of the window and watch me and hear what we said. I figured they were videotaping me.

I'd been sitting there twenty minutes or so before this big guy came in. He told me his name was Sergeant Kirk and removed my cuffs. That was a nice friendly start. He had a way of putting me at ease. Not really at ease, but at least I didn't feel like he was going to pounce on me. For some stupid reason I almost laughed at his name. I had an urge to ask him if he got demoted. The only Kirk I knew had always been a captain. But I didn't. I didn't say anything at all about that.

"Yeah, Darcy's fine." That's all I said.

He placed a recorder on the table and pressed a button.

"Just start at the beginning and tell me in your own words, Darcy," he said. "The only way I can help you is for you to open up and tell me everything. It's still not too late to change your mind and have a lawyer present."

"No," I said. They'd already asked me two or three times if I wanted a lawyer. I didn't need a stupid lawyer, at least not right now. Like I said, I made some bad choices but at least I'm man enough to stand up and admit it. Considering my position, I didn't think a lawyer could do much for me. Besides, now I didn't have any money to be hiring lawyers.

But even today, looking back, I can't honestly say I would've done anything differently. Things just have a way of creeping up on a guy.

That's the way it was when I met Angela Berry. There was plenty of warning. I should've seen right away that she was one pencil short of a gross, maybe two. But when I say warning, I'm not sure I know exactly what I mean by that, because the choices I made later on and the way things happened…I could never have foreseen them. No way. Not in my wildest dreams.

* * *

Angie was I think twenty-five. Slender and lithe. She didn't have big boobs and all that, but there was a firm catlike quality about her that stirred me and made me feel immediately that she'd be a holy terror in bed. She had a fine nose and wide cheekbones with dark hollows underneath. She had wide-set almost colorless eyes, eyes like those arctic dogs; eyes that made me feel she couldn't be trusted. And they had kind of a daredevil faraway look in them so even while I was talking to her I had a gut feeling that she was off on some cutting edge adventure all by herself and only giving me half her attention. When she looked at me, I felt like she looked right through me, at something beyond.

Angie worked at The Owl, this little chili joint where I dropped in for a bowl of chili once in a while. She hadn't been there but a few days I guess, the first time I saw her. We didn't talk that time but the lazy way she let those icy eyes linger on me told me I wasn't the ugliest guy she'd ever seen. But I figured too that maybe she was just one of those gals who like to dazzle you with a look so you'll leave a nice tip but don't get your hopes up. She had dark straight brows and dark hair that frizzed a little, especially near the roots. She wore it cut short to reveal a long slender neck, a look I thought was pretty beautiful. I never was much of a ladies man, but after a couple of visits to The Owl, something about this gal gave me the idea that she might just like me at that, at least a little bit.

The Owl wasn't a very big place. Deep and narrow and kind of gray. Back around the grill the gray had turned a sickly yellow from years of smoke and grease. A counter ran down the left side and a row of tables ran down the right side ending at the kitchen. By that a little hall led to the restrooms in the dark near all the garbage.

The Owl always smelled. Whether or not you consider that good depends on whether you like frying onions, the smell of bacon and beans and fishy grease wafting on the air. And if you sat too near the restrooms you smelled them too. The food smells didn't bother me but I usually didn't sit any closer to the restrooms than I had to.

About the third time I came in after Angie started there she was sitting at a table in the back, near the restrooms. Naturally I saw her immediately. She had her elbows on the table with a cup of coffee in front of her and an unlit cigarette held high to let the imaginary smoke drift away from those faraway eyes. If she saw me come in, she didn't let on. Even though her eyes were trained directly on me there was no sign that she was in this world. Her eyes were so colorless that it was always hard to tell. Mostly you only saw the little black pupils.

But for all that, I felt a strange sense of connection. Something about the way she'd looked at me before—maybe even a crazy feeling that somehow, someplace, we'd known each other before—maybe in another life. Who knows? Something more than just her looks pulled at me to wander on back and stop at her table. I didn't even notice the smells from the restrooms.

Now she acknowledged my presence with a faint smile.

"More chili?" she said. "Better check it if you get some."

"Check it?" I asked. I wondered where this was going. I'd already had something I thought was pretty clever to say to her. I was going to say, "Hey, do you come here often?" But that threw me off.

"Yeah," she said and nodded toward Jessie, the waitress behind the counter. Jessie had been there ever since I'd been coming in. A little taller and older than Angie she wore too much makeup and had about twenty pounds of jet-black hair piled high on top of her head. She had big soft boobs and ass all right, and a lot of the guys came in just to BS with Jessie. Her curves were too dumpy and exaggerated to do much for me. And the lazy way she moved her ass around—I could just imagine what a slob she must be at home. Not that my one room pad was anything to talk about. I hate it but every time I diss somebody a little voice reminds me that I'm not perfect either. I don't know why that is, especially in the light of everything that happened later, but I do believe I have a conscience.

"Yeah," Angie went on, "a customer pulled a two foot black hair out of his chili today and he's threatening to sue. Don't be surprised if Jessie's long gone by next week. I won't be sorry. She's been stealing tips from me."

"A two-foot hair?" That sounded pretty long even for Jessie, but I could believe it. Jessie always wore her hair pinned up, but more than once I'd seen long stringy black hairs working their way loose around her head. I remembered thinking once that if you pulled at it a moth might fly out. The thought of pulling a long black hair out of my chili kind of put me off. "I guess I'll just have coffee," I said. Then in a lower voice: "She's been stealing your tips?"

"Yeah, every time a customer leaves me a big tip, Jessie swipes some of it."

Some people are pretty greedy, I thought. I turned to go to the counter to order, but Angie reached across and touched my arm—it was like being zapped by electricity.

"Relax. I'll get it for you." She scraped her chair back and went around to the kitchen and behind the counter and poured me a cup of coffee. I liked the assured way she looked and carried herself. She looked like she was fully in charge and knew exactly what was going on. While I waited, I saw Jessie eye me and whisper something to Angie with a snicker. Angie smiled back. I guess she'd forgotten about her stolen tips already.

She came back with a mug of coffee and placed it in front of me. "You'd better talk fast," she said, sitting back down, "I've go to get back to work in a minute."

Talk fast? I'd had a hard time coming up with that line I didn't get to use. I didn't know what to say now. Like did she know what I wanted to say? I wasn't sure myself what I wanted to say to her. I just knew I wanted to be around her, to talk to her. Or I could've spent the evening not saying a thing, just so long as I could hang around her. She was like a magnet. One of those powerful magnets that grab and hold on tight without doing a thing.

I caught my breath and tried to look cool. "What do you want me to talk fast about?" I asked her.

She just looked at me, kind of sideways. "I thought maybe you were going to ask me out for something decent to drink after work."

I couldn't believe my ears. I'd always been a little awkward around women, and the few women who ever came onto me were the ones I didn't really want or need. I guess for a guy who didn't have much to offer I was kind of picky. But Angie? I gulped and tried to be cool.

"What time do you get off?" I asked.

She looked coolly through me and gave me that Mona Lisa smile. "Nine. Just wait outside on the corner." Suddenly her voice changed. She became very businesslike: "Got to go." She stood up without looking at me and picked up her mug and disappeared back into the kitchen area.

I sipped about half my coffee and stepped up to the counter. By then Angie had come around and I paid her for my coffee and mumbled something about seeing her at nine.

"I've got to go to the bathroom," I told Kirk. He got up and called for a uniformed officer to take me down the hall to the can. After that, the officer brought me back.

Kirk was very accommodating and asked if I wanted a Coke or some coffee or something and I said no, thanks, I was fine.

"Well, you just go ahead and tell me what happened next, Darcy."

* * *

Outside it was cool. Having a little time to kill, I decided it was time I got a haircut that I knew was way overdue. My boss had already made a couple of wisecracks about it and I hated that. The barbershop next door to The Owl was a small one-man affair. Conan the Barberman. I'd been there before but hadn't been back because to tell the truth Conan kind of scared me. Sometimes he'd swing those scissors around like he thought he really was Conan with a sword in his hand. He was a thin old guy with loose gray hair and wrinkled skin. He'd start off all right but then the hand that held the scissors would get to shaking and pretty soon he'd lean down behind the chair where he thought I couldn't see him and pick up a green bottle and take a jolt. Then almost immediately the shaking would stop and he'd get back to trimming my hair. I smelled booze on his breath and that wasn't unpleasant, but beneath that there was a sourness I didn't like. When it was all over the haircut looked all right but I couldn't help being relieved to get away from that shaking hand and those long pointed scissors. I'd promised myself I wouldn't go back. But that evening I went on in anyway. What the hell.

"Just a trim," I said, getting into the seat. Conan wasn't a barber to talk a lot and I liked that about him. Having been there before I realized the underlying sour smell I'd noticed before was from his drinking. Not from the drink he'd just had, but from all the drinking that had gone before. It kind of pervaded his space, even cutting through the after-shave lotions and talcum and crap. His eyes were pale and looked a little out of focus and up close the red veins in his nose were pretty bright.

He snipped and snipped and sure enough pretty soon I saw his hand was shaking pretty good. He disappeared down behind the chair for a moment and out of the corner of my eye I could see him through the mirror that ran along the wall. He picked up the green bottle that stood on the tile floor there and took a healthy jolt and I watched him stiffen for a second while he renewed his forces before he pulled himself together and came back up with hands so steady he could put a valve in your heart.

By the time I got that over with and paid Conan I took a walk around the K Street Mall. Then I fiddled around in the magazine store on the corner near The Owl until it was nine and a few minutes later I watched Angie pop through the door. She paused just outside and lit that cigarette she'd been playing with earlier and looked casually about her before she blew out smoke. It was getting dark and I wasn't sure she saw me but before I could make a sign she headed in my direction. She walked pretty fast and I liked the catlike gracefulness in the way she moved and carried herself. That was part of the reason I couldn't help watching her the first time I saw her there in The Owl.

I stood in front of the magazine store and waited as she approached. I knew by then that she'd seen me, but she didn't wave or let on until she was right in front of me.

"Hey," she said. She lowered one shoulder and gave me a little wave of her hand. She was wearing tight jeans and a light cotton athletic sweater that went well on her. She wore a little fanny pack at her waist and looked confident and ready for anything.

"Where do you want to go?"

"Someplace where I can get a nice cold glass of chardonnay," she told me.

I had a twelve-year old Chevy pickup with a banged-up tailgate parked down the street. It wasn't much before the accident and I still hadn't been able to get it fixed. I wasn't sure she'd go for riding in it, but the subject hadn't come up earlier. She hopped right in without a saying a word and that made me feel better. I drove out to a little lounge called

Embers. Their feature was really Mexican beer and tequila and margaritas. Despite its name, Embers was a Mexican lounge and almost everybody in the place dressed Western and talked Spanish. Most of the men were short and dark with mustaches and wore white straw cowboy hats and blue jeans and snakeskin cowboy boots. As usual, the jukebox was blasting Mexican cowboy music. I had already figured that in a noisy place like Embers I could get by without saying too much. And it was a comfortable place. Nothing fancy. I'd been there before and felt like it was sort of my kind of place somehow. Ever since I'd heard that song, *South of the Border* when I was a kid I'd always had this romantic idea about running off to Mexico. I even studied Spanish in high school because for a while I thought about moving down there. And I got some practice and picked up a little slang whenever I worked around Mexicans, so I was able to hold my own.

Though it was cool outside, Embers wasn't very big and because of the crowd they had the air conditioning on, but they had a gas log going in the fireplace in the center of the room too. I sat there by the fireplace with Angie and sipped Mexican beer while she played with her glass of chardonnay. It was pretty nice, sitting there.

Her full name was Angela Berry and before The Owl she'd worked at the Burger King in the bus depot, which wasn't far from The Owl.

"Every time a bus pulled out," she told me, "I was tempted to toss my apron and go hop on it." She watched the effect of that on my face.

"Where would you go?"

"Who cares? Anywhere. Just somewhere. Anyway I couldn't really run off. That was just wishful thinking. I have to stay here and take care of my grandpa. All I've got is my grandpa—I should say all he's got is me. I kind of take care of him. You know he's getting up there. To me bus stations are depressing places. Most of the people wandering around don't look happy to be traveling and they've got too much baggage with them. I think that's the trouble with all of us. We carry too much baggage around with us." She took another sip of wine and made a little face. Moisture beaded on the glass and ran down the sides leaving her fingerprints on it. "It was a lousy job." She rubbed her damp fingertips on her paper napkin. "But they're all lousy jobs when you get right down to it, don't you think?" Her eyes gazed into me, through me, steadily.

I sighed. "Well, I haven't ever found a job I wanted to consider my life's work, I have to admit that." I heard the sounds of people talking and the jukebox blaring away and smelled booze and limes and some combination of maybe colognes and beer. It wasn't an unpleasant smell. I leaned back and became more expansive, but I had to talk loud. "People are always trying to get me to become an apprentice plumber or electrician or something like that. I already know going in that I that don't want to be a plumber. And besides I haven't got four or five years to fool around before I get on a job that pays any money."

"Still, you do know that four or five years will go by anyway while you're dicking around trying to figure out what to do, right?" Now her eyes held a twinkle and I wasn't sure whether she was just kidding me or — what I had a sneaking suspicion of — maybe she was just feeling me out.

"Yeah," I admitted. "Yeah, that's what people tell me. You're right. I don't know." I looked straight at her and our eyes locked in the dark. Kind of a Kodak moment without the flash. "Maybe what I need is a good woman to set me on the right path," I said.

"Now all that was still before you met her grandfather?" Kirk asked.

I looked blankly at Kirk. I'd been kind of lost in my memories. "Grandfather? Oh, yeah. Yeah, I hadn't met him yet."

"This girl Angie, she sounds pretty independent."
"Yeah...independent."
"Well, go on."

Okay, just at that moment the jukebox stopped and Angie laughed loud enough to cause other patrons to look our way. "A good woman to get you on the right path," she repeated. "That's a hot one." She finished the wine in her glass in one swallow and stood the glass back on the little table and massaged the paper napkin with her fingertips again.

"Oh, I was just kind of kidding around," I said.

"I'm not laughing at that," she told me. "I'm laughing at the part about finding a good woman. If you want a good woman to set you on the right path, Darcy, you'd better start looking someplace else. I'm going to hell and I'm the kind of woman who'll take you straight to hell with me if you don't watch out."

When she said that her eyes had turned dead serious and I felt she wasn't joking around anymore.

The cocktail waitress came over and I ordered two more of the same.

As I said before, even when I should know better I usually go ahead and do the dumb thing.

"Maybe I'd rather go to hell with a girl like you than be on the straight and narrow with some dowdy housewife who lies around watching soap operas all day," I said.

The jukebox finished another song and stopped again. The room became almost silent for a moment.

"Give me some change," Angie told me.

I dug in my pocket and came up with a handful of change. She hadn't touched her second glass of wine. She went and leaned over the jukebox for a while looking at the selections. I liked the way her rear stuck out and shifted when she bent over the titles. She managed to move it just enough. Finally she put money into the slot. The song that started up sounded familiar—I'd heard it before.

"What's that?" I asked her. With the music playing again

we just about had to shout but for the most part nobody could hear us.

"'Las Mañanitas,'" she told me, sitting back down. "It's an old Mexican folk song I think. I don't even know what it means."

I could barely hear the plaintive voice that rose above the guitars and cornets.

> *Ya viene amaneciendo,*
> *Ya la luz del día nos vio...*

"'Las Mañanitas'...I'd translate it as The Little Mornings," I told Angie. "But I guess actually it means very early in the morning or something. I'm no Spanish expert. But I think The Little Mornings sounds more romantic anyway, don't you think?"

"She jus' mean the little birthday love song, I t'ink," a voice behind me said close to my ear. I looked up. It was our waitress. She was a stocky little gal in a white satin blouse with a red floral trim. She had her fat ass stuffed into black jeans and wore a little apron with a change pocket. "I t'ink that's what she mean, you know."

I laughed. After she'd gone about her business, I told Angie, "Forget her," I said. "I still t'ink The Little Mornings sounds more romantic."

"Romantic? I don't know..."

We sat listening to the blare of the jukebox for a little longer, sipping our drinks. After a bit Angie shifted her weight and moved her glass around on the table. Her glass was still nearly as full as it had been when the waitress brought it. Again with the fingertips on the napkin.

She leaned across the table so I could hear her. "Funny, I had it pretty good for a while," she said thoughtfully.

"How's that?"

"Before the gig at the bus depot I got hired to be a nanny for this couple that was having a baby. They're both lawyers. Lots of money. I mean money up the yingyang. You should've seen their house. What a place. There's enough room there for three or four families and still a few rooms to let out. I had my own room with a private bath and a television and everything." For a second she looked wistful.

"What happened? How come you left that?"

"Oh," she toyed with the stem of her glass, "by the time the baby was a couple of months old I just couldn't take it any more. Changing diapers, cleaning up the mustard and all that—and then the kid would get colic and cry for hours." She sighed and looked at me in that lazy way, "It was a good job, you know? But finally I couldn't take it anymore so that's when I quit and went to work at the bus station." She took another sip of wine. "I guess I wasn't cut out to be a mother."

"What were you cut out for," I had to ask.

She gave me one of those looks that said, "If you play your cards right you may find out."

I know it's dumb, but I think I must have flushed a little in the dark.

She studied me for a beat and then took a tiny sip of her wine. "But I'll give mothers credit," she admitted. "Mothers put up with a lot."

I didn't say anything and then she sighed again. "I know mine did."

"Your mother put up with a lot?" I asked.

"Didn't yours?"

I thought about that for a minute. "I suppose she did," I admitted. I thought how I always intended to send her a little extra money now and then, but hardly ever did—and then one day it was too late. "She's gone now."

Angie's eyes softened. "I'm sorry," she said and I felt like she meant it, "So's mine. I never really ever knew mine." She suddenly knocked back the rest of her wine and grimaced and pushed her chair back. "Let's get out of here," she said. "I don't like that waitress talking about me."

"What waitress?" I asked. Then I realized she must mean

our waitress. "Talking about you?"

Angie looked sideways at me as if I were a little dense. "She was talking to the bartender. She said something."

"Do you understand Spanish?"

"No—I couldn't quite hear anyway because it's so noisy, but she said something about me. I could tell. I don't like it. Let's go."

I thought maybe the waitress didn't like Angie's attitude. She could act a little bitchy. I noticed that right away. I could imagine why some women might not like her.

On the sidewalk I said, "Where do you want to go now?"

"You better take me home," Angie told me. "I'm drunk."

It wasn't real late, but we got into the truck and she gave me directions. Traffic was light. I guess I was feeling my beer because I hardly ever sing outside the shower, and nobody wants to hear me sing anyway. But that song kept running through my head. And maybe I was just showing off that I could talk Spanish, but I started singing, *"Ya los pajaritos cantan, La luna ya se metió…"*

"I didn't know you knew the words," Angie said. Maybe she was a little bit impressed at that.

"I didn't," I told her. "But it's, you know, like I have a photographic memory. I hear something once and I can repeat it…like a parrot. Even if I don't know what it means. Crazy huh?"

She laughed. "I don't know. I'm not your analyst. Turn here."

We pulled up in front of an old Victorian house on E that had been converted into apartments.

Angie sat there for a beat while I tried to think of something to say and then she opened her door and got down. I didn't know whether to get out and see her to her door or what. She turned toward me and looked at me very seriously.

"What are you waiting for?"

"I was waiting till you got inside," I said.

"I meant aren't you coming up?"

I gulped and turned off the lights and the engine and got down out of the truck.

Up close to her when she unlocked the door she smelled of smoke and onions—but under that there was an indefinable smell that was more interesting, more powerful and exciting. Not perfume. She just smelled good.

On the stairs I said maybe we shouldn't disturb her grandfather.

"He doesn't live here," she told me. "I love the old coot but he's too crazy to live with. Besides, he's a Communist. He has his own little apartment—well, a furnished room. Maybe I'll take you over to meet him sometime."

Her apartment wasn't much more than a furnished room itself. One room with a tiny kitchenette and a bath. A soft red glow lit the room enough. There was no need to turn on any lights. The room held a Murphy bed that was down and unmade. Forget Jessie being a slob around the house. Magazines and dirty cups and bits of female clothing lay scattered all over the place. Angie was no homemaker. That was for sure. The place smelled of ashtrays, perfume and stale powder and like that, but for all that I felt privileged to be inside her little inner sanctum. This was her private little nest and she was letting me share it. At the same time part of me told me I was probably only one of a string of guys who had been up here before me.

She went into the bathroom and turned on the light and took a leak without closing the door. I only had to lean sideways a little to watch her, but I didn't. I just tried to be cool as if I was used to that kind of thing. After a moment she flushed the toilet and came back out and looked at me and then went and rummaged about in her closet. She found some kind of flimsy nightie and disappeared back into the bathroom.

I was trembling inside. I anticipated what was coming and it was what I wanted for sure. But still, the actuality of it—her telling me about her grandpa and all, I'd barely expected to dump her off at the door. I was surprised and gratified that she even deigned go out with me in the first place. And now, whammo! Home run!

Well maybe...I didn't want to get overconfident. Then I heard the shower going. Steam floated out and I smelled perfumed soap.

I wandered around. There was nothing much to see in the kitchenette area. I opened the little refrigerator. Inside there was only half a carton of cigarettes, a half empty bottle of Taster's Choice and an open can of Pepsi. In the sink dirty dishes lay in an inch of black water and patches of mold had formed on them. An ashtray on the tile beside the sink flowed over with cigarette butts and two or three of those throwaway lighters lay on the tile beside it. I came back out of the kitchenette.

Her room faced the street. The red glow came from there. I pulled back the curtains and looked out at the red sign. It was across the street. Barney's Place. A little bar with a big sign. There was a streetlight on the corner but the sign from Barney's Place seemed brighter. I looked down at my pickup parked below. I guess Barney's Place was open but I didn't see any activity and the street was silent. The windows above the bar were dark. I let the curtain fall and wondered whether I should start undressing or if Angie would consider that as me taking her for granted. One thing I'd learned so far is that people, especially women, don't like to be taken for granted.

I stood by the foot of the bed feeling the steam from the shower and smelling her soap and then the shower stopped. After a few moments Angie came out of the bathroom wearing the nightie. I smelled damp steam on her. She was still drying at her hair with a towel and the nightie clung to her body, just tight enough to tease and entice. Her nipples beneath the fine material looked hard and swollen. The material clung to her tummy just below the navel and shone slightly. The nightie had a lacy trim and stopped just below her crotch. Her legs were as lithe and smooth as I'd imagined.

She stopped toweling her hair for a second. "Do you want to take a shower? There's plenty of hot water."

"Should I?" I asked. I felt like such a creep.

"You don't want to go to bed dirty, do you?" Her eyes were faintly mocking as if she was privy to a little joke I didn't quite understand.

I hit the shower and in less than five minutes I was standing there stark naked in the bathroom toweling myself with the same towel she'd been using. The scent of her body on the towel—rubbing it over my own body gave me a warm feeling, like I'd been permitted something special. I felt that she'd let me to get a little closer to her than she allowed most people. Well…at the moment I believed it.

"Hurry up," came her voice and I glanced into the room and there she was on the bed with a sheet kind of pulled up over her body. The nightie lay on the floor in plain sight by the foot of the bed.

Her mouth was wet and her tongue hot as she forced it between my teeth. She was everything I'd imagined she might be, aggressive, agile and very active. It was all I could do to keep up with her. The bed creaked and the springs squealed. The sweaty sheets got so twisted around us that a couple of times I couldn't even move—which wasn't so bad either—and by the time we wound down the whole room was a steam bath. We were both completely satisfied and exhausted.

She lay back with one hand behind her head and smoked cigarettes and blew little curls of smoke into the air. The only light came from the Neon sign outside the window. I lay with my nose in her armpit and basked in the moment.

After awhile I dozed off and the next thing I remember was her nudging me in the ribs.

"It's five o'clock," she said. "You'd better go home."

THE LITTLE MORNINGS

Reluctantly I got up and dressed in the gray light that filtered in from the street. The red glow from Barney's Place was gone.

I leaned over and kissed her.

"Come by this evening—I'll buy you a bowl of chili," she whispered. "Without hair."

"Yeah, Mexican hairless," I said. She smiled and I promised to take her up on the invitation.

In the bleak grayness of the street a few invisible birds twittered someplace above my head. They brought back the song from last night.

> *Ya los pajaritos cantan,*
> *La luna ya se metió...*

A faint pinkish light was rising in the east. I looked at Barney's Place. It stood dark and quiet. It was as if, save for the birds, the world had come to a standstill. Although it wasn't cold, I shivered and got into the pickup and turned the key.

* * *

I didn't go home. I stopped and had some donuts and coffee. Then it was time to get out to the job site.

I wasn't really what you'd call a trained professional painter, but I worked for this contractor who was such an erratic drunk he couldn't keep any real painters—so he hired guys like me. I'd been at it for a while and by now I could swing a brush and a roller all right. Actually I'd managed to learn to do very neat trim work once I got the hang of it. "Let the brush do the work," Ephraim liked to tell me in the beginning. "The brush will be your friend if you let it."

Right now we were painting the inside of an IGA grocery store over on Marconi. I guess the outfit couldn't afford to close down for remodeling, so we had to work around the customers.

Jack Bergstrom was already there. Jack was a gloomy guy who always seemed to be thinking about something serious.

I never found out what it was. When I'd say something to him or ask him something, he acted like I was dragging him back from someplace far off and I was a pain in the ass for doing it. Then, even after that he'd have to think about what I was saying for a while and ask a couple of dumb questions before he got himself situated back in the real world again and could formulate a reply to whatever it was I had said. He was a dark little guy with curly hair sticking out around his painter cap. Usually by the end of the day he had paint stuck in his hair so he looked kind of like a clown. We chummed around sometimes after work. We'd go have a bite to eat or maybe just a beer. Soon as we hit a bar he'd come up with, "You going to buy one or be one?" He didn't even know he was saying it. It was something he'd been saying for so long it was like breathing to him. Sometimes we'd go to The Owl and have a bowl of chili.

Jack loved chili but he was the strangest guy I ever saw when it came to eating it. He'd order a bowl of chili with extra cheese on top. At The Owl they didn't put cheese on the chili and he knew it, so I don't know why he always said extra. But they'd put some cheese on it for him and then he'd always look at it for a minute like he couldn't figure out just what the waitress had placed in front of him and then he'd say, "What's this crap," and if the waitress wasn't used to him, she'd say, "That's your chili," and he'd say, "I asked for extra cheese—and how about some chopped onions too," and the waitress would take it back and get more cheese and some onions, and then when it was all set up to Jack's liking he'd sit there on the stool and look at it and then we'd talk a little and pretty soon he'd pick up his spoon and stick it into the chili and move it about a little bit. Then after a few minutes of chatting and looking around he'd look at the chili again and then drink some coffee and so on like that till I wanted to dump the damned bowl over his head and so did the waitress, I'm certain. I swear to God, after he had everything just right, it still took him about ten minutes to take that first bite. He did it hesitantly as if he thought it might be poisoned or something, and then he'd make a horrible face and gnaw on it like it was a bone and make more faces like it was even worse than he ever expected and he'd put the spoon back into the bowl and stare at it some more. It would go on like that for half an hour. He might get up right in the middle of it and go study the jukebox for a while although he never played anything, or he'd go to the can for ten minutes. I don't know how he could manage ten minutes in there without a gasmask. One time I swear—as God is my witness—he went next door to Conan's and got a haircut while I sat there drinking coffee and watching his half bowl of chili for him. When he came back it was naturally stone cold and it still took him fifteen minutes to finish it.

Jack smoked too so he was always finding some excuse or another to sneak off to the can to grab a smoke. That didn't bother me, just Ephraim.

After my night with Angie I was tired from lack of sleep but at the same time I was walking on cloud nine. Normally I didn't get much sex at all to be truthful. What there was of it was okay I guess. But usually it happened when I got half drunk and picked up some skagg in a bar. Later I could barely remember what she looked like and had no idea of what her name was. And for days I'd worry that maybe I caught something. Still, every time I went over it in my mind it had a way of getting a little better. But last night. That was something I remembered all right. Something I wouldn't get over. I was still in a daze and Angie's smell still filled my nostrils. Call it what you like but I was in love. I wasn't thinking about marriage and picket fences and all but at the same time I couldn't imagine going anywhere now without Angie right there with me. From the moment I got into bed with her, the decision had already been made. It was a decision that came from somewhere outside me. It was beyond my control, and I didn't care. From now on, it was me and

Angie. At least that was my point of view. I guess I thought that would be her point of view too.

Ephraim, my boss, finally showed up. He carried a plastic cup of coffee in his hand. I could smell the whiskey in his coffee when I got within two feet of him.

"Don't you have any cleaner overalls?" he asked me. He was a skinny little guy about fifty. He might be a drunk but he was always neat. He wore his gray hair cut close and combed neatly and he shaved every day. His glasses always sparkled and his white overalls never had a speck of paint on them.

"When I was starting out we had to wear little leatherette bow ties," he told me at least ten times, "and we had to wear black shoes and keep them polished too." I don't know how he managed it because if I even walked past a building someone else was painting and crossed over to the other side of the street to boot I'd still get paint on me. I'm just lucky that way I guess. "And we wore our damned caps too," he added. "When are you going to get cleaned up?"

"I'll have some clean clothes tomorrow," I promised. "I just have to pick them up at the laundry." He knew damned well I didn't take anything to the laundry. If and when I got around to washing I went to the neighborhood Laundromat—which I promised myself to do that afternoon.

"Yeah," he grumbled giving me a sad look, "You need to clean up your act, Darcy."

Kirk cleared his throat. "So you were a painter?"

"Yeah. I worked for this contractor, Ephraim Dekker. And this particular day...it wasn't my fault even if I was in a daze. I was up on the ladder painting a pipe over a wine display and some old gal came by with her shopping cart and hit the ladder and that started a chain reaction in the wine bottles. My pail of paint went flying and I grabbed the pipe. I tried to hang onto the pipe, but it was wet so I slowly slid off and dropped to the floor falling right against the bottles.

A lot of them broke. It's a wonder I didn't get all cut up. Then Ephraim fired me.

"The manager don't want you working here any more. I mean... I got to work with management, you know."

"You mean I'm fired?" I couldn't believe it.

Ephraim shook his head. "He don't want you here any more, Darcy. Maybe I'll find something else for you in a couple of days. Go home and get cleaned up—and get some clean clothes. You look like hell."

As I went back out through the front of the store I saw Jack loaded down with rags trying to clean up spilled paint. You wouldn't believe how far a half-gallon of paint will go when you throw it off a ladder. He didn't look up and see me and I was glad to get out of there.

At the rooming house I took a long shower in the hall and then went back to my room and got dressed. Now I didn't have anything to do except ponder my fate while I waited to see Angie again. Finally the time came and I got into the pickup and drove over to The Owl and there she was. I saw her through the window before I even got inside. She was standing at the counter writing up an order for some old guy—but she must have sensed my presence because suddenly she looked straight at me, right through the window.

I hustled inside and took a stool.

"You look guilty," she said kind of bossy.

I explained what had happened and how I was lucky not to be in the hospital all cut up but she didn't seem to be too upset by all. I told her how I was hanging from the pipe over the wine display and saw some old geezer slip two bottles of wine under his shirt while everybody was watching me. We laughed at that one. I sat there and smelled grease and onions and chili and drank a couple of mugs of coffee. I didn't see Jessie.

"Did they get rid of Elvira?" I asked.

"Elvira? Oh, you mean Jessie." She smiled. "Yeah, she's

gone. The guy was threatening to sue if he ever saw her in here again and that was good enough for Nikos."

I had a bowl of chili and another cup of coffee and when it was almost nine, she told me to wait outside.

* * *

I drove her home in the pickup. While I'd been out and about I picked up a couple of joints and we smoked those and everything turned to a golden glow and we made love on the unmade bed and rested awhile and did it again—and again.

The part about the joints just slipped out and I expected Kirk to say something, but he didn't. He got up and asked me if I wanted a Coke or some coffee. I told him I could drink some black coffee. He went to the door and asked somebody to bring in some coffee. He sat back down and leaned back, all friendly and relaxed. I rubbed my wrists.

This routine, meeting Angie after work, it went on for a few more nights. In the meantime, Ephraim relented and put me and Jack out on a job painting the exterior of an old stucco warehouse somebody had rented. It went yellow with a light green trim.

That's the way things went for a few days.

* * *

I went to The Owl to pick Angie up like I'd got into the habit of doing. She came out of the kitchen with a package.

"Here," she said, handing it to me.

"What's this?"

"A present. You can open it when we get to the apartment."

It was heavy. I couldn't remember the last time somebody gave me a present. I was dying with curiosity but I patiently waited while I drove her home. By the time we got there I couldn't wait to tear it open.

It was a toilet kit: razor, shaving foam, after-shave, a toothbrush and toothpaste and a comb and some other stuff.

"Look at this," Angie said. She showed me red scrapes around her mouth. "That's whisker burn." She smiled crookedly, "And I've got some someplace else too. I want you to start shaving every day and brushing your teeth. You look like a loser. Come on." She grabbed me by the arm and pulled and we went into the bathroom. "Look at that, will you?"

I looked into the mirror over the bathroom sink. I tried to look at myself from Angie's point of view. My hair looked stiff and greasy, sticking out at odd angles, especially at the crown. I hadn't shaved in days and when I bared my teeth, it was obvious I didn't take very good care of them. I guess I was lucky not to have a mouth full of cavities. I always felt kind of ugly. Usually I'd look at myself in the morning and see a skinny face with red-rimmed blue eyes and a slightly bent nose and I didn't even notice the beard unless Ephraim or somebody made some comment about it. I'd rub a little toothpaste over my teeth sometimes with my finger and rinse.

"I want you to start a regular routine," Angie told me. "If you want to hang with me you have to get up and shave every day and I want you to brush at least twice a day, three or four times wouldn't be too much. And now we're going to wash that mop you call hair."

A wave of warmth washed over me, having somebody that actually cared about me. All at once I felt my life might have a purpose after all. She got my head down over the sink and shampooed the hell out of it and then after she'd dried it pretty well with a towel, she combed my hair neatly into place and watched me while I shaved.

"I like to watch a man shave," she told me. "I'm going to enjoy this. It's sexy."

"Shut up or I won't be able to wait till I get shaved," I told her. She liked that.

I knew she was right and decided she was worth it. I wanted Angie to like me. It was time I really made an effort to clean up my act. I wanted her to be proud of me, too.

Within days I had given up my room and moved my stuff over to Angie's apartment.

"My dad died when I was still a kid," I told Angie. A car accident. And then my mom died up in Oregon a couple of years ago. Christ, I didn't even have money to go to the funeral. My boss where I was working lent me the money. He said a person only has one mother, like I didn't know that." I sighed, remembering the little funeral. Almost nobody there. I guess she didn't have a lot of friends. I hadn't seen her in a couple of years. I always wanted to send her some money when I could, but it seems like I hardly ever managed to do it. Ever so often I think about it and feel rotten all over again.

Angie patted my arm and then pulled out a cigarette and lit up.

"What about you?" I asked.

She blew out a cloud of smoke. "Ah, my dad disappeared before I was born," she told me. "Mom and I lived with my grandpa but she died while I was still pretty small. I don't remember her. After that my grandpa took care of me until I was big enough to take care of myself. Now I take care of him. He's all I've got."

A week later Angie took me to visit her grandfather.

Never in my wildest flights of fantasy could I have predicted the profound effect this visit with grandpa was going to have on my life.

Kirk perked up at that. "So that was the first time you met her grandfather?"

"Yeah."

*　*　*

Downtown Sacramento is full of old Victorian houses that have been converted into rooming houses. Angie's grandfather lived in a room on Twenty-First Street. It wasn't much different than the dump I'd just abandoned on Eleventh Street.

The Little Mornings

But this room had to be one of a kind. When the old man opened the door the smell so overwhelmed me that my eyes began to water. It took me a minute to get my bearings. Angie appeared to be more used to it, but she still gasped and wrinkled her nose. He opened his arms in greeting but couldn't seem to get his mouth to work. He settled for giving us a half bow. He staggered back so we could come in.

"God this place smells worse than a public toilet," Angie said. She went to the window and opened it wide although I think it was hotter outside his room than it was inside. She turned and looked around her. "What a mess."

He belched softly and at last got his tongue going. He waved one arm about to take in the room, "In the words of Mr. Cabell, 'The optimist proclaims that we live in the best of all possible worlds; and the pessimist fears this is true'. As for me, here I crouch in my vile retreat and proclaim a day of rejoicing at the sight of my beloved granddaughter. Won't you join me in a glass?"

The old guy was really drunk. He tried to sound important, but he slurred his words really bad. He was a frail old dude in his seventies with a shock of white hair and a raggedy white mustache and he needed a shave too. The mustache was stained a reddish yellow. Maybe that was from the wine. He wore glasses held together on one side by a tiny safety pin and he had a big bulbous nose tinged with red. He was a mess but behind the phony glasses his watery blue eyes were warm and kindly. His face and hands had purple blotches scattered around on them like tattoos. I didn't know where he was going but he had on a shirt and tie, and over that one of those heavy old gray shawl sweaters with wads of paper towel sticking out of the pockets. The sweater hung on him like a dirty blanket. God, and I was sweating in a T-shirt. All his clothes hung on him like rags and his shirt and tie were dingy. He had dried stains down the front of his pants and the cuffs of his sweater looked stiff and black. He bent slightly and picked up a water glass half full of red wine from the table by his bed. He pointed vaguely toward another table where I saw glasses and stuff. "Please, sit down someplace. *Soyez les bienvenus.*"

I felt sorry for him. A little bent old drunk with nothing to live for but another glass of the same.

We sat there and talked. Angie smoked one cigarette after another. The old guy didn't smoke, but he didn't seem to mind that she did.

The stench didn't get any better. Jugs of wine sat around, some on the three tables he had and a lot more on the floor. I soon found out that many of the bottles on the floor weren't full of wine; they were full of piss. Later Angie told me the old guy had a bladder problem and most of the time when he had to go he had to go. He didn't have time to run down the hall to the can, which might likely be occupied anyway. So he used the empty wine jugs, except he usually forgot to empty them.

His room was some kind of maniac's library, crowded with books. He had books stacked in crazy unbalanced piles all over the place, most of them with papers sticking out from between the pages, big books on little books; books shoved out of the way under the bed. Some books lay open but most of the books were closed. From the general ratty look of them, they'd been read a few times.

He was glad enough to meet me, I think. At least he was civil.

While Angie took bottles of piss down the hall to empty them, he gave me his hand and we shook. "Jason Berry," he smiled, showing bad teeth. "Professor at large. Join me." Again he pointed toward the glasses.

Angie came back into the room and he beamed drunkenly at her through his watery blue eyes, "You always could pick them," he told her.

I wanted to be sociable so I got a glass and poured myself a little wine.

The table in the center of the room was his official desk. It held an office typewriter that was probably older than he was. Piles of paper and books lay stacked all around it. There was no television or radio.

Angie saw me looking at the typewriter. "Grandpa writes," she explained. "He's a professor—well, retired professor."

"A college professor?"

The old man smiled and nodded. "You may call me doctor, or you can call me doc..." He broke off trying to laugh. Instead he coughed and belched delicately. He smelled so bad; his breath smelled even worse. There was that Conan the Barberman sourness about him that comes from constant drinking combined with everything that goes with it and maybe his bad teeth too. I had an idea he hadn't taken too many baths in the recent past. And there was no barbershop talcum and after-shave around here to help cut the smell. He sort of staggered over to me and stuck out one thin blotchy hand again, "Jason Berry, Ph.D., Professor Emeritus or something, *et cetera et cetera,* and a tired old man who doth enjoy a drink..." he said. He leaned sideways and grinned up at me like an idiot. "I'm very pleased to make your acquaintance."

Angie pointed to the wall over his bed where several framed diplomas hung kind of off balance. I guess that was supposed to impress me.

"Grandpa writes essays and all sorts of stuff, stuff about world events, and he analyzes old time authors too; all kinds of stuff, don't you pops?" Angie smiled fondly at him. It was clear that she loved the old guy. She saw past what I saw. All I saw was a dirty old drunk who was lucky not to be living under the Tower Bridge. Angie saw the intelligent educated man who had raised her and probably spoiled the shit out of her. He was still doing that, as I was to learn. But I could see he needed her too. He needed her to come over and give him a hand or moral support or whatever. He hitched up his pant leg and showed her a sore on the side of his calf near the ankle.

"I can't get it to heal," he said.

"That's from the wine," she told him. "All you do is drink that bad wine and you don't eat properly, pops. I've told you before."

He winked and held up one finger. "'A man may surely be allowed to take a glass of wine by his own fireside'—or perhaps better," he said, winking at me and holding up the finger again, "since I unfortunately have no fireside to take a glass of wine by: 'I rather like bad wine, said Mr. Mountchesney; one gets so bored with good wine'."

"Yeah yeah," Angie said, dabbing at the suppurating wound with Mercurochrome. She placed a large Band-Aid loosely over the wound and let his pant leg drop back into place while the old guy belched and pardoned himself very politely. He wiped his mustache with the sleeve of his sweater, and caressed the back of Angie's neck. "Ah, that gracile neck," he sighed. Indeed a thing of beauty, indeed." She liked that.

We chitchatted for a while but Professor Berry was hard to follow. He kept getting off into flights of fantasy and stuff and quoted Shakespeare or somebody with every second breath. Most of the time I didn't have a clue what he was talking about. I don't think he did either.

I sipped my wine. I never particularly liked wine, but I wanted to be polite and besides, under the circumstances, it was better than nothing. He offered me another glass and I accepted.

He downed his own wine pretty fast and poured another from the half-gallon jug. I wondered if he ever got them mixed up and poured piss into his glass. The very thought made me shudder. I held my glass out and took a hard second look at it. It looked the right color.

I noticed the professor had some of those boxes of wine too, over against one wall. But he probably didn't like them because he couldn't piss in them. A stained coffeemaker stood on the biggest table by the window and a dirty dishpan lay on top of a hot plate next to that. He didn't even have a sink. Somewhere in there I realized his nightstand was actually a little refrigerator. Wonderful place for retirement.

"We have to go pretty soon," Angie told him. "I have to go get a pair of shoes for work."

"Do you have enough money?" he asked.

She shook her head. "I think so. They're pretty expensive, good work shoes."

"Oh," he jumped up. "Here, permit your old pops to write a little check for his baby girl." He fumbled around in the papers on the table by the typewriter and located a checkbook. He studied it carefully and finally picked up a ball pen. "Would a hundred be all right?" he asked.

"Oh, pops, you don't have to," she said. "You don't have that kind of money to throw around."

"I know, I know, but we can't have you working barefoot, my princess. Besides, when I need help I know I can turn to my little Angela." He tore out a check and passed it over to her.

After that we chatted a bit more so it wouldn't look like we'd come by just to hit him up for some dough. By then it had soaked in: that was exactly why we came by. She went over and let him kiss her on the cheek.

"Men," she said, looking at me. She turned back to him, "You need a shave." She rubbed his chin with the back of her hand, "as usual."

He grinned foolishly and shook hands with me again and we left him alone with his wine and paperwork and some empty wine jugs to piss in.

* * *

"Your grandpa's a doctor too?" I asked . "If he's a doctor why can't he write himself a prescription for that leg for God's sake?"

"He's not a medical doctor, dufus. He's kind of a doctor of literature or philosophy or something. I forget."

"Well, I'd need a doctor to teach me anything about literature. And he'd need big medicine," I said. We both laughed at that one.

In the weeks that followed I realized that Grandpa Berry was still taking care of Angie all right. He took more care of Angie than Angie took of him. When she went to visit him she was helpful and all. I know she loved him all right, but the only time she went to visit was when she wanted something. She had this little way of hinting around—she'd just mention that she had to get something, or that she needed something. She'd sigh and say, "Well, I'd better get going. I have to get my nails done today." Without a word he'd whip out his checkbook. To the best of my knowledge all he had was a monthly pension and whatever he got from his little essays. I didn't really think he could afford to give Angie money all the time, but somehow he managed. I don't think he ate much.

"So you're saying she used him for his money?" Kirk leaned forward and placed his bare elbows on the table.

"Oh not at all." I didn't like Kirk's change in tone. I didn't want to hear anything like that about Angie. "Well, okay, she used him, I guess. Yeah, I guess you could say that. But he used her too. Don't you see? Besides, he wanted to give her money every time he saw her. He was just waiting for a chance to write her a check."

I asked Angie, "Does he make much money on those essays and things he writes?"

She laughed. "I think he used to make a little money at it. But I don't think he sells anything anymore. He only writes when he's drunk and the he rambles on so much that nobody can follow what he's written." She shrugged. "Once in a while he gets something printed just because of his reputation. But a lot of those mags don't pay anything anyway. It's just for prestige or whatever I guess."

She smiled to herself and stared off into space. "Anyway, it makes him feel like he's doing something. I guess as long as you feel like you're doing something it gives you something to live for."

* * *

Ephraim found more work for me—in fact he gave me better jobs now that I shaved every day and started taking care of my appearance.

Angie kept me on my toes. We went to Target and she helped me pick out some clothes that looked better on me. Even Ephraim and Jack and some of the other guys Ephraim hired off and on couldn't help but mention it. The general consensus was that I was pussy-whipped, but they seemed to think that was okay. I guess I didn't mind. Besides, it was true. What the hell.

After about a month I was working every day and making more money too. Ephraim gave me a two dollar an hour raise. I was still getting less than a real professional painter would get I think, but it looked pretty good to me.

Angie got mad about something at The Owl and quit. I figured she'd get another job right away but the days sort of drifted along and she stayed home most of the time watching rented movies on her television. Things started to get a little tight on the budget, but I didn't really mind. It was sure better than what had gone before. And by now, I couldn't imagine going back to life without Angie. We were getting to be just like an old married couple.

One day Mrs. Gonzalez, her landlady, told Angie she was supposed to call her grandfather. He didn't have a phone.

Angie and I went tearing over there with our hearts in our mouths. For sure something had happened. I knew that despite the fact that Angie kind of used her granddad, she really loved him, and I have to admit I liked the old guy too. He was pretty funny when he was drunk—which he was practically all the time. He'd come up with all kinds of little cracks and he was always quoting from famous books I guess and stuff. He liked to quote from the Bible too although he told me he didn't believe in God, at least not in the kind of God most of us think about.

"'Ich lehre euch den Übermenschen'," he started once when we were over there. He held up that finger, "Mere man today, God tomorrow. Man is god becoming. When Nietzsche spoke of supermen he wasn't talking that twaddle the Nazis tried to turn to their advantage. I think rather that in his mind, man first creates that which he wishes to become, i.e. God—and then he proceeds to work toward that end. Just as you perchance visualize yourself as, say, an electrician, Darcy. First you create the idea of an electrician and then the desire to become an electrician and then you visualize yourself as an electrician and you work to become the very electrician that you have visualized. Finally one day, if you persevere, you *are* that electrician. An electrician, a reality developed from a simple thought, an idea that formerly existed only in your imagination."

Oh wow, I thought. An electrician. Just what I always wanted.

"We are working to become gods," he went on. "Gods becoming. That is our goal and our destiny. God, to me, is everything and nothing, certainly not some wrathful old senior citizen sitting on a throne watching our every move through his bifocals. But for all that, the King James Version makes for some lively and beautiful reading, wouldn't you agree? Some of the finest work in the English language." He swallowed half a water glass of wine and choked a little bit.

"Are you all right pops?" Angie asked jumping up. She looked at her cigarette and stubbed it out in a dirty dish.

He coughed and nodded. Up went that finger, "But for all that, just to be on the safe side, we do well to be prudent for, as Job so aptly put it, 'Doth Job fear God for naught?'" He laughed and wiped at his mustache. "Remember, children, the important thing in life is not to be important. Don't take me or anything I say too seriously." I figured he was right to hedge his bets. That's what I've always tried to do.

Today, after the message from the old guy, I half expected to see an emergency vehicle parked out front. After all the old dude was well into his seventies - and the way he lived!

But we were relieved and surprised to find there was nothing wrong with him, except he was so drunk he could barely stand up. Champagne bottles stood on the floor by his bed, some open, some unopened.

"A little respect and a roll of the drums if you please," he smiled, toasting us with a water glass of champagne. "Get yourselves a glass over there if you can find one, and have some champagne. If you can't find a glass, you may indeed drink from the bottle. Heh heh heh."

"My God you scared the sh—crap out of me," Angie told him. "We thought you had an accident or something. What did you do, win the lottery?"

"No, not exactly, my child. In a way my news is better than that," he beamed. "I am going to have a novel published. True," he framed a childlike smile, "it probably won't net us the millions of dollars that we might gain from six magic numbers, but imagine the prestige, the sense of accomplishment. The lottery is, after all, only chance. Anyone may win a lottery."

"But you've had plenty of stuff published before," Angie protested. I think she was a little disappointed that the good news wasn't better.

"Ah, yes," he smiled waving his glass in the air. "But this is different. "Those little essays and articles and commentaries and critiques mean nothing and pour nothing into the glass. They don't even receive a great deal of attention because no one bothers to read them. They fall into that vague and forgettable class of literature we know as ephemera.

"But in this case the publishers actually believe my novel may have merit...and a future. They're banking on it to earn some real money."

I went over by the hot plate and found a couple of glasses and wiped them out with my handkerchief and poured champagne for Angie and me.

"When did you manage to write a novel? I didn't even know you wrote novels," Angie said. "I thought you just wrote those, you know, essays; whatever was bugging you at a given moment."

"Well, of course I haven't written anything recently. That is true." He chuckled and waved his glass in the air. "No, this was rather like finding an old photograph that one might stuff into an album and forget. Actually, some years ago, under the influence of some ineffable inspiration, I wrote a few novels—during a more sober and reflective period of my life. At that time however, not getting any encouragement from the publisher that read them, I just laid them away and forgot all about them. I had other things to keep me busy." He waved one hand around and I figured the 'other things' meant wine. "Perhaps I was ahead of my time—or behind it." He leaned over and picked up a bottle and poured more champagne, spilling some over his hand. He licked the back of his hand. It was bony and covered with livery stains from old age and made my gorge rise. His nails looked dingy and ragged and the skin looked thin as tracing paper. "Can't waste this nectar," he smiled. "'What life is then to a man that is without wine? For it was made to make men glad'." He lifted his glass and drank. A little bit trickled from the corner of his mouth. He grinned like an idiot. "And I'm glad."

"How did you manage to find a publisher this time then?" Angie asked.

"Oh—well you know, I was poking around in my papers one day recently and came across a box containing the novels. There are four or five actually. I'd completely forgotten about them. I started reading one and decided that perhaps it had merit after all. It really had something to say; so I called one of my old colleagues from university days.

He has published a number of scholarly books in recent years, and he was kind enough to fire off a missive laden with praise to warn his publisher to expect my little opus. In the meantime, my landlord was kind enough to mail off my little effort. The rest, as they say, is history." He raised his glass in his shaky hand.

"Well, I hope you make a lot of money, pops," Angie told him. "You've got it coming."

He nodded and smiled in a way I think he thought was wise, "I just may do that." He placed his glass on the bedside table and held up three shaking fingers. He looked even more idiotic: "Two words: Holly Wood."

"Hollywood?" Angie exclaimed.

"The publisher expresses the possibility of selling film rights. In fact," he smiled wisely, "he expresses all the boundless confidence of a television weatherman." He chuckled over this and a little shine appeared at the corner of his mouth.

"Well, I hope he's more accurate than they are," I put in. "The weather people, I mean."

He laughed so hard I realized suddenly that he was making a little joke. I laughed too so he'd know I got it.

"So do I, my boy," he said. "So do I."

Angie wasn't much of a drinker. That first night—our first date—the way she talked about getting a glass of chardonnay, I thought she was a regular drinker, but that was just talk. She hardly did more than sip at whatever she had in front of her. So even in this grand moment of celebration she only had a taste of grandpa's expensive champagne but I liked it. It was pretty damned good and by the time we left I was half drunk. The old guy had fallen back on his bed and dropped off. Angie took his glasses off and laid them on the night table by his bed before we left.

I guess the old man's news cheered us up a little at that because for the first time in weeks we got more excited about each other, more the way we'd been before. Of course, I didn't really expect anything much to come of grandpa's big announcement.

* * *

"Okay, Darcy, don't stop now," Kirk said. He smiled as if he was really interested, like a good friend. I caught a whiff of onions from his breath and for a split second it brought back The Owl.

"Well, things went on that way for I guess about a month or so." I told him.

Grandpa kept a low profile for a spell and I pretty much forgot about his big success. Sometimes Angela and I would be at each other like we'd just met and at others we'd both be half sick of each other. I wasn't getting tired of her exactly, but she drove me crazy with some of her habits and the goofy ideas she'd get. She wanted me to be neat and clean—she always kept herself neat and clean—but the place we lived in was such a dump that even a lout like me felt uncomfortable in it. She never picked up a thing. Everything she dropped landed on the floor and stayed there. Clothing, towels, papers, magazines; you name it. Q-tips all over the place like lint. And every ashtray was always overflowing with butts.

And then she had this habit of sitting for an hour at a time staring off into space or more often, at the floor. She'd take hold of a strand of hair and begin twisting it and that was the tip-off. Sure enough, pretty soon I'd look at her and she'd be sitting there staring at the floor and working that strand of hair. Off in lala-land. I mean it's fine to be thoughtful and reflective once in a while. It could happen to anybody. But this not only went on a lot, it appeared to me it was becoming more frequent. And she became more critical of me all the time too.

At first it was only the razor and stuff. That was all right. She probably had the right idea in trying to get me to clean up my act a little and I don't regret it, but then she'd get on me about the way I combed my hair, or about the way I walked. She said I slouched. At some point in time I'd got into the habit I guess of saying 'you know what I'm saying' every other breath and that drove her nuts. I really worked on that until I pretty much stopped saying it. I don't even know how I picked it up in the first place. And I have to admit, once I'd weaned myself away from it, I thought it sounded pretty retarded when I'd hear other people saying it every time they opened their mouths. Besides, while she was spending all her time reforming me, I didn't notice her doing anything to improve her own life. She kept smoking like a fiend all the time—I got used to the smell in the apartment so I didn't notice it any more, but it still annoyed me when we were in public and she'd jump up and run outside for a cigarette all the time since most public places don't allow smoking inside anymore. And then there were these little things that always seemed to happen to her. Some woman deliberately kicked her ankle on the street. In a cafe the waitress gave her a soda straw that had been on the floor. Weird stuff like that never happened to me but it happened to Angie all the time.

In the meantime I kept on working most every day and Angie stayed home and for all I know, just smoked and watched television or stared into space and tugged at her hair. And she couldn't cook any better than I could. Mostly we ate at burger joints or we'd get frozen dinners and fix them at home.

Sometimes I'd pick up a bag of Chinese food and bring it home and we'd usually get two meals out of it. Sometimes we'd share a pizza. We never went to The Owl anymore.

Then one day when I came home from work, Angie told me her grandfather wanted to see me. He wanted to see *me*. That wasn't the same as his wanting to see us. Why me?

"What's he want with me?"

"How should I know? Anyway, he likes you. That's saying a lot. He doesn't like most people. Of course a lot of people don't like him. But he can't help that. He thinks he's so damned superior. Well besides...I guess he is pretty smart."

We got over to his place in the early evening. He'd been drinking, but he wasn't falling down drunk, although with him sometimes it was hard to tell. Even half sober he staggered around a lot and had trouble with his balance. We sat down and he offered us a glass of wine (he was back on the everyday stuff now, of course). So much for his big novel deal and Hollywood. Neither of us felt like any wine this time. I've always been a beer drinker and I'd already had a couple of beers. The wine just didn't sound good.

"My boy," the old dude said, "I've been thinking. I have in mind a little project that I believe would be beneficial to all of us." He glanced at Angie and smiled. "Angie here likes you, and I like you—and I trust you, you know."

"You do?" I said.

"Of course I do. Of course I do." He laughed. "At my age I have to trust people. And I think I have good instincts. Well, my capabilities are somewhat limited, as you see." He swallowed some wine and thought about his situation for a moment.

My feeling was that he was trying to work up to some sort of brilliant idea for me to come over and take care of him, or chauffeur him around in my pickup or some such dippy idea—and whatever it was, I wasn't going to go for it. Not even if he paid me. But he took off in a completely different direction.

"You know, this book thing is coming along, coming along."

That was a surprise. I figured he'd forgotten all about that by now.

"That was a long time ago," I said. "They sure must move slow."

"Slow? My boy, they move with all the speed and grace of a badly wounded snail, but be that as it may, they do move."

We all laughed a little at that thought. He put his empty glass down on the refrigerator table and rubbed his hands together.

"As it turns out however we are faced with a minuscule problem."

"A problem?" Angie said. I looked at her and saw sudden apprehension cloud her face. In the meantime I was wondering what in hell any of this had to do with me.

Berry smiled. "I do not believe the problem to be serious," he said. "At least it need not be."

"What do you mean, need not be? Get to the point pops."

"The thing is, my child, that when the publisher accepted the manuscript for publication and sent the contract to me, I signed it without really reading it. Why should I? After all, I wasn't in the enviable position of a star basketball player negotiating a contract after a successful season. Nor was I in a position to run out and hire legal counsel to advise me, and besides, why should I worry about it that much? As I say, I wasn't in a strong bargaining position and besides, *réflexion faite*, the publisher has a good reputation and even if I had read the contract thoroughly or had counsel, I'm not sure I could have done anything differently. In signing on the dotted line I had everything to gain and little to lose." He smiled and held out his shaking hands. "It is, I believe, obvious that I don't have a lifetime ahead of me to wait for better days. And no one else was bidding for my favors as it were. Besides, in point of fact, if memory serves, the contract did not seem at all unfair. This problem is actually such a little thing."

"So?" Angie said. Her shoulders had slumped. Her body language said grandpa had let himself get screwed by the big publisher and she wasn't a bit surprised. Neither was I.

"So what did they do?" she said.

"Well, it isn't that they *did* anything, my sweetie pie," he explained. "The thing is that part of my obligation under the terms of the contract is that I agreed to promote the book in any way the publisher deemed necessary. Now the publisher is talking about having me go on a promotional tour, you see. He wants me to travel about the country appearing on television and radio programs and signing books at bookstores, you see…"

"Well, is that so bad?" I felt the sense of relief in Angie's voice. "At least it'll get you out of this dingy room." She looked around in disgust. "God it stinks in here."

He smiled again, sadly. "I know. I'm sorry, sweetheart. Just look at me. Look at me. Take a good look. Can you visualize me, a disgusting sloppy old drunk, traveling from city to city, appearing on television, trying to discuss my work in a coherent and sensible fashion? I can't get down the hall to the bathroom and back without stumbling and falling against the wall. Can you just imagine? And even if I were determined to cooperate with my esteemed publisher, can you imagine the impression I would make on my readers? Can you imagine readers being inspired to rush out and purchase a book offered by a disgusting old drunk with shaky hands? And even if all that were moot, I'm simply not in condition to face the rigors of travel."

He cast a glance about his miserable little room. "I can't leave my happy little den." He sighed and looked down at the shaky hand holding his glass. "I just can't." He thought about that for a minute and then brightened up. "From the tone of the book and from the tone of the letters that I've received from my publishers, they apparently have the impression that I'm a much younger man than I—in fact—am…I have a feeling that if they knew my true age and — and condition — they might indeed have second thoughts about promoting the work of an unhealthy old drunk who probably has, shall we say a rather limited future. Building a reputation as a writer can take many years and I'm afraid that even if I were able to stop drinking and clean up my act, they might well feel that it would be neither wise nor prudent for them to consider investing in an author who has a very short future ahead of him, you see?"

He was probably right. Even I couldn't imagine watching him appear on television all clean and sober. Not good. Not good at all.

"So?" Angie said.

"So I have a plan."

* * *

The old guy leaned back and looked at us like we were children. "As I say, from the tone of the novel one would assume that I'm a young man in my late twenties or early thirties at most. A man Darcy's age. You know, I may look like what you see on the outside, but inside — at least in my clearer moments — I still am and remain the enthusiastic and optimistic youth of yesteryear. Even today I frequently forget that I can hardly walk, that I haven't the strength to read a good book." He directed his attention to me: "I can tell the publisher that I let you, the true author, use my name in order to give you an entree." He beamed crookedly at me and then turned to Angie. "You see, I think Darcy here is just the young man to take my place."

"Take your place?" Angie exclaimed.

He nodded. "In the first place, I can have the editor change the byline to Darcy — what is your full name, Darcy?"

"Lemarsh, Darcy James Lemarsh," I told him.

"Darcy Lemarsh. I like that. Yes, very good. D. James Lemarsh. D. J. Lemarsh…No that makes you sound like one of those music jockeys on the radio. Darcy J. Lemarsh; Darcy

Lemarsh, promising young author. Yes, Darcy Lemarsh. I like that." He studied me closely and almost looked sober for a minute. "We'll dress you up in some decent clothing and get you a good haircut and all you have to do is travel around the country promoting your book. I shall tell you what to say and how to say it and I'm certain that we will thereby satisfy not only my publishers but the general book-buying public as well, and of course the more you promote the book, the more copies we will sell. If, as I hope, and have been led to believe, it can be sold to Hollywood, we shall receive a good percentage of the movie rights. And we can divide the earnings equally, my children. I think that's only fair. Besides," he added after a little burp, "I have three or four more novels in that box over there. If this one is good, the others will be good, too. Perhaps even better. Therefore, we can turn out a new book every year or so over the next five to ten years. In reality I don't have to write another word so long as I live, and even if I do leave this earth in a year or so, you can continue at least through the last novel. At that time you and Angie can retire and simply refuse to write any longer. Who can say? Or perhaps you may choose to attend a writing class in the interim." With that he laughed out loud and finished off about six ounces of red wine at one gulp. He belched and fell back on his bed. He beamed vaguely up at us. "So, what do you think?" His glasses threatened to fall off, but he didn't appear to notice.

What did I think? I didn't know what to think. Talk about becoming an electrician. Now he wanted me to visualize myself as a famous author—and become one!

My stomach had tied itself into a knot at the mere thought of appearing on a television show promoting a book I knew absolutely nothing about, but on the other hand the idea really fired up my imagination. Being able to travel around first class and dress up and BS about a book on television and stuff. That sounded mighty good. And maybe a chance to go to Hollywood and hobnob with the stars. Well, it all

The Little Mornings

sounded good in principle, but I didn't see any way I could pull it off in actual practice. At exactly the same time this stuff was roiling around in my mind another part of me told me I was stupid to let the old guy get me fired up. It was just the wine talking. Maybe he had the DTs—nothing was ever going to come of it and I couldn't do it anyway—but still...

"I—I don't know," I said. "I mean, I—don't—know..."

"Don't be silly," Angie said. She was obviously impressed. She turned to her grandfather, "He could do it, pops. Of course he could. With me behind him to bolster him up, there's no reason in the world why he couldn't do the job to perfection." She looked through me with those pale eyes. "Of course he can do it. I think it's a great idea."

Well, for all that I still figured the old man was at best hallucinating. He drank so much all the time I guessed he was just having some sort of attack but why not humor the old guy? I didn't have anything to gain by telling him he was nuts.

"Sure," I said, "I guess I could do that. Why not? If Angie says I can do it, I can do it." Up until then I never had many pretensions. I don't have any talents to speak of, and no special skills or training, and I figured I'd be lucky just to make a halfway decent living without killing myself while I did it. The biggest event so far in my life was my traffic accident and the hope of the settlement I was going to get one of these days soon. I'd already spent the damned thing a hundred times. First I was going to fix the old boat but by now I'd decided definitely I was going to buy a brand new truck; I knew that. Maybe a GMC this time, with a king cab, but beyond that, I hadn't got very far. Every time the subject of money came up, I figured I could soon take care of that particular situation when I got my settlement. At least it was always something in the background, something that brought me hope.

I hadn't said anything about the expected settlement to Angie at first, but later on, after maybe a month, it had somehow come up. I could tell that now she was looking forward to it as much as I was. Every time something about money would come up—which was almost every day—she'd say, "Well, when we get our settlement..." Now it had become *our* settlement.

"What—what's the book about?" I asked Berry.

"Oh, it's just another novel I suppose, in a world already filled with too many novels. Although the editor did say I might just be another James M. Cain."

"Who's James M. Cain," Angie asked. I didn't know either.

"Oh my child. He was a bit before your time, but many of his novels have been turned into very successful films. You must remember *Mildred Pierce, The Postman Always Rings Twice, Double Indemnity* among others..."

"Oh. Okay..."

"Oh—those were novels?" I said.

"Before they were made into films they were novels, of course," he said. He swallowed more wine. "Books, like everything in this world, come and go in cycles. Perhaps now it's the turn of the so-called hard-boiled novel, the *roman noir*, to make its comeback. There was quite a clique at one time, Hammett, Thompson, Chandler, Woolrich; Hines; Cain, to mention only a few...But back to our own little novel: It's the story of a young man perhaps someone like you, Darcy, and a star-crossed meeting with a beautiful young woman; perhaps a woman like you," he beamed drunkenly at Angie. Up came the finger. By now I knew that meant a quotation alert: "And they're both 'Mad, bad, and dangerous to know'." He chuckled for a long time at this thought. "Now after our protagonists meet and become acquainted, they soon realize that life is usually sweeter when one has money. So they cast about for a way to get their hands on some. Now as it turns out, the girl had previously worked for a Hollywood producer in Beverly Hills. The producer and his wife had a baby and hired the girl as a nanny. Our young nanny however, unfortunately failed to share Bacon's sentiments when he said, 'Children sweeten labours...' She therefore worked for only a short while and then left. The dismal routine of tears and diapers, you know—as Lamb so aptly put it, 'To this dry drudgery, et cetera...'" He smiled wisely as his voice trailed off and he half lay there on the bed with his empty glass tilted over in his hand and a foolish lost expression on his tired face. His breathing was very shallow. I jumped up and took his glass and refilled it.

"Thank you, my boy," he said. He sounded honestly grateful. He smoothed his wrinkled tie down over his stomach and pulled his sweater closer about him. "You are indeed a gentleman. Well, as I was saying, this event took place before our Angie met our young Darcy. Eventually this however becomes a part of the plot when she remembers that she knows the house and has access to the house. And the owners of the house are quite wealthy. Through a series of mishaps our heroes devise a plan to kidnap the producer's child, collect a fat ransom, return the child safely to his parents and flee to Mexico where they expect to live happily and comfortably ever after listening to melodious guitar music." He drank deeply and I felt a little chill in the hot room. "The first part works out well. The new nanny is incompetent and therefore our Angie has little trouble sneaking into the house and sequestering the child who is now about two months old, if memory serves.

"Unfortunately, as things have an ineluctable way of doing, it turns out that the child apparently had what its parents thought was only a touch of the flu—but which, in reality, was not the flu at all but meningitis, an extremely virulent disease, and while in the care of our kidnappers, the unfortunate child perishes. Our young couple is of course devastated by the loss of the child as well as by the turn of events. But after the initial upheaval of their fortune, they manage to calm down and bury the tiny body and—since no one knows the child has died—they hope to collect the ransom anyway. This they do and they head for Mexico where they encounter a new series of misadventures. They are found out by another young man who hopes to blackmail them. Together they agree that to keep him silent, they have to kill him. This they do, but they eventually turn against each other and Angela is killed and finally our young Darcy is arrested for the murder of his girl friend and the young blackmailer as well—and for the kidnap and murder of the child—that would be at least negligent homicide—and the novel ends with our young Darcy languishing in a Mexican jail awaiting his sentence for the murders with the specter of extradition hanging over his head as well."

"Did he kill her, his girl friend I mean?" Angie asked him.

He winked knowingly, "Ah, you'll have to read the book, my child," he said.

"I never read a book in my life," I told him. I'd read comic books if that counted, but I didn't want to tell him that. I wasn't crazy about his calling the characters by our names even just for laughs, but now that he'd given us a little idea of what the book was actually about, it sounded more real than it had fifteen minutes earlier, and a little too close to home maybe, but still… "That's the only problem I'd have," I said, "convincing people I actually wrote something."

"Not to worry, my boy," he smiled. "That's the easy part. When someone asks you a question about anything at all, you simply point out you address that question in your book and imply thereby that they should purchase a copy to find out what it was that you had to say about whatever it was that they asked, and by the time they read the book they will have forgotten exactly what it was that they asked and exactly what it was that you said to them about it. And when they ask what you're working on now, you smile wisely and say you never talk about work in progress, but you are presently committed to a project that you feel will please your readers and hopefully even surpass your previous triumph." He drank another half glass of wine and looked pained for a moment. At last he smiled weakly and said,

The Little Mornings

"Well, back to our story. Now our young Darcy has been arrested and as I say, he is awaiting trial for murder. Worse, he still faces extradition back to the United States after the Mexican authorities get finished with him—I'm afraid that in Mexico, self defense and *les affaires de coeur* are still looked upon a bit differently than they are here. People often commit murder in the name of love and jealousy and get away with it or at least suffer only a pretty light pat on the wrist. And too there's always the possibility of a self-defense plea for the murder of the young man, since it turns out that he intended to kill our quote-unquote hero, so in point of fact, our young Darcy may not spend as much time in the Mexican prison as he might have done for the same crimes in the United States. But if he is returned to the United States and tried for the kidnapping and murder of the producer's child...well, the producer is a wealthy and influential man in Beverly Hills, and a vengeful man as well." He sighed as if to say that oh God he knew so much, and finished by saying, "So, as I say, our Darcy is in jail in Mexico and outside, through the bars of his window, he hears *mariachis* playing the strains of the song *'Las Mañanitas'* and he interprets the song's title as 'The Little Mornings.' He reflects on the many little mornings just before the sun came up while he listened to the singing of the birds and made plans and lay with his loved one and how, now alone, he lies awake at dawn and listens to the *mariachis* and the birds singing outside the window of his cell. He ponders his dismal fate. 'The Little Mornings,' his swan song...The End."

While I sat there listening to this an even colder chill had gripped me. I couldn't believe my ears. Him calling the girl Angie and the guy Darcy. Of course I knew that wasn't in the book, but using our names to retell the story, I don't think he knew how close to home he was hitting. Angie had worked as a nanny for the wealthy lawyers before I met her and I remembered how we'd sat at the Embers that first night talking about that little morning thing. I know we hadn't talked about any kidnappings, but it might have come up if we'd thought about it. It was downright scary. Like almost getting run over by a bus.

He looked blearily at me. "What is it my boy? You look as if you had seen a ghost."

"Oh…" I caught Angie's eye, "It's nothing. It's just that song, 'Las Mañanitas,' it sort of has a meaning for me too."

"Really? Splendid. Then it's settled. And I think we'll soon see our novel on the bookshelves: *The Little Mornings* by Darcy Lemarsh, a brilliant new author."

* * *

I took a long cool shower and tried to think. I was actually beginning to believe the old bird might not be hallucinating after all. At least it might be something to hope for. On the other hand I didn't forget that people can get carried away, especially old drunks. I remember some guy I worked with. His grandmother was an old lush. She won ten million dollars on that Publishers' Clearing House thing. The old gal really believed she had won and was making all sorts of big plans. She had a good heart. She was going to divide it up between all her relatives, including my friend. He was supposed to get about a quarter million or so after taxes and she was so positive, she had him convinced too for a while. But it all petered out eventuality. I guess they made it look like she'd really won something when in reality all she won was a chance to win something if, and only if, she had, and returned the winning numbers in time—one of those kinds of things. But they did it so smoothly they had her completely sold. I don't think old people are as observant as they think they are. I mean kids don't miss a thing. Old people act like they don't miss a thing either, but they miss plenty if you ask me.

I really didn't like to think old Grandpa Jason had brain damage from the wine and somehow got himself convinced that he was now going to be a famous author—but then on the other hand, he sort of made sense and I figured that at this point I didn't have anything to lose. Maybe he was right about publishers moving along like a sick snail or whatever it was. It wasn't costing me anything to humor him, but that was just one more thing hanging fire, like that damned settlement from the insurance company. I hate having things hang fire. You can't really make plans or get on with your life and you end up waiting around and making everything depend on what may or may not develop sometime in the future.

And speaking of my—make that *our*—settlement. I came out of the shower all cool and refreshed and there was Angie flat on her back naked on the bed with her legs spread as wide as she could get them. She was pretty acrobatic and her inner thigh muscles trembled in expectation. I forgot everything looking at that dark mound raised expectantly. My breath caught in my throat and I lunged at her like a starving tiger leaping on an antelope.

Afterward we lay there on the bed all sweaty and worn out and she whispered in my ear.

"When we get our settlement are you going to buy me an engagement ring, baby?"

"Sure," I said, half listening.

She rolled over and got a cigarette and lit it and blew a cloud of smoke up toward the ceiling. "I mean, a real engagement ring, Dar. A gold ring with a real diamond in it, a diamond you can see without a magnifying glass, got it?"

Wow I thought. I hadn't really ever thought seriously about marriage. I mean things were going along all right. I suppose if I ever stopped to think about it, Angie wouldn't probably have been my first choice for a wife and mother of my children. Christ, she didn't know how to cook and wouldn't cook if she did know how. And she was too damned introspective or whatever it was. She didn't take care of her own clothes either so how could I ever expect her to change diapers and wash them out and all the garbage that goes along with having kids. I had to admit, she was probably a lot like that gal in grandpa's book all right. She never hit a lick around the apartment.

Of course I realized I wasn't any prize husband material either. No woman who considered herself a good wife and mother would bother with me. Why should she? What's the use getting involved with a loser unless you're a loser too and can't do better? Yeah, we sounded like the couple in grandpa's story all right. I guess loser isn't exactly the right term. We were misfits. Dysfunctional. I think that's what they call people like us, Angela and me. We were both dysfunctional. At least Angie was good looking and sexy, a lot better than I really ever expected to find, all things considered. But what the hell. Who knew when we'd get the stupid settlement? We were only talking.

"Sure. I'll get you a real diamond ring, sweetheart. I promise."

She blew out more smoke. "Well, I think you should get on that lawyer's ass, Dar. If you don't stay on those guys they'll sit there on their fat butts till hell freezes over and we'll still be waiting for our settlement."

"Yeah, I'll give him a call," I said. I didn't really like to bother him. He always had a way of making me feel like I was being impatient and greedy—that all these good things come to those who wait—and besides, it was very hard to get him alone in his office. Either he was in court or in a meeting or not in the office today. It was always some damned thing or another, so I never really knew what, if anything, was going on. And then there was another consideration; I had half a feeling that if I started pushing too hard, he'd just fold and take the first offer they gave us and I'd be stuck with nothing after all this time.

Angela lay there with her hands behind her head. She didn't shave her armpits; she didn't have to. At best when you snuggled up close you could only see a few light fuzzy hairs, short and downy. I liked to rub my nose in there where it was soft and warm and smelled of Angie. But this time she ignored my cuddles and sat up on the side of the bed. The springs let out a squeal at the suddenness of her move.

"Well, you'd better get on it," she said. "We need the money." She crushed out her cigarette in the ashtray. She hardly ever smoked more than half a cigarette at a time. She got up and I lay there admiring the lithe sway of her buttocks as she headed for the bathroom. I started to become half aroused all over again.

She jumped. "Oh shit," she cried, "I'm dripping!"

* * *

It was probably a month or so later. Jack and I were up on rented scaffolding painting an old warehouse in Alkali Flat. Most of the windows had been broken out. Don't ask me why we had to paint the mullions on broken windows.

We were using an exterior latex paint and in the heat, the damned stuff stuck to the surface and started setting up before we could get the brush off it.

"Don't tell Ephraim," I cautioned Jack, "but as soon as I get my settlement, I'm out of here. I've about had it with this shit. Christ, I'm soaking wet."

"I know," Jack said. "This work sucks and looks like shit to boot. Total waste of time and money if you ask me."

"Well, long as Ephraim signs those checks every Friday night, I guess we can't complain too much." I looked through the window into the building. It was enormous and dark inside with open girders supporting the roof. There was nothing on the concrete floor below but what looked like dirt and a little debris.

"Darcy!" Angie's voice carried loud in the quiet afternoon. I looked down behind at the street below me and there she was standing on the sidewalk, hands on her hips. She had her fanny pack fastened around her waist. The sun glinted brightly off her wristwatch.

"Hey," I said. "What's up?"

"I came to take you guys to lunch," she called out. "My treat."

It was almost lunchtime so we put our material in a shady place and clambered down the scaffolding and took off our overalls. We were both soaking, but at least it was better without the overalls.

"I was just over visiting grandpa," she told me. That explained how she'd got the money to play the big shot and take us to lunch.

Jack had already met Angie several times, but he had enough sense to keep any opinions he might have to himself. He acted as if he liked her all right. In fact sometimes it looked like they were getting along a little too well to suit me, but I didn't really think there was a reason to worry.

We found a little taco stand around the corner. Jack did his usual: he ordered chili with extra cheese.

It was self-service. You ordered at the window and when they gave you your food, you'd go sit at metal picnic table. They had tables inside and outside. The tables had recently been painted, light blue, pink and white.

"What's this crap?" he said when the waitress placed a paper bowl of chili in the window. "I asked for extra cheese."

She gave him a look and grabbed the bowl back.

"Put some onions on it too while you're at it," he ordered.

We sat at a pink table outside and had tacos. Angie and I finished our lunch before Jack had done more than look at his chili and stir it once or twice.

We watched the Metro rattle by along the street. We sipped our Cokes and waiting patiently for Jack to get started.

"Our half hour's just about up," I mentioned.

"Ephraim doesn't know what time we knocked off," Jack retorted.

That was true. I decided to relax and not to worry too much about it.

"When you get off tonight grandpa wants to see you," Angie told me.

"He wants to see little old me?" I asked. "Now what?"

She shrugged, "I don't know. Something about his book, I think."

I sat there on my plastic chair sweating. Grandpa and his damned book. But my heart pounded a little faster. I wondered if, after all, there could possibly be a grain of truth in his crazy idea. Could it really happen? If he wasn't dreaming, could I actually represent? Or was he just riding along on some dumb fantasy he'd dreamed up on a gallon of wine? Besides, I was almost afraid to think about it because if he wasn't crazy, I might actually have to go through with it.

Jack wanted to know what we were talking about and I just told him Angie's grandpa needed me to help him do a little shopping.

Angie and I went over to Berry's room later, after I'd had a shower and got most of the paint off. Bits and pieces of paint stuck to me like little bits of rubber. I was always finding another bit of paint to peel off.

As usual pops was drunk. He lay back on his pillows with a cloudy water glass of red wine on the nightstand by his bed.

"Welcome!" he bellowed as if we were deaf. "Have a chair. Have a bit of *le rouge qui tache*."

"Grandpa," Angie said. "You've already had too much to drink. I think it's time for you to take a nap."

He leered at her. "I've already had a nap, my child." Then he half sat up on the bed, pushing himself up against the headboard. He reached out and grasped the glass. The front of his pants looked damp.

"Oh my, see how my hand is shaking," he said as wine sloshed over it. He looked awful and I felt sorry for the old geezer. He grabbed the flying hand with his other hand and managed to calm it down and get the glass to his lips. After a long swallow, he placed the glass carefully on the nightstand, but it fell off onto the floor anyway, spilling the rest of the wine out onto the carpet, not that a little wine made a difference to the carpet. A drink sure didn't help his shaking the way it did for Conan the Barberman.

"You see," he said. "I'm in pretty bad shape. I wonder if this can be ahe *alzheimersche Krankheit*."

Angie looked at him blankly.

"Alzheimer's disease," he explained. He smiled and a little bit of drool formed at the corner of his mouth and stuck to his mustache.

"It's not Alzheimer's disease," Angie told him, "It's old-timer's disease. You're just getting old and you drink too much."

We talked about nothing for a while and I wondered why he wanted us to come over. Finally the old guy mentioned that he'd heard from his publisher.

"He wanted to know why I chose the pseudonym, Darcy Lemarsh," he said. "I told him that in reality, Darcy Lemarsh is my real name." He chuckled like that was a stroke of genius.

"Your real name?" Angie asked, bewildered.

"Of course. I sent the book in under my own name, but when I told the publishers I wanted to change the author's name to Darcy Lemarsh, they asked why, so that was my explanation. I told them I had used the name and CV of my college professor, the erudite and charming raconteur cum man-about-town, Professor Jason Berry, Ph.D. in the hope that it might carry more weight around their editorial offices than the name of a completely unknown person named Darcy. That will explain why you are the handsome young writer that you are." He snickered and smiled wisely. "They accepted that. In fact I think they liked it. The publishers admitted that had they not thought the novel came from me, they probably would not have considered it for publication. Editors have no self-confidence, you see; they're too concerned with keeping their employment, which I believe is chancy at best."

"Okay," Angie told him.

"Okay what?" he asked.

"I mean, okay, whatever, grandpa." She sat there for a second. "What's a CV?"

"Oh, that is merely a little biographical information. Where I studied, where I taught and so on..."

I sat there smelling the piss and wine and general sourness of the room and wondered how I ever got myself into this mess. It was suffocating. I'd go along for a while thinking he was crazy and that disappointed me. Then ever so often it began to look as if the old guy wasn't crazy after all and I'd get scared-scared and excited. Now this was even scarier. He actually sounded like he knew what he was talking about. Now they were using my name and talking about it like it was just something somebody had made up out of thin air. I still half wondered if he wasn't only daydreaming and I think Angie felt the same way too. After all, some three months had drifted by without anything going on. Most of the time the old man didn't even talk about it. I mean snails or not, I would think that when you write a book, you send it in and the publisher happily sends off a check and next week the damned book is on a stand out in front of B. Dalton. Every time the professor got off on this stuff, I'd remind myself that months were drifting by—this was worse than my settlement. Then the whole thing would die down again.

But all of a sudden the old boy would start in all over again. I figured I might as well go along anyway. And every time I got impatient, I'd go through the same argument in my head. Why burst his bubble by telling him I thought he was full of shit? It wouldn't accomplish anything for me to jump up and tell him and Angie I thought they were both nut cases.

He held out the shaky hand. It was covered in purple splotches and trembled like a flower in a high wind. "Just look at me," he said. "My skin is as thin as tissue paper. At the slightest touch I collect another bruise."

Kirk cleared his throat. "Did you ever see Angie abuse him?"

"Of course not," I told him. "He didn't need anybody to do that. He abused himself."

* * *

One day the following week Angie was out fooling around someplace and I didn't have any work to do that day. I was kind of broke so I thought I'd drift over by grandpa's place and have a glass of wine and BS with him for a while.

He seemed glad to see me. His glasses rode cockeyed on the bridge of his nose. And his nose glowed like Rudolph the Red Nose Reindeer. White hair stuck out all over around his head like a halo. It seemed to me he could have afforded to get his damned glasses fixed, but whatever.

"We'll pour a glass," he solemnly said. "I'm glad you chose to come by, my boy. You're an author now. You have to learn to behave like one."

"I don't know how authors behave," I told him.

"Well most of the time they behave just as you and I, my boy. But you have to know what to say. I can teach you a good deal of what to say when you get out on the road."

I was half-surprised to see that he was starting in again about the damned book. Another couple of months had gone by since the thing had come up the last time. Even a wounded snail should have got home by now. He hadn't mentioned it lately and I'd sort of figured that, once and for all, the whole thing had blown over. I made it a point never to broach the subject when we were over at his place. But here he was back on it again. I kept my mouth shut. He shuffled around the room in his dirty pants and an old wrinkled shirt and that damned sweater. His tie looked as if the knot had never been untied since the day he'd tied it around his neck twenty years ago. He managed to pour us a glass of red and after he handed mine to me, he just made it back to his bed and fell back with a whoosh. The skin around his neck and arms was so thin and so finely wrinkled that it was painful to look at. He didn't have any muscle tone left in him. Just enough to hoist a glass. Maybe he used to go out once in a while before I came along, but he didn't ever go out any more. Over the last few months he got into the habit of giving Angie a check so we could pick up a few things for him from time to time. Mostly wine. He held the glass high as he fell back and somehow managed not to spill most of his wine. He smiled wisely.

"A man in my condition has to develop sea legs," he winked. His hand trembled and it got worse. "I wonder if I shouldn't perhaps take the purchase of a walking stick under advisement." He grabbed the shaking hand with the other hand and got his glass onto the nightstand. "Oh, just look at my hands," he told me. "I really do so worry about developing Alzheimer's disease—"

"Oh you don't have Alzheimer's disease," I assured him like I was a medical specialist they'd just flown in from the Mayo Clinic. "Angie's right, pops, it's just old-timer's disease. It's your age—and the fact that you drink a lot. Believe me, if I downed as much wine as you do, I'd be shaking too. I've always heard, with Alzheimer's you lose your memory. You don't have any trouble remembering things."

"You are very kind, Darcy. I hope you are right. Sometimes I do forget what I'm saying or doing at a given moment. 'Ah, memory fades, must the remembered perishing be?'" He nodded sagely like that meant something.

We visited for a while.

"Angie says you're a Communist," I said. To tell the actual truth, I wasn't exactly sure what a Communist did, except that I knew they used to run the country in Russia.

"A Communist you say?" He laughed. "A pacifist, that's what I am, my boy. A pacifist and a drunk. But a Communist? Never. I can't imagine…" he slowed to a stop. "I feel very guilty, Darcy, in that because I myself was living on drugs at the time of Blair's pregnancy, I did not realize that she too was living in a drug-induced coma. I sometimes wonder if that did not have a deleterious effect on our unborn Angela." He sighed. "I admit that sometimes Angela's behavior concerns me. But then again one of the few things of value that age and education have taught me is, 'Judge not, and ye shall not be judged', et cetera." Who indeed am I to judge or condemn the behavior of another?" He stared pitifully into his glass.

I sat there. Finally I said, "No wonder everybody quotes Shakespeare. I guess he was a pretty smart guy for his time."

Berry looked up and smiled. "Shakespeare? That was from Saint Luke in the Bible, young man. Haven't you ever read the Bible?"

"Oh..." I remembered something about going to Sunday School when I was a kid, but the only thing that stands out was the memory of Sister O'Donnell my Sunday School teacher. I think she was in her early twenties and she had a way of moving her body that excited even a dumb kid like me. At that time really big glasses were in, and on her they looked about as sexy as anything I'd ever seen. And what made her even more exciting was that she always wore starchy dresses and looked so prim and prissy, a perfect schoolmarm. But at the same time she had this way of giving you little glimpses of her breasts when she'd bend over by your chair. They were so soft that they trembled at her slightest movement and I couldn't swallow. Or she'd turn her back and bend over to pick up something from the floor and I'd see way up above her knees. She didn't really have a desk, just a little table and when she sat down behind her table she kept moving her legs so I couldn't take my eyes off them. And ever so often she'd spread them just enough so that I could glimpse her panties for a thousandth of a second. I remember that mostly she wore white panties, but sometimes blue or pink, or even black once. So much for what I learned in Sunday school. If she'd had it printed

THE LITTLE MORNINGS

on her panties I'd have learned the Sermon on the Mount by heart.

Mostly Berry did the talking and didn't make a lot of sense. But I politely drank his wine and listened.

"I regret many things, Darcy," he said. "You should have seen me at Berkeley in the late sixties, the early seventies. My wife and I had our ups and downs but we shared at least one thing in common: we both wore our hair long." He chuckled at that. "And we marched and smoked pot and did LSD—we were against war. We were against the action in Viet Nam. We were against the draft. I'm reminded of what Groucho Marx sang: 'Whatever it is, I'm against it'. Oh, I was full of fire in those days, Darcy. Hah hah hah. Yes, I was a regular hippie—and I had girl friends too—in fact girl friends precipitated my divorce. Angela's grandmother— ah, who knows where she is?

"Angela's mother, Blair, was still in school at the time. Although we were well into the seventies, it was still a time of flower children, you know, and I'm afraid neither Blair's mother nor I were very good examples. Before I knew it, Blair was pregnant with Angela and no husband in sight. As I say, I learned only later that during the entire pregnancy Blair had in no way changed her life style. Angela's father had disappeared in a cloud of drug-induced smoke. Then Blair died. I suppose Angela told you?" Without waiting for me to remember whether she had or not he went on: "I believe we told Angela that her mother died of influenza or something. Actually she had what we euphemistically referred to as a 'bad trip' shortly after Angela was born. I felt—I still feel extremely guilty," he said. "So I had to try to straighten up and be mother and father to little Angie."

"Well, I guess you didn't do so bad," I told him. I felt woozy from the heat and the wine and the heavy air.

After a while he appeared to doze off so I left. I didn't have many friends and sometimes it was nice to have somebody to talk to, so I sort of got in the habit of dropping by without Angie once in a while. I sure wasn't thinking about his stupid book. But it was kind of nice just to sit there and sip a little wine and listen to him go on. Actually I didn't even listen really. I just nodded once in a while to let him know he wasn't alone. And he didn't press me for information about myself. I hate when people start asking me personal questions. Maybe if I had a few things to brag about it would be different, but under the circumstances I didn't like to think about myself any more than I had to. With Berry I didn't feel like I had to say much or do any thinking. I enjoyed our visits more when Angie wasn't there because in a sense she sort of came between our man-to-man frankness. Over the course of several visits pops told me all kinds of his personal stuff. Like, he opened up and had to tell me all about his erectile dysfunction problems that had begun many years earlier. Like I really needed to hear that.

"Even in my forties I was still quite the buck," he told me. "But on this one particular occasion—this was after the divorce—I was overjoyed to have the opportunity to take an extremely popular and notorious blonde up to a so-called lovers' lane. Strange, I can't remember her name, but I remember the name of the lovers' lane. It was called Lake Herman Road. Ah, memories. And she was such a beautiful blonde with veronica blue eyes, or perhaps they were more of a periwinkle. Her hair was I believe natural and although I suspected that in later years her figure would become blowsy, she was at the moment as ripe as a sun kissed peach. Ripe and delicious. She was a graduate student. I'm not proud to admit that at the time I smoked marijuana night and day. I did LSD and sometimes tried other things. My God, I seem to recall a dry period when I was reduced to ingesting diet pills for some supposed high that I don't remember noticing. I survived on drugs. When you live on drugs long enough, Darcy, life begins to assume a dreamlike quality that alters one's thinking about everything, including ethics: right and wrong, good and bad...on a cosmic level, what is good? What is bad?" He sighed and drank a swallow of wine. "We began to see everything as through a glass, darkly. Anyway, after some heavy petting and panting, we had just begun to, eh do what lovers do under similar circumstances—" he winked, "—when at that moment a patrol car drove by and flashed his spotlight into our window.

"We managed to pull ourselves together and sat there obediently while the officer checked our identities and my vehicle registration. He left us with a stern warning. Very near to the place where we had parked, two young persons had recently been shot by some madman, it seemed, and the officer wanted to remind us of that fact." Berry used two hands now to get his glass to his lips. He sipped some wine and swallowed. "All that was of course well and good, my dear friend, but alas, when my flower reopened her petals to receive me, nothing happened. The emotional drain of having the officer shine an unexpected and unwelcome beam of light in our faces and check our identities at such a critical moment combined with the dismal story of murder within arm's reach had drained every emotion from my body. I can't even consider what might have happened if the news had come out that Professor Jason Berry got caught in lovers' lane with one of his students...I was left numb and could not react—not even to this goddess. Unfortunately she took my lack of forthright action as a grievous insult. She of course did absolutely nothing to rekindle my flame. On the contrary, she folded her arms, got into a very bad mood and told me that since I was of no use to her, I might as well take her home where she had an electric dildo that she felt would be much more cooperative and satisfying than I was. I dutifully took her home but from that time on, each time I found myself on the point of such intimacy, the terrible specter arose that I might not be able to—perform—and in fearing of course, I did experience difficulty." He sighed. "It's sad that a man's ego should be so fragile. And it hurts men even to admit such a possibility. It hurts and embarrasses us." He poured a little more wine into his glass and looked at it. "Ah," he said, and took another swallow.

I didn't know what to say. I just sat there and drank wine and nodded in understanding. I'd kind of grown to like the flavor of the wine by this time. I noticed that when we were alone Berry tended to let his hair down. He didn't throw in quite so much literary crap and quote Shakespeare or whoever with every other breath. I guess he didn't feel like he had to impress me anymore, and that was good.

* * *

I got in the habit buying a jug of wine to take up with me when I came up to visit Berry. It was bad enough that Angie sponged off him all the time. I didn't want him to think I only came up there to sponge off him too. One day I bought a jug of something red and headed up. When I got to his room he was standing shakily on his feet in the middle of the room by his typewriter. Huddled in that heavy old sweater he was crumpling up what looked like manuscripts and stuffing them into a black garbage bag. He had wet stains running down his pant legs. I guessed he hadn't been able to grab a jug fast enough. But he looked about as sober as I'd ever seen him. And he looked glad to see the wine coming.

Seeing all the paper going bye-bye, I gave up inside on any goofy ideas I still might have had about his book. I guessed he'd decided it was time to wake up and smell the roses—or whatever it was that he smelled around there.

"What's all that?" I asked.

"My boy, this is all the literary garbage I have lying about—all my drunken litanies and jeremiads—it is nothing but literary flatulence in a closed room."

I was right. There went my famous future. I knew it was too good to be true. But on the other hand, in a way it was sort of a relief too. I couldn't have handled the job anyway and I knew it.

"But I thought you had your book sold," I said. I guess I still held onto just a faint vestige of hope.

"Ah, the valuable novels. Not to worry. My dear boy, in this cleansing, novels, like batteries for a new toy, are not included. Hah hah. Since they appear to have some monetary if not great literary value, we'll keep them in the hope that the wine may continue to flow. And I want to be able to leave a little something for Angela, a lovely and wonderful girl despite the air of chthonic mystery that surrounds her…"

I'm not sure what he was saying but it sounded good and brought a sigh of relief to me. Maybe there was hope after all. I couldn't make up my mind whether I wanted this or did not want it. Every time I'd think about it, it was touch and go.

He pointed vaguely toward the dirty white cardboard file box that sat against one wall where it had always been. A dark brown sock hung off the side of the box.

"That is all I leave behind, Darcy. All this," he waved his hand over the garbage bag, "this drivel that I am destroying is the product of a diseased and drunken old mind. Even half drunk I look it over and see that I don't make sense. No wonder no one wants to publish any of it. Even *The Sacramento News* rejected my latest guest commentary for which there is no remuneration whatsoever. That, I think, puts me in my rightful place. 'Less than the dust…even less am I'. No, Darcy, the time has come to get rid of all this excess baggage. When I go I don't want to leave this sort of thing behind. People would only laugh and shake their heads. They would see what a deceitful fraud I was and they would only feel sorry for me. Now only these few novels remain. They may not endure as say, the works of Dickens do. And it's certainly not the work of a Shakespeare. Really you know, *en fin de compte*, it isn't really the author who is remembered; it is his or her creations, Captain Ahab, Scarlett O'Hara, David Copperfield, Sherlock Holmes, Hamlet, Lear…I imagine my little efforts may well be forgotten within ten years. Five. Who can say? What difference does it make? But never mind. I believe these are the equals of, if not better than much of the commercial trash to be found on display at Barnes & Noble. But as for me, I write no more, my boy. *La comeddia è finita.* I have finished. I shall beat my typewriter into a ploughshare or some such—nay, I shall rather hurl it from yon window. I lay down my plume. From this day forward shall I be satisfied to make do with the writings of others." His shoulders dropped even more than usual and he glanced aimlessly about him. Piles of books, papers, garbage…wine jugs and remains of snacks…what a mess.

"But I thought you said you couldn't read anymore," I told him. I stood bent there, crumpling papers beside him.

"Ah." He raised that finger.. "'This I cannot read, but in Nature's infinite book of secrecy, A little I can read'…" He tried to tear a fistful of sheets in half before crumpling them up. They wouldn't give. I realized how frail he really was. He gave up and settled for crumpling them together before he shoved them into the bag. "I've read too much, Darcy." He suddenly raised his head and spoke as if to an audience, "'Thou wear a lion's hide! Doff it for shame, and hang a calf's skin on those recreant limbs.' Oh Darcy, I am sorry. I am so sorry. Don't pay any attention to me. I'm disgusting. You must despise me. I'm an old fraud and a fake. All my life I have tried to gain respect and keep my pride by impressing everyone with my erudition. Lacking talent and inspiration, I steal the words that others have so painstakingly written and usurp them for my own self-aggrandizement. Through this I managed to maintain the respect of possible detractors and keep them at bay. I'll tell you something, Darcy: Any fool can read a book and memorize words. I constantly borrow the words of other writers—much easier than coining something of my own, wouldn't you agree? When all else fails, one can still impress others by reminding them how well read one is." He picked up the jug I'd brought and unscrewed the cap and filled our glasses.

The Little Mornings

I figured Berry knew what he was talking about. I took that as a bad sign, whatever it meant. I wondered if he was getting ready to poop out on us. I noticed then that he was wearing a different tie today but it still looked like he'd been wearing it for twenty years just like the one I'd seen him wear before. By now I was pretty much used to the smell around there and didn't let it bother me anymore. We drank wine and I helped him crumple up papers. I glanced at a few of the typewritten pages and I have to admit they sure didn't make any sense to me. Long convoluted sentences without commas or periods. Sentences stuffed with quotations borrowed from God knows where—words that had been x'd over and retyped, foreign words and words that had been written twice, new words right over old words so you couldn't read either one of them...and repetitions and underlined words. Words all written with capital letters. Sometimes whole sentences had been underlined. It was pretty sad. I just hoped his famous novels were really better than what I was looking at. He seemed to think so, but down deep I wasn't a hundred percent positive that he'd ever really sent that first one in. Maybe he was just trying to build up to it. I used to work with a guy who always assured the boss that he'd done something, but when the boss pinned him down, the guy'd admit he hadn't actually quite done it. But he was fixing to do it. Fixing to do it. Yeah. Maybe Berry never would send the damned books in. Maybe they were really just as bad as everything he was shoving into the garbage bag. Who knew? That reminded me of something I picked up from a Ukrainian girl I dated a couple of times before Angie ever came into my life. I was telling her something about what I was going to do one of these days and she said, "Drinking tea isn't getting the wood chopped," or something like that. I didn't quite get it at the time, but suddenly I remembered and it made sense. Maybe all grandpa was doing was sitting around drinking—only in his case it was wine, not tea. Maybe he was only *fixing* to chop the damned wood.

"It's true," he went on. "I can no longer read, but I still enjoy looking about me and seeing my books gathering dust. At least I have the opportunity to think, ah, perhaps tomorrow I shall re-read *Germinal*. It has been a while." He sighed. "Of course I could never read it again. Much too tedious. I no longer have the attention span. But even old men dream, you see." He coughed a little bit. He drank some more wine and I drank some more wine.

By the time we'd finished crumpling up sheets of paper we had a thirty-gallon garbage bag pretty well filled and we were both three sheets to the wind. When I left I took the bag with me and threw it into the Dumpster in the alley behind his house.

I sure wasn't seeing clearly and should never have tried to drive the truck in my condition, but somehow I made it home. There was still no Angie when I got there but I smelled perfume and then I found a note on the counter by the sink.

Dar, I'm going to Old Sac to hear a jazz band with a couple of the girls. Be back later. Love, Angie.

That didn't sit well with me. I didn't know she had any girl friends around—I hadn't seen them. In my own experience, when a natural girl like Angie stops to put on perfume and stuff, that's a bad sign. I passed out on the bed and slept for a couple of hours. Later I woke up and took a long shower and lay on the bed with a headache watching television. When Angela finally came in I could tell she'd been drinking more than usual and there was something private about her that I didn't like, like there was something she wasn't telling me. But I didn't want to push it.

That night I dreamed. I dreamed that Jack had come over and was drinking beer with Angie and me.

"I'm Scandinavian," he told her, tilting his bottle. "I'm really Norwegian, but my mother always taught me to say Scandinavian. She said when I say I'm Scandinavian, I'm being truthful, but if I tell people I'm Norwegian, then I'm bragging."

In my dream I laughed just as I laughed when I'd heard it twenty times before in my waking life.

But then he began making advances to Angie and I didn't like that. "Hey, Scandinavian or not," I cautioned him, "you better lay off or you're going to have a lump on your square head, buddy."

And then it got worse because I could see that Angie didn't mind his advances at all—she seemed to have forgotten all about me being there.

Then suddenly Jason Berry was there holding a glass of wine in one shaking hand. Now I was in Berry's room and I don't think Angie and Jack were there anymore.

"Look at me shake," Berry said. "My life is over."

With that I jumped up and grabbed him by the throat and began strangling him. "Your damned right it's over, old man," I told him through gritted teeth. "It's my book. It's my fucking book. They're *all* my books and nobody's ever going to say different, especially not you. Darcy Lemarsh. It's my name and my books and nobody needs a shaky old drunk to spoil this picture."

Even while I was choking him and he gasped for breath, he was still able to speak clearly, "But Angie... What about my Angie? I did it for her. I accepted you and admitted you into our circle so that when I was gone my baby girl might have someone to take care of her, Darcy."

"I'm going to take care of your baby girl, all right," I promised as I squeezed his throat. "Right after I take care of you. Don't you worry about that old man."

With that he relaxed and I continued to choke him until his body became limp and I knew he was dead. I dropped his lifeless form to the floor and went over and gathered up the cardboard file box that held his books and left the room.

Behind me, even though I'd gone, I knew Angie was there now and out of the corner of my eye I watched her throw herself over his lifeless body. "He's dead," Angie was crying. "My grandpa's dead…you killed him. You killed my grandpa."

"Shut up," I told her. I was running with the white file box of grandpa's books and the lid blew off and all the sheets of paper went flying all over the place and I was losing them, losing everything. At the same time I was standing there beside his dead body and talking to Angela, "We've got the books and that's all you or I will ever need. The old man's gone. It was time for him to go. He wanted to go. He told me so himself. He made me do it. I'm Darcy Lemarsh. I'm the author now. These are my books and you're my accomplice and don't you ever forget it."

I woke up in a sweat. My hands were shaking as bad as Berry's. I rolled over and raised my head and looked at Angie. She was sleeping quietly beside me. The tip of her tongue barely showed between her teeth. A few bright beads of sweat stood on her forehead and I didn't wonder; my own body was drenched in sweat. I threw off my sheet and looked at the back of my hands. I half expected to see purple blotches on them. I lay there shaking at the horror of my dream and wanted to go take another shower but somewhere along there I must have drifted off into a black dreamless sleep.

* * *

More weeks drifted by. Nothing new on my settlement and nothing new on our famous novel. I'd tell myself to forget the book, and then next thing, I'd find myself thinking about it, about being a famous author on television and stuff and people asking for my autograph and what it would be like. Then I'd get mad at myself. Famous author. Christ, I was lucky if I could remember how to spell my name! I worked most of the time and tried not to think about all that. But every time I'd lie back and shut my eyes, either I'd start going over the settlement or I'd start in on the infinite possibilities I worked out in my head about the novel and all the things that could happen to me if it ever came to pass. I thought about going to Hollywood. One thing Berry had been right about was Hollywood over the lottery. I think going to Hollywood would probably be better than winning the lottery, at least for me. One day I'm a so-so painter in dirty overalls and the next day I'm a famous author hobnobbing with producers and movie stars...I always thought of people like that as if they lived on a different planet. I'd never seriously thought about actually being around them, talking to them-having them consider me one of them. I'd have to get up off the bed and down a brew or take a couple of aspirin—anything just to get my mind off all that crap so I could get a little peace of mind.

In the meantime Angie tried a couple of jobs that came her way, but they didn't work out. She worked in a place that made no tears shampoo for kids. The plastic bottles were cartoon characters and she was supposed to make sure they were full as they came down the line and then screw the proper head on them. But I guess she couldn't keep up and ever so often—according to her—some of the other girls would switch bottles without warning and she'd get the wrong heads on the bottles or else they'd speed up the line and a bottle or two would get by without a top at all and spill out down the pike someplace. Nobody liked her. They were all out to get her.

Then there was the ball pen place out on Power Inn. She had a big block full of holes and was supposed to put one part of the pen in each hole and then go back and put in the next part and so on until all the holes were full of completed pens. She got paid by each block of pens she finished. The girls came in blocks too. There were blocks of Viet Nam girls, blocks of Cambodians and blocks of Mexicans and blocks of blacks. They didn't like Angie either because she was the real minority among the minorities who worked there. Angie didn't fit in I guess. Evidently some of the girls could knock those blocks of pens out fast and make pretty good money, but not Angela. It reminded me of the time when I was a kid up in Oregon. Early in the morning I'd get on a truck with a bunch of other yawning people and go out strawberry picking. We got paid so much a box but I'd dawdle along and eat every really beautiful berry I saw so by the end of the day I hadn't made enough money to pay for the can of Dinty Moore's Beef Stew I brought along for lunch. But sometimes, thinking about it, I can still catch a distant taste of the tart sweetness and the heady aroma of those fresh strawberries in the heat of the noonday sun.

Angie didn't have anybody to talk to at work so she'd get lost in thought, I think. She took forever to fill a block. And then half the pens weren't assembled right so they kicked her out of there. Of course it was totally their fault and she didn't like the job anyway. Then there was a job trimming loose threads off towels and washcloths and stuff like that, but that didn't work out either.

More and more often she'd go out with the "girls" after work and I began to notice how much time she spent getting ready. Part of what I liked about Angie when she worked at The Owl was the fact that she was normally very natural. She didn't have to shave her legs or her underarms. The bit of fuzz she had in her armpits was so light that you didn't even notice it. She usually didn't wear much in the way of makeup or perfume. She did a couple of times when we first went out together, but that didn't last. And she usually didn't spend a lot of time fooling around with her hair. She kept it short, which showed off her slender neck that me and her grandpa thought was so beautiful. She washed her hair almost every day, but just a little brushing and she was ready, and I liked that too. I hate women who wear their hair so lacquered up you could bust your nose on it.

Most of the time Angie wore little tank tops and jeans, or sometimes shorts. In Sacramento we have long hot summers and I'd even taken to wearing shorts myself a good part of the year when I wasn't working. Jack found some white painters' shorts at a Target or someplace but Ephraim didn't like that. The white work shorts disappeared as quickly as they'd appeared.

"If you're going out with the girls why get all dressed up?" I asked Angie. "You don't dress up like that for me."

"That's because you like me the way I am," she replied simply. "I just dress up a little to impress the girls, that's all. I want them to know you take care of me, Dar. Don't worry about it."

I tried to accept that as a reasonable explanation, but down deep I couldn't help wondering.

Then the next day at work Jack said something about some club he'd been to the night before. The River Rat. Strange. That's where Angie said she'd gone with the girls. If Jack had seen Angie there I was sure he'd have mentioned it. Where in the hell was she then?

I know I'm pretty slow sometimes, but finally another little idea crept into my brain: maybe she was at The River Rat all right but Jack hadn't mentioned seeing her because they were in there together—had my nasty dream about them come true? Of course I could've made a big stink about it. Maybe in retrospect I should have. It might have saved me a lot of grief down the line. But whether I was right or wrong, the upshot of the whole argument would probably mean my having to move out. Another bad choice I'd have to make and I didn't want that, not right now.

Angie and I bickered almost every day of course. Sometimes it was something as silly as the way she put the paper on the roller in the can. She always put the roll of paper on the roller so that you had to reach under and pull the paper up. I always put it the other way, so that you pulled the paper down from over the top.

"If you were supposed to pull it up from the bottom, they'd put the damned flowers on the inside of the roll," I told her and she came right back with her own convoluted logic.

"Are you mentally challenged?" she said. "They can't print the flowers on the inside of the paper." That went on half an afternoon. In the end I guess she got me. I couldn't outtalk her with the way they print flowers on toilet paper. Then there was the matter of the toilet seat. I always forgot and left it up. She'd give me hell for not putting it back down after I used it. Seemed to me it was just as much trouble for me to put it up as it was for her to put it down. But no, it was a man's duty to put the seat back down for the lady after he finished taking a leak. Okay, I could accept that. It was just hard to remember.

"Christ," I said another time, bending down and looking into the refrigerator, "there's no beer, no pop—" I looked at an empty cigarette carton. "Did I ever ask you why in the hell you keep your cigs in the frig?"

Angie gave me a long sideways glance as if to say I was indeed mentally challenged. "It keeps them fresh," she said simply.

"Yeah, well it must be nice to keep an empty carton staying fresh in the frig. At least there's something in here. Since it's empty and you're not going to put any cigarettes back into the carton, why the hell can't you throw it into the trash, would that be too much to ask?"

That started us off again. Especially when I told her she should just throw the empty carton on the floor because that's where all the rest of the trash was. Then she came back with me never offering to help a bit. All I wanted to do was lie on the bed and drink beer and watch football. Which wasn't true. I had pretty much given up sports on television because she bitched so much about it. I guess we were just like any couple that spends time together. All it would take was some little thing like the empty cigarette carton or whatever and we'd fly into another dumb argument. Sometimes we'd have a pretty good fight and keep at it until it got so ridiculous we'd break down and start laughing in spite of ourselves and then we'd make love, which was extra good, and we'd be sweet as pie to each other for a week. Sometimes she'd even buy me a shirt or a couple pairs of socks or something. But then little by little we'd drift back into the same-old, same-old…

I can't blame everything on Angie. I had never really shared an apartment with anyone before. And I wasn't used to having to consider somebody else every time I flushed the toilet. But just having Angie there with me, I was comfortable and I'd be satisfied to lie around and watch television for hours on end, even the crap she liked to watch—something I couldn't do when she wasn't home. I couldn't even enjoy a game. When she wasn't home I'd get restless or nervous and pace around and keep looking out the window at Barney's Place across the street. Sometimes I'd go over there and have a beer but I really didn't like it too much.

Barney's was a dark place, shabby and rundown. As far as I ever learned Barney hadn't been seen around there in thirty years. A guy named Big Al owned the place but he had other interests and didn't come around very often. Sometimes a woman would be tending bar and sometimes a man, but it didn't matter. It was always slow and quiet. A few old timers sitting at the bar holding onto a glass of beer or staring at a shot of whiskey that sat on the bar in front of them. Some would sit there and drink coffee. Those were people who for one reason or another had decided to quit for a while. Once in a while an old couple would play pool or shuffleboard—frowsy old gals with too much makeup on and beer bellies and crusty-faced old timers with even bigger beer bellies and rings of keys hanging from their belts. But most of the time I'd only see two or three people lounging around the bar. Nobody every played any music when I was in there and nobody talked much either. I liked it that way.

On the other hand, when Angie *was* home she wanted me to forget everything and sit there adoringly and stare at her. She had to be the center of my universe. For me to watch television except what and when she was watching something, that was unbearable. I couldn't pick up a magazine or daydream or anything else. Angie wanted all my attention all the time, even if she was looking at a magazine or watching television. But I learned to cope with that. It all got to be a big pain sometimes, but when all was said and done, I liked being with her more than I did being back in my room alone or sitting over at Barney's. And not having more than a few vague suspicions to go on anyway, I decided not to rock the boat.

* * *

The next morning Jack and I were repainting a small building that housed chiropractors and a masseuse and paralegals and stuff like that. We tried to work on the shady sides of the building and stay out of the sun as much as we could.

As I said, Angie had been "out with the girls" at the River Rat last night.

"You didn't happen to run into Angie at the River Rat, did you?"

Jack kind of froze for a flash and then went back to painting without looking at me.

"Why, what makes you ask?" he said.

"Yeah well, I just thought you guys might have run into each other—I know you both like jazz." I tried to keep it real casual and hide any real interest. "She mentioned going there too. It must be a big place…"

Jack mumbled something and painted a little bit and then said, "Actually I think I did see her, but not to talk to—you know. She was with some girls I think. Why, did she say she saw me?"

"No…she didn't say anything." I stopped now and looked right at him. Now he was painting away as if he was Michelangelo bent on getting the Sistine Chapel finished before the Pope showed up. "She wasn't with any guys?"

"I—" Jack stopped painting and stood there looking foolish.

"You didn't even say hi?"

"I—oh, well yeah—I mean I bought her a drink. That's all. I didn't mention it because I didn't want you to think—"

"Think what, Jack? You didn't want me to think you've been jumping Angie behind my back? You can't find a whore of your own?"

Now he was all red and almost shaking. "I—I—"

I'd only been half sure before but now I was positive and getting madder all the time. Jack wasn't any great shakes to look at and certainly I didn't consider him my best friend in the world, not that I had one. I'd worked with the bastard for over a year now and I certainly had no reason to think he'd manage to get behind my back and start banging my girl when I wasn't looking.

"God damn it, Jack, why would you pull something like that? I thought we were friends. I wouldn't pull something like that on you, and you know it."

"No I don't, Dar. How do I know what you'd do? Besides," he hung his head as he sort of loosened up, "it wasn't like that. I mean I didn't go looking—we just ran into each other one night at the River Rat. They had a local jazz group playing and I dropped in to grab a brewsky and listen and there was Angie. She was with some skagg—I forgot her name already." He shrugged. "Hey, I bought them a couple of drinks, you know how it goes…"

"Yeah, I know how that goes all right," I said through clenched teeth. "And then one thing led to another. You got rid of the skagg and jumped her, didn't you, Jack?"

"Hey no—no, well, I mean…not then. Not—the first time. I—"

I've only lost it a very few times in my life. A couple of times when I was a kid. There was this big kid. He had a reputation for being the school bully. Once I was coming down the stairs between classes and he was coming up. I didn't get out of his way fast enough so he nailed me and started telling me what he was going to do to me. I was so scared I almost wet my pants, but suddenly the blackness closed in around me and I lost it and popped him in the nose so hard he went flying back down the steps with me right on top of him. I couldn't even think. It was almost as if I were a bystander watching some other people. We both got suspended for a few days but he never messed with Darcy again. There had been a couple of incidents like that. And this was one of them. It was like Darcy shut down and somebody else took over. Part of me stood in the darkness by my ladder and watched somebody else throw my pail of paint at Jack's head. He ducked and paint went flying all over the face of the building and all over a woman who was just coming out of a chiropractor's office. I vaguely remember her screaming as I threw myself on top of Jack and down we went onto the concrete walkway under the overhang. I tried to slug him in the jaw but he turned his head and my knuckle scraped hard over the concrete and that only made me madder. Jack wasn't as big as I was and I managed to keep him down and finally got in a good one right in the nozzle.

Blood spurted from his nostrils. "Christ," he screamed, "you broke my goddam nose!"

"I'll break more than your fucking nose, you bastard," I yelled as we rolled around on the concrete. The woman with paint all over her was still screaming in the background and by now other people had come out of the offices. The Darcy standing by the ladder knew somebody must be calling the police by now but I couldn't stop. I was so enraged that my whole body shook as if I had hold of a high voltage electric cable and couldn't turn loose. I couldn't even cuss him clearly. All I could do was spit out weird sounds while we rolled around. Jack kept trying to duck my fists. He didn't even try to hit back now that I think about it.

Suddenly strong hands grabbed me and jerked me bodily off Jack and stood me up and held me in place.

"Put your right hand behind your back," a voice commanded and I did it before I even realized what was going on. Now, cuffed, standing there with bleeding knuckles in my dirty white overalls all smeared with paint and blood, I began to calm down a little.

"Adult male Caucasian, first of Darcy—that's David, Adam, Robert, Charles—" The cop lost me in there someplace while he rattled off names into his microphone. Jack sat up on the walkway touching gently at his bleeding nose with the index fingers of both hands and crying and the woman with the paint all over her stood there behind him with her head down. She stood with her feet together and her arms spread out like she was hanging on the cross or something. Most of the fight was gone out of me by then and out of the corner of my eye I saw Ephraim coming toward us. He might be an old drunk, but he always took care of business.

"My God," he cried, "what have you done? That's it. You're both fired. I don't ever want you on another job of mine again. That's it. You're fired." He turned around and started talking to one of the chiropractors or somebody and the woman was looking at him now.

"I sure hope you've got plenty of insurance, mister," she said. "You're going to need it." Ephraim turned to her and began buttering her up. He could be pretty good with the BS.

I thought I was going to jail for sure. The cops were all ready to take me in. They wanted to. Since they had arrived while we were still fighting, they said it was their duty. At the moment I didn't care, but as it turned out, Jack didn't want to press any charges and neither did Ephraim. He finally calmed the woman down and promised that his insurance would take care of her so she decided not to press any charges either and the people that owned the building didn't care just so long as Ephraim cleaned up the mess and got the building finished. One of the cops conferred with somebody on his radio and finally I guess they figured it wasn't worth the paper work just to have me and Jack back out on the street in half an hour. They took my cuffs off and told me I got lucky this time. An emergency vehicle came and took Jack off to have his nose looked at.

After things calmed down and the cops left, a woman who worked in one of the chiropractor offices brought me inside. She was sympathetic.

"I know sometimes bad things happen to nice people," she said. "People lose control. Sometimes I think that's what life is all about: self control." She cleaned up my knuckles and put a couple of Band-Aids on them and I went to a bar and sat there drinking beer and wondering what was ever going to become of me.

It took hours for me to get myself halfway calmed down again. I couldn't even get drunk from the beer. It was too early to go home—I wasn't ready to face Angie yet. I just didn't know what I was going to do or say. I could get indignant and grab my stuff and move out. I could shut my mouth and eyes and pretend nothing had ever happened—right!

I decided to drop by Grandpa Berry's and share a glass of wine with him. I'd already drunk a gallon of beer but it hadn't helped so what the hell. I picked up a jug of wine at the liquor store on the corner.

He seemed delighted to see me. He didn't look too drunk. His hair looked worse than usual, sticking up all over his head and his nose looked bigger and redder then ever.

"Come in, my boy," he said. He looked curiously at me. "Did you fall from a scaffold?" he asked.

I told him I got into a fight.

"Tsk, tsk. Well, let us enjoy a glass of your vintage wine."

"Yeah, the clerk said this was a great vintage," I said. "Tuesday morning."

He'd tucked his necktie into his shirtfront so he wouldn't spill wine on it—not that it mattered a bit at this stage of the game. He staggered around and caught the tail of his sweater on the table. That damned near pulled him off his feet, but he steadied himself before I could jump in to help him. He managed to get two glasses of wine poured and he sat down on the edge of his bed and I sat on his work chair by the typewriter and we sipped wine and BSd for a while. He was drunker than I'd realized at first but I was getting there too and I didn't really care. I just needed a friendly ear.

Finally I got around to telling him why I was in the fight and I told him the whole story about Angie.

He sucked in air. "You must not judge Angela too harshly," he told me. "Remember, Angela's mother passed away at a very tender age. Her father was never there. He disappeared before she was born. A passing whimsy. An era of flower children, drugs and free love—and now Angela has to pay for their sins. We heard later that her father had been killed in a car crash in Los Angeles shortly after Angie's birth. Since Angie's mother, Blair, and this boy were never married it was natural for Angela to take her mother's family name, Berry." He sighed. "I never knew the man, but Angela had to get those eyes from him. Aah, after her mother passed away, I was both mother and father. I was better—or worse—than mother and father, I was an indulgent and guilty foster parent. I spoiled Angela. I can't deny it. I felt not only guilty that her mother was gone, but to be honest with you, Darcy, for some reason I felt a closer attachment to Angela than I did to my actual daughter. It was as if Angela took Blair's place and became my daughter; not only my daughter, but my only daughter. She never had to lift a finger. I tried to straighten out my life. Because of my schedule and lifestyle

I never found time to spend with Blair, but I managed to find the time to lavish on Angela. My little princess. Blair had somehow got started on drugs in college—crazy, I know. Here I was, her dignified and scholarly, not to mention well-respected father doing LSD, smoking pot and drinking like a freshman and yet I had absolutely no idea that Blair…" He shook his head sadly. "Not in my most drug-induced flights of fancy, Darcy.

"One night when Angie was still a baby someone from the hospital called me and I learned that Blair had died of some sort of overdose of drugs." He shook his head sadly and drank more wine. I drank some more too.

"Yeah, I remember. You told me," I said.

"For what is may be worth, I raised Angela from that time on—she was about two I believe. I did the best I could. I really tried to straighten up my own life. As I say, I spoiled her. I found the time to take care of her. I prepared her meals, bought her anything she wanted; I walked her to school every morning and got her through school. I took her to Disneyland. But it became embarrassing. One day when I went to pick Angie up after school—I think she was in the fourth or fifth grade—one of her schoolmates asked, 'Are you Angie's father or her grandfather?' Well, I had to admit that I was her grandfather, but from that time on there was a difference, a difference I could sense. The other children had a mother and father who cared for them and picked them up after school; Angela had only a grandfather. Somehow to the children, probably to Angela, and ultimately to me certainly, that made a difference.

"Later, in high school my presence was less evident." He poured more wine. "I had hoped, taken it for granted in fact, that Angie would go on to college, but my pension doesn't allow for much in the way of college tuition and her grades did not make Angie a promising candidate for a scholarship. And in my weakness I drifted into drinking more and more. That means I paid less and less attention to

Angie's behavior. She got involved with the R.O.T.C. for a brief period and they hoped to drag her off into the army I think, but that blew over and of course," he looked down at himself sitting there with his water glass of wine in his shaking hand, "as I say, I was scarcely a model. Finally my drinking got so bad that poor Angie could not even bear to live with me." He chuckled. "Besides, it got to the point where I was no longer able to cook and take care of her…"

I sat there and drank my wine. My tongue felt thick and my mouth tasted sour. I didn't know what to say or what I was going to do. I tried to imagine him taking care of a kid. He couldn't even take care of himself. I almost laughed to myself as I realized something: the combination of wine and piss had almost got to smell good. I realized that I almost looked forward to coming over and sitting there in the middle of it. I remembered that first time how I wondered if he ever got the wrong bottle and drank piss instead of wine. I looked at my glass again and wondered if I was drinking piss or wine right now. Who cared? I laughed to myself. Right now everything was a-okay.

"You must not judge our little Angela too harshly," grandpa went on. "She may have her weak moments— 'Made weak by time and fate, but strong in will'—our little Angela had a difficult beginning but I believe that, down deep, she is very loyal and you may depend on her to do the right thing in the end, Darcy."

I wondered. I wondered more how I could forgive her— not to her face—but in my own heart. I didn't want to harbor any resentment inside. I didn't want to be one of those jerks that always bring all their resentments up every time there's a little fight. What the old man said made sense, and I realized that the same thing might have happened to me if the right gal came along and threw herself at me—and it wouldn't have to mean a damned thing either, but—

By the time I left there I was pretty drunk. I was so drunk I couldn't remember exactly where I'd parked the truck, which was probably lucky for me. I walked home. I didn't say anything to Angie. It was time for me to come home anyway. I just threw myself onto the bed while she sat smoking and watching television and the next thing I knew I was out like a light.

* * *

I woke up with a hangover sometime early the next morning. Angie still lay beside me sleeping peacefully. She was snoring very lightly and her hair against my face tickled. I moved slowly and got out of bed. My mouth felt like I had a dirty sock in it. In the bathroom I took two aspirin and drank two big glasses of water. By now I was in the habit of shaving every day so I washed my face and began shaving just like normal. I brushed my teeth and combed my hair with a damp comb and began to feel a little better. I went over to the range and put on some water for a cup of instant coffee. I didn't like instant but it was all we had. It didn't even taste like real coffee but Angie filled hers up with so much powdered creamer and sugar that she couldn't tell the difference. Angie didn't even know how to make real coffee. Of course, I didn't either.

I guess my stirring about woke her up. I still hadn't decided what to say or how to say it. I wasn't at all sure if I was going to be there that night or what. She didn't say anything. She lit a cigarette and blew out smoke and while she was in the can I made her a cup of instant coffee too. When she came out wearing nothing but panties and a little shift I handed the cup to her without a word. Angie took it and kind of looked at me and finally went over and sat on the edge of the bed and flicked ashes into her ashtray. She looked at me sideways.

"What happened to your hands?"

"Didn't I tell you last night?" I countered.

"You told me something but I never figured out exactly what you meant, Dar. You were drunk."

"I meant Jack and I got into a fight, that's what I meant." I tried to sip coffee but it was still too hot. I stood there and looked at the sink. For the first time I noticed a big black chink where the porcelain had been chipped off. It was shaped like a butterfly and looked like it had been there for a long time. My head started pounding again and my stomach didn't feel good.

Angie hesitated a beat looking at me. "You and Jack were fighting?"

"What did you expect?"

She just stared at me. She wasn't about to admit anything that easy.

"Yeah, I found out about you and Jack and we got into a discussion and it turned kind of bad—if you couldn't figure that out for yourself."

She looked at her cup and didn't say anything. I walked over and pulled the curtain back and looked out the window. Barney's Place was still there. In the street two druggies in raggedy jeans and shirts sauntered along, their heads close together. I waited. Finally Angie tasted her coffee and spoke without looking at me.

"It wasn't like that," she said. Her shoulders slumped even more. She stabbed out the cigarette and immediately lit another one. "I mean—it was just—we ran into each other at a club. You know, they were playing jazz. You didn't tell me Jack was a jazz freak."

"I didn't think it would turn out to be something important in your life," I told her. I can be pretty scornful when I get indignant.

"Well, he just happened to be there. What were we supposed to do? Pretend we didn't know each other? We're all supposed to be friends here, right?"

I didn't answer that one.

I moved away from the window and it was her turn to get up and wander over to look out, "Then," she sipped some more coffee, "we—everybody drank too much I guess and—

not that anything happened—that night. We just kidded around a little but then, you know, every time I'd go to the River Rat, Jack would show up. He's *your* friend. I couldn't just ignore him. He started showing me a lot of attention. Something you sure don't do anymore. I guess I was a little bit flattered. He started telling me how much he'd liked me from the first time we met. Besides," she gave me that sidelong look. "A girl likes to keep her options open. You never know what's going to happen."

"What does that mean?"

"I just—I don't know, Dar. I know you love me but you never seem interested in anything—permanent, you know?"

"I promised you an engagement ring when we get our settlement, didn't I?" I hadn't really been thinking much about that but right now it seemed like a good thing to say. Right away her eyes brightened. She got a pouty flirty little smile around the edges of her lips.

"Did you really mean it, Dar? I mean…you weren't just shitting me were you? About the ring, getting married?"

"Of course not." I put down my cup and came over to her. She looked so small and forlorn. Even though I had a headache and was still mad and hurt, watching her sit there defenseless and practically naked with that flirty little attitude got me hot and next thing I knew I took her cigarette and put it into the ash tray and her coffee went flying and we were rolling around on the bed and she was crying, "Oh Dar…oh Darcy…"

* * *

Later that morning when I went downstairs and didn't see the truck I began to remember. I hotfooted it over to Berry's and found the truck parked around the corner. I never mentioned that to Angie.

For about a week we lived off what I had coming from Ephraim who griped that I was lucky to get paid at all because of the damage I caused. Of course I knew he had to pay me anyway but I didn't push it. It wasn't his fault and he always treated me pretty good at that. He put up with a lot of stuff, especially in the beginning when I was getting started.

I made a few dismal attempts to find work as a painter. I kind of liked the work and besides, by now I felt like I wasn't too bad at it. But every time I had to tell somebody I'd been working for Ephraim, I could see they weren't going to hire me. I swear every painter in town knows every other painter.

A couple of times after that we visited Professor Berry and without actually asking, Angie managed to get some money out of him. It wasn't a lot but it was enough for us to get by on. I felt cheap and guilty taking his money. I knew he didn't really have much or he wouldn't be living the way he did.

As the days drifted by the pain and anger of Angie's betrayal dissipated a little and I began to dwell on it less and less. Especially when she finally got another job.

"You got a job?" I asked, surprised. I thought she'd retired but I didn't want to get anything started.

"Well, somebody has to work around here," she told me. "We can't live off grandpa forever." She said it like it was my idea to bum him for money all the time, and I didn't much like the way she implied that I wasn't looking for work, but I was trying hard not to start another fight. Besides, not working was really putting me down in the dumps and I didn't have much fight in me right then.

She started work in a little cafe that only served breakfast and lunch so she was home by about three in the afternoon. The owner was an old fat gal who had a thing about frogs. The place was decorated with frog pictures on the walls and little porcelain or metal froggies all over the shelves and frogs on the menus—frogs all over hell. The old gal's name was Lily, and the name of the place was The Lily Pad. I stayed away from there most of the time because I thought it might look bad if I hung around. Besides, if I caught Angie BS-ing with the customers now, after my experience with Jack, I might just lose my temper and shoot my big mouth off. Besides, looking at frogs never did anything for *my* appetite.

For the time being I figured the best thing I could do was sit tight until I got to working. Then I'd have a little more to say about the way things went around there. Or if that damned lawyer could ever get my goddam settlement for me. At least I could get some decent wheels and maybe then I *would* get out of there. Half the time I didn't really like Angie much any more. I had very mixed feelings. On the one hand she was so cute and sexy and there was something, an air of mystery about her that always excited and intrigued me. But at the same time, her sloppy way of living and her casual attitude irritated me constantly and half the time I was on the verge of saying something sarcastic. And then the thought of her and Jack would loom over me and I'd have to go through all that again. Sometimes it was all I could do to hold my breath. When I'd think about her and Jack I felt like I'd never be able to trust her again. By this time I hadn't really admitted it, but I realized down deep that Angie was playing cards with a deck of fifty-one. Maybe only fifty. I'd lie there on the bed while she smoked one cigarette after another and watched some stupid show on television. I thought about getting cancer from her secondhand smoke, but I figured nobody lives forever anyway. If I got bored and dozed off she bitched about that too. But then just about the time I'd think this is it, she'd suddenly go all soft and cuddly on me or buy me a pair of white shorts with red lipstick kisses all over them or a T-shirt or something like that.

* * *

I went over to visit Berry and we sat there drinking wine. He looked even frailer than ever. The place didn't smell any better than it ever had.

"Do you and Angela have enough to eat?" he asked. I guess he figured I came over looking for a handout.

I leaned forward on my chair and held my glass out. "Oh sure," I told him. "I've got some lines out. I hope I'm going to find something pretty soon—" I thought about it for a second, then added: "You know, pops, I know Angie loves you and you love her, but sometimes she's still a kid. I think she forgets sometimes that you're on a pretty fixed income schedule or whatever—I mean, I think lots of times when she says she wants something she's just talking. She doesn't really come out and ask you for money. I don't know whether you just think she wants help or whether she's really hinting, I—"

He laughed, waving his glass shakily in front of him. The bed springs squeaked as he shifted his weight on the edge. "Of course she's hinting. That's her way of asking, Darcy. Children take it for granted that their parents—or in this case—Angie's pops, has enough money for all her needs. But you know I love Angie, and she is so charming." He held up that finger. "Camus said that charm is a way of getting what you want without having to ask for it." You have to admit, the child has charm—and she never has to ask." He saluted me with his glass and swallowed wine as if to say, "And I'll drink to that."

I smiled too and drank. "Yeah, you've got a point there, professor. Well, I feel better knowing that you know what you're doing. I just didn't want you to think we were trying to take advantage of you. I mean, it's one thing if we come begging at the door for food, but when it's just a matter of a new pair of shoes or getting our nails done, I think that could legally wait, don't you?"

"Of course it could, Darcy. But it's my pleasure to see that contented little smile on Angie's face. When I write a check she reminds me of a kitten that has just been given a bowl of warm milk."

"I think sometimes you just feel guilty," I said.

"I do. I feel guilty and nostalgic about the past and I dread the future. What did Thompson say? 'The pang of all the partings gone, and partings yet to be'…yes, it overwhelms me sometimes. Ah Darcy, it is only natural to indulge someone you love—while you have the opportunity."

Then he started in again on his novel and my bright future. I told him I just wouldn't know what to say or how to act. By now the thrill had pretty much left me anyway. Months had come and gone. It was all BS and I knew it. But from that time on, it seemed like every time I went over there, he'd get started on the book right away and that would make me irritable. The days were drifting past and I felt it was time to move on. But I couldn't stop him. So I'd get sucked into his hypothetical world every time. Like supposing I was being interviewed or something. He'd want to teach me some pithy little thing to say, depending on the occasion. It sounded good in theory, but I still had grave doubts. Luckily I could at least remember what he told me.

"But what if somebody asks me some question, you know, not about the book but about something general, you know, like how do I feel about abortion or what do I think about Iraq or do I believe in marriage, the ozone layer, endangered butterflies or…whatever? I won't know what to say. There are so many damned questions—I think people like to hear writers' opinions. You know lately since this thing about the book came up, I've been watching writers talking about their books and stuff on television. Most of them seem to have a lot of opinions. They have opinions about everything and they act like they know what they're talking about. I don't think I have any opinions and even if I did I'm afraid I'd sound like a dork."

He chuckled indulgently. "It's very simple, Darcy. If you are asked for an opinion about for example, relationships, just say something like, 'As I point out in my book, I feel that the true depth of any relationship is directly related to the degree of mutual honesty and therefore, trust, shown by two—or more—individuals.' You see?" He beamed crookedly at me. He always had an answer. The answer was always in the book. It was in the book. The general idea was that no matter what anyone should ask, the answer was in the book. I finally got that into my thick head. Whatever it is, it's in the book. Buy the fucking book.

"Later, when a person reads your book, Darcy, he won't remember having asked the question in the first place. Even if he does, he can't be certain that you did not answer it after all in your book—and in any event, by this time the customer has paid for the book and you're in another time and place, don't you see? And the reader may think that, after all, you misunderstood his question, or he misunderstood what you said."

I still thought he was full of bull, but what the hell. Visiting pops was something to do. I guess in a way he was right. I could always remain vague and just tell people I talk about whatever in the book. Buy the book.

* * *

I still hadn't found any work and Angie was getting impatient. She started in again on *our* settlement.

"At least go talk to the lawyer," she insisted. "I mean it's not like you have anything better to do all day."

That hurt and it was all I could do to keep my mouth shut, but I managed to hold my tongue and promised to talk to the lawyer. The next day I went over and had to wait around a while.

The lawyer's office was shared I think by two or three lawyers with one secretary in the outer office. You'd go in there and sit on a bench and look at ancient magazines and wait until your lawyer stuck his head out of his door and called you in. I waited and read an old joke magazine. There was like a little comic strip with two fat women sitting on a bench at a bus stop. The first two panels showed them doing nothing but sitting and watching for the bus or looking at their watches. In the next to last panel one fat woman said, "We've been waiting so long that my butt's gone to sleep." And in the last panel the other fat woman said, "Yes I know. I heard it snoring." Hah hah...

I waited for a long time and had to piss really bad. I hated to ask, but I didn't know where the can was. Finally I asked the secretary.

"Just down the hall, second door on the right," she told me. I did that and came back and waited some more. Boy these lawyers are sure busy I thought, but then lo and behold my lawyer came in through the front entrance. He hadn't even been in his stupid office!

"Oh, hello Mister—" he began. He took my hand. He was on the heavy side and looked sweaty. His hand was damp too. He carried a big old-fashioned brown leather briefcase in the other hand.

"Lemarsh," I filled in for him. "Darcy."

"Oh, Darcy. Sure. Listen, could you just wait for a minute and I'll have some time to talk to you." He went into his office and closed the door. I wiped my hand on the side of my pants.

After about ten more minutes of waiting he came to the door and called me in.

He had a huge glass-topped desk piled with folders and loose papers and books and pens and two telephones that rang off and on. He shuffled piles of papers around on his desk and every two minutes he'd have to have a chat about something on a phone, all of which helped give him time to try to figure out what the hell I was doing there.

"Now let's see—you'll excuse me Darcy. I've been so damned busy lately. You're lucky you caught me; I have to be in court in an hour. Let's see—" He shuffled some more papers.

I told him about the accident and the anticipated settlement.

"Oh sure, of course. I was just talking to the adjuster the other day. Didn't I call you?"

"Well I don't have a phone right now, Mr. Connally," I reminded him. "Remember you were going to write me a letter when you had news."

"A...letter—sure. Well, let's see." He had a habit of scratching at the side of his neck. He scratched and then he shuffled papers around and went over some documents and moved more paper about. Finally he looked up and smiled as if to say that now he had it all under control, and started scratching at his neck again. "Okay, Darcy. Well, here's where we stand right now." He smiled grandly. "The adjuster is trying to pass this off as a big mistake and minimize your injuries. They're offering to settle for a couple of thousand dollars just to get the case closed, and—" He broke off seeing the expression on my face, "Never mind, Darcy. Never you mind. That's just talk. Of course I told him to take a flying leap. Don't you worry; we're not going to let them pull something like that on us. That's just part of the game they play. They stall and stall and try your patience until they hope you'll grab at anything they offer just to get it over with. That's what you have me for. It's a game of nerves. A matter of who can hold out longer—and believe me, they can hold out only so long. They can't keep something like this open forever. It makes them look bad. You know how it is when they advertise, they try to convince people that they settle their claims quickly and fairly."

"Two thousand dollars..." I mumbled.

"Oh, don't worry about that, Darcy," he said, waving that away. He scratched his neck and pushed his chair back and stood up. He moved around the desk and patted me on the shoulder with one hand and shook my hand with the other as he made it clear that my interview was over. "That doesn't mean anything. We're going to get you some money, don't you worry about that."

Before I knew it he was inside scratching his neck and I

was outside scratching my ass. I didn't know a bit more than when I'd gone in. Almost two hours wasted for nothing. As I trudged through the heat walking back to the truck, I had to admit I wasn't really hurt in the accident. It wasn't really much more than a fender-bender. I got shaken up a little. Going to the chiropractor had been the lawyer's brainstorm. Somehow I got the impression that the amount of the settlement would have a lot to do with how long I could string out my visits to the chiropractor and how much money we could spend, all on contingency. But I went to the chiropractor less and less frequently until I stopped going altogether. The guy drove me crazy. He'd put me on a table and roll some wooden wheels over my back and snap my neck a couple of times and try his best to get me to tell him how much better I felt. All I really felt was stupid for being there in the first place. Finally I couldn't take it any more and stopped going. I still used to get a postcard from the chiropractor ever so often right up until I moved to Angie's place. I noticed the lawyer never wrote and mentioned it. He probably thought I was still going. Great.

It didn't thrill Angela when I came home with the latest news but at least I went and talked to the lawyer. That bought me a little slack.

A couple of days later she came home from work and told me grandpa wanted us to come over.

He was half-drunk as usual but he was in a good mood and had champagne again. Just about every time I decided to shove that novel crap behind me once and for all, he'd start in again. Just enough to keep me hanging on. Like that damned lawyer. But the champagne looked promising. My heart gave a little leap in spite of my misgivings. Hey, I thought, maybe things are looking up.

"Drink to our success, my children," he said. He sloshed champagne into some glasses. "This is the good wine. A hundred dollars a bottle."

"A hundred dollars a—Christ, don't slosh it around like

that," I said, leaping forward. I drank. It was good all right but I probably couldn't have told the difference between that and the five-dollar stuff.

He sat on the edge of his bed. His glasses hung cockeyed on his nose. His tie looked as if somebody had been hanged in it and one shirtsleeve cuff was hanging out from beneath the sleeve of his sweater. The button was missing so it flapped around his hand and made his shaking look even worse. "Good news at last." He fished in the pocket of his sweater amongst the dirty paper towels and pulled out a wrinkled check. "Look."

We smoothed the check out on the table. Angie and I bent over it together. At the top it said Carrington House. It was in the amount of twenty thousand dollars...and it was made out to Darcy Lemarsh. I think I gasped. My heart pounded and my breath caught in my throat.

"All you have to do is endorse it over to me, Darcy and I shall deposit it in the bank—and we'll be on our way." He bent awkwardly over and came up with his glass. "To better days."

A real check. Twenty thousand dollars. And it was made out to me. Talk about a rush. After all this time. I couldn't believe it. But there it was, a real check. At least it sure looked real to me. I'd never had a check for that much money in my life. Man, I could take it out to a bank and cash it. I really could. Angie must have read my mind. She gave me a telling look.

There was only one thing for me to do. I looked at them and sighed.

"Anybody got a pen?"

"Thank you," Berry said when I'd signed the check over to him. "Perhaps you might be willing to escort an ailing gentleman to the bank, Darcy?"

We managed to get him downstairs and we crowded into the pickup and I drove him to the bank. Angie went in with him and I expected them to come out with a fistful of cash, but they didn't. I guess that didn't matter; grandpa had his trusty checkbook.

I was overwhelmed. Up until now I'd been about ninety-nine and forty-four one-hundredths percent sure his story about the book was all a daydream. Suddenly the reality of it struck home. This was real. He wasn't crazy—and what was I going to do now?

We went back to his dump and had some more champagne.

"Angela, I want you to take Darcy here to a clothier and get him something to wear. I think at least two suits and something...perhaps something a little more casual. You can discuss that with the tailor. Shoes—everything a promising young author would need. I've been assigned my own personal editor who will oversee the production of the book and your promotional tour. He's flying out for a meeting, just to get acquainted." He smiled benignly at me. "Oh by the way, did I mention that you're to meet him in San Francisco."

My heart leaped. "San Francisco?" I asked. God, this *was* really real.

"Eh, that was my idea," Berry went on. "I really prefer that he not come here to Sacramento where he might see me."

Angie didn't say anything to that. She sat there for a minute while the old man went on. Finally she raised her head, "Well, am I going to San Francisco with Darcy?"

Berry frowned. "I don't think that would be a good idea at this time, baby girl. Once the meeting takes place, the editor will return to New York. But when the campaign gets under way, then of course if you wish to travel with Darcy—well, I should miss you terribly of course..."

* * *

Angie found a good men's clothing store. Inside it was paneled in dark wood and had a creaky floor of wide

The Little Mornings

polished oak planks. Shelves running high around the walls held old time men's things: bowler hats, top hats, high top shoes and spats and gloves; ancient golf clubs and riding boots...Around us dark tables stood about laden with shirts and ties and stuff while the side walls held racks of suits and other clothing between full length mirrors. One table held an array of cashmere socks in all different colors. Cashmere socks...

An affable young black man about my own age and height took charge of us. He was wiry and lean and dressed like a million dollars. I could tell immediately that anything Angie said would be all right with him. He wanted us to call him Henry. He wore a big gold ring with a diamond on his right little finger and a heavy gold watch on his wrist. I'm no expert, but they looked like real gold to me. I suddenly realized that gold really looks good against black skin.

"We need some new clothes," Angie told him. "Maybe a couple of suits or something. Shirts, ties—everything. We need to start from the bottom up."

Henry was more than pleased. "Is this for any particular occasion?" he said. His voice was clear and high. He wore a yellow measuring tape draped around his neck like a shawl and had lavender suspenders although I don't think he needed them. He held his fingers intertwined in front of him, just ready to go.

"Darcy's a writer," Angie told him. "A novelist. He has to go to San Francisco to meet with his personal editor. We want to make a good impression."

"A novelist!" His eyes widened. "Wow."

I started to feel embarrassed.

"They're going to publish Darcy's novel," Angie told him. "It's his first—" she winked, "but not his last."

"That's a coincidence," Henry said. "I write too." His eyes took on a sudden wistful look. I think he was wishing he was the dude going to San Francisco to see my personal editor rather than me. And the crazy thing is that I was almost ready to trade places with him. "Maybe sometime you'd be good enough to take a look at something of mine. I mean, I don't know what it is, but everything I write bounces like a basketball."

"Tell me about it," I said. "Believe me Henry, I've had my share of rejection." This was really true in a certain sense. I've felt rejected most of my life one way or another.

"What's the name of your novel?"

"*The Little Mornings,*" Angie put in. "It won't be out for a while. You know, all that takes time."

You can say that again, I thought. I laughed inside at the way she jumped in all of a sudden and became the expert. Angie began fondling shirts that lay neatly folded on a big round table.

Henry walked us toward a section of wall near the rear of the store. "That's a beautiful title," he said in passing. "*The Little Mornings.* I like that. Wait a minute." He got a notebook out of his hip pocket and wrote it down with a little silver pen. "I'll be sure to watch for it. I don't want to seem pushy, Darcy, but I really would appreciate your opinion. I mean, if you were to read some of my stuff and tell me to stick to selling socks, then all right. I could accept that. I mean you're a real writer. But these editors, I think they're just frustrated writers themselves and when they see something good it makes them too jealous to admit they like it. Or else they don't have enough self-confidence to give an opinion. They want someone else to discover you and then they'll jump on the bandwagon. They never tell you a thing. Just—you know: it's not quite right for their needs or something like that. Or they have to be very selective. Crap like that. That doesn't tell a guy whether he's on the right track, or on any track at all for that matter." He pulled a jacket off a hanger.

"I know, Henry. You just have to have faith in yourself," I told him - like I knew what I was talking about. "That's the best thing I can tell you. I'll be glad to look at some of your stuff when I get back from San Francisco. Bring something to the store and when I come back I'll give it a whirl."

Henry was obviously elated. "I will. I will surely do that." He bustled around me looking me over. "I've never really dressed an author before," he told me. "But come here." He guided me toward a full-length mirror. "I want to show you something. Now I may not be a professional writer myself, but I can sure tell you how to dress like one. Dress for success, I always say." He held out the jacket he'd grabbed. "Now this Harris Tweed is a little heavy for Sacramento," he told me, "but believe me, in San Francisco it's going to be perfect—and I don't know why it is, but people always associate writers and teachers and people like that with tweed. Something of the Old English countryside about it. Very literary. Here, let's just slip this on for size."

I dutifully let him slip the jacket on me. It seemed like a pretty good fit at that. It was kind of a brown mixture tending a little toward a dark orange with bits of green and blue and red in it. I wasn't too sure about the color. I've always been sort of blah about colors.

"It looks kind of loud," I told Henry. "I mean...it's almost orange..."

"Oh," Henry laughed, "don't let that put you off, Darcy. Just wait till I get you put together here and you'll see. Of course you don't want too much color. I mean you don't want to look like a circus clown, but you want to show them something. You don't want to be just another face in the crowd. San Francisco is big and full of hip dudes. I want people to turn and look when you walk down the street. I want them to turn around and say, 'I wonder if that man's an educator or...a writer'. When you go into a restaurant you want the *maitre d'* to notice you right away and not make you stand around waiting. I want your personal editor to remember you—and he will. I guarantee it. You're going to be the perfect author, believe me, Darcy."

Angie wasn't much help. She seemed to like everything I tried on, but I do think she was a little disappointed by the change in Henry. When we first came in he was really all over her. It was Angie he wanted to impress, but once he found out I was an almost famous author, man, he didn't have eyes for anyone else. Angie could've taken off her jeans and done a belly dance for him and I don't think he'd even have noticed.

My first fan.

We got back to the apartment with boxes of shirts, ties, socks, belts and even a brand new billfold and two pairs of leather shoes. We had just about everything but the suits because they had to be altered to fit me just right. I thought they fit pretty okay, but Henry wanted to take in the waist a hair on the jackets and shorten one sleeve a bit—I guess one of my arms is shorter than the other, although I never particularly noticed. And the pants too, they had to be cuffed and Henry wanted to take in the waist at the back just a bit. The store had its own tailor and between him and Henry they really worked me over.

"These tattersall shirts will be perfect," Henry promised me. "This pattern is a true classic; it goes back to the eighteenth century."

Boy, he seemed to know his stuff.

Angie helped pick out some shirts. A couple of plain white shirts, a couple of light tan shirts, one with a faint stripe, and a couple of the tattersalls.

"Believe me, Darcy, you're going to play the role and look the part. And bow ties. Not everybody can wear a bow tie but I think you're just the man for it. And that's where you don't to go getting bashful on me. The tie's the one place you can afford to show a little daring, a little color and dash. With the bow tie you'll be telling them, hey, I'm me. I'm an individual. I got my own groove. I dance to my own beat, you know what I'm saying?"

"I don't know how to tie a bow tie," I told him. Actually I

wasn't too sure about any tie. I hadn't worn a tie more than two or three times in my life.

"Don't worry," Henry told me, "I'm going to teach you. That's part of our service."

I ended up with two suits, one dark blue with a fine stripe in it for evenings, the other a light tan with the faintest red windowpane design that Henry thought was perfect for warmer days. And the one he thought I'd get the most use of, the tweed jacket with a couple pairs of slacks; a pair of brass colored cords and a soft copper tone flannel.

I had a tense moment when Angie wrote out the check and Henry went off to verify it. I half expected the damned thing to bounce. From the expression on his face, Henry was having a tense moment too, but pretty soon he came back all warmth and big white teeth and loaded us up with our purchases.

That was the clincher. For the first time since I met him, I realized that, after all, maybe grandpa wasn't crazy after all. Twenty thousand dollars...

At home Angie helped me try on a shirt and between us we managed to tie a halfway decent knot in the bow tie. It was pretty big, yellow silk with kind of little blue flowers outlined on it. I felt like I was wearing a Neon sign around my neck, but Angie liked it and the more I looked at it, the better I liked it myself. When we finally got it right and I stood looking in the mirror I almost didn't recognize myself.

"You look like a new man, Dar," she said, smiling. "That's what I saw underneath the layers of crud when I met you. I knew you had something."

"What do you mean, layers of crud?"

"Well, you know. I mean you always needed a shave and you didn't take care of your hair and you dressed so sloppy. You look like a pro now, Darcy. You do look like a famous author. We're going places now." She dug a cigarette out of her fanny pack and lit it.

I looked at her. As long as we were going places I thought she could do a couple of things to clean up her own act, but I didn't want to start anything. The only time she took any extra care was when she went out with those famous "girls", but she hadn't done that since the incident with Jack.

The trip to Frisco was set for about three weeks away. While I waited for my clothes to get ready I thought I better follow grandpa's advice and read the damned book at least once so I'd know what it was about, but I never was a good reader. He had given me a photocopy that he had had made before he sent it off. I couldn't get over the coincidence of the title, "*The Little Mornings.*" It was if I'd already predicted the title before I ever heard of Angie's grandpa. I started reading and it looked better than the writings we'd stuffed into the garbage bag all right but it still had its share of typos and x'd out words and such. Each time I started reading and got a few pages along, my mind would drift and wander. I'd get to daydreaming about San Francisco and editors and going on talk shows and I'd either get so wound up I'd feel sick or I'd get on a high at being an overnight sensation. Either way I couldn't sit there and keep my mind on this stupid book. Besides, every time I picked it up I'd forget exactly what was going on so then I'd have to go back and read some of it over again. A lot of it was almost illegible anyway from having been typed over or erased or crossed out. I didn't even recognize a lot of words and I didn't have a dictionary handy either. Tessellated…what in the hell did tessellated mean? All at once I knew how pops felt when he said he couldn't read any more. I was never really cut out to read I guess—I was raised on television—and somehow even as I read, I didn't make a lot of sense out of what the old guy was saying. But after all, he was an educated English professor or something and I was just a bum who didn't finish high school. Of course I remembered the basic premise of the book. Pops had told us a long time ago and I kind of got it connected in my mind with my first meeting with

The Little Mornings

Angie: a young guy meeting this gal, her former employer, the movie producer; the kidnapping—running off to Mexico—murdering some guy who was trying to horn in on the action...

Still, I knew that if I had a prayer in hell of pulling off my end, I was going to have to convince the editor that I knew what I was doing. But I knew I'd never really get through the book and understand it before I met the editor in San Francisco. And Angie sure wasn't any help.

"Put those damned papers down and pay some attention to me," she growled. I did and it didn't take long to get with her agenda. I couldn't resist her even when I was mad at her. I still didn't like that her breath smelled like an ashtray. Most of the time I didn't notice it any more but sometimes it would bring me up short—but I didn't need to start any confrontations; we got into enough without having to look for any.

The closer to the big day we got, the more nervous I got. When I thought it was all BS—thinking that way, I managed to live with it. But this was real. I was really going to do it. I was getting pretty shaky.

I went over to Professor Berry's place a couple of times and he tried his best to prime me. But with him being drunk and me getting drunk, I don't think we accomplished too much.

"Just let your editor do the talking. Remember the old adage: people like to talk about themselves. Look wise and trust in your 'knowing ignorance'," he said, raising that old finger. It seemed he was slurring his words more now than ever. "Remember, you display a great deal more by talking than by remaining silent. You're naturally shy; keep it that way. They will a-attribute your shyness to your awe at being in the presence of a real book editor—after all, you are a young and inexperienced writer. You don't even have an agent. Just appear amenable to their suggestions and imply that you trust them and place yourself in their hands."

"Can I do that? Trust them, I mean," I asked.

Berry threw his arms up in the air and managed a kind of shrug. "How should I know," he laughed. "They will take advantage of us, certainly. This is our first book and we have very little bargaining power. Make that zero bargaining power—but remember, the contract has already been signed. That means that much of our future has already been graven in stone, so to speak. They have the book, and they have to have first look at the next two. I believe there was something in there about sharing movie rights, if memory serves. Movie rights could be a real plum."

"Yeah, I remember you said something about a movie. But I'm not sure—"

"The movie possibility is very likely. I remember now. We discussed that almost immediately upon presentation of the contract. The publishers feel that our novel has the stuff that Hollywood dreams are made of." He looked at me through his crooked glasses. His eyes couldn't quite focus and were rimmed with red. "Darcy, I thought you read the book."

I hung my head. "I tried," I told him. "I've really tried, pops, but I'm just not much of a reader."

He looked sadly at me.

"I know what you're thinking," I told him. "You think I'm going to blow the whole thing. You think you chose the wrong jerk to be your front man and now you don't know what to do about it. Christ, I tried to tell you and Angie both that I didn't think I could pull this off. All I ever read is comics and *Hustler*. I don't know anything about reading, let alone writing. And you want me to talk to some editor and convince him that I not only wrote a hot book but I knew what I was doing when I did it. Jeeze!" I leaned forward and put my head in my hands. I felt sick. I was right back where I started. Somehow, during the weeks that followed our first talk and getting the clothes and everything, I kind of got away from the harsh reality of actually going to San Francisco in a week to meet with some snob-assed book editor who would figure me out so fast I wouldn't be able to say sorry. I rubbed at my wrenching stomach.

"I'm sorry, pops. I really am, but I don't think I'm going to be able to do it. I'll do you more harm than good if I go rolling in there trying to convince somebody that I'm a writer."

"You can do it, Darcy. You have to. It's too late to change our plans now. You can do it. Just do as I say, remain calm, reflective. Look knowing, nod a lot and talk as little as you can. Remember too, writers don't really talk the way they write. They talk in the same way that everyone else talks. They don't sit down and dash off a book and send it away to their eagerly waiting editor in New York City — *au contraire* — most writers agonize for hours over every sentence, every word, changing, rephrasing, adding an adjective, taking an adjective away. They review the work making certain that they didn't use the same word several times in one paragraph; they search and search to find just the right word to add the perfect color to a turn of speech. They sit for hours staring into their thesaurus weighing two or more words. They talk to themselves and read their scribblings aloud to see how they sound. They sit for hours in pained silence wondering whether they should add or subtract a comma. They have an epiphany at three o'clock in the morning and have to get up to make revisions. The result of each sentence is the product of the many tiresome hours of work and research that is needed to bring a work to its final perfection, however perfect that may turn out to be. The editor isn't going to expect you to pronounce enduring prose every time you open your mouth, my boy."

Easy for him to say.

At home, Angie tried to buck me up.

"Just be yourself, Dar," she told me. "You don't give yourself enough credit. Just be polite and natural. Remember, they know this is your first book and your first contact with editors and everything so they'll expect you to be a little awed. And besides, if they're like everyone else I've ever met, they'll be flattered that you look up to them. And unless I miss my guess, that editor will have plenty of talking to do, impressing you with all the books he's edited and all the big things he's going to do with yours."

"Yeah, and maybe he'll ask me about my next book. I don't even know what it's about."

She smiled as if at a child. "Darcy. Remember what pops told you. Just say that you're working on it and you don't like to talk it out before you put it on paper. Besides, somewhere I think I read that writers do that. They don't like to go around talking about their book because they're afraid somebody will steal their ideas or something—and they say that if you talk about it too much, you lose your enthusiasm."

I scratched my head. "Well, I think that kind of makes sense." I tried to put on a brave face and hope for the best, but the best wasn't what I really hoped to get. Over the next few days I went to an upscale barber shop and got a haircut. No more slumming around Conan the Barberman for me!

We went back to the clothing store and a glowing Henry had me try on my pants and jackets and he checked me over as if he were tailor to the stars. I wore the tattersall shirt and the yellow bow tie and had on brand new brown loafers. Now, standing there in front of the tall mirrors with my jacket and the dark copper colored flannel slacks, I stared at the dapper successful young man who stood before me in the mirror. I didn't recognize myself. Damn! The guy in the mirror looked like he really could be a famous author at that!

Angie gave a little gasp of pleased surprise too and Henry said, "Wow!"

All of a sudden I felt for the very first time that by God,

I could pull this off after all. Who said clothes don't make the man?

"Now if you want to do this right," Henry told me, "You got to get a pair of heavy dark brown horn-rimmed glasses, Darcy."

"I don't need glasses," I told him.

"That doesn't matter, man. They'll set you off and give you a distinguished writer look. They can just have plain glass in them—hell man, you can go to some of those places and get them in about an hour. And another thing, a pipe would look great." He hesitated and frowned. "Scratch that. A pipe's a great prop but these days it might not do your image any good. A lot of people are against smoking. But if you guys got the money, go get a big fat Mont Blanc pen and stick it in the pocket of your jacket."

I think Henry had seen too many movies and I decided I could live without the glasses and the pen too. If they saw me packing a big fat pen somebody might want me to write something.

We left the store laden down with my clothing and a couple of fat brown envelopes stuffed with some of Henry's stuff.

Part Two

**The blush of dawn has found us...
The birds are singing...**

The trip to San Francisco is a blur. I remember catching a predawn bus downtown and heading west along Eighty. The sky lit up a pinkish yellow in the east and I couldn't bear to look at it. Bus full of stuffy people farting and groaning and coughing and squirming around in their seats. I sat next to a fat woman who at least had the good sense to go to sleep and not bother me except that she snuffled and snored and her elbow took up all the armrest. Once she farted and I thought about the joke I read in the lawyer's office. Her elbow pressed against my ribs all the way, but there was no place to go. I lay my head back and closed my eyes. I tried to relax but my stomach was acting up again and all sorts of crazy images and ideas flitted through my mind. I thought about Henry and his stuff. The next day, after we came back with my new suits and Henry's envelopes I thought I owed it to him at least to look at them.

I opened one of the brown envelopes and pulled out a thick sheaf of papers. It was about as thick as the manuscript Berry wanted me to read, but this wasn't a novel. It was a bunch of short stories held together with paper clips. At least that's what Henry told me. I tried to read but I couldn't. I'd do it later.

A week later Henry's stuff lay on the bureau in our apartment with an empty beer bottle sitting on them. I looked at it again. Down deep I knew I never would read the damned stuff and I wondered if I could trust the professor to stay halfway sober long enough for him to give Henry's stories a once over. Maybe he could come up with a couple of professional comments. I didn't want to let Henry down now that I'd made a commitment. Big shot author. Christ! The bus gave a little jolt. I opened my eyes and looked out the window. We were just passing the Nut Tree. I tried to think of something else.

Finally after an eternity the traffic got heavier and heavier. Then we got into the mess on the Bay Bridge, but at least the bus didn't have to stall along as much as the cars did. As we went up over the bridge under a hazy sky I began to pull myself together. I took a deep breath.

This was it.

I came out of the depot and shivered. It was a lot cooler here than it had been in Sacramento. Henry had sure been right about the weather. I wished now that I'd worn a sweater too.

I asked a kid which way Market Street was and he pointed me in the right direction. I saw a BART station. First time I'd ever seen a subway. I'd been to San Francisco before but that was a long time ago and I didn't remember much about it. I didn't have to meet the guy till eleven so I had time. It was noisy and busy. I piddled around looking in store windows, had coffee in a couple of little coffee shops and worked my way along the crowded streets looking in windows and asking here and there till I found the hotel facing a park with palm trees. It was twenty to eleven. Good enough.

I have to admit I was impressed. The hotel was too much to take in all at once. I got only a vague impression of tall blackish marble columns with gold. Heavy chandeliers hung from on high; a colorful carpet covered the floor. Stairs mounted to a gallery or something above. I was out of my element—way out. I began to quake all over again but then I caught a glimpse of myself reflected in glass and I didn't really look out of place at that.

A blonde receptionist greeted me approvingly and I told her I had an appointment to meet with J. C. Appleby. She told me to wait just a moment. She called on the phone and told me that Miss Appleby would be right down. I went over and sat on a low red kind of ottoman thing.

I sat there for a full minute before I suddenly jumped up and went back over to the receptionist.

"Did you say *Miss* Appleby?"

"That's right." She smiled. "She should be right down, sir."

I'd taken it for granted that my editor was a man. Pops had just said the editor's name was J. C. Appleby. I think he took it for granted that Appleby was a man too. Angie did too or, knowing her, she'd have insisted on coming along with me.

After five minutes a tall slender blonde came walking toward me. She didn't wear any makeup and her hair had a natural look about it that didn't look like she spent the morning in a beauty shop and her walk was awkwardly graceful. Not the pigeon-toed walk of a model, but more the confident stride of a thoroughbred. She wore a silky jacket that I think was gray but it was so dark it was practically black and under that a cream silk blouse open at the throat with the collar out over the lapels of the jacket. No necklace or anything. The only jewelry I saw were the earrings, fairly large rings set with little lavender stones. She wore slacks that matched the jacket—and silver gray high heel shoes and she carried a slender black briefcase thing. Actually I didn't see her that clearly at first. I only saw her through a sort of haze, misty and out of focus. Definitely out of my class. At first I didn't realize that she was looking for me. She just grabbed my attention and held on. I would never have talked to her in the normal course of things of course. I sat there and admired the aggressive and healthy outdoorsy look she carried about her, her long stride and the way she made me think of the upper crust horse breeder set—and she looked like a man-eater to boot.

She walked right up to me as if she'd already seen my picture, which was impossible.

"Mr. Lemarsh?" She stuck out her free hand. I was on my

The Little Mornings

feet like I'd been stuck in the ass with a hot needle. Her eyes were deep blue and intelligent, her smile just a little lopsided. Her lips were a soft pink and puffy, almost as if they'd been bruised. "I'm Joanna, but everyone calls me JC. May I call you Darcy?" She had a low throaty voice that stirred me and filled me with a vague sort of hope.

I took her hand and admitted I was the man she was looking for. Unbelievable!

"I took the liberty of booking us for lunch on Fisherman's Wharf," she told me, "I've never had an opportunity to see it before."

"What? Oh...Fisherman's Wharf. Sure. I haven't been there in a long time either." That was true. I went there once years ago but I had only a vague impression of crowds of people milling around and souvenir shops and restaurants and people in front of them selling crabs or something.

"I've never ridden on a cable car before either," she told me. We walked along by the park for a block or so and sure enough along came a cable car. Angie hadn't given me a lot of money to play with but I began to fumble around in my pocket to pay the cable car. JC smiled and touched my arm. Up close I thought I sensed a light flowery perfume and had an idea that she did wear a little makeup after all, but it was so subtly and artfully applied that it just blended right in and it was hard to be sure.

"I'm on an expense account, Darcy. Just relax and have a good time. Today is yours." For a fleeting moment I almost felt like I was the girl out with some guy who was trying to impress me. I shook my head and clang clang went the bell.

We rode on the outside and I shivered from the crisp breeze that blew in from the bay and then we were on the steep descent down the hill to Fisherman's Wharf. The smells and buildings and noise and the clanging of the bell were pretty heady. I hadn't been out of my rut in so long I'd forgotten what it might be like. I thought I was going to freeze to death and I'm sure my clothes were warmer than

JC's but she didn't blink an eye. I sure wasn't going to say anything.

Fisherman's Wharf looked vaguely the way I remembered it from years before. Picturesque but a little shabby at the same time. Maybe that was part of its charm. Tourists pushed and pulled their way through the throngs of early visitors. Nearby, other tourists lined up to get on a boat to Alcatraz.

We went upstairs to a restaurant and the headwaiter seated us at a table by the window so we could look down on the fishing boats tied up below. The view was great. The place was busy but not noisy and the food smelled fantastic. Nervous as I was I felt hungry now and was ready for anything.

JC ordered a champagne cocktail and I ordered a martini.

"Make it very dry," I told the waiter and from his look I knew I shouldn't have said that. I'd never had a martini before but I couldn't think of anything else to order. He thought I was a shit-faced punk. But in the movies suave gentlemen always ordered a very dry martini. I sure didn't want to order a Bud in a place like that. I didn't know anything about wine except for the juice the old man drank. The waiter had me figured for a phony, but he managed to keep it to himself.

"Look," JC said, "there's Tony Bennett." I followed her gaze and sure enough, there he was near the entrance with some people and the headwaiter fawning over him like he was the president of the United States. He didn't look as tall in person as I would have thought. But damn, here I was in the same room with Tony Bennett and my beautiful editor! My *personal* editor! Suddenly the full impact of it all hit me. I really was somebody after all. I was hobnobbing with a different class of people now. And I meant to keep it up. Things were definitely going my way.

"You're kind of a classic," JC remarked with a smile. Her eyes were warm and intelligent. "I like that."

"A classic?" I wasn't quite sure what that meant.

THE LITTLE MORNINGS

"Well...you're a handsome young man, yet you have the appearance and manners of a scholar from the old school—I mean your dress, even the classic martini—and the way you write; pounding out your fiction on an old typewriter just like old-timey writers used to do. A classic."

Oh shit, I thought. I don't know anything about what I pounded my fiction out on. I guess I thought all writers pounded out their stuff on a typewriter. I hadn't thought about it, but it occurred to me in that instant that lots of people probably use computers; I'd heard that you could do anything on a computer. I remember reading someplace where you could do your own desktop publishing, whatever that was exactly. I guessed that if grandpa had a computer he could've published his book himself and kept all the dough. I figured that his not having a lot of money helped explain that old typewriter; I know getting started can be tough and lots of writers and people like that don't have it easy at first. I seemed to remember seeing on television about somebody who was living out of his car when he made his first sale—yeah, and I'd swear that I read somewhere that the guy who wrote that book, *"The Shining"*, was living in a trailer park when he hit the big time. One day you're trailer trash and the next you're a famous author with Hollywood sucking up to you. *Yes!*

"Oh, well, I...I have been thinking about getting a computer actually," I told her.

Her dark eyes twinkled. "Going high tech on us are you?"

When the waiter brought the wine list I glanced at it and then said, "What would you recommend?"

He smiled wisely and I think that bought me a few points. He suggested a bottle of something and I nodded. I was back in his good graces and he thought there might be hope for me after all.

I had eaten out before of course, but I wasn't too sure about my manners. I never used to worry about them; but now...I watched JC unfold her napkin and spread it on her lap so I did the same thing as if I'd always done it that way. Usually I just left it lying on the table I think. Besides in my circles I didn't run into many cloth napkins. But I was determined to stay cool and be relaxed come hell or high water. In the meantime the Tony Bennett party got all settled down at the far end of the room and I could just barely see the top of his head sometimes when nobody got in the way, but it was very recognizable. Darcy Lemarsh having lunch with Tony Bennett...*I left my heart in San Francisco...* Yeah!

Our waiter came and went. He was very attentive compared to what I was used to. He had big black eyes and a heavy cleft chin that was close shaven but still dark blue. His whole grizzled head looked too big for his body just like Tony Bennett's.

"How's your salmon?" JC asked, poising her fork in the air.

"Oh, great," I told her. It had been lightly poached and it was really good. The waiter had suggested it to me. "How's your, your—" I pointed my own fork at JC's plate.

"Sand dabs, Darcy. They're great. When you want good fresh seafood there's nothing like a real seafood restaurant next to the dock where the boats come in. I believe in the old saying about doing as the Romans do."

"Oh, yeah..."

"Yes, don't you just hate it when people come to a seafood restaurant and order a steak sandwich—or vice versa—they go to a famous steak house and order a shrimp salad or something really atrocious like deep fried shrimp?" She made a face as if she'd just tasted a mouthful of grandpa's wine. I liked the way her earrings bobbed and twinkled when she moved her head.

"Yeah, like ordering a hamburger at a Chinese restaurant," I said although I hadn't ever really thought about it. I'd never gone to any famous restaurants, not in the sense I felt JC meant. I mean, I guess you could call McDonald's and Wendy's famous, but...I sipped my wine. I had an anxious

The Little Mornings

moment when the waiter popped the cork and handed it to me, but just at that second, across the room I saw the exact thing happening at another table and the guy smelled the cork and nodded, so I did the same thing. I followed the other guy's lead and laid the cork on the table.

The waiter poured a few drops of pale liquid into my glass and looked at me so I picked it up and tasted it. It was okay, slightly tart and almost metallic the way it cut on my tongue; nothing like the piss that poor old Professor Doctor Berry drank.

"Nice bouquet," I said. I'd heard that someplace.

"So...what are you working on right now, Darcy?"

"Right now? Oh..." I had to think fast. I remembered what Angie, or was it the professor? had said. "Actually right now I'm working on a new project, but you know, I don't like to talk about it. I find that when I talk a book out I lose my enthusiasm, my—my—"

"Impetus?" Her eyes were amused. I wasn't sure whether she was on to me or not.

"Yeah, impetus, that's it. I have everything worked out in my head and I have to keep it right there until I get it on paper. But you'll like it. At least I certainly hope so."

"I'm sure we will," JC said. "But you're probably right not to talk it out. Besides, first things first. We've got a book to publish. Let's win Best of Show with this puppy before we start worrying about the next one." She forked food into her puffy lips and chewed and we chatted and ate.

"At Carrington House we just love *"The Little Mornings"*, Darcy," JC was saying, "but you realize of course that we still have a lot of work to do." She leaned across the table and touched the back of my hand with her fork. The pressure electrified me, the same way Angie's first touch did. JC's blouse was open so wide I saw a good bit of her throat and breasts, creamy white without a blemish. Her skin was a paler cream than her blouse.

"Oh," I stammered, "...a lot—"

"I mean we don't want to change the tone of the work or anything. We like your quote-unquote voice. It's just that there are a few awkward or ambiguous phrases here and there—a few little glitches, a few typos; nothing we can't iron out as we go along. We might go over a few scenes. Those little things are bound to happen to any author. You know, you're so close to the work that sometimes it's hard to see tiny fl—things. Of course, personally, I don't intend to change a comma myself. It's your book. You're the author, Darcy. Remember that. My job is only to make suggestions where we feel that a good novel can be made great. The final decision of course will always be yours." She smiled charmingly. Her lips were so full and such a soft pale pink and her teeth so large and white and beautiful. I wondered suddenly if she'd had her lips puffed up; I'd heard about women doing that. I was so dazzled by JC's presence and warmth and the headiness of the wine that I couldn't even follow closely what she was saying. I just wanted to lean across the little table and kiss that mouth, although I knew I'd never get the chance—at least that's what I thought at the moment.

"For instance, there's the character of Carvil; he's interesting, well-developed—and of course he's the protagonist. We felt that you drew out his character very well, but at the same time we felt that you might be able to tweak him just a tad, you know. Give him a little bit more definition, something; something that would make him stand out just a little more in the reader's mind. Something that will make him and his story more poignant to the reader. I know he's flawed. He's a damaged person, a loser. But still, as I say, he's the protagonist, the hero. In this instance what we sometimes call an antihero. We just felt that he could use bit more punch. He's loose, you know. No ties. Can't hold a steady job. I mean, *I* see him as sort of an off-the-wall kind of guy—at least that's my own personal impression. Wasn't that your intention?"

I nodded like I knew what she was talking about.

"Right. So why not make that really clear to the reader? Maybe have Carvil do one or two really outrageous things. Something that will stick in the reader's memory."

I thought about my fight with Jack. I could give her that. It was off the wall all right. She shifted in her chair and laid her fork down.

"Just visualize this as a film, Darcy. An audience would want to see Carvil really out there, drawing a laugh out of the viewer once in a while despite the seriousness of the theme, don't you think? Or perhaps even doing something a bit unexpected — and shocking."

Vaguely aware of tinkling glass around me and the murmur of voices, I fought for something halfway intelligent to say. I drank some more wine and looked down at the fishing boats tied below our window. A rainbow of bright colors on the blue water, they made a great background for a romantic luncheon. Halfway intelligent! I felt a little dizzy from the wine. All I could come up with was, "Film? Do you think this might be made into a film?"

JC smiled again. "Oh Darcy, of course. We've already been working on that. We've been talking to Scorsese and the Coen brothers. We hope to have a film deal all sewn up before we go to press. That way we can tie the book in with the film and we'll create a great deal more interest, don't you agree?"

"Oh sure," I said flabbergasted. Berry had mentioned Hollywood. But he'd been drunk and the talk was so vague that I pretty much let that slide by. JC was talking now - and she was sober. When you start talking Hollywood, you're talking big bucks. You're talking movie stars and glamor. And you're talking my language. Up until this moment, I'd been content to settle for some new clothes and not having to go look for a job for a while, but now suddenly we're talking serious Hollywood. All at once the future began to look brighter for Darcy Lemarsh, budding author. A whole lot brighter.

"And you know, you look great, Darcy. With you making the circuit—wow. Maybe we can even get you on *Today*. How does that sound: being interviewed by Savannah Guthrie or Matt Lauer?"

I was on the point of asking JC who *they* were when a small voice told me to keep my mouth shut. I had a strong feeling I should know what she was talking about. The names did ring a vague sort of bell, and I know now of course, but at the time I never watched news—especially in the morning.

"Great," I said. "That'd be great."

"One thing, Darcy, if you want a bit of motherly advice; get yourself a pair of horn-rimmed glasses. It'll make you look more studious, more thoughtful."

"Horn—I don't need—" I thought of that damned Henry.

"Of course you don't, Darcy, but trust me on this: they add a certain mystique. Just try it. Get dark brown or black with plain lenses. You'll see." She put a forkful of sand dab into her mouth and chewed. "I'll be back in New York tomorrow afternoon and we'll get started. Oh, and another thing, we're going to want you to go to a really good photographer and get some photos taken. Dress the way you're dressed right now—and don't forget the glasses."

I thought of Henry's pipe idea. "Should I get a pipe too?" I guess I had a smirk on my face.

"Okay, laugh, but believe me, your face has character. Your face on the back of the dust jacket will sell books, Darcy. And that's what we want, right?"

"Right," I had to agree. "Yeah, that's the name of the game." I couldn't believe I had character, but if JC said so…

While we finished our lunch I felt downright giddy, less from the wine, I think, than from the heady thoughts of being in the same room with JC and Tony Bennett and being a big shot with television and Hollywood money rolling in. Go to a really good photographer!

Before, I was almost certain that Berry was talking drunken nonsense, and great as it sounded, I'd always been afraid to let go and swallow his story whole, but now all of a sudden the old man's drunken daydreams had turned into reality right before my eyes. I couldn't get over it. At that moment I could've hugged him, pissy pants and bad breath and all.

When the waiter brought the bill JC slapped a credit card down and her signature took care of everything including the tip—although she was gracious enough not to do all that while the waiter was standing there. When he brought back the card and our receipt, he thanked me, not JC. Of course all that may have been part of his act. Some of those waiters get pretty wise to their customers, I imagine. Especially this guy.

As we headed out I glanced over at Tony Bennett's table and for just a thousandth of a second our eyes met. I wanted to smile and wave or something but my stupid face froze and then I looked away and followed JC downstairs.

Outside we wandered around a little on the wharf. It was still frigid with the wind whipping from across the bay, but JC didn't appear to notice. She chatted about the book and I tried to follow as she brushed up against me. Suddenly she turned and brushed those puffy lips against my cheek.

"Want to go to a motel, Darcy?" Her voice just beneath my ear was more throaty and husky than ever.

For a second my knees felt rubbery. "We could go back to your hotel," I suggested.

"Oh no—" JC looked around. There was a motel within easy walking distance from where we stood.

I didn't think a big modern hotel like the St. Francis would be too picky about women having guests in their rooms, but who knows? The thought crossed my mind that JC might be married; there might be a Mr. Appleby waiting patiently back at the hotel for the return of his faithful wife, but then I remembered that JC wasn't wearing any rings at all.

My heart beat furiously as we walked to the motel where JC filled out the data. Where the card asked for a license number, she wrote something in and I guess the man at the desk could care less because he grabbed the credit card and it passed inspection for the money and that was that.

We got a room with sort of a view. If you stretched your neck you caught a view out over Fisherman's Wharf, but the view didn't last any longer than it took JC to close the draperies and move over by the bed.

"I've been hungry for you since this morning when I first saw you sitting there in the lobby," she whispered. She grabbed me and I finally tasted those luscious lips and all at once I awoke to a wild new passion I hadn't felt since the first night Angie and I had gone to bed together. We fumbled and peeled and got each other undressed and fell laughing and panting onto the bed and kissed and hugged and flailed. JC's breasts weren't any larger than Angie's, but they had thick hard nipples and they were plenty large enough for me. I basked in the warmth of her athletic body and her fresh clean smell...I decided the perfume was her natural scent. And her breath didn't smell like an ashtray...

Later we lay on our backs with our arms behind our heads and looked at the popcorn on the ceiling. I thought of the tiny neat black triangle of hair that JC had just on top of her Venus mound. Everything else had been shaven clean as a whistle. That told me that she dyed her hair blonde, but it became her and even up close I didn't see any dark roots.

"You aren't married I take it," I said after a while.

JC chuckled deep in her throat. "Married? I don't think so, Darcy. For me life is about freedom. Married women aren't exactly free, wouldn't you say?"

I nodded. "I guess."

"And you? You're not married...?"

I hesitated. "No. I've never really thought about getting married to tell the truth, JC."

She looked at me obliquely. "But you've got a girlfriend—an arrangement..." Her smile was knowing.

"Oh...I've been going with a girl for a few months, but

it's nothing serious," I lied. "We never talk about marriage or anything like that." I didn't want to tell her Angie and I lived together although I don't know quite why. I guess if I told her that it made me out to be kind of a cheat. I didn't want JC to think I'd cheat on my woman with the first gal who spread her legs for me, even if the gal had legs like JC.

We lay there for a while longer, feeling the sheets beneath us, hearing the low whir of the air conditioning or furnace or something.

"So how is it that you used to be a doddering old college professor and now you're suddenly a handsome young writer, Darcy? I've been dying to ask you all day."

I froze. I felt sweat pop out on my forehead and on my lip. "How do you mean?" I said. I knew what she meant all right, but I didn't know what to say or how to say it. I thought I'd blown the whole game.

But JC didn't appear to be too perturbed. She just smiled knowingly at me.

"Well, originally we received a flowery letter filled with praise about you—or whoever—from Professor Chandler. We've published a number of his books, although of course, they're nonfiction, but when he told us about Professor Berry's novel, how good he thought it was, and how much he admired and respected Professor Berry and of the professor's years of teaching experience, we felt of course that we should give the book a read." She dropped her voice, "You know, Darcy, we receive so many manuscripts. For all I know there may be literally hundreds of perfectly acceptable books coming over the transom each year, but it's like looking for a needle in a haystack. That's why so many publishers let agents do the pre-screening for them. We receive tons of crap that is unbelievably bad. You go outside and look around, Darcy. Look at all the people you see. You see what you think are bus drivers, garbage men, nurses, doctors, policemen, motorcycle repairmen, whatever; that's not what they're about. That's only their cover. They're really writers. They do what they do because that's what puts butter on the asparagus, but after work they go home and take off their uniform and let their hair down and become—writers. Many are good. More are bad. Some are so incredibly bad that it gives pause for thought. We get tons of material from disturbed writers who have an axe to grind or whatever. They hate somebody or something and sometimes spend eight or nine hundred pages in frenzied tirades. They repeat themselves and get lost on side paths or they can't even spell or they're so confused and confusing nobody can figure out exactly what they're trying to say."

I thought about grandpa sitting there drunk in his stinking room writing his crap and how Angie said he'd go on and repeat himself. Poor pops. JC had his number without even knowing him. I smiled. She had Henry's number too.

"That's not to say they're all uneducated," she went on. "Some of the worst offenders are highly educated." That was pops all right. "They're so superior. They talk down to the reader as if they're talking to a retard." She sighed deeply. "And with all that, I still pack home a ton of paper every night to read in my, hah hah, spare time. My bedroom looks like an editorial office, Darcy, believe me. No, despite what publishing houses would like you to believe about being open to writers, we simply don't have the time or resources to read and consider all the crap that drops into our laps. Besides, we can't even publish all the good stuff that comes our way. A person can eat only so much steak no matter how much is piled on the plate. We have to be very selective. We decide where we're going and then concentrate on trying to get there."

"So what do you do then?"

"Well, I don't make those decisions. But as a house we try to get on the right track. Many things go into the making up of a list, and often we have to rely on someone else's opinion to help us narrow down the field. Like that recommendation from your friend Professor Chandler for example. That at least bought you a considerate reading." She turned her head and looked at me and I felt her warm breath on my face, "but Darcy, let's cut to the chase: you're no dotty old college professor. Chandler said you boys have known each other for forty years." She slid one hand beneath the sheet and caressed me. "Not bad for an old geezer in his seventies."

My face had become very warm. I lay there kind of stunned for a minute while I struggled to gather my thoughts. I thought pops had already explained all that. At least that's what he told me. I felt stupid for not having foreseen something like this, but slowly I began to see what I hoped would be a way out.

"You're absolutely right about that, JC," I told her. I moved closer and pulled the sheet down and caressed her lean thigh with the back of my hand. "But I wrote and explained about that some time ago."

"Well if you did, no one told me." She sighed. "The lowly editor is always the last to know…"

"What happened in actual fact is that I was one of Professor Berry's students. After I wrote the book I didn't know what to do with it. You know, that was a few years ago. I sent it off a couple of times and got no response. I sort of gave up on it for a while. I mean I didn't know whether it was any good or not and then one day I remembered Professor Berry. He's had a lot of stuff published in the past you know."

JC nodded. I didn't know whether that meant she knew, or was just urging me on.

"Well, I know him and respect him so I looked him up and asked him to read it and give me his opinion. I told him that if he said it was no good I'd go be a—a house painter or something." We both chuckled at such a ridiculous thought. "Well it turned out that he liked it all right. He said I showed lots of promise but he felt that it wouldn't be enough just to drop it in on some publisher without a little preparation, and then he remembered his old pal Chandler who, as you say, has had some books published by your company. So he got Professor Chandler to write that letter and sure enough you agreed to read the book. So Berry sent it to you under his name. He and I both figured that if and when you decided to publish the book, then we could talk about the little deception." I shrugged. "The main thing was for someone to give it an honest reading. He was just trying to be a nice guy. Are you mad, JC?"

She smiled. "Mad? No, I'm not mad, Darcy. No. I'm not even disappointed. Hey, that's a good story in itself. It could be worse. Not too many years ago one of our biggest competitors laid out a half-million dollar advance for a book that hadn't even been written."

"A book that hadn't...?"

"That's right," she smiled. "The dude convinced them that he was the grandson of a mob boss from Vegas and proposed a book that would tell the real story of the mob in Las Vegas."

"But he couldn't write," I asked.

"I don't know about write, Darcy, but he could certainly bullshit. He was a con man. It was all a lie. And the greedy bastards went for it." She chuckled. "No, I'm just a little amused at our having been taken in so easily. Besides I wasn't the first person to read your book. I'm just a small cog in the machinery. Actually several other people read it before I did. We have weekly meetings that I'm seldom invited to attend. Only then, finally, after offering you—or the professor—a contract, did they assign me to be your editor. He or you or somebody signed the contract so it's a done deal now and it doesn't matter to me who wrote the damned thing. Just so you and the professor agree on what you're doing, I don't see any problem." She frowned and looked at me curiously. "Of course if he were to come forward later and claim any rights to the book, that could pose a problem. But he surely wouldn't do anything like that would he?"

The Little Mornings

"Oh, of course not," I said. "He's honest." But suddenly I wondered. People do funny things, and he drank so much...

"But still—worst case scenario: you're the author. I don't think you'd have any problem convincing a judge or anyone else, so we won't worry our little heads about things like that. Between us, between you and me, Darcy, we're going to get your book ready to print and fly with it. Does that work for you?"

"Perfect," I told JC. I breathed a sigh of relief. At least that was one hurdle behind me. I could breathe a little easier now. Besides, after all, as long as we kept Berry supplied with wine and a little food, he'd have no reason to complain. And I was doing him a favor even though now it began to look like I was going to end up getting the best of the deal. In any case I felt pretty sure I didn't have to worry about the old man being a problem later on. Why should he? I guess that comes under the heading of those bad choices for which I'm famous. I had no idea of how wrong I could be about pops—but not in any way I could ever have expected.

* * *

I rode home in a daze. It was night and I spent the whole trip in a blur of hazy memory, memory of our lovemaking, memory of our dinner with Tony Bennett, memory of finally riding back tfrom the motel on a cable car, having Chinese food on Grant Avenue.

I broke open my fortune cookie and read my fortune. *Notoriety not same as fame.* I wondered if the gods were trying to tell me something.

Eventually I left JC at the hotel. She became very formal at this point. Our relationship was suddenly all business. She smiled professionally and shook my hand and she promised to keep in touch. She turned and headed into the lobby with that beautiful gangling walk of hers. I'd never realized before what high heels do for a woman. No wonder women put up with the discomfort.

But I felt disappointed and deflated while I waited for my bus to take me back to Sacramento. I felt kind of like Cinderella at midnight when it was time to kick off the glass slippers and go home. I think I'd developed kind of crush on JC. When we separated she turned so formal that it hurt me a lot more than she probably knew, and a lot more than I might ever have imagined. I don't know what I thought or expected from JC, but we were so close all day and then suddenly she appeared to be done with me the way you'd be done playing with a dog or something and out I went. I can't say for sure that I was in love with her. I think I was, in a way at least. I loved Angie too, but what made this different was that before I'd never have raised my sights high enough even to think about someone like JC before. Like I'd never seriously dream about dating a movie star. They're beautiful and graceful and everything but they live on a different planet. That's the way JC was—and suddenly here we were, JC and Darcy Lemarsh and Tony Bennett, all together in the same room on the same planet—and she liked me! If she'd seen me in my overalls painting a building for Ephraim she'd walk past without ever giving me a second glance. Now that I had some decent clothes and was an author, I could actually get women like JC. I couldn't believe it. And what about Hollywood?

Still, it sure didn't look like JC had exactly fallen head over heels in love with me. She liked me well enough to go to bed with me and she evidently didn't have any complaints. But she didn't ask me to pack up and move to New York to live with her. She didn't even talk about seeing me again soon. There had only been the vague talk about getting me onto some television shows and book signings and things—but far as I knew, I might never see JC again. It left me sad and feeling a little bit hopeless and empty, but at the same time, I couldn't just drop Angie anyway. And I didn't want to. There was some glue that held us together. Angie certainly didn't have the class that JC had, or the position or anything.

Here JC was an editor in some big publishing company in New York City and Angie couldn't even hold down a job assembling ballpoint pens. But at the same time, if JC actually had asked me to move in with her, I'd have been between a rock and a hard place as they say. Hell, I could love both of them at the same time, but I sure couldn't live with both of them at the same time.

I had to do some serious reality checking. I'd somehow started thinking of myself as a real writer, an author on the first rung of the ladder of success. But in reality, down deep I knew I was still plain old Darcy who couldn't write a poem on the wall of a men's room. I laughed. Hell, I couldn't even hold down a job being a half-ass painter for Ephraim Dekker. I told myself I might as well be glad for one happy afternoon and forget about JC. JC might be gone forever but Angela was here today and she'd be here tomorrow—or at least I had every reason to hope so.

Sometimes I'd start thinking about that little incident with Jack, but as time went on, I got less and less emotional about it. And especially after having spent the day on Fisherman's Wharf whooping it up with JC, I couldn't manage to feel quite so outraged as I had before.

Angie was suspicious from the moment I got back. I don't know why, but women seem to have that sixth sense. She met me at the depot and I drove us home in the pickup. It was evening but not cold. We were getting into October but I was uncomfortably warm in my tweed jacket now that I was back in Sacramento.

"So how did it go?" She lit up a cigarette and gave me her sidelong glance. She turned her head and blew smoke through the open window but it blew right back in creating a little cloud around her face.

Maybe I still had a glaze over my eyes, I don't know. I kept them focused on the street ahead and tried to be casual. "I saw Tony Bennett."

"Who?"

"Tony Bennett—I left my heart in San Francisco…?"

"I know who Tony Bennett is. So that's what you did—you went to see Tony Bennett?"

"No, I mean, we went to lunch and Tony Bennett was there. He was having lunch too—with some people."

She gave me a long sideways look and flicked ashes. No comment. "So how did your thing with the editor go?"

I was a little disappointed that she wasn't impressed, but knowing Angie she probably wouldn't admit it if she was—as long as it happened to somebody else.

"I've never been in the same room with a celebrity before. I mean just having lunch together. You don't forget something like that five minutes later, you know."

"Okay. Did you go there to see Tony Bennett or to talk to your stupid editor? I mean, how did that part of your fucking trip go?" She hardly ever used rough language except when she was in a bad mood. Must be on her period.

"Well, it wasn't as tough as I thought it would be," I told her. "The editor took me to lunch—that's where I saw Tony Bennett. But they want me to do some revisions or something, I think. I don't know what to do. I just hope grandpa can come through for us. We're talking about Hollywood."

I rattled round a corner and shifted gears.

"So what was he like, the editor?" She watched me.

My original intention was to go ahead and let her think JC was a man, but then I told myself there was no reason to lie. And besides, I knew perfectly well that sooner or later Angie would find out and if I didn't tell her now, that would only make it even worse when she did find out.

"Joke's on us," I told her. "He's not a he; he's a she."

There was a long loud moment of silence.

"A woman? Your editor's a woman?" She blew smoke into my face and I held my breath while it dissipated.

I nodded. "Yep, I guess a lot of editors are women."

"So? What's she like? Pretty?"

"Pretty?" I laughed. "You don't have anything to worry about, baby. She's one of those librarian types. She's all books and manuscripts. She doesn't even comb her hair or wear makeup."

"Is she married?"

"I don't know. I didn't ask. We just talked about the book. She's probably a dyke."

Angela gave me another of those sidelong glances and I knew she wasn't really satisfied, but evidently she thought she'd better play it cool for the moment, not having more to go on—and there was the little incident with Jack. I could always throw that up to her.

"For openers," I said, "she knows I'm not your grandpa. They read the book in the first place because some professor they'd published before sent them a letter of recommendation. Seems him and Berry have been pals for forty years. Naturally the minute she saw me she knew I couldn't be Professor Berry."

"So you told her the truth?" Angie blew out smoke and the wind from the open window blew it across me.

"Well, not exactly. I let her think I wrote the book all right, but Professor Berry lent his name to it to get it a little respect—and she admitted that helped. But she also said now that they'd accepted the book and we have a signed contract she didn't really care who wrote the damned thing. Besides I thought your grandpa already told the people in New York about it. It was just that my personal editor didn't realize. Anyway, they want me to get a picture taken and I might be on television with Savannah Guthrie."

"Television?" Angie focused in on that one. "You really think you'll be going on television? Man, pops will go crazy when he hears that."

"Well, I'm sure he's patiently waiting to hear what happened," I said. Actually I wasn't in a great rush to get home. "I guess we can drop by and tell him what's up."

By the time we got to his place it was pretty late. Berry let us in and staggered back to his bed. The stench would've knocked a gorilla off his feet. Grandpa fell back onto the bed in a squeal of springs. He didn't have his pants on but he was still wearing his sweater over his shirt and of course, his tie. He half lay there in his underpants and tried to focus his bleary eyes on me. He waved one shaky hand in the air.

"Return, return, that we may look upon thee." He reached shakily for his glass but it was empty. I picked up the jug and poured the glass half full.

"Ah, thank you my boy." He shivered although it must've been ninety in there even at that hour. He pulled his sweater closer around his chest. He sat up a little and picked up the glass with both hands and got it to his mouth. After San Francisco this stinking room was even more intolerable than ever. God, if JC could only see her famous author right now!

I told him about JC being a woman and brought him up to speed on where we were at that point and he took it all in stride.

"You did the right thing, my boy. I did tell someone about the change—at least it seems to me that I did. In any event, I had no idea that Chandler told the editors that we have been friends for forty years. Can it really have been forty years?" He took another swallow and coughed. "Well, I believe this is all for the best, Darcy. Now you may act on your own behalf. It is certainly best for me to remain *dans les coulisses* as it were. From what you say your editor apparently likes you."

Little did he know how much she had liked me! The urge to brag was hard to ignore but I managed. "Yeah," I said. I have to get my picture taken so they can put it on the back of the book," I told him. "And I have to get a pair of horn-rimmed glasses."

Angie snorted "Just because Henry—"

I cut her off, "No, not Henry. JC wants me to get them. It was her idea, not mine. And certainly not Henry's. But hey, if they want glasses, I can wear glasses."

"I suppose if JC wanted you to run around in a bikini and

join the Communist party you'd do that too," Angie said. She wasn't smiling.

"Hey, give me a break," I told her. "I'm just trying to play the role."

"Bravo," the old man said.

"Those people are pretty sharp," I told them. "I wouldn't ever have thought about it, but JC mentioned something about the manuscript having been written on an old-fashioned typewriter," I pointed to the old machine that stood on his writing table. "I guess they think that's obsolete. I mean that was okay the first time, but when we send in the next one we should have it redone on a computer or something. Anyway I told JC I was thinking about getting a computer," I added. "She seemed to think that was a good idea."

"A computer?" Berry looked at his typewriter as if he'd never seen it before. "Get a computer?" Suddenly his haggard face broke into a smile. "A computer! That was a stroke of genius, my boy. Yes, I daresay my old manual typewriter is a real dinosaur at that. My, I never graduated to an electric machine—and now we're in the age of computers. Still, that's all I have. I don't think I could adjust to a computer."

"Well, you don't have to worry about it right now anyway. She was talking about having you—me—somebody—go over some of the work to 'tweak it a tad' as she put it. I guess there are a few things. I didn't know what the hell she was talking about, but I figured that between us we can work it out."

"Oh, yes, of course," grandpa said. Right now he was in a good mood and wasn't going to let anything bother him. Besides, as long as we did most of this crap by mail, who would know? And what the hell...if JC just needed a few *i*'s dotted and *t*'s crossed, I ought to be able to handle that. As to that Carvil character, whoever the hell he was, he'd be tweaked till he squeaked. I'd get pops to help me there. We could do it. I wasn't about to let something like that ruin our plans now. Matt and Merideth were waiting. And Hollywood was playing my song!

* * *

Over the next few weeks Angie didn't say much about JC or anything. She did promise that if she ever found out I was lying to her she'd kill me. I couldn't understand how she could be so suspicious without having a shred of evidence to go on.

Then pops started getting a flood of mail from New York. JC sent copies of typewritten pages with writing in the margins suggesting this and suggesting that. None of it made a lick of sense to me. Most of the time pops didn't even bother to open the envelopes. I'd open them up and show the stuff to Berry but he wasn't much help. He'd offer a change here and there where JC had suggested something, and sometimes he'd try to retype the page for me. But he couldn't control his fingers and screwed things up even more.

"God, I can't even type. I used to type pretty well actually," he complained.

Finally I got Angie to sit down with me and help me when she could. She couldn't type either. But at least she could use the old hunt and peck system and, with the professor halfway dictating and a little imagination, we managed to get a few things right, I think.

Then Angie got me lined up with a photographer for the sitting. I followed everybody's advice and went to an optometrist and found a pair of glasses that looked like what everyone seemed to want and told the girl I just wanted basically sunglasses with the lightest possible tint. We settled on a very light gray and when I tried them on I have to admit I looked pretty good.

The photographer was a fussy little guy with a potbelly. He oozed sweat like a pig although inside the studio it wasn't bad at all.

The Little Mornings

I wore the Harris Tweed jacket and tattersall shirt and the yellow bow tie just like JC had told me to do, and of course my glasses. I held them out and tried to look like I'd just had an idea. Angie looked at me approvingly. "You're really a handsome stud when you get dressed up," she told me. That was about the nicest things she ever said and it warmed me.

The photographer buzzed about me like a bee. He fussed at my hair and sprayed stuff on it. He arranged it just the way he liked and each time he'd get ready to take a shot he's say, "Lick your lips now."

He took a lot of shots; some up close, some farther back. Mostly I sat on a big dark red leather wing chair or leaned against the back of it. In one or two poses I wore the glasses and held a book as if I were checking something in it. Another time I held the book as if it were the one I'd written. In one I just leaned back and crossed my arms as if I had made my decision and was sticking to it. And I put on the glasses and leaned across the back of the chair and smiled directly into the camera. The photographer had me in front of a background with paneling and I guess it could've been an office or something.

As soon as we get the proofs I'll call you," he promised.

In the meantime, the revisions weren't going as well as I'd hoped. JC wrote long letters along with manuscript pages filled with markings. Nothing pleased her. "You're not following through here on page seventy-five," she wrote. "What the hell does *he was left but didn't stay* mean? And what about Carvil? I thought we talked about that." On and on she went with the letters and I'd sit there with Berry drinking wine and trying to look wise. And she griped about everybody else using the Internet for this shit. Berry's suggestions didn't make any more sense than anything else he ever did. Sometimes he'd come up with something that seemed to make sense, but then later on, looking at it a second time, it didn't make any sense at all.

JC's letters grew more frantic and then suddenly they

became less frequent. I didn't know why at the time, but later I realized that she was getting in hot water back home and had just about given up on my doing what I was supposed to know how to do: write a hot novel.

* * *

Henry started leaving messages too. I never did get around to reading his stuff. I glanced at a few pages and got the idea that, despite the cool way he acted in the store, his real concern was race relations and all that stuff. I guess maybe if I were in his shoes, I'd feel the same way. I talked about it to grandpa and he told me a couple of things that I thought would give me an out.

We met downtown and had lunch together.

"The thing is, Henry. I have to be honest with you. I think you write well and you make a lot of sense, but maybe you're going a little too heavy on the black thing."

"The black thing?" He looked innocently surprised.

"Yeah, well, you know, like my editor was saying the other day, one thing that ruins so much work from promising young writers is that too many of them have an axe to grind. They get off on their pet peeve or whatever and spend too much time on that. You know, people read to be informed and entertained. If they want to be preached to, they go to church, Henry."

I could see that he didn't like it, but at the same time I think I kind of hit home.

"We're talking about your *personal* editor here?"

I nodded.

"Yeah, okay. I see what you're saying. Then you think maybe I should be more subtle, is that what you're saying?"

"Sure. That's it exactly, Henry. I mean you can get your point across without hitting the reader right in the eye. But don't ever give up. I mean maybe instead of having a white person say he doesn't like blacks, show him doing something. Maybe he always shakes hands with everybody,

The Little Mornings

but when he meets this black man, he doesn't offer his hand. The reader will get the idea without you saying a word, see?"

"Oh, yeah," Henry said. "Sure. Yeah..."

"Sure, if you really want to do it, you can. Just stick with it." I felt ashamed at going on like I knew what the hell I was talking about, but at the same time, I was getting stuck in the role now and half the time I kind of believed it myself.

I left Henry with new hope. I walked back to the truck wondering how I could possibly talk that shit with a straight face when I really didn't have the faintest idea in the world what I was talking about. Mostly I based what I said on what pops told me or stuff I saw on television, or what I thought JC might say if she read some of Henry's stories. Then I thought of what she'd say if she really knew what was going on!

* * *

Berry didn't answer my knock but I thought I heard movement inside. The door wasn't locked so I went in. He was half sitting on the side of the bed and looked like hell. He had a big raw scrape on his forehead and his glasses were on his nose crooked and one lens was gone. He couldn't see anyway, so maybe that didn't make much difference. One arm of his sweater hung so far down it had swallowed his hand in there someplace. An empty wine bottle lay on the floor by his feet. Its dregs oozed slowly into the colorless carpet and he had another empty bottle standing on the floor beside it. I saw the lens from his glasses on the floor. I bent and picked it up and laid it on the refrigerator by his bed. His pants were open. I guess he was planning to take a piss.

"Man, you don't look too good," I told him. I tried not to breathe in too much.

He sat there belching and hiccupping and staring at me as if he didn't remember me.

"I hope the book's coming along," I said. "I haven't heard anything from JC for a while now. I think we screwed up trying to make those revisions she asked for—well I got the pictures taken the other day anyway, so that's done."

"Pictures? Oh yes, of course. Well, I'm glad my boy." He waved the arm with the lost hand vaguely out in front of him. "Can you find a bottle of wine there. I don't believe I can stand at the moment."

I looked around and picked up a bottle from the table by the typewriter. I unscrewed the cap and passed it over to him. He tried to pour a little into his glass but his hand started shaking so bad I had to grab it and pour the wine for him."

He looked at me gratefully. "Thank you my boy. Don't worry about the book. We have a signed and sealed contract. Besides, the changes can't really be important; a few typographical errors perhaps or a split-infinifinitive—" He broke off and laughed at the thought. "They bought the book the way they read it, so it can't be anything important, rememem—" he broke off and started again, "Rememember that—my boy." Suddenly he straightened and looked more sober than I'd seen him in a while. "You can do it, Darcy. Remember, you're my voice." With that he swallowed some more wine and lapsed back into a stupor.

After a while I was damned near as drunk as he was. I looked at my empty glass and got up and refilled it.

"The other books..." I began.

"Oh yes, of course." He waved toward the white file box that stood against the wall where it'd always stood. The sock was still hanging on it. "Perhaps you should take them home with you, Darcy. You and Angie can look after them better than I can—and re-remember, we don't want to issue them too quickly." He waved his glass with one finger sticking up. "'In skating over thin ice, our safety is in our speed'." He laughed and swallowed his wine. "Perhaps I have that backwards; in this case we have to skate slowly, or am I dithering?"

THE LITTLE MORNINGS

I sat there and we talked and talked and drank more wine. After a while he wheezed and fell back on the bed and began to snore.

I didn't leave right away. I sat there for a little while. I drank some more wine. I realized I was drunk, but who cared? I had another glass of wine. My head buzzed and I felt too lazy to get up and leave. I sat there for a long time and listened to the old guy's wheezing and stared into my glass.

That was the last time I saw Professor Berry alive.

* * *

We still hadn't heard anything about my settlement, but even Angie had put it on the back burner now that pops was taking care of extra expenses. Angie was still working. She may have been a slob at home, but when she had a job she tried to do it. At least that's what she wanted me to believe—until she got some idea in her head that somebody was out to get her. It usually didn't take long for that to happen.

A few days after my last visit with grandpa, Angie came tearing into the apartment while I was dozing on the bed in front of the television.

She was all teary-eyed and sobbing.

"It's my grandpa," she told me. "He's—he's gone."

"Gone? What do you mean gone?" Of course I realized what that meant. I just couldn't bring myself to deal with it that easily.

She sank down on the side of the bed and sat with shoulders slumped. She leaned her head against my shoulder. "I went over there after work to see him and he didn't answer the door and finally I opened it—God!" She put her hands to her face and shuddered. "Oh—" she kept her face buried in her hands. She mumbled, but I understood what she was saying, "He was on the bed. He was all swollen up. The smell...oh God..." Her body began to tremble and I sat beside her and held her close. I didn't know what to say. I guess sometimes there's nothing a person can say that will help. I know I couldn't feel the way she did, but I did feel terrible. I knew she loved her pops and I liked the old guy too. I'd got so I called him grandpa too. I held her and we sat there until it began to grow dark and finally she lay on her stomach and sobbed quietly.

"He was the only mom and pop I ever had," she murmured into the pillow. I sat there rubbing her back and let her sob. I wanted to say something but nothing came out. I decided it might be best to let her cry it out.

* * *

The funeral was short and sweet. Although in his heyday the old guy probably had lots of friends, his years of solitary drinking had pretty well isolated him from all of them.

There was money to cover his funeral expense but since he hadn't made out a will, Angie wasn't going to see any of the rest of his money for a long time. One more thing to hang fire. The official cause of death appeared to be that he'd choked on his own vomit. Normally I went over there to BS with him just about every day, but this time I hadn't been there since I brought the box of manuscripts home. I was sorry it had to be poor Angie who walked in on him. She hardly ever went over there without me anymore. She just had to pick that day to go alone.

He looked pasty and out of place in the suit they'd found for him. I thought they should have left him in his sweater. I'd never once seen him without it, winter or summer. He was going to miss it.

Poor Angela. I tried to be very tender. I made instant coffee every time she looked like she needed some. She liked it with lots of powdered creamer and four teaspoons of sugar. I liked mine black without sugar, cowboy style.

For about a week after the funeral Angie was very quiet. She sat for hours by the window smoking and tugging at a few strands of hair and staring out the window. In the meantime, I went down and rented a box at one of those mail places and sent the new address to JC.

At night I was tender with Angie and we made love again and I thought we were getting back on track. She was smart enough to know she couldn't cry forever.

But things weren't back on track at all. She walked over to the box on the floor and kicked it.

"I notice you managed to get the manuscripts out of the place before my grandpa died," she said.

"He told me to take them," I countered. "He said they'd be safer over here. It was his idea, not mine. I swear."

"Well, it's still very convenient," she said. "I just don't—there's something fishy about this, Darcy. That's all I can say. It's pretty damned convenient for my grandpa to drop dead now that you have the books, isn't it? Now you don't have to share with him."

I stared at her. "Share with him? Do you really think I'm so greedy that I'd try to cut him out of his money? Christ, all he ever wanted was two bottles, one for drinking and one for pissing. I wouldn't deny him that, would I?" She didn't answer, staring off into space the way she liked to do.

"Well, would I?" I persisted.

Finally she shrugged without looking at me. "I don't know, Darcy. I never thought you were greedy, but—money and fame can do things to people. Oh God, if I ever find out you killed my grandpa…"

"Killed him?" I tried to take her by the shoulders but she pulled away from me. "Angela, listen to me. Listen to me; you're talking crazy. Why in the world would I do a thing like that? What possible motive could I have? Now we can't even touch the money in the bank. We needed him."

She shook her head. "No we didn't. He wasn't helping at all with the revisions and you and I both know it. Whatever talent he may have had in the past, it was all gone. All he could do was blather along and drink wine and piss his pants. You didn't need him any more so don't pretend you did. There'll be more money and you know it. And when it came to those revisions you talk about, Henry could've been more helpful."

I guess I should've expected Angie to go paranoid on me. She could come up with some pretty strange stuff, like grandpa being a Communist—as if that was a big deal. Well, maybe it was a big deal to her, but me and the rest of the world could care less. Nevertheless I certainly didn't like the idea of having her going around thinking I had something to do with dispatching her grandpa. Next thing she'd be running around telling that to other people.

Fortunately Angela slowed down her harping on grandpa. As each day went by, she appeared to be taking the whole thing a little better. But I still felt she was harboring something.

Things weren't going well with JC. Letters came to the mailbox. She loved the photos I'd sent her and told me which one they'd decided to use on the jacket. It showed me sitting on the arm of the wing chair with my left arm up on the top of the chair. My glasses dangled from my hand and I looked off as if I'd just remembered something important. But she wasn't happy with most of the revisions they'd got so far and started all over with the suggestions. I began to get panicky.

Then something Angela had said rang a little bell.

Henry.

We met outside the clothing store on Henry's lunch break. I took him to a deli nearby and bought him a hearty corned beef sandwich while I laid out my plan to him.

"The thing is, Henry," I told him, "I'm right in the middle of my new novel and it's taking up all my time. My editor is still sending letters suggesting changes in *"The Little Mornings"* and I just don't have the time to give them my full attention. Besides, it throws me off, you know?"

He nodded and looked confused.

"I mean, I'm in the middle of a new story and suddenly I have to stop and change gears and go back to this other one— I don't know, maybe I'm too close to it to see the need for change. Anyway, I thought about you, Henry. I think you've got lots of talent."

At that his eyes lit up and he swallowed half a mug of beer.

"You do? Really?"

"I do," I affirmed. "And it occurred to me that you might like to have a hand in this. Now I don't have any money at the moment to pay you, Henry, but if you want to take some of these manuscript pages and the letters as they come in, I thought maybe I'd let you try your hand at following some of my editor's suggestions, you follow? You can make revisions and retype them and we'll send them back."

He nodded again. "This is still your personal editor we're talking about?"

"Yes. That's the one. Anyway, that way, you not only help me out of a jam, but you get a lot of practical experience, and—down the pike, I think it could be very useful when I tell my editor who really stepped in and made the revisions and when she sees that you can really write, I don't see any reason why you'd have any trouble at all in getting them to publish your first novel."

"My first novel?"

I'd just opened a door for Henry.

He showed huge white teeth. "I hadn't ever really got that far—I mean to think about writing a novel. Me, writing a novel. Maybe I could. I've got a lot to say Darcy; I know that. I just hadn't had the vision to see that maybe I should just skip the little essays and short stories and go for a real novel. Wright, Baldwin, Hines, Haley—*The Color Purple!* Some real Americana. By God, Darcy, you're a real friend. I just didn't put myself in that class. I don't know how long it might've taken me to think of that without your input."

"Then you'll do it," I said.

"Darcy, I'd be honored. Just let me get to it."

"I'll bring some of the stuff over," I promised.

Like a big shot I walked Henry back to the store. At the entrance he turned and put his left hand on my shoulder and with the other he gripped my right hand and held it tightly. His hands were narrow and sinewy.

"You know why I have so much faith in you Darcy?" he said.

"No, I guess not Henry. Why?"

"Because you took my advice and got the glasses."

* * *

I took Angie to the Embers and she tried a margarita and I drank Negra Modelo and we listened to *'Las Mañanitas'* again on the jukebox.

> *Ya viene amaneciendo,*
> *Ya la luz del día nos vio.*
> *Despierta, amiga mía*
> *Mira que ya amaneció.*

It was dark and noisy and I began to feel my old self again. It had been a long time since I'd let down and been just plain Darcy the Loser. Most of the time now I was playing the role. Mr. Darcy Lemarsh, the soon to be famous author.

Angie hadn't said anything lately about her suspicions, but I sensed very strongly that all was still not right between us. There was a barrier now, something that hadn't been there before, and I wasn't sure it would ever go away. It left me with a hollow feeling in the pit of my stomach and that wouldn't go away either— and there was nothing I could do about it.

On the publishing house side of the question however, things began to pick up again—I thought.

I put together some of JC's suggestions and took the whole mess to Henry who was delighted. He promised to get to work immediately but he said he didn't have a computer.

"That's okay, Henry. A plain old typewriter's fine," I told him. We had grandpa's typewriter. We'd brought most of his stuff up and stored it in Angie's apartment. We even had the contract for the book, but I couldn't make any sense out of it. "I can let you use my old manual typewriter."

"I've already got one," Henry told me. "It's an old portable typewriter I picked up for ten bucks at the flea market—that's what turned me into a writer. What's the use having a typewriter if you don't write on it, right?" He was all happy face.

"Perfect," I said.

In the meantime, I thought about what I told JC: that I might get a computer. I knew there were four more books in the box and I was pretty sure they had been typed just like the first one. Each one had been wrapped up in the wrapping paper that comes with a bundle of typing paper and held together with Scotch tape. When I opened one and looked inside, I saw that sure enough it had been written on a typewriter just like the one JC had. It was obviously no great print job. It was fine to do the first one on an old typewriter but I knew JC would expect something better now that she thought I had a little money. Sooner or later I was going to have to send another manuscript to her. The fact that there were people out there who would gladly redo the stuff on a computer for a fee never occurred to me until some time later.

Of course at different times JC berated me about not having a phone where she could get into contact with me whenever she wanted to, but I just put her off with some story about getting a cell phone as soon as I got back. There was no phone in the apartment. Angie got messages now and then through her landlady. She never needed to call anybody, so no need to pay for a cell phone. Recently most of the messages had been from Henry wondering about his stories. That had stopped now that he had a job to do. But I didn't want JC calling me there. I knew the landlady knew I was living there but she hadn't ever said anything and I didn't want to push it. I figured me and JC were better off to keep our business in the mail anyway.

A couple of weeks drifted by before Henry called Angie and told her he had some of my stuff ready for me. I glanced at it and it looked pretty neat, I must say.

I smiled to myself. Smartest move I ever made. I bundled up everything and took it to the post office and shipped it off to JC in New York City.

I think that by this time nearly a year had passed since the late professor had first talked to me about his damned book. A guy could grow old waiting around for these publishers to get off their asses. He was sure right about the wounded snail or whatever it was. Here I was with four more books ready to go and didn't dare send them in while this one was still hanging fire. Fame sure comes slow sometimes. At least they gave him twenty grand up front, but that didn't do Angie and me any good and there hadn't been any more talk of money since that time. I was reluctant to mention it to JC while she was all up in the air about the revisions.

But now I could breathe a little easier. In finally got a cell phone and gave the number to JC.

Henry's work looked neat and professional. He was a pretty good typist. And I was pretty certain he'd given it his best shot. And his best shot had to be a lot better than my best shot. It was just a matter now of waiting for JC to tell me everything was okay.

Unfortunately however, everything was not okay.

* * *

I sat in a taco joint near the mailbox place drinking coffee while I read the latest mail from JC. She usually sent large manila envelopes with a couple bucks' worth of postage on them. This one was extra thick.

JC had stuffed the envelope with manuscript pages, all marked up with changes and she wanted me to be sure to call her collect at what would be nine o'clock New York time. I sat there drinking coffee. These were pages Henry had typed up for me. Some suggestions were underlined with a marking pen and big exclamation points. None of it made a lot of sense to me.

And Angie didn't like it one bit that I had to go out alone and make a call.

"Listen," I told her, "this is going to be hard enough without my being conscious of you standing there hanging onto every word." I held up two fingers and held them a quarter inch apart. "We're this close now, Angie. Just let me get it over with. Once we get past the first damned book, things should go a lot better. We'll pack up another one pretty soon and shoot it in."

"Yeah—shoot it in," she said. "Your lesbo editor will love that." She turned away and went and sat on the edge of the bed.

I decided I'd better ignore the crack about JC. "I won't be long," I promised. I went down the street where I could talk quietly.

A soft female voice answered on the first ring, but it wasn't JC. After a moment JC came onto the phone.

"What in the hell are you trying to pull on me, Darcy?" she said.

"What do you mean?" I really didn't know what she was talking about.

Her voice was as clear as if she were standing right beside me. "I asked you to make some simple changes and instead of following my suggestions, you've gone off on some wild tangent and suddenly it sounds as if Annie is black and Carvil turns out to be a racist and out of left field we've suddenly got race problems springing up. From the sound of it, Carvil might as well join the KKK and he might as well take Annie off to Mexico and burn her on a cross instead of strangling her. Christ Darcy, that's not what I meant when I asked you to make Carvil off the wall. Racists aren't off the wall, Darcy; they're just off.

"Darcy, I'm giving you one last chance to do this yourself. If you don't go over the shit I sent you and clean it up and get it right, I'm going to have to do something myself whether you like it or not, got that?"

"I—I'm sorry," I stammered. "I've been under a lot of pressure lately, JC. You know I'm working on my new novel and I get all mixed up jumping back and forth. I get too involved in what I'm doing, don't you see? And besides," I added, hoping it would buy me something, "I miss you a great deal in case you didn't know that."

"I'm very flattered, Darcy, but we've got to get this damned book into print. We've got a deadline. My ass is on the line here. Did I tell you that First Look just signed a contract with us for the film rights? This book's right up their alley. They've got a screenplay in the works right now. Do you know what that means? Does the name First Look Studio mean anything at all to you? They've made some of the most acclaimed and profitable films in Hollywood. We're talking feature film here all tied in with your novel. And that means big bucks. We're talking Cannes Film Festival, Darcy. They just love these dark love stories over there. Cannes, Darcy. Cannes. And now you're turning into Martin Luther King, Jr. on me, or the KKK—or something. God, I'm not sure what. Darcy, I don't know what you're doing! Please, Darcy. Please! Work with me. Help me here! This is important."

"Sure, I understand," I said. "Eh, do you know who's going to be in it?"

"What? Oh, the film?" Her voice dropped into a more defensive mode. "Well, you know how it is in Hollywood, Darcy. They have to work with the actors to a certain extent, and they have to keep the audience in mind. And— sometimes they have to make little changes in the script. Things that work in the book don't always work in the film. I mean, well, the thing is that they want John Goodman for the producer and Frances McDormand for his wife."

"John Goodman?"

The Little Mornings

"Yes, now listen. Here's the thing. I know that in the book you depict the producer as somewhat younger and his wife scarcely gets honorable mention. They don't really appear that much in the book, I know. But in the film, the director feels it's important to beef up the part of the producer and his wife. They thought it would make an even better storyline—film-wise that is, if the parents were a little older. Their children are grown or at least teenagers; so here's the producer's wife thinking motherhood's all behind her when she finds she's pregnant again. There's a big scene where she tells the producer the news. They're thrilled beyond belief. This is all shown in flashback, you see, while she's holding her new baby in her arms or something like that. Well, the audience is clearly shown what an unexpected joy all this is to a family that otherwise has everything, and yet, without a child in the house, has nothing. And then after that's all been clearly established and the audience shares in the couple's newfound joy, your bozos come in and kidnap the baby. That makes the whole business all the more poignant, because now the audience knows the producer and his wife. And even though they're rich and powerful, they're really nice people and the audience is happy for them. The kidnappers might as well have been the Manson gang. The audience is going to be devastated."

I couldn't think of anything to say.

"So, what do you think, Darcy? I know they're changing some of the plot, but for very good reasons. That won't make too much of a difference will it?"

I didn't have a clue what she was talking about. "Who's going to play the leads then?" I asked.

"Oh, well, they don't want name talent to play the leads because basically Carvil and Annie are a couple of losers. If they got big stars to play those parts the audience might not buy them being losers, you see? Fans don't like for their big stars to be losers, right?"

"Oh…yeah, right," I said. I wasn't sure about that, but it sounded like she made sense.

"You know, sometimes they go against type or reputation, but that can backfire. Filmgoers pay to see their hero do what heroes do. You see? As to the leads, believe me they're important parts. Those are the kinds of parts that make overnight stars. The leads may not be stars in this picture but they'll be stars in the next one, you can bet on that.

"That's why they want to beef up the parts of the producer and his wife. They need some names on the marquee to bring in the audience, and if you're going to have big talent like McDormand and Goodman, then you have to give them something to do. I mean the parts are too just big to be cameo roles, you see?"

"Oh, sure, I understand," I said. "Yeah…"

"Anyway, those Hollywood people know what they're doing. That's why they're in Hollywood and we're not."

I laughed. JC laughed too, but I felt her laugh was a little forced. In the background it sounded like the other female was putting in her two cents worth too, but I couldn't make out exactly what she was saying.

"Okay, I'm sorry about the mix-up with Carvil. I didn't intend to get any racial issues in there. I must have got confused with the book I'm working on right now. I'll fix it," I promised. "I'll try to do what you suggest." But I'd already made up my mind to do exactly what JC said, let it go and let her and the damned director finish the story any way they wanted to and they could change the kidnapped baby to an alley cat for all I cared.

And as to Henry, mild-mannered clothier by day and militant activist by night, this was a parting of our ways. From now on I was going to buy my clothes at Penney's.

* * *

At last came the fateful day when the book was due out. I hadn't heard from JC for a while and didn't know whether she'd abandoned the project or was rewriting the damned thing herself like she threatened to do. Maybe she was just mad at me. I wasn't in a position to worry about it. I couldn't try to call or anything without getting Angie all up in the air. Beside I was half afraid to talk to JC. I know I wasn't any help in making all those revisions, and if I talked to her it might just make things worse. Evidently she lived through it. And although they hadn't released the movie, they were advertising it already and so-and-so was giving it two thumbs up and a bunch of bull. First Look Studios had done it again. God forbid the lowly author should get any mention. I guess I was down there with the fifth assistant director someplace. I didn't recognize the names of any of the other stars, but true to JC's word, Frances McDormand and John Goodman were basically *the* stars. At least they kept the original title. That was a surprise since I knew most of the time when a book gets to Hollywood they change the title.

I'd been expecting to go to Hollywood when they started the movie. In fact I'd been counting on it. Night after night I dreamed about meeting the stars and going to swank restaurants and wandering around movie studios. Maybe they'd even fit me in the picture someplace, even if it was what JC called a cameo role, like *Erin Brockovich*. I remember the real Erin Brockovich turned up as a waitress in the movie. Angie told me that. Angie always sat there in the theater and read all the titles after everybody else had gone. She knew almost all the actors and actresses by name— big stars and all the character players too. She's say, "Look, that's Jonathan Banks. Bad guy. Don Gibb. Bad guy. Peter Greene, bad ass. Louise Latham; I thought she was dead. Of course this flick was made a long time ago. Veda Ann *Borg*! Boy this *is* an oldie." Whatever. It seemed to me they'd want the author to be involved in the movie-making process, too. As it turned out, nobody invited me and the picture got made before I even realized it. That was pretty disappointing.

Maybe if I'd really written the damned book, I could've insisted on helping oversee the screenplay or at least being there to give approval or something. Maybe I could even help write the screenplay—but for me it was a challenge just to fill out an employment application, so since nobody invited me I had to let it ride. Maybe next time.

Over the couple of months that passed since grandpa died, relations between Angie and me had been off and on. Sometimes we got along like everything was back to normal and at others I'd be aware of her sitting across the room staring sideways at me with those pale faraway eyes, chilling in their icy anger. I saw that she wasn't really going to give up on this notion that I had something to do with helping old Berry into the next world.

* * *

JC got hold of me. The book was out.

"We've got our initial run of a hundred thousand copies spoken for so we've ordered another hundred thousand."

I got a dozen copies of the book by UPS and a notice that they were going to provide me with a car and hotel vouchers and an itinerary.

The book looked great. The cover thing was kind of abstract on black paper. *The Little Mornings.* A sketch of a group of mariachis stood near the bottom of the dust jacket playing their tunes, and slightly off to the right and just above them a girl lay on a bed with a black and red coverlet while two birds fluttered above her, and above that, the sun was in the background peeping over a cactus. And on the back there I was, Darcy James Lemarsh, the Author. It was a good pic.

I finally got confirmation to pick up a car. This trip was going to be a swing around the western states. I guess they wanted to see how I did before they brought me back east.

We were to go to Portland first. After I made some excuses to JC about money, I also got an expense check made out in my own name for five thousand dollars. I'm sure JC thought I was going alone, but of course I had to take Angie with me.

"I don't like it," Angie complained. "But I'm not going to sit here and sweat while you run all over the country and spend my grandpa's money. Now that he's gone, his share is mine and I mean to stay with you till I get it."

"Angie I never dreamed of running off and leaving you here," I told her.

"Well, it's not that I don't trust you, Darcy, but I don't."

"What the hell does that mean?"

She walked over close and looked at me. Her face could be incredibly cold when she wanted it to. I looked into those icy colorless eyes. It was almost as if she were some kind of alien from another world.

"Sometimes I hate you so much I can't stand it," she said. "I look at you and see you strangling my grandpa and I absolutely loathe you—but the worst thing is that, no matter what, I can't imagine me going on without you anymore. I don't know what to do."

"He wasn't strangled, Angie," I told her. "He died in his own vomit." I tried to soothe her. "Maybe we're soul mates. Maybe we knew each other in previous lives." I didn't really believe in that stuff but I thought it sounded good.

Angie looked through me, "If this is life, then one's enough, thanks." She stood there and folded her arms. She glared at me. "You killed my grandpa. I just know it. Down deep I know."

I threw up my hands and paced.

"He was everything to me," she went on. "Mother, father; my best friend. He loved me just the way I am, good times or bad. It didn't matter. He didn't love me the way you love me. His love was unconditional."

"Angie, don't keep talking like that. I didn't kill your pops, and my love is unconditional." Whatever the hell that meant.

"It doesn't matter," she said. "I forgive you. I have to. I can't deny you anything, Darcy."

"Oh Christ," I muttered. I went to the window and looked down at the traffic in the street below.

I wondered if and how I was ever going to get this idea out of her head. With that coming between us it was no wonder that our relationship was strained. We couldn't go on like that forever.

* * *

I didn't have a bank account so it wasn't all that easy to get the check cashed. I went to the check place where I used to cash Ephraim's checks. It cost me, but I got it done. I was off!

Of course even though I was elated, my heart was in my mouth since I still wasn't quite sure what I was going to say or do. Closest thing I ever had to an interview before was to sit down and have somebody ask about my experience and why I left my last job. Of course, over the past year or so I had been paying more attention when I saw interviews on television. I especially watched for anything to do with writers. Of course, most of the time, when they interviewed an author, the book was nonfiction about some current event, or an exposé of the CIA or maybe about a famous murder case or something. It seemed to me that very few had anything to do with fiction—but I learned later that unless it's pretty newsworthy you're lucky if you don't have to pay the station to let you come on and promote your stuff. I guess they figure why let you advertise for free. I can relate to that.

The car was a nice Honda.

"Check it out," I said, feeling down beside my seat. "Look, it's even got a little latch to pop the trunk and the gas cap down here."

"That's why they put that stuff there," Angie said, not in one of her better moods. "For dufuses like you to play with."

Anyway, we were all set.

THE LITTLE MORNINGS

Then next morning while we were getting ready to leave, I fumbled around with the papers and stuff and dropped the whole mess onto the floor right by the bed. I had to get down on my knees to gather them back up and then my eye caught sight of something almost on the other side, under Angie's side. I got up and went around while she still lay there in bed puffing on a cigarette and got down on my knees and reached under. I came up with a package of Trojans.

I froze for a minute while it soaked in. Angie and I didn't use any protection. I know it sounds stupid since I hadn't ever decided whether or not we were going to get married. I guess we were just lazy. Lazy and stupid. I don't know. I hardly ever thought about it. All I knew in this moment was that the rubbers weren't mine.

I held them up for her to see. She gave them that lazy sideways glance and then glanced at me.

"What? Oh, you think they're mine?" She sat up blowing smoke into the air while I waited, unable to speak.

"Maybe they belong to the landlady?" I suggested in my most sarcastic voice. She ignored that.

"You remember Nancy."

I didn't. She had spoken of some of her girl friends once in a while but I never paid any attention.

"Come on. I told you all about her. Nancy's married but she doesn't get along with her old man any more. Anyway she met a guitar player in Old Sac and they've been seeing each other. He's married too so they couldn't leave the damned things at his house and they couldn't leave them at her house, so she asked me to keep them for her. I mean, she doesn't really even see the guy very often."

I stared at her. "You expect me to believe a bullshit story like that, Angie?"

She hopped out of bed all furious now. "*Don't* believe me. I don't care. It's the truth, damn it. I let her use the place a couple of times when we were out and about. I'll bring Nancy over here and you can ask her yourself."

"Yeah, like that's going to make everything all right," I said. "I mean I'm sure Nancy wouldn't lie. She slips around banging guitar players behind her husband's back, but when it comes to her damned Trojans, Nancy wouldn't lie. Christ, if I can't trust you for five minutes when I'm out of the house...Angie, I've got to have a woman who doesn't keep secrets."

She stabbed out her cigarette in the ashtray and put her hands on her hips, taking a stance. She was only wearing a short shift and thong panties and for a second there she looked so hot I almost forgot what we were talking about, but as I looked at the package I was still holding I got madder and madder. Some guy had been right here, here in our apartment, in our bed. That took nerve. She knew I wasn't working so there was no real way to know when I was coming home. I opened my mouth but she came right back at me.

"Secrets? You talk about secrets? What about my grandpa? You killed him, Darcy. I know it. I know it in my bones. He may have been a Communist, but he didn't deserve to die like that. You killed him because you were afraid he'd be a problem for you and your future down the road and you'll never make me believe otherwise. And you talk about secrets."

I watched a fly slip in through the open window and land on the table by her ashtray. I sighed and took a deep breath. That darkness was closing in around me and I fought against it.

"Angie, if you believe something as crazy as that why the hell are you still here? Why don't you dump me, turn me in to the police or something? Why? Because you know you're full of shit, that's why. Just like that Communist shit and everything else you go on about. And besides, that's just camouflage to get me off the subject of Nancy's rubbers. All that kind of crap doesn't have anything to do with me finding rubbers under the bed."

"I told you: they're Nancy's." She turned and ducked her head and grabbed another cigarette. The fly took off in a spiral and shot past my head. She lit up and blew out smoke and looked at me as if to say, "Prove otherwise meatball".

I couldn't talk. I really couldn't think what to do. I had to get control of myself. I looked down and saw that my hands were trembling and inside I felt as if I were shaking too.

I moved on wooden legs to the bathroom and cleaned up and got dressed while she waited around smoking and watching me out of the corners of her eyes. She sat there on the edge of the bed, a cigarette in one hand and a strand of hair in the other, twisting and twisting it around. I tried not to pay any attention.

Finally I was dressed and ready to leave. By now I had calmed down a little — but it had been closer than Angie knew. During that time she hadn't done a thing. I could leave her sitting right where she was of course, but that wouldn't solve anything. Especially if she were to go to the police with those crazy accusations. She might decide tell the cops that I'd stolen the damned books from her stupid grandpa. Here I was passing myself off as The Author. That sure wouldn't make me look very good if they started any kind of investigation. Besides, mad as I was at Angie — and hurt, I still loved her. I'd made sort of a commitment to her. And then I thought about JC and the motel at Fisherman's Wharf. I couldn't help but feel guilty, and that took a lot of the steam out of my anger. I knew that the first time JC hooked her finger at me, I'd dive right back into bed with her too — and I wouldn't have to hide any rubbers either! I ran my hand through my hair and took a deep breath and let it out slowly. Maybe I should just say tit for tat and let it go. And aside from that, I didn't feel like I could run off and abandon Angie — not so much for her sake maybe — I'm trying to be truthful here — as for mine. Much as I hated to have to admit it, I guess I needed Angie. Maybe I needed her more than she needed me, even though sometimes I half suspected she was one rose short of a bouquet.

I sighed. "Better get dressed," I told her. "We've got a long day ahead."

I'd wanted to get the feel of the Honda so a couple of days before, on Saturday, I drove Angie out to the flea market in Roseville and we bought, among other things, a couple of suitcases so we'd be ready to roll. I realized later that I could've got a garment bag too, but since the suits came in a nice black plastic cover with the store's name on it in gold, I figured I could get by.

"Are you sure you still want me to come?" Angie asked. Suddenly she was all sweet and timid. She stood there not looking at me at all. Instead she studied the end of her cigarette. "I mean, if you feel can't trust me..."

"Don't push it Angie," I told her. "If the shoe were on the other foot you wouldn't believe a phony story like that for a minute. I know you." I moved over to her and put my arm around her waist. I pulled her and she melted against me as if she didn't weigh an ounce. "Angie, I'm going to try to believe you. I want to believe you—but I want to know that you're not ever going to cheat on me. I need to know that."

She snuggled against me, holding her cigarette out away from us.

"Maybe it's crazy, but there's something that holds us together, Angie. You know it and I know it. We belong together and I want us to stay together—but we have to have trust. Don't you see that?"

She didn't say anything. I held her for a minute and then said, "Well, you'd better get your shit together. We've got to go."

I opened the box of manuscripts. Each one was pretty thick. I laid two in my suitcase and two in Angie's. Our tickets to Hollywood! Well maybe...

The furniture went with the apartment. The only real possessions Angie had aside from her clothes and an old

The Little Mornings

television were a couple of pots and pans and maybe the sheets and towels, none of which were worth twenty cents put together. We'd given all Berry's books and stuff to the Goodwill except for his typewriter and a couple of things, but there was nothing much of grandpa's that I wanted except for the contract. I stuffed that into my suitcase too. I couldn't use his typewriter and besides, I'd already decided to see about a computer or something.

We left the apartment behind without saying a word and went downstairs and got into the Honda. The November sky was gray but there was no sign of rain. We were all settled in but then I thought of the pickup. I got back out of the Honda and put the key in the ignition of the truck.

"What're you doing with the truck?" Angie said.

"Fuck it," I said. "This is the end of an era, Angie. We're not coming back—at least not to this old bucket and that ratty apartment we've been sharing. This is a new beginning for us. A new life. Whoever gets to the truck first can have it."

She looked at me curiously and lit a cigarette. I was getting worse jitters by the moment. That was the first time I'd ever done anything so daring: just stick the key in the ignition and walk away. The excitement of actually getting the new car and an itinerary and motel reservations and money in my pocket took a lot out of me and Angie too, I think. She laid her head back and closed her eyes. I took her hand and sat there for a minute. Then I took a deep breath leaned over and kissed her hard on the mouth and started the car.

* * *

We went blazing up Interstate Five and stopped at places like McDonald's along the way and lived on hamburgers and coffee. Most of the time Angie smoked or leaned back with her eyes closed.

By the time we were getting close to Portland it was raining.

The motel reservation was in my name only, but the lobby was big and full of people milling about. Nobody said anything about Angie.

"Wow, nice room," she said. She danced around and lit up. It *was* a nice room. Better than the motel room where JC and I had passed that Fantasy Island afternoon in San Francisco.

* * *

I'd never been inside a television station before in my life. Angie came with me and we walked through confusing rooms without ceilings. There were ceilings I guess but they were dark and high above the tops of the partitions. And lights, mostly turned off, hung down from them all over. A young fellow with a fistful of papers and a clipboard lead us carefully over jumbles of heavy cables on the floor and we finally came out onto a set where it looked like they did the news. To one side there was a smaller raised set with two chairs, a small table between, and on the floor just beside one chair, a big green plant. A small wooden panel stood like a wall just behind the table and in front of that, a small table with a lamp.

People moved around and they had huge cameras on dolly things and lights all over the place. The guy led us past that to a small area just beyond where we came to a little room that looked something like a barbershop. A flighty young black man seated me in the chair and started fixing me up with makeup and playing with my hair.

As it turned out, the interview was for a later broadcast so we weren't going to be talking live. So much the better because this was my first big test.

"You just relax my man—we'll have you all fixed up in a jiffy," he said.

"Do I need this?" I asked him.

He sprayed lightly at my hair. "Hey, you want this to look professional or you want it to look like your cousin

The Little Mornings

Izzy filmed you with his cell phone?" He showed bright white teeth.

"Of course—yeah—we want to be professional all right," I agreed.

"You look beautiful," he told me. He beamed at me and I couldn't tell whether he was being sincere or BS-ing me—or if he just liked all the boys. He stepped back and made a frame with his hands and studied me. "Damn if you don't look like a young Tom Cruise with a good haircut." He winked at Angie. "As for you, darling, while Mr. Cruise here is busy with the taping, I want to show you something,"

She beamed all over at this attention. I didn't worry about him and Angie being alone together because he was far too limp-wristed to want to mess with her. Besides, his telling me I looked like Tom Cruise didn't exactly make him my enemy. Of course I knew he was full of bull, but still…

Eventually a heavyset guy with lots of makeup and a hairpiece came out and shook hands with me. "Where's that fucking book?" he yelled to nobody in particular. Somebody brought the book and he placed it on the table between the chairs.

He had a deep artificial tan and heavy makeup. And, up close, his hair looked ridiculous, but he was the guy who had to wear it. He still had a tissue sticking out of his collar. We got seated and an assistant did a last minute touch up on him and then somebody hooked us up with tiny microphones wired around to a box on our waist and we did a voice test and finally we got started.

"We're here today to talk about the hot new novel, *The Little Mornings*." He held a clipboard in his hand but apparently didn't need to look at it.

"I'm Jeff Barrett. And today we're very pleased to have the book's author, Mr. Darcy Lemarsh here with us in our studios." He went on a little more and then got to the interview.

"Mr. Lemarsh, I understand this is your first novel?"

I hesitated too damned long before I could get my wits about me. Somebody yelled, "Cut," and we had to start all over. Barrett gave me a look, but decided to be pleasant about it.

This time I nodded and said, "Yes, I've been writing for some time, Mr. Barrett, but this one finally made it."

"Yes, by all accounts you're getting off to a very successful start," he said. "We know most first novels lose money, but we understand that—what is it again?"

"*The Little Mornings*," I said.

"*The Little* Mornings, right. Great title. Intriguing." He held the book up so that the viewers could see it. "We understand that your publishers hope to have a great success with this first novel. It barely hit the bookstores and it's already going into a second printing—and how can you go wrong when Hollywood snatches it up? Read the book, see the movie." He had a hell of a voice, deep and resonant, and a big smile. After he'd say something I felt like a sissy when I opened my mouth. I found out later that they beefed my voice up a little, to sort of even things out.

I tried to smile, "My editor says sales are getting off to a very promising start," I told him. And with the movie tie-in. Besides, my tour is just starting, so…"

"Yes, and of course the movie by the same title is about to be released in many of our larger cities, including right here in Portland," Barrett said. He kept looking at the camera even when he talked to me. "Now we've heard stories that *"The Little Mornings"* is strictly fiction, yet other stories that come in say that it's at least partially autobiographical. In fact *The Globe* implied that it was based on a factual case. Was there actually any factual basis for the book?"

"No," I said, "not really." I pulled out my phony glasses and put them on my nose to stall for time. I smiled. "Besides, if it were based on a factual case, then it wouldn't be fiction would it?" I was getting warmer by the minute and ever so often—while the camera was on my host I guess—an assistant would duck in and pat my forehead with a tissue.

"But of course many authors put much of themselves into their fiction. Tell me, Mr. Lemarsh, how much of your book would you say is autobiographical?"

Autobiographical? I wasn't completely sure what that meant. I had an idea that it meant true as opposed to made up, so I smiled. Suddenly I was back in the room smelling piss and wine. The professor was rambling along in my ear and I smiled at Mr. Television and relaxed, "Well, Mr. Barrett, even when a work is fiction, I believe the author must put a great deal of himself into it. I see the writer as a sort of ragman. He goes around picking up rags and threads wherever he finds them. Some are red and some are blue. Some are heavy yarn and some are fine silk, and none of them match. Never mind; he picks them all up and saves them in a box until one day he has enough thread in his box to enable him to weave a garment out of it. At least I believe that's what I do. My novel is the product of all these bits and pieces I've picked up over the years. Now all I can do is look at what all these threads have produced and hope it will be of interest to someone."

I saw by the expression in Barrett's eyes that he was impressed and that tickled me. Good old grandpa and his ramblings. Actually even with his help I was impressed that I'd managed to say anything halfway intelligent at that. It wasn't like me. But pops had told me a lot of BS during our visits. More of it stuck to me than I realized at the time. That's the funny thing: sometimes when I'm not even paying attention, I hear something and by golly, a year later I can repeat it word for word anyway. And besides this author thing was beginning to rub off on me. I remembered old pops saying something about people sort of creating a picture of what they wanted to be and then slowly, maybe even subconsciously, working toward becoming that person. Oh yeah: he'd been talking about electricians. Well, this was one hell of a lot better than becoming an electrician! All things considered the interview went pretty well. At one point I got in another lick that Berry had taught me. Jeff Barrett asked me some dumb question about the book and I smiled wisely. I was on a roll now. I pulled my glasses off and held them in front of me for a second and then put them back on as if I was getting ready to read something and touched the book on the table between us.

"Yes, I treat of this rather extensively in my book actually. Indeed that was one of the reasons that impelled me to pick up pen, as it were, and dramatize this philosophy in what I hoped would be an entertaining as well as informative manner."

Backstage Angie was beaming too and back at the motel she told me how good I'd looked and sounded on television. "You looked like a movie star. And you sounded good too. I'm not shitting you, Darcy," she told me.

Later we had dinner in the coffee shop next to the motel.

"That kid, Hilaire, the one who did your makeup," she said. "He told me something interesting today. "He said that if I were on television my eyes are so pale that they wouldn't show. He said that if I was going to go on television with pale eyes like mine, they'd have to get blue contact lenses for me. Did you know you could do that?"

"No—I guess I didn't," I admitted.

She lit up a cigarette and blew out smoke. She was in a good mood today. "He said I'd really be amazed at the difference." What he also told her and I didn't learn until much later was that most people associate those pale eyes with a person not being sincere or trustworthy—or in my own translation: scary. Which fit Angie and her eyes just fine.

* * *

Seattle, and then Spokane and Helena and Billings, Montana. Each stop got a little easier. It turned out that in many stops I was on radio instead of television. That was

The Little Mornings

even easier because I knew nobody could see me and I felt more comfortable. Sometimes they'd take calls from listeners, but that was easy. I'd pretty well memorized my shit by now. Then on to stores for book signings. The signings weren't hard. The hard part was getting a lot of people to show up to them. Then we dropped down to Boise and drove to Salt Lake City and finally to Denver. By then we were in the middle of winter and had deep snow. Even with chains and traveling in low gear, we slip-slided along the highway like a fish in panic. And my tail was getting sore from all the driving, and at night in my sleep I'd see the road unwinding ahead all covered in layers of snow. By morning I felt like I'd been driving all night too. When we got to Denver it stopped snowing for a while and luckily I didn't have to spend more than five minutes at a time out in the cold. Part of the time Angie stayed in the motel and part of the time she came with me and stood around in the background. I liked it better when she waited in the motel. I didn't like knowing that she was just out of sight watching me. After the television thing I spent part of the day in a department store and then went to a big bookstore where I signed more books. More people showed up this time. And that evening I was finally able to take Angie to see the famous movie.

For the first time I was going to really find out what the stupid book was about. Up until now I'd started shaking inside every time someone mentioned anything about the book because I really didn't have a clue. Now at last, by God, we were going to see everything.

Once we knew the movie was going to be made I began to try to cast the parts in my mind. That was hard because I still didn't know what was really going on. Mostly I only knew about the guy, the gal, the baby and the movie producer. There had to be other characters. I knew John Goodman was going to be in the picture of course, and Frances McDormand. I remembered her from *Fargo*.

Seemed to me she'd even got an award or something for that. Other than that, I was in the dark. Well, Angie and I sat right in the middle of the auditorium with our feet stuck to the floor and ate popcorn and drank Cokes and watched the movie from start to finish.

The lead guy and his girlfriend weren't anybody I knew, but all in all, I thought the producers made good choices. Everybody fit the part. John Goodman sure looked like a Hollywood producer. He was important and had lots of money and he was used to waving his arms around and giving orders. As it turned out, Frances McDormand played his wife and she was great. She was likeable but still tough as nails as far as everything else was considered and was obviously used to kicking ass around the house. She kept the servants running scared. But when it came to that baby, she and the producer were pure mush. JC had already told me the movie people were going to make the producer and his wife more important in the movie and I guess they did. The nanny was a dork who really had her head in her ass. The young man was good-looking but down deep right from the start I could see that he was a loser all right. Just like me. I thought too how Angie had worked for that rich lawyer and if things had gone another way, it could've been Angie and me who kidnapped a baby—and look what could've happened to us. Anyway, I knew from the start that things weren't going to turn out well for this guy, Carvil, or for his girl friend either. She didn't look anything like Angie. She was blonde and looked a little shortsighted. She had a squeaky little voice. Still I guess you could call it good casting because she played the part really well, and she was a little paranoid too. I didn't really like it too much, but they reminded me a lot of Angie and me. I almost felt sorry for them because they hadn't set out to do anything really bad, like hurt the baby. They just wanted to get their hands on a little money. They didn't expect anybody to get hurt. When the baby's fever began to climb they almost went crazy. They got stuff from the drugstore and they gave the baby cold baths and everything. But there was nothing they could do. It looked to me like they felt almost as bad as the baby's parents. Then it died on them. But it was too late to turn back so they went on and finally got the kidnap money. They took off to Mexico, but pretty soon here came this other guy. He was about the same age as they were but he was a slime ball. He realized who they were and wanted the money, or at least most of it. So sure enough they decided the only thing to do was to kill the dude. They got busy and plotted his murder and carried it out. And by God later on Carvil did end up killing his girl friend even though you could tell he loved her just like I loved Angie. The end of the movie left us knowing that he was going down hard for the kidnap and for the murder of the baby because they had that one hung on him good, and the big producer had a mean eye now and was demanding justice and it looked like he was going to get it. Then at the end of the picture the young guy got his best moment, I thought. He was alone in a Mexican jail cell listening to the musicians just outside his window. They were all dressed in those black outfits with lots of silver and had big black and silver sombreros. They were playing *Las Mañanitas*. A little fat guy played the cornet in sad clear tones. I remembered Berry telling us the story. *His swan song...the end.*

"Well?" Angie said outside. We stood bundled up and shivering in the snow. "What did you think?"

"Wow, I don't know," I told her. "I guess it was pretty good at that. The guy was a jerk but I couldn't help but feel sorry for him too, didn't you? I mean I don't think he was really bad. He just got sucked into something. Everything just went wrong—I guess that was the message maybe: when you start out to do something you know is wrong, you can't expect everything to turn up roses or whatever. I don't know."

"I guess. The girl sort of got sucked in too," Angie said. "But I didn't like her. I bet in real life she'd cut your throat to get a part. I didn't like the popcorn. It was stale."

We found a coffee shop and had something to eat and then beat it back to our motel. I decided I should see the damned movie again first chance I got. Of course, I understood that they'd changed a lot of stuff in the movie. But that was the best I had to offer: the movie version. I figured it was better that the zip I had to go on just yesterday.

On the heels of that our love life began to pick up again, but it was getting more and more regular for Angie to get into one of her depressed moods and sit there staring and thinking—and I kept having this uncomfortable feeling that she resented me.

Somehow she couldn't shake this idea that I had something to do with pop's death and she wouldn't let go of it. "Even if he was a Communist, he didn't deserve to die like that," she'd say for the twentieth time. When she got like that I tried to leave her alone. I couldn't bear the thought of watching her get started.

We headed to Albuquerque and Phoenix. Then San Diego. At least the weather was better. The television people came and went. Most of them looked phony as hell up close. They'd be all made up and looked artificial and while they all smiled a lot and carefully intoned every word before the camera, a lot of them were real assholes the rest of the time, bitching and grumbling and making sarcastic remarks. They were the big stars of their little productions and they didn't want anybody to forget it. Of course some of them were pretty nice. Most of them had hair so hard that you could bust a knuckle on it.

* * *

I was in the back of a bookstore in San Diego patiently waiting for a customer to offer me a book to sign. Outside it was raining and only a few damp and dripping customers wandered about the store and evidently they weren't too excited about seeing Darcy Lemarsh sitting at a table in the back.

Then this fellow about my own age sidled up to me. He wore a crew cut and had a kind of rolling walk and I wondered if he was a sailor. He had a slick sneaky air about him that I didn't like. He had on a silk suit over a white T-shirt. The suit was too shapeless and modern for my taste, but it looked like it cost money. He held a wet umbrella out away from him. He held his book out for me to sign.

"What's your name?" I asked.

"Just make it out to Ron," he said. While I was writing he ducked his head a little closer. "You know, Mr. Lemarsh, I really enjoyed your book and I want to go see the movie. Say, you know, a friend of mine is gone for the weekend and he lent me his apartment. He has CDs and DVDs up the yahoo and a bar. A very well-stocked bar. I thought maybe we could go see the movie together and then, you know, go up for a drink or two and listen to some music…I mean I suppose you don't know anybody in town here."

I looked up at him and his eyes looked so hopeful. I could see in them too that he already knew I was going to say no.

"Well, that's okay," he said. "Listen, if you get in town again and want some action, I know some good places. If you ever want to get screwed, chewed and tattooed, look me up. Here." He gave me a card and took his book. He had to move aside because a middle-aged woman behind him was beginning to grunt. Later I looked at the card. Ronald "Ron" McGuire. I guess he wasn't a sailor after all. He sold real estate.

* * *

The lights were bright and the makeup heavy. We were in L.A. This time I had a woman interviewer. Up close she was a lot older than I'd realized. She had perfect blond hair and so much makeup I didn't really know what she looked like. But her throat and her hands gave her away. She was an old hand and for some reason she decided to give me a bad time. At least to me it was a bad time. But by now I was getting a lot better at swordsmanship with these interviewers. Sometimes I surprised myself.

"Well," I said, putting on my famous glasses, "it's my personal belief that the writer is like an actor playing all the parts in a movie. One minute I'm the sheriff in khaki with a spare tire around my waist and a chaw of tobacco under my lip—and then the next minute I'm a sexy blonde with a short skirt and a fetching smile. Then I'm suddenly the straightlaced librarian or the handsome leading man—in all these quick changes I have to feel the part and sort of become that person for whatever time it takes to play the scene." I relaxed my shoulders and sat back, "And then I move on to the next character or the next scene." I smiled wisely and took my glasses off and polished them with my handkerchief.

"Yes, I think I see," she said. "But unlike an actor, you don't have to memorize your lines; you make them up as you go along."

"Right," I laughed. "That's exactly right, I make them up as I go along—but of course I agonize over every word, every comma. And I always have to know where I'm going, which way I'm heading—you know, so I don't get lost."

"And does that ever happen, Mr. Lemarsh?" Her blue eyes were searching. "Do you ever get lost or off the track?"

"Oh, all the time." I remembered something grandpa had told me. I leaned back, comfortable and expansive. "Usually I bring myself up short and get back on track, but sometimes I like the direction I find myself going. The unknown road ahead looks interesting so I turn loose and follow it and I find that often that's where I do some of my best writing. Sometimes I'm just as eager to learn what's going to happen next as my reader will hopefully be when the book is published."

The Little Mornings

"I like that," she said. I think I'd won her over by then. "Then sometimes it's almost as if the book is there, waiting—and you're the first person to read it."

"Exactly," I said, pouncing on that. I smiled happily. "I think you've got it exactly right there."

Then for some unannounced reason there was evidently some sort of tie-in with a baseball team. The Louisville RiverBats were in town to play the Padres so they introduced a pitcher that I was evidently supposed to recognize. He got to say a few words and talk about the game that evening. I never followed baseball so I didn't know who he was and didn't care. As part of the gimmick, he presented me with an autographed baseball bat and I had to smile and act impressed and give him an autographed book to take back home to Kentucky. He told me the bat was what they call a Louisville Slugger. I think I was supposed to be impressed. I managed to act happy but I didn't know what any of that had to do with me. Evidently the television people figured they'd kill two birds with one bat— or book.

"What am I supposed to do with a baseball bat?" I asked Angie later. I don't follow baseball. They could've given me a Kings T-shirt maybe…or something."

* * *

I was all excited about getting to LA so that I could see Hollywood, but as it turned out, all I got to see of Hollywood was a shabby Hollywood Boulevard and the front of a couple of studios. We didn't even have time to take the Universal Studios tour. JC hadn't given me any intros to producers or anything and I had no idea where to look. Just another tourist in the city of smog. It was pretty disappointing. I didn't see one movie star. Not one. I guess I had some vague idea they'd be strolling along the boulevards signing autographs for everybody or jogging or something. When we'd go into a store, I always looked around to see if any stars were shopping there, but none were. I had an idea too that JC would arrange for me to meet some of the people who made the movie. At least a tour of the studio or something, but as far as I could tell, nobody in Hollywood ever heard of Darcy Lemarsh.

We managed to see the movie two more times in between and by now I had it down pretty much by heart so I felt like I could at least talk about it without looking like a complete fool.

We came out of the theater in the evening. It had been sprinkling earlier but now it was pleasant. We walked along the street. The hollows in Angie's cheeks looked deeper than ever. She hadn't been eating well. We usually shared at least one meal together. The other times I'd have to grab a bite on the way to a television or radio studio or grab a sandwich between book signings. I didn't know how much money the book and movie were generating. It kept our bills paid I guess, and I figured I'd get some sort of accounting when we got to New York. Angie and I had both forgotten about my famous settlement back in Sacramento. That was small potatoes now.

* * *

"What do you think?" Angie said. We got to San Francisco a couple of hours earlier and she'd gone out while I tried to recover from the drive up from LA. I looked at her. She had a dress on. That was different. She looked good in it. A flowery dress with a little belt, a sweater and high heel shoes. She looked just a little bit awkward in the shoes but she looked good.

"You look great," I told her. "You look great." I stared at her. There was something about her, the way she was dressed. She looked almost like a different person. "I love the high heels."

"Do I really look nice?" She looked suddenly so vulnerable and hopeful that my heart went out to her.

"Really," I said. "Come here."

The Little Mornings

She stood there for a sec and then came closer. "Look at me."

I looked. She looked different all right, but I wasn't sure just what. Then it hit me: her eyes. There was something about her eyes. She batted them expressively and smiled. Then I had it. Of course. She didn't have those pale eyes any more. She had deep limpid blue eyes. I had to admit they made all the difference in the world. She looked warm and sincere. If she'd been wearing those contacts the day I found the Trojans, I think I would've believed her phony story about Nancy. I'd believe anything she said though I knew damned well she couldn't be trusted out of my sight.

"Your eyes," I said. "You went to an eye doctor."

"You really like them?" She moved closer.

I took her in my arms and held her close to me and stared deep into her new eyes. "I love them," I said. "Do you have to take them out to screw?"

* * *

We lay back on the bed in our motel room and stared at the brocaded ceiling. Smoke curled up from Angie's cigarette and faded away as it rose above our heads.

"They comfortable, your eyes?"

"Sure. They're soft lenses. They're basically phony, just like your glasses. They don't affect my vision." She rolled over and faced me. "I got a joke for you. The optometrist told me about a customer who got a speeding ticket. When she appeared before the judge, he said, 'It says on your license that you must wear glasses, young lady.' 'Oh but your honor,' she said, 'I have contacts.'

"The judge got all indignant and said, 'Look, miss, I don't care who you know. You still have to wear glasses!'"

We laughed our butts off. I guess it wasn't all that funny but we were in a good mood and pretty soon we made love again.

Later she was on a chair staring out the window with a

cigarette in one hand and a tangle of hair in the other. Suddenly she turned and looked right at me.

"I have an idea that you're a Communist too," she told me.

"You do eh? Do you know what a Communist is, Angie? Hell, I don't even know what a Communist is. And what difference does it make anyway?"

"It makes a difference, Darcy. It makes a hell of a difference. "Communists want to overthrow the government."

"Well, I don't know a damned thing about the government and I don't care. That's what we have politicians for. They cause enough trouble without my help. I've never voted in my life and at the rate things are going, I probably never will." I laughed. "A Communist. That went out with the Soviet Union."

"That's what they want you to think," she said as if she was in on some secret FBI information. She lit a cigarette and turned back to the window. After a while she turned and stared accusingly at me for a long time. I went into the can and closed the door. When I came out she was off in lala land again.

* * *

I had to get to the television studio. I bulled my way through the interview and after that I picked up Angie and we had lunch at a restaurant on Fisherman's Wharf but not the one where I went with JC. I dropped Angie back off at the motel. Then it was off to a department store in Union Square near the hotel where I first laid eyes on JC.

I handed my book to a good-looking girl about seventeen and looked up to see who was next but there was no one standing in line. A person would expect a line in San Francisco when a famous author is autographing his novel, especially after having seen me that morning on television. I was clean and shaven. I had on my tan suit. I had my glasses in my jacket pocket with one temple hanging out. In one of

The Little Mornings

her sentimental moments Angie had followed Henry's advice and found me a Mont Blanc pen in a discount stationery store. I sat there with my fat Mont Blanc pen in hand and so far in the first twenty minutes I'd had only two signings. I looked around me. The store was pretty busy but the book department wasn't particularly full. A couple of women were looking at some kind of picture books or cookbooks or something and I heard another one asking where the diet books were. She didn't even glance at me.

Then I spotted this little guy waddling in my direction. I recognized my book in his hand. He was short and furtive with a balding head and round shoulders. He walked slightly pigeon toed, but his clothes didn't look bad. His walk reminded me of The Penguin. He was wearing a dark suit with a little checkered sweater underneath. Only the knot of his tie showed above it. He wore little gold-rimmed glasses and when he got up to me he smiled and stuck out his hand.

"Mr. Lemarsh. I'm so glad to meet you. My name's Leo. Leo Ballcock. Now don't say anything. I know it's a shitty name but I'm stuck with it." He clung to his book as if he wasn't about to hand it over to me to sign.

"Hey, we don't get to choose our names—Leo," I said. I shook his hand. Despite his mousy attitude I kind of liked the guy. I held my hand out for the book.

He hung onto the book. "You know," he said earnestly, "I've already read *"The Little Mornings"* two times, and I saw the movie. They didn't do your book justice, I'll tell you that—aah, I'm sure you already know that. Are you going to sue them? I already have a copy at home, but I wanted to meet you so I bought another one. I like the way you handled that girl friend in the book. I really do."

"You did—you do?" Personally I thought killing her wasn't a particularly good solution to Carvil's problems.

"Yeah," he kind of hung his head and almost shuffled his feet. He kind of raised his head and briefly met my eyes. "Have you ever been abused, Mr. Lemarsh?" He looked away again real fast. His voice was a little bit high and the way he said it sounded whiny.

"Abused? I guess I can't really say I have," I said. Out of nowhere I suddenly remembered the guy who cocked his leg up and kept leaning closer and closer in a movie once when I was about twelve. He kept leaning his weight against me more and more until finally I pushed back and said, "Excuse me".

He said, "You want some popcorn?"

That's another time when I lost it. It was one of those few times when everything went black and I started hitting and kicking and somebody dragged me out of the theater and left me standing on the sidewalk. I was so mad I was trembling all over remembering the bad smell of the guy's breath in my face. Here I paid my hard earned money to go to a movie and he had to ruin it and get me thrown out. I had an idea he was thinking about some kind of abuse, but I sure didn't let it get that far. I felt like a sap and besides, the stupid thing was that the movie turned out to be in Spanish and at that time I didn't know how to say *la cucaracha*, so I didn't know what was going on anyway. It was a cowboy movie. I remember that.

"Well," Leo said, "my wife abuses me. I know it sounds kind of wimpy but it's true. A man shouldn't have to take that shit from his wife." He was still clutching his book— my book. He held it even closer now.

I tried to look concerned. "Your wife abuses you?"

"Yeah—she's pretty insidious, Mr. Lemarsh. He glanced furtively about him and leaned closer. "She can be a real bitch." I smelled Old Spice on him when he leaned closer.

"Does she throw stuff at you?" That was the only abuse I could imagine from a wife. I've seen plenty of that in old movies.

"No...oh, you'll laugh...but like—" He paused and took a breath and let it out: "She makes me wear my socks to bed."

The Little Mornings

"She makes you wear your socks to bed?"

"Yeah," he said. "Because she says I scratch her legs with my toenails. I keep my nails cut. I mean, in the winter it's okay because sometimes I get cold feet, but in summertime, my feet sweat and here I have to wear socks all night long."

"Yeah," I told him. "I just never thought of that before. I don't know whether that comes under abuse or not, Leo. I guess it's an inconvenience…"

"Yeah, and if I forget and leave the toilet seat up she makes me go in there and put it up and down fifty times."

"I hear you," I said, remembering. I looked around wishing somebody else would buy a damned book.

"You had to do that too?" he asked.

"Well, we've had our arguments about it, my wife and me."

"Yeah, and she watches me and keeps count, how do you like that? And she's hell on wheels when it comes to money too. I mean devious. You know, right after we got married we were in Safeway and there was something slick on the floor. Well, I slipped and fell down and quick as a flash she kicked me right in the nose and made it bleed and started screaming."

"You're kidding," I said.

"No, I'm not kidding at all." Light winked on a bit of saliva at the corner of his mouth. He kind of smiled at the memory, "They ended up giving us a thousand dollars just to shut her up. That was the down payment on our first car."

"I—"

"I'll tell you something else," he went on. "When I say she's insidious, I mean really insidious." He leaned closer again and I got another whiff of Old Spice. He assumed a more confidential manner, "Once when I went to the barber shop for a trim she followed me—to see if I was really going, I guess. And by God she looked through the window and saw me reading a *Penthouse* while I waited and you know what?"

I shook my head and waited.

"Well when I got home she tried to wash my eyes out with soap and water!"

"You're kidding," was all I could say.

"No— no I'm not even kidding." He smiled shrewdly. "But I didn't let her do it. That's where I drew the line." He paused and looked sad. "But she was mad at me for a week. I thought she'd never get over it."

I didn't know what to say. I looked around again hoping some more novel buyers would come up but nobody did. I noticed a skinny guy about my own age. He stood off to one side watching us. I almost felt like I'd seen him before. Watching. The guy looked kind of like a hippie type with raggedy hair and glasses. He wore a fuzzy blue sweater under a light golf jacket and had torn jeans over his spindly legs. He didn't look like he could afford twenty-eight fifty for a book. But in San Francisco, you can never tell about people. I figured he was waiting for Leo to shut up and move on so he could buy a book too. I wished he'd come on over for an autograph and get me out of this, but he just stood there watching. Our eyes met once but he quickly looked the other way. I remembered the day when I met Tony Bennett. How our eyes met anyway.

I looked back at Leo. "Well, there you go. Even if she gets mad, can't you just refuse to do what she says?"

He shrugged. "I guess I could Mr. Lemarsh, but you know, that would bring—repercussions. You know what they say: hell hath no fury…and like when we order Chinese take out. If she's in a bad mood or I did something wrong she makes me eat my dinner with one chopstick. Did you ever try to eat Chinese with one chopstick?" He made motions of scooping his food into his mouth with one chopstick.

By now I was sure he was putting me on. "No, I guess I never have, Leo," I told him. "Hell, I probably couldn't eat Chinese with three chopsticks. I use a fork." What did I know about that stuff? Once when we ate in a Chinese restaurant

The Little Mornings

I remember some Chinese people at another table, and they ate with forks. At least I think they were Chinese people.

Ballcock looked around him and lowered his voice. "And she insists on reading the fortunes first and then she takes the one she likes and I get the other one. Sometimes I hate her so much I want to kill her and that's the truth."

"I don't think you have to go that far, Leo," I said.

"Sometimes I'd like to. I could. I'm all set. I've got it all figured out. I could get away with it too, Mr. Lemarsh." And then he went into this long involved plan he'd dreamed up to dispose of his wife.

This was turning kind of dark and I didn't know what to say. "Couldn't you just leave her, Leo? I mean, hell, just pack up and get out."

"Oh, no…I couldn't do that," he told me. He looked at me sincerely. "I couldn't ever leave her, Mr. Lemarsh. She needs me."

I told Angie about my strange visit with Ballcock, the abused husband.

"Chinese food with one chopstick," I told Angie. She looked at me like I was nuts.

* * *

"Sometimes I think that a writer must, to a certain extent, be schizophrenic," I said, holding my glasses in my hand. "Inside he has all these alternate realities, these different people, which is to say, aspects of himself. And they're all scrabbling and fighting to get out, to express themselves. But instead of letting them all out at once, succumbing to an alternate reality, and landing in an insane asylum, the writer maintains control. He sits at his typewriter in, as Shakespeare says: 'The very witching time of night, when churchyards yawn and hell itself breathes out'. And surrounded by these fantastic presences there at his keyboard, the writer steps aside and lets these different people spew their vitriol out one at a time in a controlled way so their thoughts and feelings may be clarified and stabilized on the printed page. He can be a monster, a man, a woman, a child or all of the above at the same time. And his salvation is that he gets all this out of his system without ending up in the booby hatch and, if he's lucky," I smiled, "he makes some money too." I looked at the face of my interviewer, a stocky woman with horn-rimmed glasses and a hooked nose. She was indeed impressed. She almost had tears in her eyes. By God, I thought, I'm really getting good at this. I went on and on. It was almost like I'd turned into Professor Berry. I rattled out homilies and quoted Shakespeare and God knows who else and it just rolled off my tongue smooth as silk. Way to go, Darcy!

I woke up slowly. I couldn't figure out where I was for a minute and then it came to me. I was in our motel room. Dreaming. No wonder I'd been so eloquent. It was light outside. I heard Angie moving around in the bathroom. It had been so real. God, it seemed like I was so polished, so smooth, just rattling along like the professor used to do. My head still whirred. At least while I was dreaming it *seemed* like I was pretty suave. Now that I was awake, maybe it wasn't so great after all. In real life when I talked to interviewers I think I came off all right considering, but lots of times I felt like a fool trying to figure out what to say when my interviewer asked me a question. I worked on it in my spare time. I thought back about all the different things Berry used to say, and I still watched anything I could on television that had to do with writers and so on. At least I've always had a good memory and that helped, even if I didn't know what I was saying.

When the interviewer asks you a question you have to say something and say it fast. And you can't just sit there and answer yes or no. When they ask you a question and you see that light they expect you to start talking till they let you know it's time to shut up.

The Little Mornings

I spent part of the day signing books and I was all lined up to appear on some radio talk show the next morning.

I took Angie to a late lunch in a little Italian restaurant but she only played with her fettuccini. We stopped at a lounge on the way back to the motel and I had a bottle of beer. Angie ordered a glass of wine, but she barely touched that either. She sat there dabbing her damp fingers on her napkin just the way she always did. The way she did the very first time I took her to Embers. Sometimes that seemed like a long time ago, and then sometimes it seemed like only yesterday. Then I'd remember Ephraim and Jack and for some strange reason, I got a whiff of Conan the Barberman and chili at The Owl.

We just got back inside our motel room when we heard a knock at the door. I turned back around and opened it to a young man about my own age. He had eyebrows so pale that they were almost invisible. He wore glasses and had blue eyes and needed a shave and a haircut and wore jeans. He had a light golf jacket over his fuzzy sweater and stood there looking forlorn and kind of lost. He looked familiar. Suddenly I remembered.

"I know you," I said. "I saw you hanging around the store..."

"Yeah," he said. He had a very soft high voice. He looked worried and timid as if he expected me to slam the door in his face.

"I—yeah, I was sort of watching, Mister...Mr. Lemarsh. I—I wanted to talk to you." He looked hopeful but at the same time he looked like he expected me to tell him to get lost. Actually that's what I meant to do. I just hadn't had a chance to think how to do it without being impolite. But something about him made me feel sorry for him. And too, I was a little bit curious.

Angie came up behind me. "Who is it?"

"Uh—okay, come on in for a minute," I told the guy. I opened the door wider and he slouched into the room.

"Aren't you going to introduce me?" Angie asked. She looked at me suspiciously.

"Oh," the guy said. "I'm sorry. I should have introduced myself." He smiled showing kind of sharp uneven teeth. "My name's Arthur. Arthur Haviland. Just call me Arthur—Artie...everybody calls me Artie." He didn't stick out his hand. He just stood there.

"Well," I said, "what was it you wanted to talk to me about, Mr. Haviland... Artie?"

He looked around our motel room. It was okay. Just a motel room. Queen bed, nightstands, television and dresser. A table with four chairs by the window. It had real wallpaper, a pale striped pattern.

"Well, it's the book. It's about that book, *"The Little Mornings"*." He stared bleakly at me, looking for understanding.

"Yeah, well, I always sign them at the bookstore, you know. I'd have been glad to sign it for you while you were there...Artie."

"Yes..."

Angie had moved up closer.

"Well, okay. I don't understand, eh, Artie. I guess I don't understand what you're getting at."

"The book," he said. "Well, I—I take it that you know Professor Berry."

Suddenly I sensed an uneasy chill.

"I mean when I first heard about the book coming out— I mean, I thought Professor Berry—"

"Oh, Professor *Berry*. Yes, of course." I turned. "This is Angela Berry. She's the professor's granddaughter."

"Ah, you're his granddaughter? That explains a lot." He stopped for a beat and glanced around again. "Where's the professor?"

"Oh," I said. "I guess you didn't know. He passed away a few months ago.'

"Oh, I'm sorry," he said. "I had no idea. I always liked Doctor Berry."

"You knew him then?"

"Knew him? Oh, yes. Yes, I knew him. I studied under him for a semester at Berkeley just before he retired.

This fellow knew I didn't write the damned book. He had to know the professor was the real author.

"Okay, have a seat," I told Haviland. I led him over to the table by the window and he sat down and laid one arm on the table.

"I think I know why you're here now," I said. "Are you here basically to tell me you know I didn't write the book?"

His eyes lit up and he smiled again. "Exactly. That's it exactly. I—I didn't expect you to come right out and admit it so readily, I must—"

"Look, Artie," I cut in, "it's really not a big deal. It wasn't meant to be a national secret. Okay, this is the way it happened. The professor wrote the book a long time ago. At the time nobody showed any interest and nothing came of it. So he filed it away. Then not long ago he tried sending it to another publisher and they decided to buy it. You know, by that time the old guy was well into his seventies. And he drank. He drank a lot. Well, they wanted him to go on tour to promote the book. He knew he wasn't up to a tour so he asked me to take his place. It was all in the family. Nothing suspicious or illegal at all, I can assure you. It was all his idea. Even the publishers know all about it." I took a breath. That wasn't quite a lie. I think JC kind of suspected something. "Unfortunately, like I say, the professor passed away since then, but Angie here is his granddaughter and his sole heir, so if you thought I was trying to get away with something... I'm not taking money that—" I kind of foundered there.

Haviland shuffled his feet and looked even more uncomfortable while he absorbed all that. We stared at him. Finally he opened his mouth again.

"But the thing is," he said, looking at Angie, "What I've been trying to tell you ever since I got here...I mean, he didn't do it."

Angie took my arm. "He just said that," she told him.

He looked back at me. "No, I know you didn't write the book eh, Darcy. What I'm trying to say is Professor Berry didn't write *"The Little Mornings"* either."

I stared stupidly at him. "He didn't? I mean...he didn't?"

"No," Haviland said, He didn't." He cleared his throat and his face reddened. That's when he dropped the bomb.

"That's my book. I wrote it."

Part Three

**The moon is down
And rain is coming...**

Our jaws dropped. I can't swear about Angie, but mine sure did. This was the last thing I'd ever expected. I figured this Artie had known pops when he wrote that crap. He just wanted to set the record straight or something. I thought I just had to convince him that Angie and I weren't doing anything wrong. The last thing in the world I ever expected was for some cockroach to crawl out of the woodwork and tell me the professor didn't even write his own novels. I stood there dumbfounded.

Angie squeezed my arm hard. Then she released it and somewhere behind me she paced about the room. She stopped suddenly and looked at Artie.

"That can't be true," she said. "My grandpa wrote everything himself. He's been writing all his life. He didn't have to steal books from anyone."

"Hey, I don't know why he did it," Haviland said. He sounded whiny now. "I don't know what to tell you, except that I wrote it. I really did."

"Okay," I said. "I have to admit I'm confused. Maybe you can set the record straight for us…Artie. Just what in hell are you talking about?"

"Well, he said in his soft voice, "I mean I wrote *"The Little Mornings"*.

"Yeah, but that's only a title. Just because you wrote a book with the same title. I mean you can't copyright titles, Artie." I'd picked that bit of knowledge up on one of those television book shows somewhere.

"No," Artie said. "I'm not talking about just the same title. I wrote the book. It's my book. I mean there've been a few changes. But that's still my story. That's why I'm here." He took a breath. "I wrote five novels while I was at Berkeley. Professor Berry taught my English Lit class. I worked nights in a McDonald's and went to school days and I still managed to find time to write five novels."

"Five novels," I repeated like a dummy. Yeah, one down and four more in the cardboard box...

"I did it in my spare time on an old portable typewriter I bought at a penny market in Alameda. I was on a roll. At least I thought I was. I pounded on that typewriter every spare moment. Finally, after I was well into the second novel, I read in a magazine about an agent—you know, in one of those writer's magazines—so I sent *"The Little Mornings"* to her but it got lost in the shuffle I guess. I was doing this on an old typewriter you know; word processors were available, but I certainly couldn't afford to think about buying one. When I inquired about the manuscript the agent not only said she had no record of receiving it, but politely told me to get lost anyway. She only considered 'literary' works by known authors whatever that means. Just that one episode took months. I had a bad carbon copy so I slowly but surely retyped the whole thing. Well, I think I made it better anyway, so it wasn't an entirely wasted effort.

"A couple of other agents said they couldn't read unsolicited material. Nobody was even willing to look at my stuff. Then I found an agent who was very nice and he called me on the phone one Sunday morning and got me all excited, although in retrospect the main thing I got out of his enthusiastic praise was that I'd done a good clean job typing the manuscript, which wasn't particularly true. I was never a really good typist. And then he segued to the part where he wanted me to send him three hundred fifty bucks to 'generate a contract' on his computer.

"Well, by that time I'd read about phony agents who charge up-front fees like that so I politely told *him* to get lost. Artie hung his head and appeared to fall into thought for a minute. "Besides I didn't have three hundred fifty bucks.

Well, finally one day I thought about Doctor Berry. I'd always admired him and enjoyed his lectures. I found out he had recently retired, so I got his address and looked him up." Artie hesitated and looked around like he needed something to drink maybe, but I didn't say anything. He looked back at me. "By then I had five novels completed but I hadn't bothered to send anything out after the trauma of the phony agent. I didn't know whether my stuff was any good or what to do with it. So I put the whole mess in a box and brought it up to Doctor Berry and asked him if he'd be kind enough to read some of it. I figured at least he could tell me whether to go back to McDonald's or to keep on writing.

"He'd always been very nice and he was very nice that day. You say he drank a lot. Looking back I think maybe he had been drinking that day. But we chatted like old buddies and the upshot was that he promised to read my manuscripts and get back to me, so I left them with him and went back to San Jose where I was staying at the time."

"I'll make us some coffee," Angie said. She got up and went into the bathroom.

Artie nodded.

Angie made instant coffee on the hot water thing in the bathroom and brought out three plastic cups of coffee. Then she sat at the table across from Artie smoking one cigarette after another. If it bothered him, he didn't let on. Artie thanked her and drank a little coffee.

I watched Angie stirring her syrup. I couldn't tell how she really felt about all this. She appeared to be taking it calmly.

Artie moved his cup about and started talking again, "Time rolled on the way it does you know, and I never heard a word from Doctor Berry. Months drifted by actually and finally one day I decided to write him a letter but I never got a response—and you know, sometimes I'd think about those books and feel that they were pretty good, but then the next time I'd think they were worthless and I was sure he was too polite to come out and tell me so. About a year later I wrote another letter to him. I thanked him again for being kind enough to offer to look at them and told him that if they were no good, just to toss them. I don't know what I expected him to do. Well, I still got no response. I sort of figured he had done exactly that: tossed them. And now, with some distance between my novels and me it all seemed like a bad dream anyway. Finally I decided to stop wasting my time and to forget the whole thing.

"At Berkeley I always worked hard and thought I'd get someplace, you know? I studied and worked and wrote and kept my nose clean. That wasn't only because of my temperament, but I was always very shy. I know I'm no live wire. So I wasn't asked to participate in many of the social functions that went on around me. That was all right. I had things to do and I kept busy.

"Then after that second letter I wrote to Doctor Berry I fooled around for about a year working with a traveling carnival. Boy you wouldn't believe how fast we could hit town and set up all the rides and booths and then a couple of days later we'd tear it all back down and away we'd go. I slept at night in a storage bin under a trailer. As to the books, I let myself forget about all that. After all, if the professor thought my stuff had any value at all I was certain he'd have got into contact with me. He was always very considerate."

"Well," I told him, "he drank more and more, you know." While this guy was talking, a lot of things were clearing up in my little head. I realized suddenly why all the professor's other crap was worthless drunken rambling. And suddenly I remembered that day when he'd been standing there crumpling up papers.

"From this day forward shall I be satisfied to make do with the writings of others...Lacking talent and inspiration, I steal the words that others have so painstakingly written and usurp them for my own self-aggrandizement."

The words that others have so painstakingly written...

Sure. Of course. I thought he was just talking about being so high and mighty, always borrowing from Shakespeare and God knows who else, but now it made sense to me. He wasn't talking about that at all. He was really talking about the theft of Artie's books. The old reprobate. I wouldn't have thought he had it in him. Looking back I think that if he hadn't been such a drunk he'd never have done it in the first place. Besides, maybe he did try to find Artie but the guy was out and about. So what was more natural than to go ahead and sell the damned books anyway? I know he told me he'd written his novels some time ago, but now the more I thought about it, the less they sounded like the professor. Even the theme. That story didn't sound like some Shakespeare-quoting old professor talking. It sounded more like a loser. Like Darcy Lemarsh or Artie Haviland talking. No wonder I'd fallen into the role so easily. I should have caught on before. I knew instinctively that Artie wasn't lying. Artie wrote those fucking books. *"The Little Mornings"* by Arthur Haviland, mild-mannered ex-carnival roustabout. Then I realized in that same instant that I'd been stealing too. Darcy The Author, stealing lines from the professor, stealing words from JC and Angie and from Henry too. Hell, I stole from grandpa and every writer and interviewer I saw on television. Is that what we all do, steal from each other? I jerked my cup to my lips and gulped some coffee. It went down too fast and I choked on it.

"Are you all right?" Angie asked.

I nodded.

Artie looked at me for a minute and then at Angie. "Yeah, I thought about the drinking—that Professor Berry might have been drinking. But you know—I guess I've just never had much confidence in myself anyway. That's why I gave the stuff to him in the first place; I was hoping he would tell me I was pretty good, but down deep I don't think I expected anything to come of it. So in retrospect I wasn't surprised when he didn't answer my letters.

"Anyway, I got sick of San Jose and I got a chance to go to Mexico on a tour. Well, I had eight years of Spanish under my belt. That's how I came up with that title, *"The Little Mornings"*. I guess it sounds stupid, but in the Spanish class the instructor taught us that by adding the diminutive, *ito* to a word you change it to mean little. Like girl was *muchacha*, so *muchachita* was little girl. I guess it sounds corny but in my own mind I translated *las mañanitas* as the little mornings. Well. Anyway, I thought Mexico would be very romantic (this due to certain books I'd read over the years). When I got back from the tour I sold everything I had and went back to bum around down there alone. I—"

"Listen," I said looking at my watch. "I'm sorry, but I've got an appointment, eh, Artie. Why don't you come back over in a couple of hours? We need to talk when we have plenty of time to relax and straighten out this situation, okay?"

Artie looked doubtfully at me. "You aren't going to take off are you?"

"Absolutely not, Artie," I promised. "Even if I did you wouldn't have any trouble finding me."

I don't think he liked it but he left and I turned and looked at Angie. She looked at me and lit a cigarette.

"My grandpa wouldn't steal his damned books," she said. But she didn't sound too sure of herself. "Even if he did, he did it for me. He didn't want to leave me penniless."

I nodded. "He did say something about that. He drank so much, maybe he ended up thinking he really did write the damned things."

Angie smiled knowingly. "I think Artie wanted to make it with me."

I threw her a bitter smile. "That's a big help."

I walked to the window and back and then back to the window. I looked into the street one story below. It was getting late and gray clouds covered the sky. I saw a yellow Shell sign down the street. Cars rolled back and forth but I think the windows were double-pane. I didn't hear a thing.

I turned back to Angie. "Your grandpa probably tried to find Artie." She didn't answer. "I guess he couldn't find him. I'll give the professor the benefit of the doubt. Whatever's done is done anyway. The question is: What are *we* going to do?"

"Good question," Angie said. "What *are* we going to do?"

"I'm trying to think," I said. "Have another cigarette. If one's good, two ought to be twice as good."

"Well, I see our friend got you into a great mood," she said. "You don't need to take it out on me."

"I—" I broke off. She was right. It wasn't her fault—only indirectly. If she hadn't introduced me to her grandpa this would never have happened. But here we were.

"I can't really believe your damned pops would steal that guy's work either," I told her after a while. "Hell, maybe he was a Communist after all. I thought he had more integrity than that."

"He used to, Darcy," Angie said. She blew out smoke and folded her arms and walked to the window. "I don't think he ever would have done it but you know—that guy, Arthur. He was long gone, and I suppose my grandpa just figured he'd never come back. When he finally got around to reading some of it, he thought it might be worth some money."

"Yeah...some money." Now I was scratching *my* neck. Maybe I should've been a lawyer.

"Besides," Angie went on, "you were right. What you said about my grandpa. If Artie really did write those books, then I'm sure my grandpa tried to find him at first. I bet he did. That would've been just like my grandpa. But I suppose he couldn't find him and I don't think he could legally sell the thing if he couldn't produce the author or at least some evidence that he was acting as the author's agent or whatever.

THE LITTLE MORNINGS

I don't know."

"Well, it sure gets complicated," I said. "Not only I didn't write the damned thing but neither did your grandpa. Now we got three authors for one book and—life being what it is—sooner or later the shit's going to hit the fan. That's all I know."

"Not necessarily," she said.

"What do you mean, not necessarily? I know this guy's quiet and shy and talks soft, and maybe he doesn't want a scandal and all that, but after all, he wrote those books with the sweat of his brow and now he comes back to find everybody in California claiming to have written them. Yeah, and taking all the gravy too while he's standing around in raggedy jeans. How long do you think he's going to hold his water? Really?"

"That's why I said not necessarily," Angie repeated. "One way or another he's going to blow the lid off our little operation. Sure, they may not be able to get back what they've already paid out. But we're getting low on fundage and your editor damned well won't give us another dime, you can count on that. We'll be hitchhiking back to Sacramento and be lucky to do that. More likely we'll ride back in police custody. I'm no lawyer, Darcy, but I've got a feeling that stealing somebody's book is just the same as stealing his car or whatever." She stubbed out her half-smoked cigarette in an ashtray and got another cigarette from the nightstand and lit it and plopped down on the foot of the bed. "When—and I said *when* Darcy, not *if*. *When* he decides to go public with his story we're going to be in hot water. I wish my grandpa had never started this as much as you do, but we're in it now and it's up to us to get ourselves out." She started twisting a curl of hair and I guess that meant she was thinking.

I walked over and picked up my cup from the table. The coffee was cold but I drank some anyway. I needed something stronger than that. Stronger than beer too at this stage of the game.

"Okay," I sighed, "what are we going to do then, forget the book? Pack up and sneak out in the middle of the night?" Actually, a dark half-plan had begun to take shape in the back of my mind, but I didn't want to look at it.

Angie looked up at me. "Are you really willing to give all this up now that you've got it?"

"Well no. Of course not, but—"

"Neither am I, Dar. This is just the beginning. We still have four more books to go, Darcy. Four more. And movie rights...and didn't your famous editor say something about a paperback edition coming out later on? That means more money."

I nodded. "So—you've got a master plan then?"

"We don't need a master plan, dork. There's only one thing to do and it's very simple. There's only sure way for us to get rid of Arthur."

I felt a sudden chill. "And?"

"We have to kill him."

Despite the fact that the thought had already crossed my mind, I stared at her. This was too much like the characters in that stupid book. Talk about cold-blooded. I would never have thought the girl had it in her. I'd seen Angie do some goofy things, but I never thought she could sit there calmly and talk about murdering a guy she'd only known for less than an hour.

"Damn," I said. It wasn't really the plan that shocked me so much as the fact that Angie just whipped it out so casually. "That's serious. I didn't think you thought that way. I mean—*damn*!"

"Don't look so shocked and innocent," she told me. "You've done it before and you can do it again." She looked at me like she hated me.

"Angie—" I started, but she cut me off.

"I don't want to hear it. You killed my grandpa. Maybe

you'll never admit it but you did. You know it and I know it. So don't try to bullshit me, Darcy. You killed him without even having a good reason. Why? Just because you got greedy, that's why. He'd probably have given us practically everything and you were getting all the glory. Why would you be so selfish and greedy, Dar?" Before I could say anything she went on, "So don't tell me you're going to wimp out on me now when we really need something taken care of."

"Angie, I didn't. I didn't kill your grandpa. Why do you keep saying that?"

"Because I know," she said simply. "I just know. For the same reason we have to kill this bozo. You were afraid that sooner or later grandpa would come forward and ruin your act." Sometimes she could make things look so simple.

But she had a point. And the idea had already been trying to form in my mind. There was no way I could think of to ensure that Arthur would keep his mouth shut. I could see that Angie was right. Knowing human nature it was certain that one way or another Artie was going to screw us over before he finished. I didn't really know what his plan was, if he had one. But if he didn't already have a plan, he'd get one. We could give him money and everything. It was just like the blackmailing guy in the book. I'd have been willing to pay a little blackmail—Christ, I wasn't really as greedy as Angie seemed to think. And maybe Arthur wasn't all that interested in money and fame. But something told me that no matter what he thought or promised right now, sooner or later his artistic pride would come to the top like scum on dishwater and he'd decide he couldn't go through life letting people think somebody else wrote his novels. And speaking of novels, Angie was right there too: we still had four to go. The thought of handing them over to Arthur was not pretty. Not pretty at all.

Angie continued to smoke and watch me. I paced back and forth and finally I headed for the door.

"Where you going?"

"I've got to get something to drink," I told her. "Be right back." I went out and found a liquor store a block away and bought a fifth of whiskey. I don't even know what it was. I just pointed to the bottle on the shelf behind the clerk and he slipped it into a paper bag like that's all he'd ever done since he graduated from high school.

In the room I opened the bottle and poured a couple of fingers into my coffee cup. There were still coffee dregs in the cup but I wasn't exactly doing a wine tasting. The stuff burned all the way down and hit my stomach like a sucker punch. An instant later it hit my brain.

"What…what would we do?" I asked Angie.

"Somehow we've got to get him alone long enough to whack him. We can't do it here."

"Whack him? *Whack* him?" Now she was a professional hit woman. I know that I lose it sometimes, but just to stand there and talk about whacking some innocent guy… "How am I going to whack him? Give him a karate chop or what? We don't even have a gun."

"It's him or us. We'll have to think of something, Darcy. Use your brain for once."

"We couldn't do it here," I said after a while. "Do you think he'd trust us enough for us to get him alone someplace?" I poured another slug of whiskey into the cup.

She thought for a minute and lit another cigarette. "I think he kind of liked me," she said after a while.

"Yeah, you told me. Were you flirting with him when I wasn't looking?"

"No…" She started to get mad. Suddenly she changed her mind and became the innocent schoolgirl. "But I could tell. Maybe I could get him to take me someplace—you know, to be alone, and you could hide in the trunk or something like that and then, at the right moment, you jump out and—"

"Yeah, you're the girl who could handle your end all right. You've got experience."

"Don't start, Darcy. I thought we agreed to forget about the past and get on with our lives." She went into the bathroom and bent back putting her contacts in.

"All right, let's not fight about that again, but there's no way I'm going to hide in the trunk. We'll have to think of something more practical."

She came back into the bedroom. "Darcy, people hide in the trunk all the time. Duh!"

"Oh wow. Man. I don't know." I just couldn't keep up with this. I'd never stood around and planned a murder in my life and I couldn't believe we were doing it now. Just like a couple of hit men with a contract. Wow. One minute I'm an up and coming young author and the next I'm a hit man for my sweetheart. Still...

"You think we could really pull it off and not get caught?" I asked. "I mean it's one thing to be exposed as a fraudulent author, but to be pulled in on cold-blooded murder-that's... Besides, I'm not sure I could just—I don't even know how I'd do it. He's as big as I am. I couldn't just you know strangle him with my bare hands or something. We don't have a gun or anything. I've done a few things in my life, but I mean this—this is a whole other ballgame."

Angie folded her arms. "We'd better think fast. He'll be back here in less than an hour." She thought for a minute and suddenly looked back at me. "What did you say? Whole other ballgame?"

I didn't know what to say to that and she looked at me like I was a total retard.

"What about your Louisville Slugger?"

***

"Okay, here's the plan," I told Angie. I'd thought all about it and decided her idea, her plan, was right in the first place. We had to whack Artie. Except now it was my plan. "When Arthur comes back you'll feed him a drink or two and come on to him. In the meantime I'll make some excuse to leave and I'll hide in the trunk with the baseball bat. You convince him to go for a drive and head down the coast past Pacifica. There're lots of cliffs along there over the ocean. It'll be getting dark by then. The first time you see a lonely turnout by the ocean, pull over and start making out. We'll have to have a blanket in the back seat and you get him onto the sand or whatever and then when he's busy I'll sneak up and let him have it."

"Christ I don't want blood all over me," she said.

"No, a bang on the head won't cause blood to spurt all over you," I assured her." For a split second I wondered, but I was pretty sure it wouldn't. "Once I hit him you get the hell out of the way. When I finish the job, we'll dump him into the ocean and take off. Nobody knows we know him and far as I can tell he doesn't have anyone who's going to wonder what happened to him. We just can't have any witnesses. He'll wash up on the beach someplace later on. If we're lucky he'll never wash up at all. They have sharks out along there you know." I had another drink and thought about it. I closed my eyes…

It was hot and cramped in the trunk of the Honda. The car rolled smoothly along the highway and I could faintly hear music. They had the radio on. Finally after what seemed like forever, I felt the crunch of gravel under the tires and the car rolled to a stop.

After a moment the lock on the trunk snapped and I waited a beat before raising the hood a hair. I could barely see out. There they were. Angie and Artie walking out toward the cliff over the ocean. They were arm in arm, swaying against each other and almost falling. They were laughing. She didn't have to enjoy it so damned much. As they reached the edge she turned and raised her face to his and he leaned forward and kissed her. As she turned slightly putting his back to me, I slipped out of the trunk with my Louisville Slugger and ran lightly across the gravel.

Artie was so lost in Angie that I could've brought a *mariachi* band with me and he wouldn't have heard it. Out of the corner of her eye Angie saw me and suddenly pushed Artie back away from her and I let him have it right in the back of the head. He went down as if he'd been shot in the heart with a forty-five. No blood at all. Piece of cake.

"Good," Angie said. "That's done. Yuk, I hated it when he put his tongue in my mouth."

"Yeah," I said. "I could see that. Here, help me lift him up."

I grabbed his shoulders and Angie grabbed his feet and together we lifted him up over the railing and down he went. Below the cliff the ocean crashed against the rocks, waiting for Artie, and as his body hit the water with a splash, I saw fins circling in the water just beyond. A job well done...

I opened my eyes and found myself sitting in the motel room. My hands were shaking. I took another slug of whiskey. I'd had a few, but I didn't feel a thing. I shuddered and looked at Angie.

"We can do it," I said.

She lit a cigarette and looked at me.

I looked at her, sitting on the edge of the bed. "*What?*"

"I don't feel too good," Angie said, and she didn't look good either. The hollows of her cheeks were darker than ever and she had dark rings beneath her deep blue eyes. "It does sound pretty cold-blooded. Are you sure you can handle it?"

"Hey this was your brainstorm. I don't feel too good about it either, but I'm going to handle it. If you think *you're* not up to it—"

"We'll do it," she said. She headed for the bathroom. "We'll just stick to the plan."

But as usual things had a way of not working out according to plan.

Arthur came up to our room right on schedule. I'd already put the bat in the trunk and laid a blanket on the back seat.

"Hi," I told him. "Come on it." He hesitantly stepped into the room and I handed him his coffee cup with two fingers of whiskey in it. "Sorry I had to have you come back," I told him. "Business, you know…"

"It's okay. Thanks." He took a sip, then another.

"Need some water?"

"No, no, this hits the spot actually," he said. He kind of giggled. "I already had a couple. Eh, on television it sounded like you were ready to send in another book." He looked concerned but not exactly mad.

"Oh no…no. That's just television bull. You know, you have to tell them what they want to hear. I haven't done anything at all, Artie," I told him. "Actually, I'm glad we met and got this out in the open. I was hoping to discuss the whole thing with you. You know, before we do anything. We need your input, especially now. Frankly, at this point I'm not sure how we should proceed. Besides, I'm no kind of writer at all. I'm really not. We need you to help with revisions."

"Revisions?" He swallowed more whiskey and grimaced as it went down. His eyes looked slightly fuzzy.

"Oh yeah, they always want to make a few changes here and there," I explained. Like I knew what I was talking about. "You know editors: they like to show you who's in charge."

At this point Angie came out of the bathroom and I almost had an erection. She wore a skimpy halter-top that accented her nipples and then below her belly button a pair of short-shorts made even shorter by her not having buttoned the top button. It didn't look like she was wearing panties at all. The effect said that she was practically undressed and couldn't wait to rip the rest of her clothes off. She smelled good too. I don't know what it was, but she was wearing some kind of perfume I hadn't smelled before. She gave Artie a sleepy smile.

Arthur's eyes kind of bugged out behind his glasses, but he only said, "Hey."

I made an excuse to leave and told them I'd be right back. I lit out. I went to the car and crawled into the trunk. It was black inside and a lot more uncomfortable than I had expected. I wasn't sure I could keep my legs cramped up for maybe half an hour. The trunk smelled of gas but I didn't think I'd have any trouble breathing because actually the seats folded down in the back seat so it wasn't that airtight. And if worst came to worst I guess I could kick my way out.

The damned bat jammed into my crotch and I couldn't get it out. I waited what seemed like an eternity. My legs were already cramped up. My watch was supposed to glow in the dark but I couldn't read the damned thing. Every time I moved my head I scraped it on some piece of metal on the top of the trunk. I started to sweat and get claustrophobia. I felt a sudden wash of panic sweep over me and I realized that if something didn't happen pretty soon, I was going to lose it. Then I thought I heard noises.

The trunk popped open and there stood Angie.

"*What?*" I stared up at her. "What the hell's the matter now?" I looked past her but I didn't see Arthur so I pulled myself painfully back out of the trunk and onto the concrete. God it felt good to stand up again. My feet tingled.

Angie did not look happy. She looked at me with suspicion and disdain. "Looks like *I* have to ride in the trunk."

"You ride in the—what the hell are you talking about?"

Her look became even more suspicious. "News flash, Darcy. This just in: It's you he likes. He likes you. He likes guys, and evidently you're his kind of guy." Her look turned even more suspicious, as if she had just learned something I'd been hiding.

"He likes *me*?" I never thought about a possibility like that. No wonder she was giving me that suspicious look. She probably wondered if I'd come on to him or something. "You mean like he's gay?" I asked.

"Fruitier than a can of Dole pineapple. You'll make a lovely couple, Dar. He likes you. He told me so. He got all sorry and goofy and hoped I wasn't jealous." She almost let down and smiled. "He got friendly and told me that's why he's being so easy about this whole thing. He thought maybe you were bi. And he told me lots of people are bi. Are you—? Bi, I mean?"

I gave her a dirty look filled with all the sarcasm I could muster.

"He wanted to know if I'd be too upset if you two—" she giggled, "you know."

"Jesus." I thought for a minute. "Where is he now?"

"He's still in the room. He's half drunk already. He was too bashful to talk to you himself anyway, so he asked me if I'd feel you out. He said if you didn't want him, it was all right and he'd understand."

"So?"

"So, I'm talking to you. Go tell the little fruit you love him or whatever you boys do when you get together."

"Christ Angie, I can't…" I dribbled to a stop. I tried to think. We had to get this done.

"Darcy, you don't have to have sex with the guy. All you have to do is drive him out just the way we planned and then instead of you, I'll pop out of the trunk with the bat, and once I get in that first blow, you take over.

I stood there like an idiot.

"Do it, damn it. Just do it."

"Yeah, okay. I guess it'll work," I said.

"Okay. Go tell him that I went to Fisherman's Wharf or something. This is your big chance to be alone with him."

"What if he insists on staying in the room?" I asked. Anything was possible now.

"Tell him you're expecting some people over. Tell him I'm bringing back some friends. Tell him you want to take him someplace quiet, you want to show him something. Whatever. Just get his ass in this car. I'll be in the trunk."

I don't think I'd ever realized before how cold and practical Angie could be. It kind of scared me.

I tried to kiss her but she quickly turned her head. Even though I was doing what she wanted me to do, I think she was mad at me because she was going to be stuffed inside the trunk thinking about me and Artie alone together. He'd probably put ideas in her head about that so now she was thinking I wasn't only a Communist but a gay one at that. She got into the trunk and I gently closed the top down on her till the catch clicked.

* * *

"Like a little music? Let's play a little music," I said. I turned the radio up fairly loud just in case Angie should move about or cough or anything. If anything tipped him off…

Before Angie told me, it had never crossed my mind that Arthur was interested in me, other than as the guy who sort of stole his book. I mean he wasn't one of those obviously gay guys. Sure, he looked gentle and was soft-spoken, but that doesn't make a person gay. I'm pretty gentle and soft-spoken myself.

Once I came back to the motel room and found him waiting, he was a different person. He was all calf eyes and even shyer than he'd been before. And Angie was right; he was about half drunk.

"Hey," I said.

"Hey." He ducked his head.

"Angie took off," I told him. "She's supposed to meet some friends. They're coming back in a little while." I tried to laugh. "I think she's a little jealous."

He grinned foolishly.

"How about we take a ride? I've got the car outside."

"I'm up for anything," Artie said. "Where're we going?"

"Oh, I thought we'd take a ride down the coast. We'll have a bite to eat along the road there someplace. Nice places to stop. Lots of good seafood places. You like seafood?"

"That's what the guy said when they asked him why he hung around San Diego: He said he just *loved* seafood," Arthur said. He giggled.

I realized there was something there between the lines from the way he looked at me, but it took a minute to soak in. Finally I got it. Lots of sailors in San Diego. I suddenly remembered Ron the real estate salesman. Wonderful. This was going to be an exciting evening. But immediately my mind turned back to the job at hand and my heart began beating harder. Please God let this go down easy, just the way I imagined it. We got up onto the freeway and headed down 101. Traffic was pretty heavy but not impossible. We cut off into Westlake and headed across onto the Cabrillo Highway. The sun turned deep red, dying in the western sky. But the sky was clearer and as we headed south it got cooler by the mile and I picked up the scent of the ocean.

Arthur chatted sometimes and once in a while I felt him look at me out of the corner of his eye. I don't think he ever suspected a thing. I passed the half-full bottle of whiskey to him. He took a slug and coughed.

"This reminds me of one time when I was in Mexico," he said. He laughed. "We were on a train in second class. Somebody opened up a bottle of tequila and then somebody else brought out a guitar. In Mexico it's tequila and guitars everyplace you go. Once the tequila came out and the guitar started strumming everybody sang and we passed the tequila around and everything was rosy and then somehow the question came up about whether or not tequila would burn." Now Arthur was really laughing. He had to stop for a minute to get control of himself. My heart pounded harder and I felt bad that I was sitting here planning to kill this suddenly happy little guy, a guy who was probably a lot like me—except he wrote the goddamned book. He was a real author, not just an illiterate phony.

"Next thing you know people were placing bets on it so somebody sloshed some tequila out onto the floor of the coach and lit it up. Remember this old coach had a wooden

The Little Mornings

floor and wooden benches for seats." Arthur laughed again at the memory and I almost shared it. "Well, the tequila burned all right. They had a hell of a time putting the fire out and we got our asses kicked off the train to boot. Down there in Sinaloa in the middle of the jungle somewhere. I thought I never would find my way to a town. And they have *alacranes* — scorpions — around there. The very thought scared the shit out of me. I shook one out of my shoe one morning." He had another shot of whiskey and passed the bottle to me. I took a short one but I still didn't even feel anything but a kind of dull woodiness.

"And traveling in busses with people and dogs and chickens and so forth — that's something else too. It may look quaint in old movies, but I have to tell you, in reality it isn't the most comfortable way to get around. And one bus I was in had to ford shallow rivers and one place we pulled up by the riverbank and we all had to disembark and ride across a river on a sort of raft affair only to find an ancient school bus on the opposite side that was half the size of the bus I'd just left behind. Up until then I'd had an assigned seat for which I'd paid extra, but now all the seating was up for grabs. And there wasn't much of it. I ended up standing as if I were in a subway train during rush hour. This was all right at first but after four or five arduous hours of bumping along over bad roads and smelling sweat and chicken shit a person gets pretty well exhausted. And when the driver stopped in the middle of nowhere for a rest stop, everybody just ran out and turned their backs and did their thing. Even the women. But they were very modest about it. My fellow travelers were pleasant enough. Somebody always had a guitar and would begin to strum and sing Mexican folk songs and some of the passengers would always join in. This helped enormously and eventually, after someone passed a bottle of tequila or mescal around, I began to feel better and even try to join in." He laughed out loud as we turned. The ocean off to the right flashed blood red in our eyes.

"One night I was staying with people near some little village or another and we ran out of tequila. I was pretty drunk but I said I'd walk into town and get some more. Well, there was just a narrow dirt road above the river that led into town and normally there were little sixty watt light bulbs hanging ten feet overhead every so often along the path but tonight there was no moon and no lights either, not that they were much help.

"Well, all at once I sensed something. I wasn't alone. I'd heard stories about gringos getting robbed and killed down in Mexico where anything can happen. I was wearing this stupid *jorongo* that somebody had lent me—"

"What's that a—jor—"

"*Jorongo*. It's like, you know, a poncho. Anyway, it hung down in front of me and I got my hands tangled in it and couldn't get them out in case I needed them.

"I had hardly any money on me, but...and down there a lot of the men don't like *jotos* either." He snickered. "So what else is new? Anyway, I stopped and stood there. I suddenly felt a lot more sober. Nothing. Not even a cricket. I took a couple of steps and realized there was definitely somebody there. I stopped and stood perfectly still. Nothing. '*Buenas*,' I said out loud but nobody answered. I took another step. Nothing. I told myself I must be getting the DT's and took another step and bam. I bumped into something solid and I stood stock still while I got my hands untangled. I reached out and realized I was standing right up against the biggest damned pig you ever met in your life! He must've weighted six hundred pounds and was standing right smack in the middle of the road." Arthur's eyes shone faintly and waxed nostalgic. "Listen, I wanted to put my arms around his neck and hug him," he said. "I was never so relieved in my life."

Great, I thought. He doesn't just like me. He likes pigs.

"I'm telling you, Darcy, for a minute there I thought that was going to be it."

"So what did you do then?"

"Do? Oh," he said, "I patted my friend the pig on the head and continued on into town. He was gone by the time I came back."

I tried to laugh but my laughter didn't come out too well. I started quaking inside. I was afraid to drink more whiskey.

"So what did you do after that?" I asked.

He shrugged and looked at me warmly. "Later I gave up on Mexico and came back to the US and joined the Peace Corps. Off we went to Africa for a couple of years. That was a bad trip." He frowned. "And then I came back to America and started doing odd jobs. I worked as a dishwasher, a wannabe carpenter; I pushed an ice cream cart, whatever. I was in New York. I worked on a ride at Coney Island one summer. I worked a while for Manpower. That led to some interesting experiences. And I'll admit something I'm not proud of, sometimes I had to sell myself on the street to get by. Life can be pretty hard sometimes." He smiled ruefully. "I know you must think I'm a real underachiever, Darcy, and I suppose I am. Yes, I am. But somehow I got off track early on and could never decide what to do or which way to go. And my parents weren't very understanding. I'll tell you one thing, Darcy, education doesn't necessarily equate with ambition." He laughed ruefully. "I still don't know what I want to do when I grow up."

We laughed at that one. I didn't tell him that I didn't know either.

"But didn't you ever write anymore?" I asked. "I thought you liked to write." I was thinking that if I had a talent like he did I don't think I could just give up and let it die like that, but…

"I did. Yeah, I did. I wrote a couple more novels, but it's so heart breaking, you know. I'd send them in and lots of times I'd never hear back at all, or agents and editors would give me the brush off. The only time any editors or agents were nice to me, it was because they wanted money from me. It got to the point that I saw it coming. They loved my work. Had great possibilities. They wanted to encourage new talent. And they always wanted money for reading fees or editorial services, or they'd publish my book if I'd agree to buy a thousand copies or something. Always something. The more they baited me with praise the more I knew I had to look for the hook. And it was always there. Finally I got to where I'd get a novel started and get in there twenty-five or fifty thousand words and then…"

"What, get writer's block?" I asked. I'd heard them talk about that on *Book Notes* or someplace.

"Well not exactly," he said. "I'd just kind of lose interest in the project. Maybe it was the way the publishing world works. Maybe I burnt myself out in college when I banged out those first books so quickly. Maybe that was all I had to say. Even writing in my spare time it only took a few months for me to write all five of those books. Of course later I did considerable rewriting. And I did all my own research. I wrote *"The Little Mornings"* long before I stepped foot inside Mexico, you know. But by God," he smiled proudly, "I was right on the money. All from research at the library."

The crazy thing is that by now I felt so stupid for not realizing a long time ago that Angie's grandpa never wrote those books. Grandpa had all he could do to sign a check let alone write anything that made a lick of sense. Looking back, I couldn't imagine why I needed Artie to come along and set me straight.

I studied the roadway unwinding ahead of us, thinking. Finally I looked at Artie. "Well, where does that leave us now, Artie?"

"Oh," he said. The minute we talked business he looked so damned uncomfortable. "Well…that was really my book you know. Do you have the rest of them too?"

"Rest?" I tried to look vague. I knew Angie was right. We definitely had no choice. I swallowed.

"There should be four more," he said. "I thought you must have them." His look had become accusing.

"Oh, I guess in grandpa's things maybe...what was it you wanted to do, that's what I'm trying to find out, Arthur? I mean, I realize you have some rights here, but at the same time, we don't want to cause a big mess—a—a scandal. I mean, you know, any problems could blow the whole thing for all of us."

"Look," Arthur said. "I'm trying to be fair here. I don't really believe you intended to cheat me out of anything. I don't even think the professor wanted to do that. I'm sure he probably tried to find me after he learned the book was going to be published, but of course I was all over the place and nobody knew how to get into contact with me. Still...I don't know. I like you, Darcy. I want us to be friends. I think we have a lot in common, Darcy. I want to work out something equitable for both of us. I don't know what's fair. I mean, on the one hand, the book is my own work and I feel I have every right to it, but you know, on the other hand I don't want to start a big controversy—or end up in court or anything. I don't really want to make trouble. I'm not very good around people. And I couldn't go on a tour like you're doing anyway. I just couldn't do that."

"Then you're saying you might be willing to stay in the background—kind of work behind the scenes...is that what you're saying?"

He nodded. "Well, sure, something like that." He gave me a sidelong shy half-smile. "We'll get along, you and I, Darcy. We'll be friends. When we're up, we're up together and when we go down, we go down together." He giggled.

I didn't know what kind of sense that made but I nodded and handed him the bottle.

"But I would like to look over the other novels," he said. I wanted to go over them again. I'm sure I could do some rewriting and make them better now. I have a lot more depth and experience behind me now than I had back in college."

"So what are we going to do with the next book?" I asked him.

"What do you mean, do?"

Now the wind was picking up so I rolled up my window. With the radio playing I didn't feel I had to worry about Angie making noise. The only thing that worried me was that she might be too stiff to get out once we found a place to pull over.

"Well, I mean they're already asking for another book. They don't know there are four more already finished." I glanced over at him. "Look, I know it's your work, Arthur, and I appreciate that, but now that old Berry got this ball rolling it's not so easy to stop. I guess you could go over it and redo anything you think and we can turn it in. That works for me. Sound okay to you?"

"Works for me, too," Artie said.

"I was thinking," I said. "You're a good writer, Arthur. You've proven that by the success of the book. I know you can write a lot more. I was thinking that you don't have to say anything to anybody. We just go along at least with the first two books and we'll split the money. Then while you live on that money, you could turn in the third book under your own name and sort of you know, phase me out." This was all bullshit of course, but I wanted to sound reasonable and put him completely at ease while he was alone with me. "In the meantime you can start churning out books under your own name too and the neat part is that I have my own personal editor now. I can personally recommend you and she'll not only read your stuff but she'll be glad to print it and you'll die an old and very rich man. If worst comes to worst, we can break down and tell them that you had me impersonate you because you were to shy to go on those tours and everything. I'm sure a lot of people would be dying to get their hands on anything you wrote." I could've bit my tongue. Why did I keep talking about death? I was doing my best not to give him any ideas.

Actually the idea about the books didn't sound bad at

that, even though down deep I knew he'd never be able to stick to the bargain. He looked doubtful. Something just told me he wouldn't be able to do it. Besides, we'd committed ourselves now. Angie might be a cold-blooded little bitch, but when push came to shove...crazy or not, she was right.

We came up over a rise and around a curve and began a downward descent. Before we only got teasing peeks at the ocean with the sun dying in the distance but now the Pacific Ocean lay there before us with the blood-red sun sinking into it. In the distance the sky was still deep red but a mist rose up around us now. My stomach was so tight I could scarcely breathe.

On the one hand you could've hit me on the head and I don't think I'd have felt a thing, but on the other hand, my nerves had reached the snapping point. Artie kept chattering on and I wanted to tell him to shut the fuck up. But of course I had to bite my tongue and politely listen to him as if he was the most interesting and fascinating person I'd ever met.

We continued on downward while Arthur loosened up and began to chat about other things. He told me about his time in Africa. He told me how he learned to find all sorts of plants and fruits that are medicinal and how you can eat grubs and locusts and worms.

"I learned to survive in the jungle," he said. "It's not always easy or pleasant, but it can be done. Boiled crocodile tail."

I guess he'd tried it all from the sound of it. "What?" I said. "Tastes like chicken?"

Artie laughed. "Well...but the worst day was when I went to this medicine doctor because I had a sore on my finger that was getting all full of puss," he told me. "I picked up some sort of little doll. He called it a *gri-gri* or something, and anyway I barely picked it up and the head fell off. The bastard got all excited and he took every cent I had from me to pay for it. He might have been a medicine man in the jungle but he knew all about money. And the worst thing is that I still think he put a curse on me."

Boy, was Artie right about that! I laughed and he caressed my arm.

"We're going to be good friends, Darcy. I know."

Oh God I was thinking. It was hard to swallow.

We came down through Pacifica almost level with the ocean now. To our left houses and buildings pushed back into the foothills where a pale moon peeped over the hilltops. To the right the beach led right down to the surf. But it looked cold and foggy and gray with only a faint red glow far in the distance. Only a few hardy souls stood or ran about down near the water. Then we drove back up and around through eucalyptus trees or something and over and up and around we went.

It was almost completely dark when I pulled onto a turnout near Devil's Slide high above the ocean below. I didn't unlock the trunk yet because I wanted to check things out first. Arthur and I walked together over to the edge. A steel cable had been strung across at the edge to remind us where to stop. It was very steep. I looked down over the jagged rocks to the crashing surf eighty feet below but it made me dizzy. My stomach ached and it was hard to breathe normally. The air that rose up on the deafening crash of waves was damp. The spray didn't quite make it to the top. I pulled back and looked around. It was almost night. Now the rising moon was brighter than the remains of the sunset. Only an occasional car passed by on the highway and nobody looked like he wanted to stop. Just down to our right a juniper tree shielded a little hollow.

"Go over there" I told Arthur. I touched his arm. "I'm going to get a bottle and a blanket." I headed back over the gravel to the car, moving like a robot. I reached in and grabbed the bottle and the blanket and reached down by the driver's seat and snapped the trunk lid. "Okay," I hissed. I hurried back across to the edge where Arthur still hadn't moved.

"Come on." I grabbed his arm and together we ducked down under the first low hanging branch. I tossed the blanket onto the gravel and duff and stood the bottle precariously on top if it. I stood in the middle of the blanket facing him. I wanted his back to be to Angie as she made her approach. I felt like a fool and I wasn't quite sure what to do now. I felt like I'd been filled with Novocain, but my heart pounded in my ears. Then I caught sight of Angie coming up just beyond the branch. She was carrying the bat in both hands.

I smiled and made as if to take a step toward Haviland and suddenly in a burst of passion he jumped forward and grabbed me to him and pressed his mouth hard to mine. The whole move was so totally unexpected that I couldn't react. He cocked one leg around my legs and held me close and jammed his wet tongue into my mouth and moved it about, but it wasn't exciting like it was when Angie did it. It was horrifying. It was as if somebody had stuffed a hot slimy towel in my mouth against my will. I struggled to push him away and at that moment he abruptly pulled his slobbery tongue back and bit down hard on the inside of my lower lip. His teeth were sharp and his bite was vicious. An excruciating pain shot through my mouth like I'd been slashed with a serrated knife and I tasted the gush of warm blood. I pushed back hard and shoved him away with all my strength and he almost lost his balance and had to put his arms out to keep from falling over backward.

"Jesus Christ Artie," I cried. "You bit me!" What kind of freak are you? What the hell are you trying to do? What are you some kind of masochist or what? Jesus!"

His little glasses hung half crooked on his nose and for a terrible moment he made me think of grandpa. He had a goofy half smile and licked his lips like a drunken vampire and just then Angie stepped in behind him with the baseball bat.

She loosed a massive swing.

I think she was aiming for his head. That's what I'd told her to do, but naturally she missed.

The blow slugged hard across Artie's shoulder and spun

him about and he went down sideways with a grunt. His glasses flew from his face.

"*What?*" His eyes shone white with pain and fear as he tried to understand what was going on. His arm came up to protect his face just as the bat slammed against him again. The surf below drowned the smack but his arm took the brunt of it. I thought I heard bone crack. He screamed and tried to right himself. The arm flopped at his side, useless.

Somehow I'd been imagining one good smack in the head. One good smack to drop him like he'd been shot with a forty-five. Oh yeah.

He screamed. He started begging. He threatened. He tried to scrabble away from Angie but his feet slipped on the edge of the blanket as the bat slammed at him again. This time his other hand closed on the bat and hung onto it. He pulled Angie over and she crashed down on top of him. They rolled over in the dirt growling like Tasmanian devils in heat and the bat went flying. I bent and grabbed it up and yanked Angie back away from him. He struggled to his feet but he was leaning too far back, off balance and doing the limbo. Just as he recovered his balance and began to straighten toward me, I hit a home run right in his face.

Even above the roar of the crashing surf below us I heard the crack of bone and his nose went sideways spurting blood. He screamed in agony and waved his good arm around. Now in his pain and confusion he wasn't even trying to defend himself. Stunned, he just cried and flopped around on his back like a fish out of water. Well, I could fix that.

"Grab his shoulders," I told Angie.

He writhed and screamed and kicked. Blood spewed from his broken face. I finally managed to hold his feet together and we dragged him the few feet to the edge and in one final burst of power, we got him over the low cable and threw him out into the air.

He was supposed to fly down into the ocean but he didn't.

He bounced off the rocks one after another. He made me think of the ball in a pinball game. Bounce bounce bounce... His mouth gaped wide open but the noise of the surf drowned his screams. He bounced and bounced again and finally his body slammed to a rest on the rocks below just above the water line. I leaned out and looked down. In the darkness I could barely make out his body.

"Shit," I said. "He didn't go into the water." I closed my eyes and took in air. I was shaking all over but numb at the same time.

Angie held my arm and looked down. "We can't get down there," she said. "That has to do. If we're lucky he'll drift out on the high tide or something."

I stood there shaking and breathing hard too. I pulled my eyes from his body and looked at her. "And if he doesn't drift?"

"There's nothing more we can do, Dar." Angie could be so damned matter-of-fact. "Besides, nobody connects us to him so, if and when he turns up, nobody's going to be knocking on our door—and even if they do, we won't be there. We'll be long gone, right?"

I looked back down again and shuddered. I looked at Angie. She was pretty disheveled too. But I didn't see any blood on her. I brushed a bit of dirt out of her hair. "Yeah... I guess you're right at that." I looked around suddenly remembering that I'd completely forgotten about where we were. Luckily there was no one about and by now it was fully dark. I took a deep breath.

"Let's go," I said.

Suddenly Angie stopped. "Wait! His glasses."

"Oh Christ." I bent looking around and finally I picked up his glasses. I moved closer to the cliff and hurled them out into the air above the ocean. I grabbed up the blanket and shook it out. Angie picked up the bottle.

I picked up the bat and was on the point of slinging it out into the ocean too but Angie stopped me.

"That thing will float," she said. "And they may be able to trace it back to you."

She was right.

"Let's get the hell out of here," I said.

She shuddered. "I have to take a pee."

* * *

At the motel I shook out the blanket again, over the tub this time, and tossed it by the bed. I had blood on my shirt but I didn't know whether it was mine or Artie's. I decided to get rid of it just to be safe. I touched my lip and looked at it in the mirror. It was raw and swollen at the inside edge but the bleeding had stopped. I rinsed my mouth with whiskey. That burned like hell and had to do some good. I got into the tub and washed the bat thoroughly. It must've been made from good wood; it hadn't cracked.

"They can still get DNA from that even after you wash it," Angie told me.

"I know that," I snapped. I kept scrubbing with a washcloth. "What do you want me to do with the damned thing? Besides, they have to connect us and the bat to Artie. Even if they find the body, it'll be pretty hard to tell that a bat got Artie before he went down over all those sharp rocks. There's absolutely nothing to connect us to Arthur Haviland."

But I had terrible dreams about Arthur. He kept trying to kiss me and shove his tongue into my mouth and bite my lip. Then he'd try to take my book away from me. First he'd berate me for stealing his book, and then he wanted to kiss me again and tell me he was sorry for causing so much trouble. Then when I let him kiss me, he bit me again.

I tossed and turned all night. I killed Artie over and over. I hit him time and again, each time splashing blood. Like the bucket of paint when the old lady hit my ladder at the IGA, like that day at the chiropractor's office. Like the day I threw the pail of paint at Jack. All night. Gallons of paint.

Paint flying, staining. Only now it was blood red. Blood flying and splattering like gallons of deep red paint. Then out of the mist, Artie came scrabbling back up over the edge of the cliff and grabbed me and tried to bite me again. I woke up at intervals sweating and trembling all over. Remembering made it worse. My swollen lip tasted raw and hurt like hell. It throbbed all night.

I awoke in the morning still shaking.

Suddenly, like a hidden surprise, a new thing hit me: I was a cold-blooded, calculating first-degree murderer. It hadn't really soaked in before. It was a nightmare. Before, even when I was a kid, whenever I did anything bad or got into trouble it was because I lost it. Everything closed in and my heart pounded and the blackness covered me like I was being enfolded in venomous black velvet and afterward I'd barely remember what happened—but this... This was different. Sure my heart pounded. But this time Angie and I coldly planned what we were going to do. I relived it several times in my mind before the act and plenty of times last night. And when it did happen, it was cold-blooded. I didn't dislike Artie. I wasn't interested in his weird sexual fantasies, but I wasn't mad at him. And this time I wasn't wrapped in any black velvet to protect me from the reality of what I was doing, and I wasn't really even drunk. I was wide-awake and completely aware of each instant as it played out in slow motion. Each time the bat struck. My swing at Artie while he bent over backwards, as he tried to get his balance and right himself; as he came up and slammed his face right in to the bat. Blood spurting violently. His screams. His whimpering. This was something I'd have to remember the rest of my life.

I shuddered and rubbed my eyes. I sat up on the bed and looked around me. Angela was down on her knees by the bathroom door. She held a cup of instant coffee in one hand and a cigarette in the other. She was using the hand with the cigarette to rub the blue carpet by the door.

"Does that feel good?" I asked her.

"It's not funny," she grumbled. "I dropped one of my contacts. They're so hard to see..."

"Great," I said. Lots of luck." I stood there looking at her for a minute. "Jesus, you just got the damned things."

She didn't answer or look up. "Here," I said. I knelt down beside her. "I'll help you." Then I suddenly thought again how like Artie's book this was, we met and did something wrong, that is, instead of the kidnapping I pretended to be the author of a book I didn't write. But then just like in the book, we kill a guy who's trying to horn in on the action. What next? I didn't feel good. I got busy helping Angie look for her lens.

We felt around together for a while and I got up and looked around in the bathroom. "Christ we'll never find it, Angie. Those things are practically invisible." Then I looked right at her. Her face was haggard and the hollows of her cheeks gray. Her eyes pale and rimmed in red. "How do you feel?"

She blew out smoke and looked up. "What do you mean?"

"I mean, how do you feel—about last night?"

She looked through me for a second and then went back to caressing the carpet. "How am I supposed to feel? I never killed anybody before. You're the expert. Maybe you can tell me."

"God damn it, Angie," I began. I caught myself. "I mean are you upset, relieved, scared...or what?"

Angie got up. She brushed at her bare knees as if she had dirt on them. She swallowed coffee and pushed past me into the bathroom and threw the butt into the toilet. "I don't feel anything, Darcy. I'm not happy. I'm not sad either. It was something that had to be done. Can't you see that? Are you going to be a wimp now and cry about it?"

"No, why should I?" I was pissed but I couldn't let her see that. "I just wondered. It'll be all right." I made up my mind never to mention the subject of Artie again. Turn the page. No more Arthur Haviland. A fresh beginning. I guess Angie could do that better than I could. But I could do it.

She knelt down and started grubbing around on the carpet again.

"How the hell did you let that fruit talk you into those things in the first place?" I said. "You don't need them." I was thinking that her real eyes suited her better. They made her look as distrustful as she really was. "Fuck it," I said, "if you absolutely have to have them we'll get you some more as soon as we get another check from Carrington House. Let's go get some breakfast. We've got a long drive ahead of us."

* * *

The phone rang. It was JC.

"How's it going?" she asked.

"Well, we're selling books," I said. Angie was hanging on to every word so I had to be careful what I said.

"I think we're ready to bring you east. The second printing is coming out next week. You'll do a tour in the eastern half of the country and we'll wind it up in New York. How's the new book coming?" Her voice was so low and throaty is was almost as if she were right in the room with us and I felt the surge of the same desire I had when I saw her in San Francisco. Since that time her attitude always seemed distant and I wasn't sure whether she was mad at me or just no longer had any interest. Maybe she was the kind that just likes one-night stands.

"Well, I hope to be sending you a copy of the new book any time now," I promised. I figured that would cheer her up. She promised to send me a new itinerary and a check right away.

Then while Angie and I sat in the coffee shop having breakfast she started in again about her grandpa and even said something about Artie. Right in the restaurant. I started thinking about my old friend Leo Ballcock. I caught a vision of his shiny bald head and his little gold-rimmed glasses, the timid pigeon-toed way he walked up to my table and his one chopstick joke. It had to be a joke. I even caught a whiff of his Old Spice.

"Yeah, I played it smart," Leo told me. "You know, we go on little trips all the time. I sell plumbing equipment and travel around all over the state. Of course Merrilee, that's my wife, Merrilee. She goes with me lots of times because she's pretty jealous."

"She is?"

"Yeah," he said. "She's always afraid I'll take up with some hussy or another. You know women. Boy, she can be kind of devilish. She knows I enjoy a nice glass of wine sometimes. Well, not long ago she bought me a nice wrought iron wine rack with little wrought iron doors. It holds six bottles of wine. Well you know what she did then?"

"I—"

"She put a padlock on the doors so when I want a bottle of wine I have to go ask her to open the padlock for me. Sometimes she says I don't need any right now and makes me wait an hour." He stared at me. "That's not right, is it, Mr. Lemarsh?"

I nodded agreement and mumbled something.

"Well, guess what? I watch a lot of television, you know. I like that *"Forensic Files"*; stuff like that. They show you all the mistakes people make so you can avoid them. You can learn a lot on television."

A faint shine glinted off his bald dome.

"I watch a lot of shows where people poison their wives or husbands or whoever. Well, far as I can see most of those poisons are too hard to come by. At least for a fellow like me. I decided the best one was good old arsenic. It's easy to find."

"Arsenic is easy to find?" I asked.

Easy for Leo maybe.

"Oh, the easiest way to get it is rat poison. That's just about all rat poison is: arsenic."

"Yeah, but it can be traced," I said. "Even I know that."

Leo looked at me. "Well, of course. Sure, you'd know that. You're a writer. Sure. It can be detected long after a person is dead, so you have to be on your toes...but you know that."

I nodded like he was right, of course.

The more he talked and got warmed to his subject the more I smelled the Old Spice and I began to think I'd never be able to use it again myself without thinking about arsenic and Leo Ballcock. I noticed a little spot of food sticking to his tie. I felt like reaching out and brushing it off. I could tell he'd be fastidious about stuff like that. But I resisted the urge. I didn't really know Leo that well, and besides I didn't want to do anything to cement our relationship any more than I had to. I kept thinking that somebody—maybe that guy who later turned out to the late Arthur Haviland—would get in line any minute now and Leo would leave. No such luck.

"What I did, Mr. Lemarsh, was every time I'd go out of town, even when Merrilee went with me, I'd buy a box of rat poison and tuck it down into my toilet kit. I started saving it up and right now I've got enough rat poison to kill all the rats in Hamlin Town and a couple of other towns too." He leaned close and snickered.

"But then, as you say, it's so traceable."

He beamed at me triumphantly. "That's the beauty of it, Mr. Lemarsh. If I bought it all right here in town it could be traced back to me, sure. But buying it as I did, over a year's time in small quantities all over the state, nobody would ever be able to trace it back to me. I always paid cash, of course. So even if authorities should discover that she'd been killed by rat poison, they couldn't trace any of it to me. I've never bought any—not that anyone can prove anyway. And of course I never bought any here in town." He chuckled at his own cleverness.

"But like you said, it would remain in her system."

"Ah, yes. But when you give somebody a little arsenic over a period of time they just get sick and then they get sicker. Ah, you already know that. You're just testing me. Well, when I saw she was getting pretty sick I'd take her to the hospital and then slip her a good hefty dose at the hospital and then she'd die. If you die in the hospital they don't require an autopsy. And besides, the minute she died I'd insist she be cremated according to *her wishes*. End of story." He glanced shyly around and chuckled.

I sat there not knowing what to say. This sounded pretty cold-blooded.

"You don't have to kill her, Leo," I said. "Can't you just leave her? I mean, hell, just pack up and get out."

"Oh, no...I couldn't do that," he told me. He looked at me sincerely. "I couldn't really kill her either. I know that. I'm just letting off steam. Buying the rat poison is just my way of getting even. Something to do to get back at her. I couldn't really leave her. "

I remembered how Leo looked at me.

"You couldn't?" I said.

"Oh no." His face turned sad and dreamy. "Not really," he said. "Merrilee needs me."

Funny how all that suddenly came back to me. I thought about Angie. I was going to have to watch her. I sat there eating my ham and eggs with that stupid conversation rolling around in my mind. I loved Angie. I needed her too. I did need her. But the question was did I need her enough to spend the rest of my life in the pen? It was becoming clear to me that just a roll of the dice was all that kept Angie from selling me down the river. If I ended up letting her get me in prison I'd be separated not only from her but from the fame and the money too. I was just at that point now; right on top of the world. Next book I was going to Hollywood. One way or another I was going to work it so they had to let me come to Hollywood while they were making the picture. Maybe I could be a consultant or something, or at least have a small part in the movie like Erin Brockovich did. If Angie said just one stupid thing I'd be worse than back to square one; I'd be some big slug's boy toy up in San Quentin. I'm no psychiatrist, but Angie was going over the top. I looked at her. She was having a Denver omelet. Without the blue contacts her eyes were pale again and rimmed in red and her cheeks were unnaturally hollow, more so than ever. Angie was sick. There was no longer any way to ignore it. And I didn't like the way she looked at me. At first the murder of Artie didn't seem to bother her at all, but now...now she had his murder to hold over my head. Never mind that it was her brainstorm in the first place and she was an accessory. When a person's crazy, who knows what they'll do? I thought back. I remembered Jessica stealing Angie's tips, and her grandpa being a Communist and women deliberately kicking her on the street. The people at work who made her lose her job. All that crap could be true I guess, but it seemed like a lot of strange things happening to one strange girl. And even if grandpa had been a Communist, all he did was sit in his room and drink wine. I don't think he was much of a threat to our national security.

But in some ways I was like Leo and his wife. No matter how bad things got, I'd been willing to put up with Angie just to be with her. I didn't try to pretend that she needed me. Maybe she did and maybe she didn't. But I knew I needed her. I loved her and she knew it. And I believed that whether or not she needed me so much, she did love me. But...

God, I was already a first-degree murderer. They say once you start killing, it gets easier every time. Maybe they're right at that. I thought about my movie again. The guy, Carvil, he ended up killing his girl friend. He had to. Some way, somehow, it almost seemed like that damnable Artie Haviland had Angie and me in mind when he wrote his stupid book. It was almost like he was telling our story.

"A Name So Terrible" by Arthur Haviland—Arthur Haviland... I'd never looked at the damned thing before.

"Just change the name to Darcy Lemarsh," I told her. "That Haviland thing was a pen name I was going to use, but my editor likes my real name better."

"I just loved *"The Little Mornings"* she told me. What's this one about?"

"Oh, you'll see when you type it. You're the first person to see it, actually. But don't talk about it to anyone. Promise?"

That really thrilled her. "Oh, of course not. Professional ethics, you know. Besides, I usually don't read what I'm typing, Mr. Lemarsh. You know," she giggled. She held up her pudgy hands and flickered her fingers, "I just type away. By the time I've finished I couldn't tell you anything about what I just wrote..." I guess she was a fast typer because she promised to have it ready for me the day after tomorrow—almost four hundred pages.

I left with a strong feeling that she was going to read it before she even starting typing—but I didn't care. All I wanted was to send something to JC that looked like I had just finished it. That old typewriter crap from the first time wouldn't work very well again. And I sure didn't want Arthur Haviland's name coming into the picture either.

I spent the afternoon signing books and later we had a good dinner at one of the casinos. I'm not much of a gambler but Angie had a hell of a time playing the one-armed bandits. Naturally she swore they were rigged.

"Every time one gets ready to pay off big," she said, "they trip a switch and make it skip. I saw the guy do it."

On the third day I picked up the manuscript. It looked beautiful. I made sure there was no Arthur Haviland on it. My stenographer gave me a little disk too. "There's your own copy so that you can print out another one on any computer," she told me. I couldn't believe it, a whole book on one little round disk, like a DVD movie. I just hoped to God the gal hadn't tried to fool around too much with it. I'd

THE LITTLE MORNINGS

never know because I never looked at the damned thing. I got the manuscript and the disk wrapped up and sent it off to JC at Carrington House in New York City, The Big Apple.

I'd been watching television but nobody mentioned Haviland. I never read papers, but I bought one and sure enough, on an inside page they mentioned a body having been found on the rocks along the coast south of San Francisco. It just said that authorities felt there were some suspicious circumstances surrounding the death and were investigating. They could wonder, but there was no way they could tell whether he'd jumped, fallen, or been helped. I felt that was just something cops say. When they get interviewed they probably do what I do: if they don't know, they make something up. Besides, the beating from the bat wouldn't show up after what Arthur's body had gone through bouncing down the side of that cliff. Angie read over my shoulder. She looked at me but neither of us said a word.

We went back through Salt Lake City and then on to Cheyenne and then aimed for Kansas City.

In the meantime, I kept slipping rat poison to Angie. The stuff came in little pellets and I dissolved them in a little bit of water. I kept the water under the sink in the bathroom and when the pellet had dissolved, I mixed a little in Angie's coffee whenever I made instant in the morning. Sometimes we'd have coffee late too, and I'd slip some in then too. She used so damned much powdered creamer and sugar she wouldn't have known if it had grandpa's piss in it.

Each time I did this she drank her coffee just like always, but other than complain about a little nausea or a bellyache once in a while, she didn't show much signs of being ready to go to the hospital.

* * *

We headed east. In Kansas City I signed books and did the television thing and later went on a radio talk show too. Angie and I were having a quiet early dinner and for once we seemed to be getting back to normal when suddenly, out of a clear blue sky, Angie jumped up in the damned coffee shop and yelled, "You're a monster Darcy!" She turned and ran out of the place screaming, "He's a monster. Murderer! He killed my grandpa. He's a murdering Communist!"

All the other customers watched her as she shot through the door and then they stared at me like I was Hannibal Lecter.

I didn't know whether she was on her way to the authorities or not. If she was, it was too late to stop her now.

But when I got back to the motel, Angie was standing by the window with a cigarette in her hand. She didn't say a word or even turn to look at me.

Later I was in the bathroom trying to dissolve another pellet into a coffee mug. This motel had real mugs instead of plastic ones like most of the others. I got to looking at the box. Active ingredient, Bro—brometh—bromethasomething. Shit. Far as I could tell there wasn't a drop of arsenic in my damned rat poison. I figured rat poison was rat poison. It said harmful or fatal if swallowed by humans, but…was that dumb Leo Ballcock as stupid as I was or did he know something I didn't know? I shoved the box in my pocket and headed for the door.

"Where you going?" she asked.

"I'm going to pick up a six-pak," I told her.

"Well, get me a carton of Marlboros too, will you. Hard pack, hard pack." That was because the last time I forgot and bought her the soft pack although I never did figure out what the big difference was.

I dumped the rat poison in the dumpster outside the motel and went to a big drugstore full of light. They had a whole section devoted to pests and insecticides and weed killers and stuff like that. I checked everything they had that looked like poison. Once I started looking I saw that not one damned box of rat poison or insecticide or anything else that I could find had arsenic in it. Or if it did, they had it labeled under some other name so I didn't know what it was. Some had that bromestuff in it and something that started with di—something and another one had broderick or something like that. I didn't really read the names. I was just looking for arsenic— and I didn't find it. I only knew the rat poison I'd been using was only making her a little bit sick. I hadn't been giving her very much. I wasn't sure the rat poison was what made her sick at all, the way she smoked and didn't eat right. It might kill her eventually but hell, at that rate I might die first. I wasn't sure how much to give her, and besides, if I tried to give her too much in one dose she might just get wise.

Just then a clerk asked me if she could help me. She was a little blonde about eighteen. Cute, but a little dumpy. I wondered at first whether she recognized me from the television.

"Could I help you find something?" she asked.

"Oh—I was just looking for a good rat poison," I told her. "Got rats in the garage."

"Oh, any of these are effective," she told me. She looked at me with big blue eyes. "But you have to be very careful, you know. Especially if you have kids or pets. My neighbor, Mrs. Hanson, she had the most beautiful Himalayan cat, Cuddles...? And all of a sudden poor Cuddles fell ill and Mrs. Hanson took her to the vet but before the vet figured out what she had, Cuddles died. Nothing they could do. It just made poor Mrs. Hanson sick, losing Cuddles like that, and she felt like it was all her fault, that's the worst part, I think. And she's such a nice person. She lets me swim in her pool whenever I want to."

"What, the cat got into some rat poison?"

She laughed. "Oh no, that's why I said you have to be so careful. No, it turned out Mrs. Hanson's radiator leaked a little bit and there was antifreeze in the driveway and Cuddles licked it right up."

"Yuk. Why would a cat lick antifreeze?" I asked.

"Well—antifreeze is very sweet—and cats and dogs like that. They lick it right up and then later," she lowered her voice as low as she could get it, *"Hasta la vista,* baby."

"Wow," I said. "I never heard of that. Well, luckily I don't have any kids or pets to worry about. And I don't have a leaky radiator."

"Don't forget your neighbors either," she said like a schoolteacher. "Their kids and pets get into everything too, you know."

"Yeah, isn't that the truth," I told her. "Well, I guess I'll skip the rat poison. Maybe I'll get a trap instead."

They had an automotive section in the drugstore but the girl was still hanging around. I bought a six-pak of beer, a carton of Marlboros in the hard pack and a rattrap. I dumped the rattrap into the trashcan outside. I went to an automotive parts store down the street and bought a gallon of antifreeze. In the parking lot outside the motel I chugalugged a can of beer and filled it half full of antifreeze. I put the plastic bottle in the trunk of the Honda.

Later on I asked Angie if she wanted some coffee. She sat on the bed in a cloud of smoke staring at the television. She didn't answer. She was twisting a strand of hair in her fingers the way she always did.

"My stomach doesn't feel so good," she murmured.

"You smoke way too much," I told her. "Do you want a cup of coffee?"

"Heh? I don't know. I don't feel too good... Yeah. Whatever." She sat back down and rubbed her stomach. Every time I looked at her or said anything, she looked like I was interrupting something important. Starting to get more like Jack all the time. And every time she started twisting at that strand of hair I knew she was thinking bad thoughts.

I made two mugs of coffee in the bathroom. Instead of sugar I poured a good dose of antifreeze into Angie's mug. I wasn't sure how much to use but I figured that with all the cream and sugar she normally used she wouldn't notice the difference. I'd see how that went. If that didn't have any effect, I might have to increase the dosage a little. I was just going by trial and error. It wasn't like I could run out and ask a doctor or anything, but if a little spillage worked on Cuddles, a good dose ought to work on Angie.

I brought the mug over to the bed and handed it to her. She took it but just held it in one hand and her cigarette in the other. Slowly her eyes moved from the television screen to me.

"I'm sorry I yelled it out that you were a Communist and killed my grandpa," she said. "I know you don't want everybody to know that. I didn't mean to blow your cover, Dar. But the more I think about you killing my grandpa the more I hate you. I can't help it Darcy. I love you and hate you at the same time. But I don't think I can live with it any more. If I'd known you were a born killer I'd never have taken up with you in the first place." She took a swallow of her coffee and made a face but didn't say anything. She sipped a little more.

"A born killer?" I'd promised myself not to talk about Artie again but it slipped out, "What about our little pal Artie?" I asked. Whose brainstorm was it to beat him to death with a fucking baseball bat? It sure wasn't mine, Angie. In case you forgot, you came up with that one all by yourself. And speaking of taking up with people, if I'd ever dreamed the kind of shit you and your nice grandpa were going to get me into I'd never have taken up with you either so you can go fuck yourself. How do you like that?"

She looked at me and slowly and carefully stubbed out her cigarette in the ashtray on the nightstand. Then without the slightest sign of warning she hurled her coffee into my face, china mug and all.

The edge of the mug caught my cheekbone with a sharp pop. Hot liquid stuck to my face and burned. I jumped and grabbed at my face.

"You dirty little bitch!" I screamed at her. And that dark cloud gathered about me.

With that she leaped up at me and tried to claw me with her nails. "You're a murderer. Murderer! You killed my grandpa!" She flailed her arms at me. "I'm calling the police," she screamed. "I don't care if we both hang. I don't care any more. You're going to pay for what you did. You killed my grandpa."

I tried to grab her wrists but she moved so fast I couldn't get a good hold on them and suddenly I had my hands around her throat. The darkness closed down and grew more intense and my head pounded. We fell back onto the bed with me on top and the more she flailed and kicked at me the darker it got and the tighter I squeezed. She squirmed and twisted her torso beneath me. I couldn't see. The skin of her neck beneath my fingers turned sticky and I kept squeezing. Dimly, through the blackness I saw a dark red face. Her eyes bugged at me in horror and anger but slowly they grayed out and disappeared into the blackness. I couldn't think. And I couldn't stop. It was as if I were only a disinterested bystander, just a few steps away, watching, watching Angie die. She kicked and writhed and fought at the guy who bent over her but her movements grew weaker and her face darkened as a glaze formed over her eyes. Slowly but surely her life ebbed away. After what seemed like an eternity her entire body slowly relaxed beneath his weight and he pulled back and only then, after she lay back on the bed and I looked at her did I come to and realize that I was that guy. I was the guy squeezing her throat...and Angie was dead. It took a while to soak in. She was dead.

I'd killed her. I'd killed my love.

I tried to stand up but staggered like I was drunk. I slumped to the floor beside the bed and sat there leaning against the side of the bed rubbing my cheek where the mug has struck me. I was breathing like I'd just climbed forty stories to nowhere. I must've drifted because the next thing

The Little Mornings

I knew the false light of the little morning filtered through the window of the motel room and I realized where I was. Slowly it all came back to me. I sat unmoving for a long time. My inner lip throbbed and my cheek ached where the coffee mug had struck me. Out of the corner of my eye I saw the mug lying on the carpet nearby. I didn't dare stand up and look at Angie. I knew she was still there, but I couldn't bring myself to look at her. It was as if she wouldn't be dead if I didn't look at her body lying on the bed.

Finally I made a great effort and got to my feet. There was Angie lying on her back on the bed, right where I'd left her. She was stiff and cold. My little Angie.

I sat on the edge of the bed and laid one hand on her tummy. My mind was numb. I'd finally done it. I'd killed the one thing I really loved. Never mind that I'd been planning to poison her already. Maybe I would have and maybe I wouldn't. I couldn't honestly say if I would have gone through with it, but this…it was done. I couldn't say I was sorry and make it right.

Angie lay so still. Her colorless eyes were open and sightless. We hadn't had a chance to get the new contact lenses for her. I was sorry now that I hadn't taken care of that. She really liked them. They did look nice on her. Her lips were slightly parted and on one side a speck of moisture clung to the corner. Her cheeks so hollow and skeletal. It was as if she'd been rehearsing for death all along.

I went out to the coffee shop and drank a couple of cups of coffee to try to pull myself together. I began to think. It was done now. I had to do something with Angie. I couldn't just go off and leave her in the motel room. I rubbed my cheek where the coffee mug had hit. It hadn't broken the skin but it felt swollen and hurt like hell. I think it bruised the bone, and my lip wouldn't heal over either. It stayed raw and tender inside and at least once a day I'd accidentally bite it and get it started all over.

Coming back to my room I ran into a maid on the balcony.

She was standing beside a couple of laundry carts. One was empty.

"Can I borrow that to take my stuff downstairs?" I asked her. "I've got a lot of luggage."

"I guess so—you'll bring it right back?"

I gave her a five-dollar bill and wheeled the cart to the room. Inside I tried to lift Angie from the bed. She didn't weigh anything but her body was so stiff that I had a hell of a time getting her knees bent enough to get her into the cart. I was afraid I was going to break something, but I managed it. I packed our stuff into the suitcases and piled everything on top and wheeled the whole mess out and down to the elevator. The elevator opened to the parking area one floor below so I didn't have to go through the lobby or anything. I wheeled it to the car and got the trunk open and then fooled around with bags and the bat and stuff and made sure nobody was watching. I managed to get my arms around Angie and slipped her into the trunk. She hardly took up any room at all. I shoved the luggage in on top of her and slammed the lid shut.

I wheeled the cart back to the elevator and returned it to the maid. The end of an era..

I came back down and got into the car and drove away from there.

* * *

"Sometimes I think the writer must be a little schizophrenic." We sat in easy chairs in front of the camera. My interviewer was supposed to be the local literary critic or something. He was a skinny guy with big writer's glasses and long straight hair hanging down over his forehead like a six-year old kid. He had a big mouth and ugly pugnacious lips and I could see he thought he was one of those really intellectual dudes. He wore a bow tie too. But thank God for my good memory. Just as the going got hot I remembered somebody I'd seen on television when I was watching every writer interview I could find. And as time went along I sort of got to expect some of the questions. I swear every single interviewer would ask, "When did you first know that you wanted to be a writer?" The exact words weren't always the same, but they'd have to get that one in. Or they'd ask how I came to create the narrator and how much of it was autobiographical. But I'd learned to sidestep that. I repeated the same story I'd told before, "The writer has all these different people or aspects of himself inside his mind, you see, and they're just dying to get out. But instead of acting out in the street and ending up in an asylum, the writer sits down at his computer and lets these different people express themselves, their thoughts, their feelings—their needs and desires—through his writing. He can be a man one minute, a woman, a child, or all of the above all at the same time as he writes his little opus."

"Or even an animal," the interviewer said. "I say that because suddenly the conservationist, James Oliver Curwood springs to mind." The bastard just had to get in something intellectual.

"Yes, Curwood. Even an animal, that's right," I said. I didn't have a clue what he was talking about but I managed to smile easily. I acted like I'd been thinking the very same thing. Never heard of the guy, but I could tell the little dude didn't get that and he was impressed in spite of himself. Hell, *I* was impressed. Between watching other television interviews and bringing back crap I'd heard from pops, I damned near had myself convinced that I really was an author.

Now with a couple of weeks passed since Angie and I had lost it, I'd begun to feel a little better. Of course I was riddled with guilt and I missed her horribly at first, more than I'd ever dreamed. When she was still alive I didn't realize how much I really did love her, crazy or not. But once she was gone and there was no way I'd ever get her back, I slowly realized fully what I'd done. I couldn't remember the details clearly. It seemed like a dream. But I still knew. I sat there rubbing my tender cheekbone. Well, it didn't turn out to be cold-blooded murder exactly, like with Artie, but I did it all right. Not that I could have done anything differently. I keep saying I always make bad choices. It's true. I don't think I'd know what a good choice was if I saw one.

It had been particularly horrible at first, driving around with Angie crumpled up in the trunk. Every time I'd hit a bump in the road or something I'd worry about her for an instant—then I'd have to remind myself that she didn't care whether I hit any bumps or not. She wouldn't care whether pops and I were both Communists preparing to overthrow the government, and she'd never get jealous over JC again. She wouldn't ever hide any rubbers under the bed again either, I told myself. Got to get over it.

Driving around I found a side road that led me out along the levee along the Missouri River. I took that and drove along until I was running down in the bend close to the water parallel to the river. I found a lonely place where I could pull off the road under some trees. I wanted to act fast because if some cop came along and saw me parked there he might ask to look in the trunk. They do that sometimes.

There wasn't a soul in sight so I opened the trunk and pulled the suitcases out and worked Angie's body up out of the trunk. It wasn't easy and she'd already begun to smell. That's not a smell a guy can forget soon either.

I felt really terrible, looking at her. In a way she wasn't Angie any more, just a bundle. But still, I'd loved her. It wasn't like I was just throwing out the trash. I carried her down to the river's edge and gently rolled her body off the embankment into the water. Without looking back I hotfooted it back to the car and got out of there. By the time anyone discovered the body I'd be in Little Rock, Arkansas. Then I was supposed to hit Memphis, and then some other city and work my way on to New York. Then on the way back I had to go through Oklahoma I think and Texas. I'd be on the move for a long time.

I didn't want to sell the police too short. I realized that sooner or later there was a good chance they'd trace Angela back to me so I got my story all prepared for when they did.

* * *

Two days later I was in a motel room watching for news about Angie but nobody said anything. I wondered if her body hadn't been found, but then I figured someone had probably found her all right, but something like that doesn't make big news out of state. I was clear up in Nashville now. I just wondered if and when. If they did find her, I wondered how long it would take to connect her to me…and then to find me.

I went down to Miami and then northward through Atlanta and Charlotte and headed for Washington. Hell, all the towns I stopped at on the way to New York became a blur. But I was getting there.

Once I was on the final leg of my journey to New York I began to feel really excited. Most of my depression had been left behind with all the books I'd signed, and I was so busy I didn't have a lot of time to think about Angie and all the other bad stuff. The worst time was driving. I'd get to thinking all over again. Driving was bad, but I forced myself to think about the road in front of me and the next town. And at night I drank half a pint of whiskey and that did me in for a few hours.

JC had called me in Washington and told me she liked the new book but—same old story—it was going to need a lot of work. But then she added something I didn't like.

"You're going to be on your own on this one, Darcy," she said.

I tried to get out of her what she meant by that but she hung up on me.

When I finally did get to New York I managed to find

Carrington House on The Avenue of the Americas. I found the floor and the receptionist showed me where to go. I was a little disappointed that JC's office wasn't the grand oak-paneled executive suite I'd somehow expected. Her "office" was really only a partitioned section of a much larger room filled with the same sort of compartments. It wasn't very big and her desk was a mess of piled documents.

But she still looked very chic. Same JC I'd left behind in San Francisco. She was wearing an off-white blouse with a dark gray pants suit that swished elegantly around her when she moved. And she still wore high heel shoes. She took my hand as if I was only a business acquaintance. Her hand was cool to the touch.

"Well, Darcy, you finally made it to the Big Apple," she said. She smiled but I felt the smile was cold. "Come on. I'll take you to lunch."

In the elevator I said, "Wow, they don't give you much of an office. I thought a big editor must make about a million bucks a year and have an executive suite."

"Hah," she said. "The pay is lousy and I'm not a big executive. My family has a little money, thank God. Otherwise the only way I could live in New York would be to stay at the Salvation Army Shelter."

We went down to a deli just off the avenue and had corned beef sandwiches with Cole slaw on them. First time I'd ever had anything quite like that but I liked it. I had imported beer and JC had a diet Coke.

"I've got good news and bad news, Darcy," she began.

"Well, what's the good news?"

"We've got you on *Today*. Savannah Guthrie is going to interview you. That's a real coup, Darcy. We don't want to blow that. Are you ready?" She looked smiling and expectantly at me.

I shrugged and swallowed. Savannah Guthrie. I tried to look confident, "This is big?"

"Darcy, don't you have any idea of what a plug like that

does to boost sales? They don't interview new authors every day on national television." She stared at me like I was mentally challenged. "Yes, Darcy, this is big."

"Well, I'm about as ready as I'll ever be. I've had quite a bit of practice talking to interviewers. I've met all kinds traveling around the country."

"Good. You'll be signing books at Barnes and Noble this afternoon and Brentano's maybe tomorrow while you're here. There's a radio interview. Tomorrow's your interview on *Today* and tomorrow evening you'll be going to the star-studded screening. That should be fun. People pay big bucks to hobnob with people like you." She looked at me funny, and added, "Believe it or not."

"Is that the bad news?" I was thinking that ay last I might get to visit with some real movie people.

She looked me almost as if she felt sorry for me. "No, Darcy. The bad news is that I'm not going to be your editor on *"A Name So Terrible"*."

"You're not?" I didn't understand.

"No, I'm not." She laid her sandwich down on the plate and leaned across the table. "Darcy, I don't know exactly what kind of bull crap scam you're running here, but I practically had to rewrite *"The Little Mornings"* from start to finish. I had to do it all myself. That, in addition to all my other work. Why should I spend my time writing your novel? That's not my job. But I was stuck. My ass was on the line. We had a schedule and you didn't help at all—actually any help you offered only made my job that much harder. I should get a byline for writing the damned thing—and half the money. That book should really have my name on it as the author. I mean yes, it had a lot of raw power, but man! It still needed a lot of work. And it was dated. We had to bring it into the twenty-first century, Darcy."

Now the damned book had *four* authors.

JC leaned back and looked at me. "I just don't know, Darcy. It's almost as if somebody else wrote the whole thing.

It's hard to put into words, but sometimes when we talk about it I feel like you don't have a clue."

"That's ridiculous," I told her. "Of course I know what it's about. I mean, I wrote it..."

"Well, I won't press you Darcy. What I do want you to know is that I don't trust you and I don't want to be involved in your next book. I've asked that it be assigned to another editor. That way we can remain friends." She smiled engagingly in a way that told me there were no hard feelings but that she meant what she said.

* * *

I spent the afternoon at the bookstore signing books. My heart wasn't in it because I realized that JC was on to me. She couldn't really put her finger on it or accuse me of stealing somebody else's book, but she knew damned well that something was seriously wrong with the picture I was showing her.

Later I went up to her office but she had gone.

"Damn, it's really important, too," I told the receptionist.

"Perhaps I could take a message, mister—"

"Lemarsh," I said. "Darcy Lemarsh. She wanted to see me this afternoon too."

Her pretty blue eyes widened. "Mr. Lemarsh? Oh I just adored *"The Little Mornings"*. Well, listen, if it's really important, I could give you her address. It isn't far."

It sounds crazy now, but I had this little idea in my head that if I went up and sweet-talked JC I could not only get back into her good graces but maybe into her pants too. I stopped by a florist I passed and got a nice bouquet of flowers to bring her.

The place had a doorman who opened the door and let me in. It was almost like a hotel. At the desk the clerk took my name and called up. I couldn't hear what he said, but after a moment he told me I could go up. Room 2609.

The elevator was self-service. They didn't have an operator

like those fancy New York apartment houses in the movies, but it was very elegant. I shot up to the twenty-sixth floor and found myself in a wide carpeted hall. The doors were a soft ivory white with little gold numbers on them.

A tall sultry black woman opened the door. She was very slender, like a model. She looked at the flowers and then at me.

"And you must be Darcy," she said. She gave me a long elegant hand and stood back for me to enter. She had a ring on her finger with a huge lavender stone. She wore a strong musky perfume that went well with her. We were in a short entryway. Just to the side of the door a small marble top table held a crystal bowl of flowers and an open silver box held a small stack of bills. Tips I guess, for deliverymen or something.

"I'm Laruena," she told me. I'm JC's roommate. Come in."

She led me into a spacious living room with deep white carpeting and wide windows that looked out at other wide windows. Lots of light shone in but you couldn't see any sky from where I was standing.

The furniture was light in color too, heavy soft looking couches and chairs, all in off-white colors. Only the pillows and things like that gave off bright splashes of red and silver, orange, white or blue. A black bust that looked like Laruena stood on a white baby grand piano by one window. A vase on a table held a bouquet of flowers three times as big as the one I brought.

JC came out of another room wearing a long open negligee over nothing but panties and a little see-through shift. Her hair was still damp as if she'd been in the shower. She didn't look happy to see me but she didn't look surprised either.

"I see you smooth-talked my address out of someone at work," she said.

"Well, they thought it was important business," I said.

"And it's not?" She patted at her hair. Off to the right Laruena moved to a wet bar and began mixing a drink or something.

"Here," I said. I was embarrassed now that the bouquet was so small, but I held the flowers out to her. She took them without a word and laid them on a low table.

"Well," I said. It had suddenly hit me when I saw Laruena. Her roommate. No wonder JC hadn't wanted to take me to her room when we were in San Francisco. Sure as hell Laruena was up there waiting for her. Maybe JC didn't believe in marriage, but I had a pretty good idea they were like married or something anyway. So much for my plans to come up here and seduce JC. Maybe she was bi or whatever Artie called it, but I was clearly no contest for Laruena; that was for sure. And I saw from JC's eyes that this wasn't going to be the happy occasion I'd hoped it might be.

"I just thought maybe we could sit down and talk for a minute," I said. "I guess maybe I owe you an explanation." I was only saying the first thing that came to mind now. I couldn't let down and really tell her the truth. Even far as we'd come, I was afraid she'd go to her boss and they'd dump *"A Name So Terrible"* as fast as they'd snapped it up. It didn't take a brain surgeon to figure they want to make money but they don't want to be involved in a literary scandal. They might turn into the laughing stock of the publishing business like that guy JC told me about, the wannabe mobster that conned a publisher out of half a million.

"I—I'm sorry for giving you so much trouble about the book," I said. I glanced around for a good place to sit but JC didn't offer me one.

"And?"

"And, well...all right, the truth is, the professor did help me. I mean I wrote the book all right. But it was pretty rough—even rougher than it was when you read it—and the professor helped me get it—in order, and he used his influence to get me a reading here in New York. That's why I wasn't much help in the revisions. I guess I'm just not very good at revisions. Once I get something done, I don't seem to know how to change it." When I said this, I was thinking of Angie. "I was thinking maybe I'll take some night classes in writing…"

"Well, what's done is done, Darcy. I bear you no grudge." Her tone was kind of a dismissal.

"Then you'll change your mind about being my editor?" I asked.

"We'll see how you come off with Savannah Guthrie tomorrow," she said. "We'll talk later." She accepted a drink from Laruena without offering me anything. She led me to the door.

At the door I turned and spoke very softly. "Are you and Laruena…?"

She looked at me curiously like—as Angie used to say—I was mentally challenged.

"What do you think?" she asked.

* * *

We sat in easy chairs with a bookcase full of books behind me. By now I was pretty used to interviews, but suddenly I froze up. Today was special. I had to fight to keep from twitching around. This was the big one. National television. If I messed this up, the whole country would be laughing at me.

Savannah Guthrie sat with her back to the window. A row of books stood on the window shelf behind her and a blue screen over the window kept people from seeing in I think, but I saw them down there waving their little signs and stuff. Plants stood on little side tables and the whole effect was to look like my office, I guess, where I turned out important books night and day.

Miss Guthrie held up a copy of my book so that the camera could see it and then laid it on her lap. She was wearing a soft rose sweater over a white blouse and a darker rose skirt. When I saw the interview later on television it looked so intimate, but in reality we were surrounded by people and lights and God knows what.

"I know this is your first novel, Mr. Lemarsh. Were you surprised by its immediate acceptance?"

"Surprised?" I smiled. I was as tongue-tied as that very first interview in Portland, but suddenly that damned old Berry appeared my shoulder, standing there on unsteady feet. He even had a glass in his hand, I swear. I didn't really see him, but I even smelled him. A calm settled over me like a warm blanket.

"Just do as I say, remain calm, reflective. You can do it, Darcy. Remember, you're my voice. You're our *future."*

Renewed, I smiled confidently at Ms Guthrie. "I was floored. I was surprised and thrilled just get it finished, actually. I didn't even submit it for publication for a long time because…I didn't know anything about that end of the business."

"I'm sure you've been asked this question before, Mr. Lemarsh, but could you tell us when you first knew you wanted to be a writer?" She wasn't the first to ask that one all right, but she did it so well.

"I—you know, it's hard to say. When I was still pretty small I started writing little stories—I guess you could call them stories if you used your imagination."

She laughed at that.

"But then as time went on, I realized that it was a way I could express myself. I could collect my thoughts and put them in writing in a way that was impossible for me to do otherwise. I've never been a good speaker. I've always been rather shy and lonely and I really didn't have anyone to confide in. So I just began jotting down my thoughts on paper."

"Then *"The Little Mornings"* wasn't actually your first effort?"

"Oh no, but up until then I confined my work mostly to essays and short stories, stuff like that. I never tried to sell any of it. It was really just a pastime, like reading or going to the movies. Like keeping a diary or a journal."

THE LITTLE MORNINGS

"I see. And today how do you feel you fit in as a writer?"

I tried to think. "Well actually I don't think of myself primarily as a writer," I told her. I remembered that writers always like this line of BS: "When I think of writers I think of people who write nonfiction, you know, history books, true crime and so on. I don't really see myself as a writer. I see myself rather as a storyteller. Ever since the dawn of man, people have been sitting around the fire recounting exciting stories of faraway adventures, something to entertain their audience and pass the evening. Today I believe I'm continuing in that tradition. I don't recount history and I don't have a message to preach. I just like to tell a good story that will entertain my readers and enable them to pass a couple of hours with a good book."

I almost floundered then but suddenly I remembered Henry and his typewriter story. Or was it Artie? I put my glasses back on.

"So anyway, here I was keeping a sort of journal just for myself when one day I found an old portable typewriter at a flea market. Once I got my hands on that—" I paused and tapped my teeth with my glasses, "I don't know. It seems to me that the typewriter galvanized my thoughts and feelings in such a way that before I knew it I found myself writing *"The Little Mornings"* on my new acquisition. The idea was a little vague at first of course, but the moment I'd lie down in bed, instead of going to sleep I'd begin imagining scenes for the book and I'd have to jump up—*three o'clock in the morning, Darcy*. Sometimes at odd hours like three in the morning—and get them down on paper. Of course even then, I wasn't at all sure there might be a market for my work. I wasn't really thinking about that."

"So you were a pretty lonely fellow, sitting in your room typing away every night, telling your story to the typewriter?" She smiled sympathetically as if she understood something I didn't.

I smiled and went on, "Writing is a very lonely profession.

And so many interviewers ask me about the book I'm working on at the moment, but personally I dislike talking about work in progress—not because, as people sometimes suggest, I'm afraid someone will steal my ideas—I mean, hey, the ideas are out there. But rather because I feel that talking about a project weakens it. I'm always afraid I may just "talk it out" as it were. Sometimes I think it's a little bit like being pregnant. A woman has to keep her project in hiding for nine months. She can't show off her infant until it's time, and then *voilà!*"

"Well, I won't ask that question then, Mr. Lemarsh, but do you really believe that writing a novel is as painful as having a baby?"

I laughed. "It can be pretty painful." Easy, this was delicate ground. "I'm sure it's nowhere near the pain of bearing a child, of course. Mothers have my deepest respect, believe me. And writers have another advantage: where a mother has to accept and love her child pretty much as-is, no refunds, no exchanges, the writer can work on his project. He can change, purge it, shape it and mold it and hone it—he can tweak his characters just a tad wherever necessary. He only shows it off when he feels it's ready to be seen by the entire world."

"And speaking of the entire world, I understand "*The Little Mornings*" is scheduled to appear in translation as well."

"Yes, it should be turning up soon in France and Germany and I believe an Italian translation is in the works. Oh, I understand there's a Spanish translation too." I was on a roll now. "And of course I hear the movie is doing well too. I should mention that I'll be at a special screening tonight at the Music Hall. I'll be there with Frances McDormand and John Goodman."

She checked her notes. "Some critics have likened you to the late James M. Cain. What is your response to that, Mr. Lemarsh?"

I took off my glasses again and held them in front of me.

I leaned forward. "Well, Ms Guthrie, I believe people are like snowflakes: there are no two alike. There was only one James M. Cain and there'll never be another. I wouldn't for a minute want to take anything away from a writer of his stature. If some choose to compare my work to his, I'm flattered. But I'm an individual too. For whatever it's worth, there'll never be another exactly like me either. If I'm remembered at all, I'd like to be remembered on my own merits."

"I know we agreed not to talk about projects in the making, but I understand you do have a second novel nearly ready to go to press, is that right, Mr. Lemarsh?"

"That's true, and although I'm not prepared to talk about it at this time, it follows in the same tradition as *"The Little Mornings"* and my editor gives me every reason to believe that it will prove to be just as popular."

"Will this continue? I mean sometimes an author has a notable success with one or two books and then his work seems to fizzle. Do you feel you have the staying power to become a major player in today's crowded book scene?"

"Who can say?" I shrugged expansively. "Usually, after I finish a project I'm drained. For weeks, months, I feel that I'm finished, washed up. I'm convinced that I'll never have the inspiration to write another word. But getting back to giving birth, I suppose a person might liken this to what they call postpartum depression." I smiled and tapped my teeth with my glasses again and went on, "But then time rolls on and suddenly the grain of a little idea creeps into my squirrel of a brain and I began to gnaw on it."

She laughed.

"And then slowly but surely this little grain or germ or whatever it is begins to grow and expand and suddenly before I know it, I'm right in the middle of another project. Of course writers have miscarriages too, you know. Often the idea that seems so promising today turns out to be a dud and fizzles tomorrow. But when everything connects,

I'm off and running and as long as the public is interested in reading my books, I'm going to be in there pounding on that keyboard."

"Speaking of keyboards, I understand you wrote "*The Little Mornings*" entirely on that old portable typewriter from the flea-market, Mr. Lemarsh."

"Yes…yes, I did. Only recently was I able to graduate to a computer. What a difference!"

"Of course there are always detractors. There are those who feel your sudden success is a flash in the pan. What's your response to those who feel that way?"

"Remember that it's enough to be remembered for one book. Darcy, like…"

"Well, only the reading public can decide that. Many novelists are remembered in the public mind by only one novel, titles like *Gone with the Wind*, *The Catcher in the Rye* and *Moby Dick* spring to mind. Everybody has heard of those books, yet most readers evidently find it hard to remember anything else the authors have written. It's as if they sat down one day and wrote one book and then retired. But I'm sure that being remembered even for one book is a far better fate than that suffered by most writers: total oblivion." I smiled in a way I thought made me look wise. "I'd settle for one book."

"I'm sure many of today's writers would have to agree with you there, Mr. Lemarsh. And do you have any closing thoughts, perhaps a word of advice to others who are writing their own novel—I'll steal a line from Willard: even as we speak?"

"I can only say that a writer has to have faith in himself, Miss Guthrie. This is a game where the players don't get much encouragement and sometimes it seems as if there's a conspiracy to keep them from getting that novel published. But believe me, the most important thing about writing, more important than education, talent or discipline; the most important thing of all, is dogged perseverance."

"Darcy Lemarsh," she said. She held my book back up and I knew we were finished. "Author of the best seller, "*The Little Mornings*". Thank you for being here and for sharing your thoughts with us today."

"Thanks for having me." I stood up and an assistant got me unhooked.

They had scheduled me to sign books that afternoon at Macy's. I'd already turned in the car. I didn't need it in New York anyway and they were supposed to get me another one for the next leg of my tour. After that I had a few hours to kill. Since the interview, I couldn't stop thinking about Berry. I hadn't really thought much about him for a while, but now I felt a sudden sadness. It was just as if he'd been standing right there alive and well. I wished the old guy could be here with me to enjoy all this success. I really did. I tried to shake off the melancholy and took a nice long shower and just got dressed to go down for a cup of coffee when someone knocked at the door.

Two stocky men stood there. My heart gave a leap. I didn't need a crystal ball to tell me they were cops. They had that unflinching way of standing there, staring without blinking. Everything about them said, "I'm here and I'm not going away. Live with it."

"Mr. Lemarsh?" They were both somewhat older than me. Probably in their forties at least. The one who spoke was older than the other cop. He had graying hair and black brows. He had thick features and his face was slightly pockmarked. He had a mean curl to his lips. He wore a dark suit, kind of gray.

When I nodded, he held up his hand. He'd been holding it down at his side but now he opened it up and showed me a badge.

"I'm Detective Bellini," he said. His voice was low but carried. "This is Detective Egan."

Instead of showing me *his* badge, Detective Egan turned slightly and lifted the knit bottom of his leather jacket so that I could see the butt of a gun on his hip. That worked for me. He was about the same size and shape as Bellini, a little shorter and maybe a little younger. His hair was graying too, curly. He was chewing gum but tried to act like he wasn't. He had light blue eyes. Not as light as Angie's had been.

"We'd like to come in and ask you a few questions," he said.

I stood back and let them into the room. There was nothing I could say. They glanced around and then got back to me.

"Sorry to disturb you, sir," Bellini said. He pulled a little notebook from his pocket and read. "Do you own a Chevrolet pickup registered in Sacramento, California?"

"A Chevrolet pickup?" Whew! A sudden wave of relief washed over me. It was like the condemned man just got a last minute reprieve. I gulped air and tried to stay casual, "My Chevy pickup? Oh, *yeah*, my old pickup."

"Why," Bellini asked. "You thought it was about something else?"

"Oh no," I lied. "I mean— I didn't know what— I couldn't figure why...my pickup, yeah, I mean it's still in California. My publisher gives me a rental. Why, is there some problem?"

While Egan, the other detective, walked around looking at the room, Bellini checked his notebook again and then looked back to me. "Well, there's been a little problem, yes," he said. "We understand you haven't been in California for a while— did you lend or sell your vehicle to someone?"

I guess my jaw dropped. What the hell? "Lend...? I— no. Last time I saw it, it was parked in front of my apartment."

"So then it must have been stolen, Mr. Lemarsh, eh?"

"You mean somebody stole my pickup?"

"Oh, then if it was stolen and you didn't know, you couldn't report it stolen, could you?" His eyes had a steady glazed look as he stared into my eyes, probing.

"Stolen," I said. "No, no I didn't know it was stolen." All of a sudden I realized the stupidity of leaving the keys in the truck. I was still responsible for it. I tried to gather my wits. "If I would've known it was—" I kind of broke off. Something wasn't right. I suddenly asked myself why this was important enough to send two detectives to my door.

"Well, it's not such a big deal," Egan said, stopping suddenly right in front of me, "but the thing is that whoever was driving your pickup slammed it into a telephone pole. Broke the pole clean off at the bottom and totaled the truck. But he must've been okay because he took off and left the truck for you to find."

"Yeah," Bellini said looking up from his notes again. "I guess the truck wasn't much, but the electric company there, SMUD they call it, they want you to pay almost four thousand dollars for the pole and repairs. See, if you'd reported the truck stolen in a timely fashion, then you wouldn't have been held responsible, but..."

"But you had insurance," Egan suggested. His eyes were steelier—and a lot colder—than Bellini's.

"Insurance?" Christ I didn't know what to say. All I knew was that right now the four grand for the pole was the least of my worries. "Insurance? Oh, sure, of course. I mean I've been awfully busy lately. Maybe I let it expire, I don't—"

"Well," Bellini smiled coldly, "I guess it won't be too big a problem. But the vehicle is registered to you so you're legally responsible for the light pole. I suppose a man like you can afford to pay for it. Maybe you can get a lawyer to dispute their charge. You can do that." Up close he smelled of tobacco. Suddenly it was if Angie had come out of the bathroom or something and I got a really bad feeling.

"Well, I'll take care of it," I promised. "I'll be out that way again next week I think. The truck wasn't worth much anyway." I smiled to show them the interview was over and they looked as if they were on their way out, but suddenly Bellini turned really sharp and looked at me. He hesitated for a second and then he hit me.

"Oh, something else."

I stared again. "Something else?"

"Yes, there was another thing."

I felt like an idiot. "Another thing?"

He nodded. "Do you know a woman named Angela Berry?" he asked. His eyes were black and steady and they never blinked.

Suddenly a light flashed over me and I knew the real reason why they were at my door. Of course. They wouldn't send two New York detectives to tell me somebody stole my old pickup truck way out in California. I took in air.

"Angela? Sure," I said. I really hadn't expected anyone to catch up to me that fast but I knew that sooner or later…I wasn't totally unprepared. "Is—is something wrong?"

"Wrong? Why? Did you expect something to be wrong, Mr. Lemarsh?" This was from Egan. He sounded like one of those Mafia guys in the movies. He gently began to grind on his gum again.

I didn't know what to say and I just stood there looking blank.

They both looked around the room at the same time. There were only two chairs to sit on—and the bed.

"May we sit down for a minute?" Bellini asked.

I indicated the chairs and I sank onto the foot of the bed. I felt almost too weak to stay on my feet. I felt like they could see my heart pumping in my chest. I put my hands behind my back so they couldn't see they were trembling.

"You say you were expecting something to be wrong," Egan persisted.

"No—I mean I hadn't heard anything from her for a week or so. I guess I wondered…"

"Weren't you traveling together, Mr. Lemarsh?" Bellini said.

"Oh—yes. Yes we were," I admitted, "but someplace back there, Denver maybe... I don't exactly remember. Anyway we got into an argument and she took off and headed back to Sacramento. That's our home. We live in Sacramento. Well, you know that."

Egan nodded. "Yeah."

"Well," I started to say Angie, but her name stuck in my throat and I couldn't say it. I said *she* instead. "She wasn't really supposed to be with me anyway, so I didn't try to stop her. I thought maybe it was all for the best. My book—my editors were really only paying my expenses, if you know what I mean..."

"What did you argue about," asked Egan. Now *he* had a notebook and a ball pen out.

"Argue about? Oh—" I tried to smile and look casual. "I don't know. I mean just stupid things. We argued all the time and then we'd make up." I smiled disarmingly. "You know how it goes."

If he did he didn't let on.

"But on that particular day you argued."

"You mean the day she left—yes..."

"What did you argue about on that occasion?" asked Bellini. He cocked one foot up on the other knee and stared into my eyes.

"Argue about? Let's see—oh, yeah, now I remember. Well, you know, I hate to say it but Angie w- is a little bit off. She has this crazy idea that people are Communists. She even embarrassed me in a restaurant. She jumped up and accused me of being a Communist right in front of everybody and then ran out of the place. You can check on that."

"But you're not a Communist?"

"Of course not. I'm not even exactly sure what a Communist is." I laughed at the absurdity of this idea. Nobody else laughed.

"And then you came back to the motel and argued some more?"

"Well...yes."

"And that's when she took off?"

"Mr. Lemarsh, didn't you almost say Angie 'was' instead of 'is' just now?" Egan said.

"Was? No, no of course not. Aren't you going to tell me what's going on?" I was sweating like a pig now. I *did* almost say 'was'.

"Mr. Lemarsh," Bellini said, "I have some bad news for you. Angela Berry has been found dead."

"Dead? Angie's dead?" I sank back on the foot of the bed. "Oh...no—no, she can't be dead. I mean we had our arguments but down deep we loved—" This was tough. Just talking about it was tough, but now I didn't really quite know how to act. I didn't want to act like I didn't give a damn, but still I didn't want to collapse and act all broken up. Until right at that moment I hadn't thought about how I'd act about it. My heart pounded harder and I rubbed my wet hands against the bed behind my back.

Egan got up and walked past me then turned suddenly and looked down at me. "Actually Mr. Lemarsh, as we understand it, Miss Berry didn't leave you in Denver. She was last seen with you in Kansas City. People at a motel in Kansas City heard something going on in your room, an argument maybe. And people remember her calling you a murderer in Denny's. We have people who remember that. And the next morning the maid remembers you tipped her five dollars to borrow an empty linen basket to wheel your luggage to the car."

"Oh yeah, that's right. I remember now. Kansas City. Yeah...yeah, I did that. That thing at Denny's, she was just mad. That didn't mean anything. Sometimes when she was mad at me she liked to say things to embarrass me."

"But you borrowed the linen basket."

"Well, yeah. It was empty and I was tired of hauling luggage around. That's all." They didn't have anything. They were fishing. I felt like one eyebrow was twitching and struggled to control it.

"You carry around a lot of luggage do you?" Bellini looked at the two bags in the corner and the plastic garment bag hanging in the open closet. And that goddam bat.

I just kind of shrugged. "Not a lot. I just got tired lugging stuff around," I said. "The maid was right there with an empty basket, so..."

"You left the room in a mess," He said. "It looked like there'd been a fight."

"Oh...yeah, I guess. She throws—she threw things sometimes when she got mad."

"We looked at a picture of that laundry wagon," Bellini said. "You could put a body the size of Miss Berry inside one."

"Put a—whoa there! Just because we had a fight and she took off. I mean...I figured she hopped a bus—hell, maybe she tried to hitchhike. That can be very dangerous. Maybe..."

"Mr. Lemarsh," Bellini went on, "do you know what else authorities in Kansas City found? They found traces of ethylene glycol in the motel carpet and they also found an open box of rat poison in the dumpster outside."

I tried to look innocent and keep that damned eyebrow from twitching. "Rat poison? So? Maybe they have rats."

"No, Mr. Lemarsh. The motel has a service contract with a pest control company. They never keep poisons on the motel premises. Never."

"And," Egan cut in, "Miss Berry had traces of rat poison in her system. I can't imagine why a person would eat rat poison, can you?"

"She died of rat poison?" I didn't know what to say now.

"Oh no," Egan said. "She didn't die of rat poison."

I breathed a sigh of relief. I thought for a second there the rat poison had killed her after all.

Bellini said, "Police in Kansas City also checked that laundry basket you used to roll your luggage out to the car and guess what. They found a bit of saliva in it. The saliva came from Miss Berry and it also contained traces of ethylene glycol. She had minute traces of that in her system too."

I just stared.

"But that's all right, you don't even know what ethylene glycol is so you, Mr. Lemarsh?" Egan said.

I tried to smile agreeably but my lips felt stiff and dry and Artie's bite began to throb. "No, as a matter of fact I sure don't." That was true so where would that take them.

Bellini stepped nearer. "Ethylene glycol is antifreeze, Mr. Lemarsh. Miss Berry had a trace of antifreeze in her system." He smiled maliciously. "But that didn't kill her either. There wasn't much, just enough to trace. And there was antifreeze in the tiny bit of saliva we found in the laundry cart too. Her saliva."

I couldn't move. I couldn't breathe. I just sat there feeling the pounding of my heart. I wondered if they could actually hear it.

"You know, a thing like that kind of looks suspicious, Mr. Lemarsh. We're paid to be suspicious. That's our job. You know how a thing like that looks to us? You buy rat poison and evidently antifreeze—or did you already have it in the trunk of your vehicle?"

I couldn't nod.

"Well, like I said, we're paid to be suspicious, so in a situation like that the first thing we think is that somebody is trying to poison Miss Berry. And since you two were so close the first thing that occurred to us was that maybe you were trying to poison your sweetheart," Bellini said. "Maybe the rat poison was going too slow for you. Then maybe you tried antifreeze and that was too slow for you too. Or maybe she tasted it in her drink or something and spit it out. Maybe you just got impatient."

Egan shook his head. "Some people have no patience."

"That's ridiculous. I—I don't know anything about poison. I don't know anything about all that." What could they prove?

"We don't think Miss Berry even took her clothes with her," Egan said. "The maid said she remembered you bringing in two suitcases and a garment bag and she saw them piled in the linen wagon when you left. Why would Miss Berry go back to Sacramento without taking her clothes?"

"Oh..." I hadn't expected anybody to count how many damned bags we took in or out. "She took some clothes. She did take some. She just didn't take the bag. She was mad because I bought it for her, that's all. She just threw some stuff into a shopping bag. That's what she did. I remember now."

"Angela Berry's body was found just outside Kansas City in the Missouri River, Mr. Lemarsh," Bellini said. "That's as far out of town as she ever got. And that was northeast of the motel. Doesn't sound like she was heading to Sacramento, does it? Why wouldn't she head for the bus station or take a taxi to the airport?"

"Northeast? I—" That hadn't occurred to me when I said she went back to Sacramento. In the first place I never expected anybody to pin down just when and where I last saw Angie. Jesus. "Well, hell I don't know," I said. Inside I was still shaking like a leaf and that one eyebrow wouldn't stop jumping. I felt like a fighter up against the ropes. This wasn't how it was supposed to be.

"Too bad," Egan said. He caught himself snapping his gum and stopped. A pretty girl like Angela being found like that."

Suddenly I sensed a trap. I had to be careful not to let them know I knew anything I wasn't supposed to know. "Like what?" I asked.

Egan stood there looking at me and Bellini got up and began pacing slowly. "She looked pretty bad, Mr. Lemarsh. A few days in the water can do a lot of damage to a pretty girl." He watched me, but I didn't flinch.

"Well you mean she drowned?" I asked. That seemed like a reasonable question.

"She didn't drown, Mr. Lemarsh," Egan said. "She was strangled. Her hyoid bone was badly fractured." He touched his Adam's apple. "Right here. She must have stared right into her killer's eyes while he strangled her." He shuddered at the thought, but I knew he was only trying to get a reaction from me. "People used to believe that when you strangle a person like that, their image remains in your eyeballs."

I blinked like an idiot. Only one thing was saving me right now: I barely remembered it happening. Everything had gone black and I hardly remember seeing her eyes while she died. I wasn't even there. It was like I was standing in another room watching through a window, completely out of the picture. "She was choked to death," he went on, "and then tossed into the river. Nice way for a pretty girl like Miss Berry to leave this world, wouldn't you say?"

"Well...no, it's horrible. I mean you say that like I had something to do with it. I told you she left. Maybe she did try to hitchhike. That's probably what she did. And she—met the wrong guy. There's a lot of weirdoes out there. I don't know what she did. I was busy on my damned book tour. I don't go around killing girlfriends."

They both sat back down and looked at me.

I admit I was badly shaken but I figured I was still in pretty good shape. At least that's what I tried to tell myself. They might suspect. It was natural for them to look hard at me. After all, when a woman gets killed their first suspects are always the husbands or boy friends. *Before you look for the outlaws, look at the in-laws.* I heard that on television. Yah yah, but in this case all they really had were vague suspicions. So they found some rat poison in the dumpster. Angie didn't die of rat poisoning. She had traces of antifreeze in her saliva. Maybe she had a little on her hand and wiped her mouth. It sure didn't kill her. That's nothing. A maid says I borrowed her laundry basket. So what? Nobody saw me kill Angie. Nobody actually saw a body in the laundry basket. Nobody actually saw anything and the only person who could tell the cops what happened was Angie—and Angie wasn't going to say a word. None of that crap meant a thing. The maid probably threw our dirty linen and towels in the laundry wagon. That's how Angie's saliva could end up in the laundry wagon. Nobody saw me put Angela's body in the river. Nobody witnessed a damned thing and there was really nothing that could connect me directly to her murder. I didn't need a lawyer to tell me that. Let them suspect all they wanted to. Besides, tomorrow I was going to be on my way west and I didn't plan on staying any one place very long either. I figured I was still in pretty good shape all right after all. Yes, I was in good shape. To hell with them and their vague insinuations. My eyebrow calmed down and I suddenly had to fight to keep from smiling.

But it was like when they advertised the sequel to that shark movie: *Just when you thought it was safe to go back in the water.*

Bellini stood up and nodded like he was satisfied and I thought they were going to go, but suddenly he swung around and cocked his shotgun and let me have both barrels.

"Mr. Lemarsh, does the name Arthur Haviland mean anything to you?" he asked.

He might as well have shot me dead with a real shotgun. My chest tightened up in a vise and I couldn't breathe. I think my heart even stopped pounding.

"Arthur Haviland?" How in God's world could they possibly know anything about Arthur Haviland? How could they connect me to him? Nobody even knew who he was. I tried to think. My chest squeezed so tight I felt like I was having a heart attack. I debated whether to admit ever knowing him or whether I should deny it completely. I couldn't believe anyone had seen us together. Even if a clerk at the motel had seen us getting into the car. Maybe Artie asked for me at the motel desk...no, impossible. He'd been following me. He wouldn't ask at the desk. What? Even if some dumb clerk did see us together for a minute he couldn't positively identify Haviland and me together. That was a month ago. In fact no clerks saw me more than for a minute when I checked in. In fact, Haviland and I hadn't been anyplace together except for the few minutes it took for us to get into the car. Besides nobody was around. Angie and I both were careful not to let anybody see anything. Nobody in this world could swear we even knew each other except Angie. And Angie sure wasn't going to talk.

As usual however, I was wrong. I said before that women don't like to be taken for granted. Well, that was Angie all right. They say women always have to have the last word. I said before that I couldn't trust Angie to keep her mouth shut. Angie might be gone now, all right. But as it turned out, she talked. And she had plenty to say.

Bellini stood and moved closer to me. His stare was steely and I felt Egan's pale eyes on me too.

"Arthur Haviland. San Francisco. You don't remember him?"

Suddenly their detective faces faded and I was someplace else and I had a clear vision of Savannah Guthrie sitting in her luxurious dressing room looking at her television monitor.

"Oh my God," she said to somebody behind her. "That's that cute writer I interviewed yesterday, the one that looks like a young Tom Cruise. He's been arrested for murder!" But then she morphed into JC sitting on her white couch with Laruena. They were both wearing only panties and bras, and Laruena's thigh gleamed darkly against the white material that covered the couch.

"My God," JC said. "Listen to what they're saying: Darcy Lemarsh, *Time Magazine's* newest Con Man of the Year. Biggest American literary hoax since Clifford Irving in seventy-two." Tears of hurt and anger rolled down JC's face. "That little shit. I knew there was something phony about Darcy the very first time I laid eyes on him in San Francisco. He's no writer. He couldn't write a joke on a bathroom wall.

I knew it. Down deep I just knew it. Oh God, I'm ruined. I'll never work in this town again. And he's been arrested for murder. Murder…" Laruena leaned close and put her arm around JC's shoulder. "It's not your fault, darling," she murmured. "You didn't volunteer for the job. It was just an assignment." She brushed her full lips against JC's cheek and JC melted into her arms sobbing.

I felt like such a bastard. I wanted to tell Miss Guthrie and JC I was so sorry. I was only…

"Arthur Haviland," Bellini was saying, "you don't remember him? Doesn't that name mean something to you?"

I tried to clear my head of these horrible visions. I tried to think about what Bellini was saying. They were just fishing. There's no way. Take a chance.

"No," I said. "No, that name doesn't ring any bells at all." I shook my head. "No, I never heard of the guy. What's he got to do with me?"

Bellini straightened and took a turn around the room. "Well, I'll tell you. It's kind of interesting. This Arthur Haviland was sort of a drifter. He worked here and there at odd jobs all over. He even worked in the Peace Corps in Africa, but mostly he got by working as a male prostitute, did you know that?"

"A male…no, of course not," I said, and that was at least partially true.

"Yeah. A male prostitute. Well, to make a long story short, Mr. Haviland turned up dead too," Bellini said.

"He's dead? He died?"

Egan smiled. "A young fellow. He was about your age, Mr. Lemarsh. Yeah, he died. But he didn't die a natural death. Died is what happens when somebody throws you off a cliff down south of San Francisco. His body was found below on the rocks. Battered to a pulp. Whoo-ee. I got to tell you, Mr. Lemarsh, something like that isn't a pretty sight to see — and the seagulls…"

Egan didn't know what Artie's body looked like. He

hadn't been there to see anything. It was all bull, about the seagulls.

"Jesus…" I said. I was getting sick. "I don't understand. I mean I still don't understand what this has to do with me."

Bellini stepped close. "You don't understand what it has to do with you?" His eyes were frosty. I looked back at Egan. Egan's eyes were even frostier. He didn't seem to have any neck. His curly head just sat there on his shoulders and he stared at me with those eyes. Bleak and wintry eyes. They looked even lighter now, even more like Angie's. He shifted his bulk in his chair and I saw the butt of his gun again just beneath the knit bottom of his leather jacket.

Bellini sat back down and studied me for a second.

"You know, it's a funny thing, Mr. Lemarsh," he said. "This Haviland fellow was gay. He was actually pretty well-known in the San Francisco gay scene. Investigators talked to a friend of Haviland. You know, when your book came out Mr. Haviland got very upset. Real upset. He went around there telling everybody it was his book. He said you stole his book." He shrugged. "Of course nobody believed him. Everybody who knew him considered him a real loser and he had a lot of problems." He looked at Egan and then back at me. He smiled in a nasty way. "So nobody believed him."

"Well, I wouldn't know about that," I managed to say. "He was probably just trying to get some attention or something…"

Bellini was bluffing. That shit didn't mean a thing. I almost breathed a sigh of relief. They didn't really have anything after all. I could see that now. So Artie went around telling his fruity pals somebody stole his book. Obviously Artie didn't have anything to prove he wrote the book. Bellini was just bluffing but I was still glad when he finally gave up on that. He nodded like he was satisfied. I hoped they were

THE LITTLE MORNINGS

getting ready to go, but then he stood up again and looked around for a minute and then shifted back to Angie.

"I guess you still have Miss Berry's suitcase there with most of her things then, don't you? Except for the things she took with her I mean...in the shopping bag."

I didn't mean to look toward the bags but I guess I did. What difference did it make? I should've dumped the damned thing someplace a long time ago but I just hadn't got around to it. Actually I guess it was a mental thing. That was all I had left of Angie. Just her bag with a few clothes in it. Bellini followed my glance.

"Mind if we take a look?" he said.

I shrugged. "It's the one on the right." I had to stay cool. I had nothing to hide.

While Egan sat there and stared at me, Bellini stepped over and picked up the bag. When he did, it jostled the bat and the thing fell over with a dull thud. That really shook me, but he only glanced at it and came back and laid the suitcase on the bed beside me. I stood up and watched him unzip it and open it up. He pulled out jeans and panties. Slippers. He pulled out the one bra that Angie owned but never wore.

"Funny, when Miss Berry's body was found there was no mention of a bra in the inventory of her clothing," he said.

"She didn't wear a bra."

He held the bra from the bag up by two fingers. "This was hers wasn't it?"

"It was hers, yeah. She had that bra," I said, "but that's the only one she had. She never wore it. Hardly ever." Man, they couldn't overlook the slightest detail no matter how stupid.

He looked at me for a minute and finally nodded and continued picking up blouses and things like that. Tampons, makeup and toothpaste. A comb and brush. He'd hold up each item for us to see and then lay it on the bed beside the suitcase. Then he came up with the little white double cup thing that held her contact lenses.

"Miss Berry wore contact lenses? There was no mention of her wearing contact lenses when her body was found."

"Oh," I laughed. Boy they don't miss a thing. My laugh was probably too hearty and I regretted it. I had to stay cool. "Her eyes were fine. She didn't need glasses. She just had very pale eyes. Some fairy makeup guy in Seattle told her she'd look better if she got colored contact lenses. That's all. She got some blue lenses. They did make her look better I think."

He studied the little lens holder. It had two sides on it, one for each lens. He popped them open. "Blue lenses. Well, I'll be damned." He studied the lens box. "That's funny though," he said. He held the lens cup out for me to see.

"Look. There's only one lens in here, Mr. Lemarsh. Did you know that?"

"Oh, yeah, I remember now," I said. I really had completely forgotten all about it. Boy they were sure stretching to find something to hang on me. The bastards. Christ, not one tiny detail without a ten-page explanation. Why wasn't she wearing a bra? Why did she have only one lens in the cup? If I'd had more guts I would've told them to get out. But I didn't. I just looked at the lens cup he was holding. "That place where we were, Denver or Kansas City or wherever it was," I said. "She dropped one lens on the carpet I guess. The carpet was blue. You know, a blue lens on a blue carpet. We never did find it. Blue on blue. We just couldn't find it. That's all. I was going to get her some more. No mystery."

"Are you sure?" Bellini said stepping close.

I stared at him. "Of course I'm sure. I promised her."

"I mean are you sure that's where she lost it?"

I nodded. "I was there." My heart was starting to pound all over again. Now what was wrong? Where the hell else could she lose it? What was the big deal on this? So she didn't wear a bra and lost a contact lens.

"You're absolutely sure that's where she lost it? On the

carpet? In the motel?" He stared at me with those unblinking eyes.

I couldn't even nod.

"Well then, actually I'd say there is a mystery after all, Mr. Lemarsh. Strangest thing. You see when they inventoried Mr. Haviland's clothing, they found a blue contact lens stuck in his sweater. His sweater was blue too, just like that carpet you were talking about. A nice fuzzy blue sweater. And nobody could figure out where that lens came from or how it got there. They learned that Haviland never wore contacts; he wore glasses. Yeah… They've really been scratching their heads over that. A little blue lens just like this one—stuck in Mr. Haviland's blue sweater. Can you imagine that?"

"Stuck—sweater?" I couldn't get the words out. I felt like I was having a heart attack. My chest squeezed tighter and tighter as the pounding of my heart throbbed and shook my body. I saw her again on the ground wrestling around with Artie. She didn't even know she lost it. Not until later.

"Funny, isn't it," Egan said. He gently snapped his gum. "Funny how a guy can go over a cliff like that and get pounded to death on the way down and yet a tiny little blue contact lens sticks in his sweater—like a marker. I don't suppose you've ever heard of the Locard theory have you?"

I just stood there.

"Locard was a French cop. He said: 'Every contact leaves its trace'. Ironic, isn't it? Contact…" He stared at me without smiling.

I couldn't breathe. I gasped for air and pointed at the lens cup. I watched my finger shaking but I couldn't do a thing.

"You can't take that. You don't have a search warrant."

"We don't need a search warrant," Egan said smoothly. "You gave us permission, Mr. Lemarsh."

I felt faint and my head whirred. I wondered if I was really having a heart attack. My God, I was too young to have a heart attack. I tried catch my breath and clear my mind. I had to think. I'd been so sure I was in the clear. I'd been so positive. Nothing could go wrong. I never dreamed they'd connect me to Haviland. There was no way they could connect me to Haviland, and there was no way to prepare for such an eventuality and no reason I should have to. That Angie. Her and her damned contact lenses. I thought I'd shut her up for good, but she had to come back to get in the last word after all. I still couldn't believe it. I got up and stood there bloody and bowed. I thought there was nothing more they could possibly do to me, but I found Haviland wasn't finished with me either. Bellini reloaded his shotgun and that lip curled and he took terrible aim and let loose with both barrels again.

This time he used Magnum slugs.

"People who knew Mr. Haviland say he was very quiet and modest, but when he got mad, look out." He smiled. I already hated that nasty smile. "Maybe it's a gay thing like a woman scorned or something. Anyway he swore that book you're promoting was his book. He swore he wrote it when he was in his last year of college. And he was outraged. In fact, he was so outraged he told everybody who'd listen to him that he was going to find the bastard who stole his book and kill him."

"Going to find—and...kill him?'

"Yeah, he was going to kill him. That's what he told everybody. I guess that meant you, Mr. Lemarsh."

"You're saying he was planning to kill—me, because he thought I stole his book?"

"That was the word in the Castro neighborhood. I understand a lot of gays hang around there and he hung around there too. I think that's what Mr. Haviland planned to do, all right." Bellini took a few steps and scratched his chin. "You know, the late Mr. Haviland may or may not have been a pretty good writer—I wouldn't know about that. However I do know one thing that he definitely was: he was a spiteful little bastard. He didn't like people very much. I don't think he liked himself much either, really.

And when he didn't like a person, especially if he thought somebody wronged him; hell, sometimes just for no logical reason at all, he'd decide to kill them." Bellini looked at me. "You're a lucky man, Mr. Lemarsh. We have it on pretty good authority that Haviland set out to track you down and kill you."

"He was actually planning to kill me?"

"Oh yes. Haviland was a real killer, Mr. Lemarsh. We only found that out after the fact of course. A dangerous man. And he had his own style when it came to taking care of enemies. Do you know what his weapon of choice was?"

I stared blankly at him. My chest squeezed even tighter. Somehow something was going on around me but it was escaping me. I felt like I was just on the edge of some intangible thing, like Artie sensing the pig in the road that night in Mexico. I felt dizzy and I wasn't even sure I understood what he was saying, but I managed to get out, "Weapon of choice?"

"Yeah, weapon of choice," Bellini said. His smile turned even nastier. He looked tougher than Egan. "Yeah, you know, like some people prefer a gun. Some a knife, and others use the garrote."

Egan looked over at the bat that still leaned against the wall by the other suitcase. He looked back at me. "Some killers even use a baseball bat," he said.

Bellini nodded agreement. "But if a killer used a bat, he'd get rid of it, wouldn't he?"

I couldn't even nod.

"Well, Haviland didn't have to use any of those. He had his own secret weapon, Mr. Lemarsh. Haviland had AIDS. His weapon of choice was AIDS. It turns out he's already infected half a dozen people around the Bay Area, people he didn't like. And those were people who didn't even steal his book. Yep, AIDS. He picked it up from a dirty needle or dirty sex or whatever when he was in Africa. He brought it home as a souvenir of his days in the Peace Corps. Yep, he planned to catch the guy who stole his book and give him AIDS."

I suddenly remembered what Artie had said about Africa. "That was a bad trip." *A bad trip.*

"That was his plan," Bellini went on. "He told all his friends. Can you beat that? He was going to kill you with AIDS. But as it turns out, looks like you got him first. You're a lucky man, Mr. Lemarsh."

I couldn't move. My chest was crushing me. I stared at Bellini. A lucky man?

His teeth were sharp and his bite was vicious. An excruciating pain shot through my mouth like the slash of a serrated knife and I tasted the gush of warm blood. Jesus Christ Artie, you bit me!

I moved my tongue and touched my lip. It was still raw, tender and swollen inside from Artie's kiss and I continued catching it in my teeth.

Arthur had given me the kiss of death...

"Mr. Lemarsh? Mr. Lemarsh, are you all right?"

Bellini's face wavered as the light dimmed and he turned into the edge of the ceiling. The room darkened and closed down around me. The blackness moved in and I couldn't move. I couldn't see. All I felt was the pressure on my chest and the throbbing of my heart. Then that stopped. It was as if I had been welded in place and the whole room tilted up sideways around me.

Everything went black.

* * *

"That's it, Sergeant Kirk," I told him. "That's pretty much the whole story. I guess I'm glad it's over. I don't know what stupid thing I was thinking. I should've known from the get-go that I couldn't pull it off. But it sounded so great. Nobody was supposed to get hurt. Travel, nice clothes. A little respect." I chuckled. "Funny, the crazy thing is that ever since I met Angie my life has kind of paralleled the damned book that started it all in the first place. It's almost like that guy Haviland wrote my story out before it ever happened and there was nothing I could do to change it."

"I never read the book," Kirk said. "Maybe I'll get a chance later." He stared at me for a minute. His expression seemed sympathetic. "I'm glad you're willing to talk, Darcy," he said. "That may help your case. You know we got DNA from that baseball bat you had."

"The Louisville Slugger," I said.

"Yeah, the Louisville Slugger. I guess you got him before he got you. I suppose some lawyers might make a case of self-defense out of that."

I remembered the guy in the story. Didn't he claim self-defense?

"Do you think a jury would buy self defense?"

Kirk looked at me. "No," he said. "I don't."

"Yeah...well anyway," I said, "as it turns out I didn't get him before he got me. You don't know the best part. Just at the last minute, just before he got it, he grabbed me and kissed me. It happened so fast. I knew he was gay. I thought he just liked me. The bastard bit me hard. He had sharp teeth and he bit my lip. He was spitting in my mouth and mixing it with my blood. I didn't even know what he was trying to do." And we'd been drinking whiskey from the same bottle too. I don't know if that made it worse. It sure didn't help.No use feeling sorry for myself because of Haviland. Besides, I hadn't been tested yet anyway. Maybe I wouldn't test positive after all. Yeah, *right!*The thing that really bothered me was the thought of what people would think. Savannah Guthrie thinking how she'd interviewed a phony loser instead of a brilliant author. JC thinking what a bum I was and hating me for everything I'd done to her. I hated the thought of people thinking I was some kind of monster. Just like they thought the guy in the book was a monster because he killed his girl friend and they believed he killed the baby just like Angie believed I killed her damned grandpa. I couldn't understand it. I couldn't understand how I ever got myself into this mess. I'd never in my life thought about killing anyone. Not even when I was mad at somebody. Thinking back I never in my wildest dreams ever thought of really hurting anyone, much less actually committing a murder. I just don't understand how these things creep up on a person. I mean I guess it's all pretty clear for serial killers and everything. Seems like that's what they set out to do in life. But not me. I was never a violent person. Well, just once in a while when something would really hit me really wrong, then everything would go black. But that fight with Jack had been the first fight I'd been involved in since the eighth grade when I got into a fight with some kid. Then there was that guy in the movie theater. In high school I had a run-in with a guy who threatened to get me after school, but he didn't show up so I worried all day for nothing.

I didn't even kill flies. I usually ignored them or shooed them out the window. I never could see any sense in going around killing things. What's so great about that?

Yet, when push came to shove...well, I'm still sure Angie had been right about Artie. It had to be. I mean it was either give up everything that meant anything to us, or give up Artie. It came down to him or us. That wasn't really a tough decision. That simple. As to whether it was a smart choice, like I said, I usually make a bad one. Christ, if I'd had any idea beforehand. I should've gone with my first impression: that grandpa was full of BS. If I had, none of this would have happened and I'd never have got involved in the first place. But now here we were. For the first time in my life I was somebody. Not just another loser, a half-ass house painter, a counterman or dishwasher in some garbage can of a restaurant. I was a person that people respected. Henry envied me. People looked up to me. They asked my opinion. I dressed nice and had a little money in my pocket and a future—well, a future for as long as the rest of the books lasted.

I know this other guy Artie actually wrote the books and I suppose he deserved better than he got, but the way he came at us, it was all or nothing. No, it was worse than that. Besides as it turned out he wasn't such a Mr. Nice Guy either. While I was planning to get him, he was planning to get me. I never suspected that. Besides, wasn't a lot of it Artie's own fault? Christ, he's the dude who dumped the books off on grandpa years ago and took off. He never checked back to see what was going on. He as much as said he gave up on them. Nobody would ever have heard another word about it if grandpa hadn't sent that damned thing in and then told the publisher that I wrote it.

I looked back over at Kirk. "Even with grandpa…it wasn't like Angie thought. She kept thinking I killed him out of greed. She was wrong there. I liked the old guy. He knew I liked him. I never dreamed of killing him. I wouldn't have hurt a fuzzy old white hair on his head. If somebody else had jumped the old guy, I'd have been right there to help him.

"But that day… Of course, I knew he was drunk. I was drunk too. I hadn't gone there with any intentions of hurting him at all. I just wanted to visit and maybe share a glass or two of wine like I always did. I kind of enjoyed sitting there and getting mellow and listening to him BS.

"But all of a sudden he got himself into one of those belligerent moods drunks get into sometimes. I said something he didn't like and he decided I was getting a little bit too possessive about his fucking novels.

"Just bear in mind that those are my books, young man, not yours. You're the front man, but remember that you hold the position at my discretion only. I'd certainly not like to think that you might harbor some crude idea of taking possession of them and attempt to usurp my position as author.' I guess he saw the dumfounded look on my face and he laughed and drank some more wine. 'Of course, I know you wouldn't, Darcy. I know that. I'm just speaking hypothetically.'

"I laughed too. Maybe he was speaking hypothetically all right, but all at once JC's words came back to haunt me. Lying there on the sheets that crinkled when we moved, smelling JC's fresh clean smell and relaxing in the glow of our lovemaking. I remember she said she didn't care who wrote the damned book.

"*Just so you and the professor agree on what you're doing, I don't see any problem. She frowned and looked at me curiously. Of course if he were to come forward later and claim any rights to the book, that could pose a problem. But he wouldn't do anything like that would he?*

"*Just so you and the professor agree on what you're doing, I don't see any problem.*

"Any problem.

"I sat there drinking wine and watching Berry shift about on the edge of his bed, shaking and wobbling.

"*Of course if he were to come forward later and claim any rights to the book, that could pose a problem. But he wouldn't do anything like that would he?*

"I drank some more wine. My head was pounding. The room began to darken. JC's words kept pounding in my head.

"*If he were to come forward later…* Like a hammer they kept pounding and pounding…

"Would he?

"I got up and staggered. It was so dark I could barely see. God I'm drunk I thought. I moved to his side and poured some more wine into his glass. Night had fallen in this sick room. The old man was sick. Shaky and infirm. Too damned old. He really didn't have anything to live for and besides, for a person in his condition, life really wasn't worth living was it? If I were in his shoes I'd wish for somebody to come along and put me out of my misery. I swear I would. I mean, Christ, he was utterly worthless. He couldn't even get out of the house any more. He pissed his pants. He could fall down the stairs, or he might go off and leave the burner going on the hot plate and set the place on fire. He might fall off the bed and bust his head.

The Little Mornings

"*Of course if he were to come forward later and claim any rights to the book...*"

"Pounding, pounding. I stood there in the dark staring down at his barely visible form on the cot. I couldn't stand it.

"He managed to put his half empty glass on his little refrigerator nightstand and lay back. His eyes closed. He looked like he was dozing. I emptied my glass and tossed it aside. It landed someplace on the floor with a thud. I bent and carefully took off his glasses and laid them on the table beside his wineglass. I gently pulled the pillow from beneath his head and held it down over his face. For a second nothing happened and then suddenly his body bucked. It was as if I was standing to the side watching. He didn't try to talk that I could hear. I don't think he was awake, but his body was. It fought with a lot more force than I'd ever have thought possible in such a frail old frame. But it was too late to stop now. JC was right. Blackness. Just about the time we began to get someplace the old fart would come out and ruin everything, sure as hell. I could see it clearly. We couldn't allow that. No way. We just couldn't take the chance. The darkness had overcome me. Angie might not want to see her grandpa dead, but she sure wouldn't want to see him tip over the applecart later on, not any more than I would. He had his time. Now it was my time. Something began to smell even more horrible than the normal smell of stale piss and sweat.

"In the blackness his body pushed up and struggled against me and twisted sideways. His hands scrabbled at the pillow and his feet flailed in the air, but I held my breath and closed my eyes. One part of me watched while another part held on and tried not to listen to the scrabbling of his fingernails against the pillowcase. I turned my head away and opened my eyes trying to see. Flies stuck on the outside of the closed window and for some crazy reason or other acted like they wanted in. That was all I could see. I almost had to stop. I was getting tired but I was just drunk enough to have a staying power I normally wouldn't have. I closed my eyes and held. I held longer than I'd have thought possible and slowly grandpa's body stopped bucking against me and finally, at last, just like in that dream so long ago, he fell limp beneath me. I reached out with one hand and took his glass from the table and finished the wine that was in it."

As I talked, Kirk just sat and stared at me. His face was a total blank.

"Finally I moved the pillow aside. The smell overwhelmed me. The pillow and his face were all covered in a thick yellowish wine-soaked puke. No wonder it had smelled so bad. I got up and put the pillow back over his face and then slowly got his whole body turned so that he was lying face down on the pillow in his own vomit. What more natural way for a man in his condition to die?

"I was staggering slightly as I took my own glass over and shoved it in among the other dirty glasses and stuff on the table where he kept them. I gathered up the file box with the books in it like he'd told me to do and closed the door quietly behind me and left.

"Angie had known. She'd known from the start. I don't know how, but she knew.

"I didn't really mean to talk about that, but... Maybe it's just something I need to do."

"Excuse me for a minute," Kirk said. He got up and went to the door. He came back a minute later and sat back down. "Somebody's going to bring us a cup of fresh coffee," he said. "I think we both can use some."

After a bit a cop brought in two paper cups of coffee. We drank coffee and waited. I didn't realize at first that we were waiting, but we were.

Kirk smiled, not unkindly. "That's some story Darcy. You're really going to need a lawyer," he said. "Have you got any money?"

"Just—well I'm expecting a settlement from an accident."

The Little Mornings

"Good. You don't want one of those public defenders, believe me."

A quarter of an hour later the cop tapped on the door and Kirk conferred with him again. He came back and dropped down heavily with a sigh.

"I'm glad you told me about Professor Berry," he said. "Old guy drowning in wine and vomit. Natural death. If you hadn't told us we never would have known. But we like to clear things like that up. I'm glad you told me. Better for you too. You don't want things like that weighing on your mind."

I didn't regret telling. I never felt right about that day. I was drunk. Besides, in a way talking about it did make me feel a little better.

AIDS. I tried to think about that. It wasn't easy. Even my settlement wasn't going to help there. I saw myself wasting away in a narrow bed someplace in some prison hospital. Wasting away just like grandpa, but at half his age.

Then a strange thing happened. Like in a theater the lights dimmed around me and slowly the window on the wall behind Kirk began to glow in a golden light and there stood a group of mariachis. They wore those black charro outfits all trimmed in silver. They had dark skin and black mustaches. They had on big black sombreros with bright silver borders. And they strummed guitars. They were backlit with a deep golden light. One guy had a silver cornet and they started playing *Las Mañanitas*. The Little Mornings. And as the notes rang sweet and clear in my ears the golden light rose behind the musicians and it became lighter and brighter.

My whole life came crashing back down on me, meeting Angie, hanging with her grandfather. Somehow without even knowing where this was going or even when I did know, I couldn't stop. My life had ended up just like in the book. I remembered the time Angie's grandpa told us about the book and how it ended.

"He ponders his dismal fate. The Little Mornings, his swan song...The End."

Suddenly I was back in Embers again and the words rang out silvery and clear just like the notes from the cornet:

> *Despierta, amiga mía*
> *Mira que ya amaneció.*
> *Ya los pajaritos cantan,*
> *La luna ya se metió.*

And then Angie pushed through between the musicians and stepped up to the window and looked through me with those pale faraway eyes. She just looked at me. She didn't say anything but I knew what she was thinking: she was telling me that she knew it all along, that I killed her grandpa. She knew it all along. I gasped and pushed back but the chair didn't move.

As suddenly as it had begun, the music died, the room fell silent and the lights dimmed behind the window and the lights in the room came back up and all I saw was my frightened face reflected in the dark glass behind Kirk.

"Yes?" he said. "What is it?"

It took a second to understand what he was saying. I looked at him. I tried to get him in focus. "Nothing," I said. "Nothing. I guess I'm all through."

"Well I guess you had it pretty good while it lasted," he said.

"Oh yeah, it was nice. I got to hobnob with some famous people. Savannah Guthrie...Tony Bennett. I was supposed to meet Frances McDormand and John Goodman at the screening tonight. I guess I won't make that."

At the mention of Tony Bennett another vision opened before me. Mr. Bennett was standing in shirtsleeves in front of a television set. He was holding a glass in his hand. "My God," he said, "there's that young writer we saw at Alioto's. The one that looks like a young Tom Cruise. Remember, he was there with his personal editor." He took a sip from his

The Little Mornings

glass and shook his head in disbelief. "I can't believe it. Such a talented young man. The kid's been charged with murder."

I felt so terrible. I wanted to take Mr. Bennett's hand and apologize. I never intended to let him down.

Kirk stood up and stretched and I tried to get him in focus. He yawned as if he hadn't seen a bed in a week. "Well, I hope you feel better to get all that off your chest, Darcy. I know I would."

"Yeah...like I said, I made some bad choices."

"We all do that, Darcy." Despite his policeman stare, Kirk looked like he really empathized with me.

"Yeah, I guess," I said. "I just hate to have everybody think I'm some kind of monster."

"Oh, I wouldn't worry too much about what people think, Darcy. They don't sign your paycheck. Things happen. One day you're a nice guy and the next...well, sometimes bad things happen to nice guys."

I remembered the nice lady at the chiropractor's office. *"Sometimes bad things happen to nice people."* And then she said something about self-control. I should've listened.

"Well," I told him, looking up, "maybe I am a nice guy at that."

"Yeah, How's that?"

"Well, they always say nice guys finish last and one thing you have to admit, I'm sure going to finish last."

Kirk didn't say anything. He stretched again. He turned off the recorder and went to the door and opened it. I got the idea and stood up.

"Don't forget your glasses," he said.

I looked at my glasses lying on the table. My writer's glasses.

"It's okay," I said, "I don't think I'm going to need them anymore.

The End

About C.M. Albrecht

C.M. Albrecht has been fascinated with crime from early childhood, and later worked as a private investigator. The main lesson he learned through his experiences is that most people are quite normal—until you get to know them.

He brings these experiences to his novels whether mainstream or mystery, because crime is catholic and endless.

C.M.Albrecht's Website
http://www.cm-albrecht.webs.com

C.M.Albrecht's e-mail
albrechtcm@gmail.com

Made in the USA
Middletown, DE
21 September 2025